Dead Man's Share

Books by Yasmina Khadra

The Attack

Autumn of the Phantoms

Double Blank

In the Name of God

Morituri

The Sirens of Baghdad

The Swallows of Kabul

Wolf Dreams

Yasmina Khadra

Dead Man's Share

TRANSLATED BY

Aubrey Botsford

The Toby Press

Dead Man's Share

The Toby Press LLC

First English language Edition 2009

POB 8531, New Milford, CT 06776-8531, USA
& POB 2455, London WIA 5WY, England
www.tobypress.com

Originally published as *La Part du Mort*,
© Éditions Julliard, Paris 2004
English Translation © *The* Toby Press LLC 2009

ISBN 978 1 59264 269 4, *paperback*

A CIP catalogue record for this title is
available from the British Library.

Typeset by Koren Publishing Services

Printed and bound in the United States

Part one

Eleventh commandment:
If the ten commandments haven't succeeded in saving your soul, if you persist in having no respect for anything, tell yourself you're not worth much.

Chapter one

Y ou'd think the world had stopped turning.

I feel as if I'm falling apart by the minute, as if every second that passes takes away some of my essence.

A dispiriting calm weighs on the city. Everything's fine. People go about their business, grandmas are in no danger, there's no drama in the streets.

For an energetic cop, it's like being in dry dock.

Ever since the Scalpel Psycho* was neutralized, Algiers has breathed again. People go to bed late and seldom get up early. The providence-state savors its idleness with as much detachment as its decision-makers. From dawn till dusk, the common folk move idly from here to there, picking their noses and staring into space. Everyone knows something terrible is on the way, but they don't care. We Algerians react only to what happens to us, never to forestall something that might happen to us.

While waiting for the storm, we carry on with our rituals. Our

---

* The Scalpel Psycho: a reference to Yasmina Khadra's novel *Le dingue au bistouri* (Algiers: Laphomic Alger, 1990), Superintendent Llob's first outing.

patron saints take good care of us, our garbage cans are overflowing with food, and the planet's impending economic crisis is as distant as a comet—to us.

In short, life is good.

Yesterday, it rained all night. The wind blew its heart out till morning. Then, from dawn on, the sky cleared and a sun worthy of Rembrandt stripped off its clothes above the city's buildings. Winter hasn't even packed away its gray canvases and summer is here, supplanting spring and everything else. In the freshly cleansed streets, girls enter your awareness like shooting stars, their faces joyful and their buttocks quivering. A real feast. If I were twenty years younger, I'd marry them all.

I try to catch the wall doing something wrong, so I can investigate it. I've been twiddling my thumbs for months. Not a single burglary, not even the most trivial dognapping. It's as if Algiers is refusing to cooperate.

I've licked the bottom of my coffee cup clean, one by one I've deciphered the countless arabesques I've aimlessly doodled on my blotter, and I still can't get the hands on the wall clock to move. It's three fifteen, and time is beginning to drag.

The president's serious eyes mock me from the gilt frame in front of me. A thousand times I've got up to take it off the wall, but a thousand times I've been afraid to unleash a thunderbolt from heaven. I'm resigned now, and patiently endure my suffering while I wait for the next revolution to bring us an Aeolian god who is less searing.

And then, suddenly, Lino bursts into my cubbyhole without even bothering to announce himself. "Hey, Super, what do you think?" he exclaims, showing himself off back and front, delighted with his look.

The lieutenant is dressed up like a prince of Monaco.

Radiant, he stops giving me vertigo, positions himself in the dead center of the room and casually takes off his colonial eyeglasses.

"Today," he says, "I'm on cloud nine."

"Good going: yesterday you were only in seventh heaven."

This cracks him up, but then he looks at me and frowns. "Don't you like me?"

I show him my wedding ring.

He giggles, turns to face the french window and examines himself in it. Satisfied, he puts his glasses back on, runs a finger delicately through his brilliantined hair, which is parted severely in the center, and then, to put me fully in the picture, shows me the lining of his jacket and recites, "Pierre Cardin: nine grand. No reduction for good behavior. Lacoste trousers: five grand. Kenzo shirt, pure silk: two grand. Dodoni shoes, real alligator skin, *kho*:* ten grand."

"Now I see why some rebellions founder for lack of weapons. Was it the lottery? Or blackmail?"

"Payslip and piggy-bank locked and bolted. Harem money's not my thing, *kho*.... What do you think?"

"Weird."

"You can be a real killjoy, you know, boss. Anyway, guess where I'm eating tonight."

"No idea."

"At the Blue Sultanate, the most exclusive joint in the bay. The food's so refined it can pass through your guts and be turned into fast food without treatment."

"You must have won the lottery."

"Wrong. Yes, I've drawn a good number, but we're talking female companionship. I've got a date with her in thirty minutes."

"I don't see your gun."

Lino sees what I'm getting at. He wrinkles his nose, grimaces and says, irritably, "There's no need for that, Super. She's not some tart. This time it's the real thing."

"In that case it must be a transvestite."

I've wounded him.

His good humor vanishes abruptly and his previously pink complexion darkens. He slips his finger under the collar of his shirt, straightens up and, disgusted by my grinning face, turns and leaves.

Lino doesn't take his shadow away with him. The brightness that was bathing my office suddenly becomes gloomy.

Three nineteen, the sluggish clock insists.

* *Kho*: brother.

I pick up the telephone and call the boss on the third floor. Inspector Bliss answers, and my hemorrhoids flare up.

"Yes?"

"Superintendent Llob here."

He sighs, the little bastard.

For those who don't yet know Bliss, I might as well warn them now: he's a shameless weasel, the kind who will bite off your finger if you give him a helping hand.

"What do you want?" he whines.

"What the hell are you doing in the boss's office?"

"Working."

"Cut the crap and give me the big man."

"*What* did you call The Director?" I want to reach down the receiver and grab him by the throat. "Listen, Llob. I've got work to do. The Director is on a two-day tour of inspection. If you have a message for him, hand it over."

"I didn't know you worked as an answering machine too."

He hangs up in my face, despite my age and my stripes. I boil for a couple of seconds and then, putting a brave face on it, pull myself together. But hanging about in the office for one more minute is out of the question. Especially when a GMT* is temporarily in charge.

The boss is away, and like any good, self-respecting Algerian I get my jacket, stand up straight and blow off work.

Wandering as my fancy takes me, I end up at Mohand's bookshop. I deduce that Fate has an idea in her head and decide to play along. Monique is arranging a pile of books on the shelves. She is wobbling about on a stepladder, her skirt indiscreet. I can see right away that her habits haven't changed in the slightest: she persists in wearing men's underwear. I cough into my fist to calm myself. Monique almost falls into my arms, she's so happy at my visit. She comes down to floor level immediately, flings her arms around my neck and gives me a kiss that would arouse a tree trunk.

"It's been ages, I swear! What brings you here?"

* GMT: Genetically modified turd.

"A hunch. Bookshops have always harbored subversive meetings. Since I've been unemployed lately, I've come to nose about behind the curtains."

"And have you got a search warrant?"

"Why do people keep asking me questions I don't understand?"

Even though she's a proud Alsacienne, Monique has Norman cousins. She's two heads taller than me. Which is why I avoid posing next to her at all costs.

She holds me out at arm's length and examines me as if I were a pair of boxer shorts, tilts her head right and left, squinting. Satisfied, she says, "You're looking good."

"That's because I'm shallow."

"Don't start that, please. Since you're not being tedious for once, allow us to rejoice in it."

I resolve not to spoil her happiness and cobble together a smile. She scolds me: "Did you lose your way?"

"My readers think there aren't enough women in my work."

She rubs my shoulders with her hands—to comfort me, I suppose.

"Now you're just trying to get me excited."

"I left my night-stick at the office."

Monique bursts out laughing, and it's the sound of a whole stable whinnying as the sun goes down over green pastures.

"Really really really? You're going to talk about me in your next book?"

"I'll have a word about it with my ghost writer, I promise."

"You could have warned me. I would have brushed my hair."

I first knew Monique in 1959, at Ighider, where she was teaching history and geography. Her father was a teacher too. After the war, and the waves of horrific reprisals that followed it, the family went into exile in France. Monique stayed behind. She married Mohand, a *d'Erguez** from the high mountains who loved books. On their wedding night, apparently, while their friends kept watch for the telltale

---

* *D'Erguez* (Kabyle dialect): "real" man. The Kabyles are the largest of the indigenous Arab (Berber) groups of Algeria.

undergarment from the terrace, the two lovebirds translated Kabyle poems until dawn. Later, when the *douar** was no longer big enough for their passion, they bought a small bookshop at Bab El Oued that had fallen on hard times, and ever since then they have spent more time reading than fooling around.

"Come and see who's here, Mohand," Monique calls out to the back of the shop.

"There's only one person who stinks like that," replies a nasal voice from offstage.

I lean toward Monique and say, "He needs to disinfect his moustache."

She lets off another of her ancestral bugle calls.

There's nothing like a woman's laugh to get you back on an even keel. A curtain parts, and Mohand emerges from his rathole. He's a little man, a hundred and ten pounds including tax, with an arrogant nose and round glasses. If nature had not burdened him with such startling baldness, you might be tempted to adopt him.

"Brahim Llob, as I live and breathe," he says, looking me up and down. "So, just like that, you forget about your childhood friends."

"I'm a bighead now."

"He's going to use me in his next book," Monique informs him, quivering with excitement.

"Lot of good that'll do us."

Mohand pretends to be an old curmudgeon. I know he's fond of me and is very upset that I neglect him. Erudite and bilingual, he is a formidable encyclopedia of knowledge. No author leaves him indifferent, no news passes him by. He knows by heart El Moun-falouti, Confucius, the musings of Rousseau and the controversial prophecies of Nostradamus. I used to go to his shop regularly; he put his entire stock of books at my disposal. Everything I have read, I owe to him, as well as a good part of my own literary output. And it's thanks to him that I love a folk tale from every culture and a god from every mythology.

"Have you come to renew your subscription?"

---

* *Douar*: nomad encampment; later, the name for an administrative region.

"That's right. I've been short of inspiration lately, and I thought I might be able to turn up something to plagiarize if I rummaged through your old books."

He glares at me for a couple of seconds, then invites me to follow him into the back of the shop. Inside, there are enough volumes to sustain a campful of vandals for a whole winter. We are forced to walk in single file so as not to unleash an avalanche. Mohand pushes a small step-stool up to a row of tomes with moldering covers, moves a spider web aside, searches, searches, and comes down again tapping his temple with his finger.

"I had an Akkad here somewhere."

"Take it easy. I'm not a trapeze artist," I remind him.

"So what?"

"You mustn't set the bar too high."

He raises an eyebrow and heads for a stack of novels packed up in a corner.

"They were due to be pulped," he tells me indignantly. "Monique's brother picked them up for me. Can you imagine? Thousands of works are thrown on the trash-heap because no one will buy them, when you could make a whole nation happy by donating them to a library in the 'South.'"

"They send sacks of rice like that too."

"Life isn't just about your belly…. Look, here's something interesting," he goes on, holding out a massive volume. "This Rachid Ouladj, he's not very well known here, but it won't be long before he's being talked about."

"Not the guy who criticized the FLN?"*

"Let's say he's a bit hard on the system."

I push the book away with my hand, disgusted. "You can keep it. These petty little cookie-cutter reactionaries who suddenly discover their talent as soon as they get to the Ile Saint-Louis, I've known a few, and let me tell you, they're not fun…."

"What are you talking about? You haven't even flicked through it."

---

* FLN: *Front de Libération Nationale* (National Liberation Front).

"There's no need. I know the mold he was made in."

Mohand is shocked by my poor taste.

I don't give in. In truth, I'm just doing what any writer from my country does when faced with a fellow countryman's success, especially if the jackpot he hits is in France. If I, Brahim Llob, incorruptible public servant and disinfected genius, were one day to shine among the stars in the firmament, I would no doubt be labeled a scribbler in the pay of the regime—just because I'm a cop—or an Arab Uncle Tom, if praise came from the overseas media. That's how it works in Algeria, no other way. We take a sort of malicious pleasure in missing the distinction between other people's success and heresy or felony. This prejudice serves as an itch that is both painful and pleasurable; we would rather scratch ourselves till we bleed than give it up. What do you expect? Some people are made like that: devious because they can't be straight, wicked because they've lost their faith, unhappy because, deep down, they love it. We have never, in living Algerian memory, really been able to imagine a reconciliation with our own reality. And what can you prescribe for a nation when the cream of her youth, the part that's supposed to rouse her conscience, starts off by traducing its own?

Anyway....

After a bit of a commotion, I choose a Driss Chraïbi and hurry to leave the place, because its fustiness is beginning to harm the most important tool of my trade.

Mina has put on some lipstick and a hint of eyeliner on her eyes. It's her way of making amends. Things didn't go well between us yesterday. Over nothing. I was in a bad mood, and I went a bit far.

She rewards me with her madonna's smile and hurries to remove my jacket. In return, I behave like an oaf. I know I'm being crass, but I can't stop myself. When I was a kid, I greatly admired my father. I don't remember ever seeing him smile. He was a real *d'Erguez*, strict and perpetually constipated. He would tip his soup into my mother's lap for nothing and then fetch his stick. And my mother, who was so afraid of him that she would go pale at the sound of his steps in the street, only venerated him the more as a result. So on the rare occasions when he said thank you, it was like hearing an angel trilling in paradise.

I think that's where my machismo comes from.

Two of my offspring are in the living room. Mourad has dozed off, overcome by a program on national television. He's snoring, with his mouth wide open and his head slumped over the arm of the chair. Beside him, his older brother Mohamed is stretched out on the padded bench, his hands behind his head, looking up at the ceiling. I can tell from his behavior that he's a hair's breadth away from imploding. If it were up to him, he'd pack his bags and set sail for some improbable land of milk and honey.

"Did you see the boss?" I ask him.

"Yeah," he answers, disgusted that he has to spill his bitterness out onto the carpet.

"Did he treat you badly?"

"He was polite, but he didn't have much to offer me."

"For example?"

"Office junior."

"You should have accepted, while you look for something better."

He scratches his nose so as not to have to look me in the eye. "I didn't spend four years working my tail off at university to end up with nothing, Dad. I graduated from Ben Aknoun, after all, top of my class."

I sit down in front of him, so that I can see into his thoughts. "Do you think I'm not making enough of an effort to see you well placed, son?"

"I didn't say that."

"But you think it."

"I know it's not your fault, Dad," he grumbles, exasperated. "It's this country that's making me ill."

"It's the only one you have."

He heaves himself up into a sitting position and stares at the palms of his hands. With a sigh, he gives up and goes back up to his room, muttering, "You can't understand, Dad."

Mina interjects, "what can't your father understand? I forbid you to speak to him like that, do you hear?"

I see my son's silhouette make a weary gesture in the corridor and then disappear.

Salim, the youngest, appears in the doorway, a schoolbook held to his chest.

"Ah! You're back, Dad. I've been waiting for you for hours," he adds, slapping the book onto my lap. "This time the teacher's gone too far. He's asked us to describe an oasis, if you can believe it. I've never set foot in the Sahara." Making sure there's no chance his mother can hear him, he whispers, "What do you think, can we make a deal? You polish it up a bit and I wash the car this weekend?"

"Not a chance. It's your homework, and it's up to you to handle it."

"In that case, take me into the desert right away. I'll do the essay tomorrow."

"Go back to your room and finish your homework, and stop bothering your father," Mina intervenes again, extremely protective.

Salim doesn't make her say it twice. He picks up his book and beats a retreat, cursing the heavens for saddling him with parents who are not only selfish but also fail to notice his suffering.

I stand up and go and get in Nadia's way in the kitchen. Nadia is my very own daughter. She's nineteen, and she turns the heads of all the young bucks in the neighborhood. True, her shoes are always one step behind the fashion and she dresses herself from the second-hand shop on the corner, but she has only to bat her eyelids and she can take Cinderella's place for a fairytale evening.

She wipes her hands on her apron and gives me a hug.

"What are you cooking up for dinner?"

"Beans."

"What about my onion soup?"

She points at my own casserole simmering away on the stove.

"You know what I'd like?" I whisper.

"No."

"A little trip over to Taghit, or perhaps to the Hoggar Mountains, just you and me."

"And mom?"

"Mom will stay at home. Someone's got to receive our postcards."

She roars with laughter.

When my daughter bursts out laughing, I'm willing to forgive everything. But her joy is so short-lived that I don't even have time to gain inspiration from it.

Chapter two

Good morning, Superintendent."

I start.

As usual, I'm having a snooze, as I do every time the city forgets it has police stations and that there's no way a cop can get ahead by twiddling his thumbs. But no matter how hard I try, I can't get the big man to see that he has to invent suspects and set up phony cases to keep us on our toes. There's no way to make him wise up.

Inspector Serdj is standing in the doorway, waiting for me to invite him in.

"I've finished the report," he mumbles apologetically, having violated my solitude without the slightest warning.

I wave him condescendingly to a chair.

He puts a folder down on my desk and deposits his bony backside on the chair.

He's killing himself by degrees, Serdj. His cheeks are about to butt up against his subconscious thoughts. With his white hair and his pathetic moustache, he's like a ghost, lost in an outfit that would make a homeless bum feel pity.

Sympathetically, I say, "You didn't have to spend all night at it."

15

"I thought it was urgent."

"There's no rush."

His head sags.

I sink further into my chair, pull the file over toward me and leaf through the report.

Serdj notices me grimacing. "Is there a problem, Superintendent?"

"Hmm…."

"If you like, I can pad it out some more."

"Your reports have always been fine. The problem lies elsewhere."

"What do you mean?"

I look him in the eye. "Who is this addressed to?"

"The director of the SIA…."

"And who's that?"

"Well, he's a superior."

I shake my head, like a teacher who is disappointed by the gaps in his dunces' memories.

"You see? You never learn. 'Superior,' that's for nuns. In our hierarchy, at every step, we have a small but perfectly formed god. These are ultra-sensitive types, sticklers for protocol. They're so fond of little gifts they think everything that lands in their office is one. And a report, if it's to be an 'offering,' must be perfumed, neatly wrapped, and tied up with a ribbon. And what do you do, Serdj? You type your blah-blah on flimsy paper that's unpleasant to the touch and leaves a thin film on your fingers. That's not clever. The director will interpret it as a lack of respect. Do you want to be labeled a reactionary?"

"No, Superintendent."

"Then take your draft and try to retype it on the right kind of paper."

"Yes, Superintendent."

He gathers up his paperwork and stands up stoically.

Just as he reaches the door, I say to him, "Find some top-quality 'extra strong' paper, pure white, with razor-sharp creases…just in case the big cheese decides to wipe his ass with it."

He nods and disappears, furtive as a shadow.

In the cubicle next door, my secretary, Baya, is purring like the cat that got the cream. I can visualize her squirming like a maggot, with the telephone jammed between her shoulder and her chin. The guy on the line has probably heard it all before.

A virgin at thirty-five, Baya has given up on suitors and seems to be getting by on telephone sex more and more. Naturally, to save face, she lets it be understood that it's her choice not to be tied down, in the first place because her independence is important to her, and then, mainly, because she finds it humiliating for a woman to play the part of a sock every night in case *monsieur* decides to take his pleasure in her. Whatever the reason, every time the telephone rings, Baya touches up her make-up before answering. If it's the sex maniac on the line, her moans soon merge with the creaking of her chair and the silky rustling of her robe.

The conversation goes on forever. While waiting for the sex maniac to lose his hard-on, she forgets to bring me letters to sign.

My patience at an end, I ring for her.

Baya takes her time before appearing with her notebook, back straight and nose in the air, steps measured to the nearest millimeter, walking like an air hostess advertising the seriousness of her airline.

"You called, Superintendent?"

"I certainly did!"

She smiles.

"I'm listening, Superintendent."

She has put too much crimson on her lips, which gives her mouth an obscene shape; and her hair, which was raven-black yesterday, is now dyed platinum blonde.

"What an inflammatory look!" I exclaim.

"Don't pay any attention to me, Superintendent," she coos, swinging her hips. Then, looking into my eyes, "You really think so?"

"With that look it won't be long before Headquarters is on fire."

She has to clench her buttocks to contain herself.

Baya used to be pretty. She dressed simply and did her best to be discreet. In those days, "men" had a weakness for discreet women. They were probably well-brought up girls, and therefore bred to the estate of beast of burden, which, in a society that traditionally owned slaves, was a shrewd investment. Then the mentality changed. Today, emancipated girls are preferred, girls who can shout with laughter

17

and swing their hips enough to challenge both taboos and rivals. In Algiers, no one believes in living within himself any more. It's too much like colonial times. Ostentation is in fashion. Since people are only worth what they excite in others, everyone does his best not to pass unnoticed, even to the point of stripping off in the heart of a mosque. Baya joins in the game willingly. Now that she is more or less sure to end up a spinster, she tries to save face by changing her look according to the order of the day.

"What's on the schedule today?"

She goes back to being serious and pulls her dress down over her knees. But the slit is so deep that even a mole could make out the pattern on her petticoat.

"Sy Abbas has cancelled his appointment, Superintendent. He asks you to excuse him and promises to continue your discussion as soon as possible," she reads out of her calendar, punctiliously. "Inspector Redouane arrived at his destination without any problems. He'll be back at the end of the week.... Your wife asks you not to forget to go and pick her up at six o'clock...and, finally, I remind you that you have an appointment with Professor Allouche at eleven o'clock."

I look at my watch. "What time is it?"

"Twenty past nine, Superintendent."

"As advertized by my watch. Lino seems to think today is a public holiday."

Baya claps her hand to her forehead. "It's my fault. I forgot to tell you that the lieutenant called in this morning. He says he's sick. A stinking cold."

I grit my teeth. "If he calls again, tell him to bring in a doctor's certificate when he comes back. He and his constant fevers are beginning to get on my nerves. I hope he hasn't kept the car."

Baya looks down in confusion.

"The son of a bitch! How am I supposed to get around? My Zastava's been at the mechanic's for three days."

"Take Inspector Serdj's car," she suggests.

Baya has always had a bit of a soft spot for Lino. An affection that is sometimes friendly and sometimes, when my back is turned, daring. I forgive her because it fosters team spirit. But if this solidarity is going to turn into complicity at the expense of my authority, then I'm no longer in favor. That's why I point out to my secretary that her dress is missing a button at the neckline, to show her she would do well to pay some attention to her private garden instead of trying to court an embittered old gardener.

*   *   *

Professor Allouche is an eminent psychoanalyst.

Frantz Fanon was a friend of his.

But what can an educated man do in a revolutionary country where charisma swears enmity to talent, where genius is outlawed?

He is the author of a large number of books, all published in France, for want of interest in his own country (at the time—as indeed today, and no doubt tomorrow—the "elite" of the seraglio conscientiously made sure that the average Algerian's IQ was kept at the same level as that of his keepers, which is to say somewhere around the crotch), and as such he has had no end of harassment from the authorities, who saw subversive maneuverings in his scientific works. It is, after all, difficult to explain to a donkey trainer that a book is not necessarily an instrument of counter-revolution; nevertheless, in an Algeria peopled with snake-oil salesmen, an excess of zeal was seen as the best outward sign of vigilance, and an insult as the descant to every oath; it was always comforting to sit in villas of questionable provenance and hear the sound of boots echoing in the underground jails. Like all people of good will handed over to the tender mercies of a bunch of messianic thugs, Professor Allouche was subjected to several abductions, imprisonments, harassments and simulated executions, and was even forced into exile. His sojourn in Europe, even though it brought him worldwide recognition and earned him countless honors, didn't go to his head. If no man is a prophet in his own country, no man is master in another's either. Our eminent savant quickly realized that the respect of his western colleagues was a juicy trap, that the prizes he was awarded left an aftertaste of payment against future favors, and that his scholarly work took on political overtones the longer he spent hanging about in NGOs' editorial offices or seminar rooms instead of university lecture theatres. No one applauded his research any more; people saluted his pronouncements against the dictatorship flourishing in his country. The people who came to listen to him had brutish features and left a trail of documents with official seals in their wakes. In short, he was being manipulated, like a common-or-garden puppet. This affected him greatly. Intellectual honesty or the gestures of a politician, swindled nation or well-stocked wallet: the question had to be resolved definitively and precisely. Sitting on the fence was not an option, especially when you had spent the best part of your life getting shafted. There were no half measures for the professor. He rendered unto Clovis that which belonged to Gaul and, like the salmon that will never suffer the intoxication of the ocean, he came back to commune with the river of his birth, where the pebbles lack the majesty of coral but the reeds can hint at nobility even among straggly oleanders. He taught at the university right up to the day knowledge was thrown on the scrapheap. Credits began to be traded on strictly pornographic terms, while degrees came by way of the love hotel. Horrified, Professor Allouche tried to salvage some sticks of furniture from the wreckage, but this greatly displeased his colleagues, who balked at jumping their students on the bare floor…. To sum up, the age of gangrene was taking over from that of the computer. Somewhere, in a high place, the first markers were being laid out for the "drift" that Professor Allouche denounced in a French newspaper. Result: six months in prison for association with the former occupant.

When he came out of jail, the professor was no longer in full possession of his faculties. He was "transferred" to the asylum and there forgotten.

Nowadays, Professor Allouche doesn't really know whether he is still under observation or being consulted. He has an office at one end of a squalid hut, with a room on the floor above, and he dedicates himself completely to his patients, any other activity being risky, if not more or less suicidal.

I find him waiting for me in the parking lot of the psychiatric ward, his hands behind his back and his head lost in worries. His white coat lends a ghostly air to his lanky frame. He is so tall, perched on his wading-bird legs, that his back is beginning to slope more and more alarmingly. His wispy hair floats about his head like a puff of smoke. He looks like a phantom emerging from the mist. And keeping his troubles to himself is a waste of time: his distress is so blatant it makes his reticence absurd.

"One more minute and I'd have caught sunstroke," he says.

"Bad news, for a hothead."

He wipes the sweat from his brow with a finger and flicks it away, then lifts his thumb up to the sun, which is bleeding the sky white. "You'd think it was July."

"The fifth or the fourteenth?"*

"I'm talking about the time of year."

"Ah...."

He squints one eye at me and looks at me side-on. "Well, aren't you in a bad mood."

"It's in my nature."

"Am I to understand that you're not delighted to see me again?"

"On the contrary. I feel less out of place in an asylum than anywhere else."

"In that case, I'd be glad to put you up."

I open my jacket to show the strap of my shoulder-holster. "I've already got a straitjacket."

He smiles at last, and offers me a hand that is so clean I hesitate to take it.

He asks me to follow him. Having learned never to turn my back on an enemy, I let him go ahead of me, even though the professor is not on my blacklist. He shrugs and leads on, the back of his neck bright red, his steps slow in the intense heat.

The asylum is vast, like an empty building site. A good place to go round the bend. An old man is picking his nose in the shade of a tree. There is decay in all directions. Unsavory-looking huts, mournful as tombs, try to make themselves visible amid the rampant vegetation. Their padlocked doors are shocking, the bars on their windows distressing. Notwithstanding the unruliness of their tenants, they seem uninhabited. Here, society's rejected beings go to ground and wait to

---

* 5 July: Algeria's Independence Day; 14 July: France's Bastille Day.

be buried. I can imagine them behind the bars, their eyes elsewhere and their hands grasping at shadows, keeping watch, between two over-generous doses of sedatives, for this gravedigger who thinks it's beneath him to dig them a hole.

I have always been ill at ease in cemeteries, but a lunatic asylum grieves me more than a charnel house. There's no hell worse than a morgue haunted by the living.

"They're unpredictable, not wicked," says the professor, as if reading my thoughts. "Some of them were successful executives."

"Sometimes, to be mad is to be too gifted."

"Do you remember Chérif Wadah?"

"The African Che Guevara?"

"Well, he's here; him too."

"I don't believe it!"

"It's true, I promise you. He had a few disagreements with the revolutionary Family. Questions of principle. They ostracized him, then they started persecuting his family. One morning, he left his house and couldn't find his way back again. He was found near Staoueli, dressed in rags and with a club in his hand, cursing both gods and men at the top of his lungs. He doesn't remember any-one. His wife and kids come and visit him. He refuses to see them. Sometimes he goes for days without saying a word. Other times, he launches into incomprehensible diatribes until he passes out."

"That's so sad."

"Can you imagine; an icon like him."

"Algiers doesn't believe in heroes, Professor. She prefers martyrs."

He stops and raises his index finger to show his agreement.

"I hope you haven't called me in to mess with my mind," I add. "I've got kids; it would be tedious if I couldn't remember them."

He nods.

We enter a small graveled courtyard opposite a grim build-ing. A man is sitting cross-legged at the entrance, wearing a paper hat like a circumflex accent on his head. When he sees us, he sits up, joins his hands beneath his chin and salutes us like a Buddhist monk.

The professor's office would fit in a pocket handkerchief. It's not much bigger than a closet, and it reminds me of those obscure little rooms in the basements of police stations where you grill the hard nuts. A formica table, a worn-out armchair, a metal chair and, on the wall, a child's picture of a dog with two heads. At the back, on a shelf, an old tape recorder of Russian manufacture, grotesque with its huge reels and cardboard lid.

The curtainless window looks out over a cracked irrigation tank. In the distance, a feeble-minded inmate believes he is a fountain. With his trousers around his ankles, he is urinating while rotating on the spot.

"He's proclaimed himself the king of the big cats," the professor explains. "Every day, at exactly eleven thirty, he comes and marks out his territory."

"He's right."

"Coffee?"

"No thanks."

"Tea then?"

"Am I here as a friend or in my professional capacity?"

"Both."

"In that case, a glass of water will be fine."

The professor takes my order but doesn't ring for anyone. I understand that his budget is limited and that the customary niceties are purely symbolic. Besides, there's no cup or jug to be seen anywhere, not even an ashtray. Apart from a few crumpled sheets of paper, a prescription and an unused exit permit, the place would pass for an irreproachably clean urinal.

"Here," he says, opening a file in front of me and taking out a photograph of an apparently rather well-bred young man. He immediately settles down in his armchair and folds his arms across his chest, like a man who has finished his presentation.

First, I fiddle with the picture. On the back, a leaky pen has added a date, a serial number and some notes. I fish out a few slips of paper from the file. There are reports on consultations, recommendations addressed to the governor of a prison, an identifying cover sheet—all irreconcilable with the heat burning up my skull.

"I suppose it's up to me to work out what the hell this is about."

"Not necessarily."

Outside, the patient has finished urinating. Now he is facing the window and displaying his sex as another man might display a sword.

The professor reverts to his previous, more cheerful, mood, rests his elbows on the table and consents to explain: "Nobody knows where he's from. One morning, he woke up and he'd completely lost it. Everything between sucking his thumb and losing his cherry was a complete blank. No name, no relatives, no address. We thought it was amnesia: the man has the memory of an elephant. We thought he'd gone mad: the patient turns out to be as clever as a conjuror. So what's going on? Nobody can come up with a theory. One evening, our friend decided to hand himself in to the cops. At that time, which is to say more than ten years ago, he was quite handsome, just over twenty years old, an intelligent look about him. As soon as they brought him to me, I said to myself that this man was from a good family. Very classy, very smooth. A bit too much so. But plausible. A university graduate? We looked, but we didn't find. A young executive? We looked, but we didn't find. On the report, we wrote a note: Refuses to reveal his identity. Later on, we wrote SNP.* He didn't object. What does he want? To be locked up in a fortress so that he doesn't commit any more atrocities. He states that he has killed a lot of people, but he doesn't remember where he buried or left the bodies. His first victims were two old people that he didn't know from Adam and Eve. His car had broken down at the entrance to a small village. It was dark. He knocked on a door and asked for help. They put him up for the night. He left very early the next morning, leaving the car behind. A stolen car. Two days later, a neighbor noticed the smell of decomposition. The police found the old couple in the outhouse. This was in 1970.... Two months later, he's hitch-hiking on a remote road. Two months after that, a forest ranger finds a van hidden under a tree in the woods. Inside, the corpse of a livestock dealer. Then, one evening, he goes to the nearest police station and gives himself up. He confesses to seven murders. Then ten, and then

---

* SNP (*sans nom patronymique*): no family name. These initials were used to identify orphans of the war of independence in the 1960s.

24

twenty-odd. Apart from the old couple and the livestock dealer, no details of his other victims."

The man in the photo suddenly seems to snicker. I hurriedly cover it up with a folder.

"If you've brought me here thinking you're going to impress me, you're mistaken," I warn him. "I've got far more frightening files at the back of my desk drawer. Serial killers we don't talk about because we don't want to inconvenience our *zaïms*,* but our taboos don't make them proliferate any more slowly or make them any less of a nuisance. I've seen many go through our premises. Each one more unhinged than the last. I've even had conversations with some of them; as a result, I have nightmares every other night."

"This one's different!"

The professor is shouting. His fist has struck the table. What I read in his eyes tells me I should calm things down. I draw him into a discussion: "What's this all about, exactly?"

He relaxes his fist, slips it under the table and rubs it discreetly. After a considerable while, he confesses, hoarsely, "The shock of my professional life."

"I suppose that's meant to terrify me too."

"Certainly."

"Is it the story that's strange, or is it just you shitting yourself?"

"Both."

"And our friend?"

"He keeps me awake at night."

"Do you think he enjoys it?"

"If he does, he hides it well."

I examine my fingernails, to look like a man who is considering the matter seriously, and continue the discussion. "Where is he now?"

"In prison."

"And where do I come in?"

The professor wrings his hands to show his discomfort. He gets up and switches on the tape recorder. "Listen to this for me, Brahim,"

---

* *Zaïm*: originally a Turkish chief heading a mounted militia also called a *zaïm*. By extension, a leader.

The reels creak. Suddenly, a cavernous voice echoes around the room:

"The wheel has come full circle. Here I am, back at square one. I should have known. There was nothing for it, I had to move around. That's been obvious since the beginning. The *fellagha** who butchered my family wanted to prove something to me, that's for sure. What exactly? He didn't know. He couldn't offer me any explanation. Having a particular reason to kill isn't necessarily enough to justify murder. I should have heeded my childish inertia; if I didn't understand the significance of the horror that was happening to me, perhaps it was because there was nothing to explain. Too easy. I absolutely had to understand. To have a clear conscience, to go back to a normal life? Can you regain your zest for life after witnessing the massacre of your family? Maybe. It wasn't for me. Something wasn't right. So I decided to see things clearly. I wanted to understand. Now I do. It's been long and hellish, but I've made it: *I understand!*"

The professor: "And what do you understand?"

The cavernous voice: "That there was nothing to understand. Nothing…. All those killings were just so many red herrings. I'd been had. I was wearing myself out trying to find the answer to a question that didn't even need to be asked. Why do people kill? When you kill, you don't ask questions; you act. Action becomes the only expression. The killing begins at the point where you no longer expect an explanation. Otherwise, you'd do without. Don't you think? You kill so as not to try to understand. It's a product of failure, a signed abdication. Murder is the killer's inability to reason, the point where a man rediscovers his atavistic reflex, where he stops being a thinking entity. The wolf kills by instinct. Man kills as a vocation. However many possible motives he professes, he won't justify his action. Life isn't within his sphere of responsibility, so how does he dare to dispose of it as he sees fit? His decision isn't based on any admissible argument; it's born of his insignificance. Anyone who doesn't respect the lives of others hasn't understood his own. Nothing. From nothingness to

* *Fellagha*: partisan who fought for independence from France, especially between 1954 and 1962.

26

nothingness, from the opaque to the shadowy, he looks for himself and can't find himself. Don't we say, 'Silence! There's killing to be done'? Why ask for silence when the universe is about to echo with intolerable howls? I've often thought I had the power of the gods, to the point that I was convinced I was the master of my victims' destiny. The result? The victim dies, and everything departs from me. I'd find myself as alone in the world as Heaven on the day after the apocalypse.... What good has this done me, ultimately? Even if I've understood, where have I got to? Precisely back to where it all started. So much waste, such a disaster. I'm my own failure incarnate. I'm not worth any more than the bodies that have paved my way. A complete nobody, a murderer who, having lost his bearings, will soon lose his soul, that's where I've got to. I despise myself, now that there's nothing to hold me back. I don't exist any more. I'm a dead rat, a piece of rotting garbage. I'm the abyss that's sucking me down and tearing me apart at the same time."

The professor stops the tape recorder and sits down again.

He clasps his chin in his hands again.

"He said that after his first stay behind bars. The prison authorities handed him over to me to see whether he had recovered his memory and whether he had calmed down. It seems he had suddenly stopped wreaking havoc."

"You didn't agree?"

"No."

"Was he raving?"

"In a sense."

"Did you send him back to jail?"

"Not a chance. He interested me. He spent seven years in my asylum. Every time I thought I was within an inch of understanding his personality, he would manage to retreat behind another, more complex, more terrifying one.... Listen to this one too. These are his words, three years after the ones you've just heard."

The reels start up again and the voice, clear this time, grips us again:

"Do you know why God doesn't let angels and demons kill each other? Because if they declare war on each other he won't be able to tell which side is which or tell them apart. Once hatred has taken up residence somewhere, everything is demonized, the just as well as the base. War isn't a game of chess. It's checkmate. A moment that can never be understood by people living in peacetime. It's all very fine to condemn violence from behind a Martini or from the depths of a comfortable living room. But what do we really know about it? Nothing. We can become indignant, we can protest, we can hold our heads in our hands—the hell we can! Violence has its own logic. It's just as rational as desertion. It has its values and even its own morality; values that have nothing to do with conventional values, and a morality that doesn't conform at all to Morality, but which are nonetheless valuable and constant. At the very moment that the desire to kill becomes the only route to salvation, the wildest animals will beat a retreat in the face of man's savagery. Because, of all the hydra-headed monsters, man is the only one that *knows* how to cross the line into animalism while remaining lucid. There is nothing more monstrous than human rage. It's perfectly aware of its ignominious nature, which makes it more horrifying than the suffering it inflicts. It's called barbarism, which is to say something neither hyenas nor ogres are capable of imagining, let alone carrying out. And you ask me why the mouth, which used to kiss, suddenly starts biting; and why the hand, which used to caress, starts destroying? It's precisely because I don't know the answer that I kill. I kill to understand. And I'll go on killing as long as I don't understand what pushes a human being to excel in the art of lavishing the most excruciating torments on his fellow men. I'd like to *know*, know what prevents a man from resisting the demands of his madness, how he manages to bring it to life so admirably."

The professor switches off the tape recorder and stares into my eyes. He sees very quickly that I'm not following, purses his lips and sits back in his chair.

"After that, I was afraid to keep him. My patients weren't safe any more, and my warders weren't up to guarding him. I handed him back to the penal authorities…. In prison, he isolates himself. Completely. Not a word for months on end. Then, one morning, they hand him back to me. And I discover a stranger. A saint filled with fervent piety, hands pressed together beneath his chin, kneeling in front of the skylight, praying to the point of exhaustion. Frantz Fanon himself would have handed in his notice."

"Had he descended into Islamism?"

"He doesn't know what it is."

"Could somebody have indoctrinated him?"

"I tell you this is nothing to do with the Islamist movement. His is an exceptional case."

"Do you have a theory?"

"I've had several. Right now, I'm fresh out. My traps are child's play to SNP, no worse than slip knots."

"And then what?"

"Back to prison. Five years of piety. Docile. But taciturn. Clean. Always performing his ablutions.... He's got me completely turned upside-down, I tell you. The moment he's standing in front of me, my guts turn to water.... That man," he adds, gathering up the file, "is convinced that he came into the world just to make his fellow men suffer."

"I still don't see what you expect from me."

"I suggest you start drinking two liters of coffee a day. Because you won't want to close your eyes from now on. Our friend has been granted a presidential pardon. He'll be free on the first of November. When I heard the news, I got in touch with the governor of the prison immediately. The man told me that the list had been drawn up by a committee of experts, which had declared that the subject could be freed. I wrote to the committee in question. I got the Ministry of Justice involved. The committee is completely independent, they told me. I alerted the Ministry of the Interior. Nothing. I even informed the press. A woman journalist came to see me. No follow-up. Time passes, and SNP is already dreaming about his next victims. That's why I called you, Brahim."

"If I understand correctly, I'm supposed to go to the president and ask him to revoke his decree?"

"It's very serious, Brahim."

"What can a lowly cop like me do once a presidential decree has been signed, Professor; when the ministers responsible won't lift a finger; when the whole world doesn't give a damn? Pick him up as he leaves the prison, book him for something and throw him back in the slammer? I don't see how I can stand in the way of someone who's been rehabilitated by justice."

"Watch him."

"With what? For how long? In whose name? Honestly, Professor, do you think it's worth it?"

"Because I tell you he'll start up again."

"Do you have any evidence?"

"I'm a psychiatrist, for crying out loud. This man is my patient. He's extremely dangerous."

"Did he make trouble in the slammer?"

"A hawk in a cage is no better than a crippled sparrow. SNP is clever. He's waiting for his prey. Once he's breathing free air, he'll gorge himself. He's a predator. He takes pleasure in hovering over the flock like a bad omen, choosing his prey, preferably without any selection criteria, and swooping down on it. You have to hear him describe how he decided, on the spur of the moment, just like that, how the man on the road, the child or the old peasant woman he met by chance at the corner of a path, *had to* disappear. Not because they had some sort of deplorable attitude, but just because he had decided that that was the way things stood. His happiness, all his happiness, lies in catching the world off guard, without the slightest motive, merely so that he can be aware of his utter *freedom*, the kind of freedom that puts him beyond the reach of the most basic doubt. It's a unique case, the most serious and the most worrying I have ever had to study, Brahim."

Chapter three

So I left Professor Allouche with a few butterflies in my stomach. I feel cold despite the heat, and I am going numb from head to foot. I drive all the way to Ben Aknoun in third gear, with the accelerator pressed to the floor. At no point do I notice the shrill screaming of the valves. I don't have any particular reason to get myself into such a state, and yet something is fermenting in the pit of my stomach, spreading its aftertaste into the back of my throat. The problem is that every time a premonition like this hits me, I can be sure that misfortune will strike.

When I get back to Headquarters, I bump into Inspector Bliss. Seeing him gives me goosebumps. If Bliss welcomes you at the gates of Paradise, you can be sure that Hell has taken up residence.

"Lino called," he announces. "He wants three days' leave."

"*Niet!*"

"He says he has a problem."

"I thought he was sick."

"Maybe it's a health problem."

"I don't give a damn. I want to see him tomorrow, in my office."

Bliss wrinkles his snout and confides, "I don't think Lino will

31

be in tomorrow. Lino's asking permission to be away is just a professional reflex. He's been going where his mind takes him, that's if he's got any left."

He casually raises a finger to his temple, runs down the steps and heads for his car.

"And where are you going?"

"The boss asked me to take care of a matter of some delicacy," he says. "His way of telling me to piss off." Then, spreading his arms: "*C'est la vie.* Some people work their butts off to make ends meet, at the risk of electrocuting themselves. And some milk cows with their gloves on."

"Careful, you pygmy, some cows have only one teat."

"I always test the ground before I commit myself." He snaps his fingers suddenly: "In fact, that reminds me. From now on, if you need me, ask the boss first. He insists."

And he vanishes, like a malign genie summoned by a spell.

The next day, first thing in the morning, I find Lino in his office, hunched self-importantly over some papers, editing something. He's trying to fool my cunning Kabyle brain into thinking he's working non-stop, but a glance at the chaos surrounding him is enough to see that he's absorbed in recopying, word for word, an old report that was found unacceptable. Naturally, Lino persists in this silly play-acting: he pokes out his tongue as he forms the capitals, leans into his commas, scratches his ear to flush out the right word, so intent that he nearly hits the ceiling when he "notices" me in front of him.

"Is it eight o'clock already?" he exclaims, with a straight face.

"Am I to conclude that you've spent all night on your draft?"

"You know I leave nothing to chance when it comes to my work, Super."

I look him up and down. "I thought you were down with something."

"Yes, something serious. I asked for leave. Baya told me you refused. Okay, so I returned to my post. I'm no mutineer."

"How touching."

He looks down.

"Tidy up that lead-swinging paperwork of yours and follow me. We've got work to do."

Lino starts. "Will it take long?"

"That depends. Why?"

"Well, Super, I have an emergency this afternoon."

"I don't care."

Reluctantly, he puts his jacket on and hurries to catch me up in the corridor. Once we're in the car, I ask him, "Will you let me have the recipe for your potion?"

"What potion?"

"The one that cured your stinking cold faster than a session of hypnotherapy."

He smiles. Lino always smiles when I catch him out. It's a nervous reflex. I point my finger at him. He raises his hands in surrender, engages first gear and takes off at top speed.

The prison at Serkadji reminds me of a time I prefer not to dwell on. So I'll spare you the details. A ghastly institution, period. The jailer—who seems to have been created by the Lord purely as support for a tangled bunch of keys—throws back several latches, opens the grille and leads us down a series of grim corridors like a tale within a tale. He is as big as sin, tall as three inner tubes set atop one another—his ugly mug, his belly and his behind—three reasons why his self-important movements are wasted on us. Every now and then, he looks back to see whether we're following him and scowls when he sees we haven't turned back.

Finally, he stops in front of a massive door, bangs on it and steps aside to avoid being blown away by a voice fit to bring a shrouded mummy back to life.

"Y-e-e-e-e-s?"

The jailer announces us. The voice calms down, and we are greeted by a mammal of some kind barricaded behind an unconstitutional moustache.

There are people who insist on believing that a man's virility depends on the strength of his handshake. Our host is one of them. His grip is intended to be ebullient; mine is rather sensitive.

"Well?" he says, briskly.

I notice that the only chair in the room is his padded leather throne. I deduce that our friend has no more regard for his visitors than he has for the galley-slaves in his custody, who obviously have a hard time of it at his insatiable pleasure.

"Can't we relax somewhere and have a little chat?" I ask him.

"This is a house of correction, Superintendent, not a tea-house."

"Ah."

Taken aback by this reception, Lino's eyes flick left and right while he digests his indignation.

The governor puts his hands on his hips in a sign of boredom. "You want to talk to me about what?"

"If you're too busy, we can come back another time."

"I'm always busy. Let's get it over with."

"Very well, Kong," I mutter, a hair's breadth away from punching him.

"My name is Mr. Boualem."

"Well, Mr. Boualem. I've heard that some of your residents may be released as of the first of November."

"Do you have something against the president's decisions?"

He is trying to put words in my mouth. To wrong-foot me. I take a deep breath, take inspiration from the explosions pounding in my temples, screw up my eyes to distill my bile, and confide in him: "Strictly between you and me, Mr. Boualem, I don't give a shit about the president, his eunuchs or anyone else who thinks a cop doesn't have the right to beat up all the little bastards who'd like to think they're the guardians of the Temple." He steps back, which allows me to gain some ground. "True, you're the master of this particular fairground ark, but I'm an animal of a different stripe, and I hate apprentice lion-tamers. So you can keep your over-zealous act for your menagerie, okay? I'm here on business."

The gorilla's backward step was only, it turns out, a tactical retreat, because he now turns it into a run-up and charges: "The hell you are!"

Lino, standing beside me, is disoriented. Not by the gorilla's aggression but by the moderation of my response—normally, when my yelling is unpersuasive, I give it an escort of blows. But Lino isn't one to strain his neurons. He needs a diagram. If he had cast an eye over the file instead of copying out old reports to impress me, he would have known that Mr. Boualem is the brother-in-law of a poisonous nabob,* and that he is only the governor of a jail so that he can follow his family's vocation, which is to bring recalcitrant souls to heel so as to have cowed ones at their disposal.

I say, with a *sang-froid* I wasn't aware I possessed, "It's about SNP...."

"Again?"

"Professor Allouche..."

"Professor Allouche is a degenerate. He's mad, he's off his head, he's hallucinating. A committee of experts studied the whole list of inmates proposed for release by presidential pardon, case by case. SNP was interviewed, probed, challenged, submitted to various chemical tests, and declared Fit for Release. By an official committee, competent and credible, made up of eminent psychologists and respected officials. That's good enough for me. A presidential decree has been signed, Superintendent. You're a civil servant, surely you understand what a decree like that means."

"Very well...may one see this man who is Fit for Release?"

"Do you have a warrant?"

"Only a credit card."

"Sorry, Superintendent. Jailers don't have the same options as cashiers."

"I'm prepared to mortgage my shirt. I won't be long. I want to see him."

He shakes his head contemptuously. "Out of the question."

And he turns his back on us.

Lino sees my rage welling up. He grabs me by the elbow and tries to steer me away from an irreparable mistake. I allow him to do it. It's not that I lack the desire to kick this boorish lout's ass, but

---

*   Nabob: business leader, member of the elite.

I don't really see the point. Sometimes you can right a wrong, but you can never cure wrong-headedness. It's a question of mentality.

* * *

Professor Allouche calls me just as I am getting ready to go to bed. Mina hands me the receiver and disappears. I wait until she has closed the door behind her before I start the conversation:

"Yes?"

"I've been trying to reach you at your office all day. Your secretary said you were out."

I understand that this is his way of asking whether it was down to me shaking my head at Baya.

"She wasn't lying to you, Professor. I was frightening myself, as you recommended."

His tone hardens: "You went to see the prisoner?"

"The governor prevented me."

"Why?"

"My shirt wasn't sufficient collateral."

The professor mutters something that is covered by the sound of frying, sniffs, goes on thinking aloud for five seconds.

"Furthermore," I reassure him, "I had a word with a lawyer friend of mine. He listened carefully and politely, but he was absolutely clear."

"Meaning?"

"SNP will be set free in five days."

"What do you mean?" the professor cries, with a lump in his throat.

"It's pretty clear: our alleged madman will go home and lead a normal life again."

The professor spits out another string of curses and concludes with a baffled sigh, "This is terrible. They're making a dreadful mistake. Nobody has the right to treat such an explosive case lightly. Why won't they listen to me?"

"You would have done us a big favor if you'd just given him an injection."

"You're not serious."

"Maybe not, but I'm tired."

A glance at the clock on the wall tells me that I'm ten seconds away from passing out.

After a stream of indignant protestations, the professor inquires, "What do you intend to do, Brahim?"

"Sleep."

Chapter four

I am at the end of the corridor, and after a while I notice Lino chatting up his reflection in the bathroom mirror. He's inspecting himself from every angle, pressing down a hair here, checking the creases in his jacket there, so fascinated by the Olympian geometry of his profile that he doesn't notice me.

Eventually, for fear of being stuck there for the rest of the day, I slip in behind him and coo in his ear, "Mirror mirror on the wall, which Algerian flatfoot is the biggest turkey of them all?"

Lino looks me up and down. He's not happy about my intrusion and is beginning to find me meddlesome.

"What's your problem, Super?"

"You're the one with a problem, son."

"So what business is it of yours?"

"Let's say I have an interest."

He stares at me in the mirror.

"You haven't got enough worries of your own, Super?"

"We're none of us alone in this world. Whether we like it or not, everything around us involves us."

"I don't follow you."

"There's a rumor going round the town…"

"Let it," he interrupts me coldly. "That's what it's for."

"Yes, but it's dragging you along like a scandal."

He clenches his jaw. He's ready to explode. I'm not intimidated.

Lino sees clearly that he can't win against me. Like a good subordinate, he throws in the towel, steps aside so as not to stain his tie on my belt, and heads for the exit.

"Try not to forget everything between the sheets."

He considers my words, then comes back and places the silk of his burgundy shirt a few centimeters from my threadbare jacket.

"Can I ask you a question, Superintendent?"

It's not the first time he's called me that, but never in this tone of voice.

I spread my arms: "Why not?"

"Would it be too much to ask you to let me stand on my own two feet?"

"You'd trip over your shoelaces."

He nods, ground down by my abuse of authority, runs his hands through his hair, and leaves.

Lino is not in good form. Normally, when I wind him up, he gives as good as he gets. For the last few days, it's as if he can't bear anyone. He comes in in the morning with his nose in the air, plants himself behind his desk and locks himself away with his thoughts. It's not Sunni. A notorious skirt-chaser, Lino spends most of his time lurking in dubious alleyways in search of a well-padded and not too expensive whore. Occasionally, he manages to flaunt one of his less desperate conquests in a grill-room before investing in a quick session upstairs or a tumble in the bushes in the forest of Baïnem. The next day, he spends the morning describing his coital prowess, and seems proud of causing the overexcited cops clustered around him to salivate. It never lasts long. In the afternoon, I find my lieutenant buried in his files again, conscientious and methodical, so worthy that I would willingly entrust my own sister to him for the weekend. But Lino has changed. He pays more attention to his center parting than to the consistency of the times in his reports. Besides, he's practically never here. We see him roll up two hours late, rifle through his drawers without the slightest conviction, knock back a coffee and, the moment my back is turned, puff! Vanished.

I watch him go. There's something in his manner I don't like. If he thinks he's old enough to steer his own ship where he pleases, he's free to take the wheel in his own way. After all, what business is it of mine? It's just that, well, my instincts as Lino's Little Big Brother, forged in the purest FLN tradition, tell me that my apprentice helmsman's compass is off-kilter and, if I don't keep a close eye on him, there's a good chance he'll founder on hidden rocks.

My suspicion becomes stronger when Inspector Bliss comes over to spoil my lunch in the Headquarters canteen. He puts his tray down on the table and sits opposite me with an abject smile.

"I hope I'm not disturbing you?"

"You'd disturb a mummy in his sarcophagus," I tell him.

The bastard ignores the disgust he inspires in me, looks right and left, as befits those who always have some ghost or other on their tails, and leans over my dessert to murmur, "The fish isn't fresh. I saw a cat coming out of the kitchen just now. He wasn't feeling well."

"Maybe he didn't like the look of your face."

He removes his emetic visage from its position over my yogurt. The director worships him, and he is capable of showing insufficient respect to me, so I have half a mind to sink my fist into his pathetic jaw—I who have managed to keep my hands clean despite the pool of shit I stir all day long. His fingers fiddle with his fork, toying with a piece of whiting, go back to a dubious-looking bone, then dislodge an olive lurking under a lettuce leaf. I understand that he's choosing his words and start tapping the side of my plate with my knife to put him off.

"Llob, my brother," he sighs, "if I've chosen to sit with you it's in no way because your company stimulates my appetite. I know what you think of me, and you know what I think of you; there's no point going over that. I just came over to draw your attention to that idiot Lino of yours.... I'm not in the habit of playing the last-minute savior, and nor am I disinclined to report to the boss—God alone knows how much I enjoy opportunities of that kind—and yet, if I prefer to speak first to you, my immediate superior, it's because you're the only one in a position to wake him up—"

"Can't you cut to the chase? My sole is beginning to smell bad."

Bliss chuckles. A pack of hyenas couldn't do half as well. His two-facedness sends shivers up and down my spine. The piece of tomato I've been savoring suddenly fills my mouth with a bilious secretion.

"How stupid can you be?" he mutters.

He picks up his tray and gets up. In his opinion, he has done his duty; he doesn't care about anything else. He even takes malicious pleasure in the idea of holding me responsible for the future of my principal team-mate, To rub it in, he adds, loud enough for everyone else to hear, "I thought you had more consideration for your men...."

Then, his expression as cutting as a knife, he goes and joins a group of officers who are obviously disgusted by my attitude.

"You ought to listen to him," someone behind me whispers.

I turn round. Lieutenant Chater, head of the Special Section, winks at me. The twinkle in his eye leads me to put my arm over the back of my chair.

"You seem to know something about it too."

Chater, who has finished his meal and is getting ready to return to duty, hesitates for a moment, weighing up the pros and cons.

"What's going on?"

"It would be best to talk to him about it, Superintendent. Lino needs someone to take an interest in him."

"Meaning...?"

Chater's embarrassment is obvious, but the seriousness of the situation gains the upper hand over other considerations.

"No one in the farmyard wants him to end up in the soup, you understand?"

"What is it that's got you all stirred up?"

"The guys at Headquarters are gossiping. They think Lino's going a bit far for a minor functionary whose salary is just enough to keep him from starvation. He changes his outfits more often than a film star."

"So what?"

"So I don't know what to tell you. Lino is free to flirt with

Queen Elizabeth, if he thinks he has a chance of getting past her praetorian guard. Unfortunately, the woman he's seeing doesn't have a praetorian guard, and Lino doesn't have a chance of being slowed down on his way up shit creek."

Upon which, he says goodbye.

Once I am alone, I realize I no longer have any desire to eat, from which I deduce that the fish must in fact not have been fresh.

That afternoon, I catch Lino telling Inspector Serdj to mind his own business. They're in Baya's office, and the argument is getting more and more venomous, amid a storm of flying paper and creaking chairs. Serdj is trying to calm things down with sweet-talk. He's standing against the wall, his hands held out in front and his neck swallowed up in his shoulders. Lino has him cornered and is waving a furious finger about in all directions. Baya, for her part, can't get a word in. She can see that the situation is about to degenerate but, being a female relegated to the rank of less than nobody, there's nothing left for her to do but watch the men with imploring eyes.

She's relieved to see me in the doorway.

"What the hell is all this racket?" I roar.

Serdj gulps convulsively. His respect for me, in combination with the coarseness that has just poured out of my mouth, is almost suffocating. Lino, on the other hand, continues to treat his finger like a machete, not giving a royal damn for my commanding yell. His burning eyes are fixed on the inspector's as if to kill him. I have to grab his shoulder to hold him back.

"That's enough, four-eyes! When the boss says 'Down!' you hit the dirt, understand? This is my patch, and I don't allow anyone to raise his voice louder than mine."

Lino finally steps back, without taking his eyes off the inspector. He wipes his throbbing lips with his fist, quivers for five seconds, sniffs fit to burst his nostrils, and returns to the attack:

"I'm an adult, fully grown," he screams at Serdj. "I don't need any lessons, least of all from a bumpkin like you. My life is my business. I'll go out with anyone I please and I'll dress according to my taste. Am I getting through your thick skull?"

43

"Okay," Serdj concedes. "I take back what I said. I didn't mean to be offensive."

"You were being worse than offensive, *kho*, you were being an asshole. Did I so much as ask you the time of day?"

"No."

"Then what business is it of yours?"

Lino remembers my hand on his shoulder. Using two fingers, he removes it as if it were a detonator. The rudeness of his gesture staggers me, but I hold back. The lieutenant is a comma away from imploding, and I have no desire to pick up the pieces. His labored breathing machine-guns my face, while a milky froth ferments at the corners of his mouth. It's true to say that, like all his kind, Lino is a drop of nitroglycerine in search of the slightest jolt, and yet this is the first time he's worked himself up into a rage like this.

"Can I speak to you?" I ask him.

"About what?"

"Come into my office."

"I don't have time."

"Don't behave like a fool, follow me. It won't take long."

"I'm not in the mood, Superintendent. I'd rather bring this to a close right now. I'm tired and I need to go home."

"It's not closing time yet."

Lino persists. His eyes rake fiercely over Serdj, he adjusts the collar of his shirt, almost pushes past me and heads for the exit from Headquarters.

"I said it's not closing time yet."

"I'm not deaf," he growls, telling me to take a walk.

When the lieutenant has gone, I ask Serdj to enlighten me. The inspector tries to make light of the incident. I bang on the table; he raises the white flag. It's as though he was just waiting for this, so that he could pour out everything he had trouble digesting. He starts by explaining that Lino has been acting strangely lately—to be precise, ever since he fell for a certain upper-class lady.

"He's asked me for money," he tells me. "'I'll give it back tomorrow, first thing,' that's what he promised. Fat chance…two days later, he hoodwinks Baya into giving him half her paycheck. 'I've got plans,' that's what he told her. Fertile plans, because Lino doesn't know the difference between a colleague and a money-lender any more. He'll latch onto anyone. Within three weeks, he's into half the guys at Headquarters for money, and it doesn't seem to slow him down.... This woman's beyond his means. I thought she'd realize, and dump him. Lino's burying his head in the sand. He's getting more and more of a taste for luxury and extravagance. His colleagues are worried sick about him. They're certain that, at this rate, the lieutenant is bound to make a mistake, a serious one, if you know what I mean. So I came to have a chat with him, hoping to make him see reason. You just saw the result. Lino's gone off the rails."

I pinch my chin between my thumb and forefinger and think about this story, while Baya studies my frown. After my meditation, I say to Serdj, "What gives you the right to claim Lino is being taken for a ride by a gold-digger? Do you know the lady? Has she come among us as a trainer, do you have proof that she's stringing him along?"

Serdj puffs out his cheeks.

"Not really."

"In that case, why the drama?"

"It's the general feeling at Headquarters, Superintendent. Lino is living beyond his means. And because he can't keep up with the pace of this woman he's already out of breath. He's on edge from morning till night. It's not normal."

"I don't think it's a crisis," I suggest.

"I don't share your opinion," Serdj insists, stubbornly. "Lino's feet have come off the pedals. I know him. When he reacts the way he just did, it's because he's lost his way."

With a gesture, I ask the inspector to keep his cool.

"Serdj, poor Serdj, don't you see that Lino is finally going through puberty? It's plain and obvious: he's in love, that's all...Lino's in love."

"You think so?"

"It stands to reason."

Serdj is skeptical.

I explain: "Love is a delightful improbability, a wonderful upheaval; it's a fabulous catastrophe. And Lino is right in the middle of it. He's being born again, do you see? He's finding himself, becoming aware of his true capacity and, rejoicing in his good fortune, making a complete fool of himself. Like all lovers, since the dawn of time."

"It's happened so quickly, Superintendent. There's haste in the air, and Lino is clumsy."

"It's love at first sight. It doesn't give you time to adjust your aim. And there's nothing you can do about it."

"Love at first sight?" Serdj frowns. Serdj, who can't possibly know what it is because he was married at seventeen, to a girl he didn't know from Adam or Eve, as is customary in conservative families.

And now I feel queasy.

Love at first sight!

The resonance of such a phrase, within a cubicle with about as much romance as a dentist's office, catapults me through a thousand fairy tales. Unbeknownst to me, my voice softens, my soul bends like a weeping willow, and I hear myself telling a story: "I experienced love at first sight too. It's worse than sunstroke. I remember: the country had won its independence and Algiers was getting its last fix of the struggle. We laughed, we pranced about, we drank ourselves stupid between lynchings; in short, we were being dragged back into the world with forceps. It was intolerable and amazing at the same time. And in the midst of the delirium and the dazzling colors there was a suburban train station, gray as an island, lost among all the shipwrecks. A station that was keeping its peace. Other, less fortunate people were getting ready to leave the country and go into the unknown. Among the families clustered among their bundles, amid the vacant stares and the shadows of silence, *there she was*, sitting on a bench in a corner, a little apart, suspended between the jubilation in the streets and the despair of the platforms. The light from the windows clothed her in a glow that I've never been able to rationalize. She was French, twenty-three, twenty-five years old, as beautiful as you like, with eyes bigger than the Mediterranean. She was wearing a sad little hat and no earrings. Her cardboard suitcase was probably the extent of her wealth. Her long black dress went all the way down to her ankles, and her short jacket was almost hidden by its big padded buttons. The fabric left something to be desired, but the cut was impeccable. Only a refined and calm hand, such as hers, could have married such modesty to such perfection…. That day, I thought I was the happiest of men. I had danced in all the boulevards and drunk in all the bistros, and then came searching for something at the end of that suburban station where I had no reason to be. Maybe it was because of her that I was there, frozen by her slight smile, unable to see straight on that great day of victory. Outside, the sun refused to go down. In the station, it was already night. Suddenly, she looked up at me; it was like being hit by a wave…."

I fall silent. Brutally. A lump in my throat. Serdj looks down, moved. Baya whimpers imperceptibly, with her nose in her handkerchief. You could have heard a mosquito's whine around us. Shaken by the reappearance of such a memory, I take refuge in contemplating my hands.

"And what happened next?" asks Serdj, in a faltering voice.

"Next," I told him, raising my head…. "Next, Mina dug her elbow in my back and I woke up."

Chapter five

The road, long since orphaned by the loss of its paving stones, has become a track fit only for goats, their progress partly halted by a dead end in the form of a pile of debris. On both sides, tired buildings await the next earthquake so they can bury the poltergeists that haunt them once and for all. A sergeant spots me as I try an acrobatic maneuver among the heaps of garbage. He signals to me to park to one side. I nod and leave my old wreck at the foot of a decapitated lamp post.

"Over here, Superintendent."

He leads me through the ruts until we reach a large building, then starts shouting at the rubberneckers who have gathered at ground level:

"Make way for the superintendent!"

A fat housewife turns to see what the "local authorities" look like. My gut and jowls reassure her. She joins in and starts shouting at the others to make way.

The assembled company parts before me, like the court before its monarch, and I climb the protesting steps of the staircase. The floor on the landings is in such a state that you could see what is going on downstairs by simply striking a match. I grope my way forward, one hand on the wall, the other to my nostrils because of the stench. There's no point looking for a light switch; there isn't even a piece of wire to bring you to your senses.

A cop is standing guard outside the apartment at the end of the corridor, fingers pinching his nose; I have to push past him to get in. Inside the room, which is cluttered with the bundles of firewood so beloved of the poor, a woman sits on a mattress with three frightened children against her chest. Her wild hair and empty gaze freeze my entrails.

Serdj lifts a filthy curtain and joins me in the hallway. I'm surprised to see him there. Normally, Lino handles this kind of situation. But ever since he discovered certain affinities with Narcissus, Lino is nowhere to be found. Serdj notices my irritation and shrugs discreetly, telling me that when a colleague makes himself scarce there's nothing wrong with keeping his seat warm, even if it burns you up.

"The lieutenant had another engagement," he lies.

"What kind of engagement?"

Serdj deduces that I am not in a good mood. He gulps, to get rid of the lump trying to replace his Adam's apple.

"To tell the truth," he says, "I couldn't get hold of him."

"He was supposed to be on call."

"I don't know where he's got to."

"Yeah, right...."

Serdj looks down.

"So what's the situation here?"

He looks up again and leads me to the back of the apartment, where some officers are trying, without conviction, to reason with someone who is barricaded behind a locked door.

"His name is Rachid Hamrelaine, forty-six years old, five kids, of which two have gone missing. The neighbors say he's a respectable guy, discreet, no record. He's been locked up in his room for more than five hours. At first, he was yelling at everyone to leave him in peace. Now he's gone quiet. I think he hasn't got the strength to yell."

"How is he?"

"I had a look through the keyhole. He's losing a lot of blood."

"I suppose we can't just kick the door in?"

"He threatened to throw himself out of the window."

"Maybe he's bluffing."

"Maybe, but who would dare put it to the test?"

I look round at a window with smashed panes, consider the cylinder of butane gas stuck any old how in an alcove that serves as a kitchen, the battered saucepans and the thick layers of dirt moldering on the walls. There's not much to choose between this apartment and a stable. Poverty has made itself at home here, and has even allowed itself to show excessive zeal.

"It's not domestic bliss, I grant you, but why choose to end it all?"

Serdj asks me to follow him into a dismal laundry room, so that we won't be overheard by the children.

"He used to work in a state-owned enterprise, doing deliveries. He had a car accident on the job and lost a leg. In eight years, he hasn't been able to sort out his situation with the social security department at his ministry. They haven't even awarded him a provisional pension. From one day to the next, they stopped paying his salary. According to the neighbors, he's tried everything, including several hunger strikes; no good. A few days ago he got an eviction order. It was too much. This morning he spoke to his wife and children and told them that since no one down here would listen to him, there was nothing for it but to take his case to God. He went into his room and opened his veins. He was already bled dry when we arrived. We've tried to reason with him. He refuses to listen to us."

"Has he taken anything?"

"His wife confirms that he's never touched drink or drugs. He's a pious man."

"Have you called an ambulance?"

"It's on its way."

"Okay, I'll talk to him. Just so we keep him awake until the stretcher-bearers get here."

Suddenly, a commotion. Shouts echoing in the street. We rush to the balcony. The poor wretch has thrown himself into the void. He's lying there, three storeys down, with his arms folded and his face to the ground, his artificial leg twisted up beside him.

I lie awake the whole night.

In the morning, I arrive at the office before the security guard. I wander up and down the corridors for a good ten minutes, in search of who knows what. Then, as the first of my underlings begins to arrive, I close and double-lock the door to my cubicle and try to decompress, my mind empty. Baya arrives in due course, made up like a Chinese dragon. She says something I don't quite catch and then, faced with my moody expression, chooses to take up her usual position and pretend not to be there. After an interminable hiatus, I resurface and try to pull myself together. Nothing to be done. The poor wretch's contorted body on the ground pulls me down again. I close my eyes and dive down into the mire of my obsessions once more.

The telephone intrudes.

It's the boss.

"Brahim?"

"Director."

"Do you have a minute?"

"Of course."

"Then shift your fat ass and get yourself up to the third floor, now!"

When the director gets on his high horse like this, it means there's a windmill on the horizon. I'm not wrong. The director has every reason to abuse his prerogatives: he has Haj Thobane himself as a guest, which is to say, an inexhaustible supply of free drinks and other incidentals.

Haj Thobanc is an influential person in Greater Algiers. A piece of history. According to him, he was the one who kicked De Gaulle up the backside. In my country, of course, a legend like this has such a thick hide that a rhinoceros wouldn't rub up against it. And yet, despite the striking implausibility of his feats of arms, Haj Thobane has at least two merits, one philosophical, the other alchemical. First, he blows to pieces Darwin's famous theory that man is descended from the apes. Haj Thobane came down directly from his own personal tree. Second, in order not to be swept away when the wind changes direction, he concentrates twenty-four hours a day on keeping his pockets full, never producing a wad of banknotes from them unless he can immediately replace it with a bent cop; if he clinks a few coins together, the whole city salivates, like good little dogs. With him, nothing is lost, everything is won back; men as well as history, including the hand I refuse to hold out to him. And yet, despite the disgust inspired in me by his type, I'm almost glad to see him there, in the boss's office, as comfortable on his sofa as a cobra in a fakir's turban. They may flop stage left, but large fortunes make it big time stage right, which does have one advantage: from time to time—revolutionary principles watch out—we are lifted out of the prevailing gloom.

The boss introduces me: "This is our Brahim."

Haj Thobane, attempting to be charming, throws me a smile. Since I left my glasses on my blotter, this leaves me as cold as a slice of sausage. How many times have we met, Haj Thobane and I? Five, ten times? Maybe a few more. Whenever there's the slightest problem he turns up at our place, because he's a good friend of the boss. And yet, every time, he pretends not to remember where he has "seen me before." In comparison with this species of shark, we're just small fry, it's true, but there's no need to exaggerate.

The boss offers me an armchair. His solicitude worries me. I sit down opposite the nabob and hold my legs together warily, like a pious hypocrite who won't believe that all gynecologists are impotent.

"You're looking well," says the boss ingratiatingly as he joins us.

"Thank you, Director."

"Would you believe he's fifty-five years old, Haj?"

Haj Thobane pretends he can't get over his surprise.

"No kidding!"

"I promise you. Our Brahim celebrated his fifty-fifth birthday less than a week ago."

Haj Thobane leans back in stunned admiration. I, on the other hand, keep my guard up, continuing to play the game so as not to rub the boss up the wrong way. Ever since I applied for my first mortgage, I've tried to live up to it.

"He's a writer, too," the boss adds.

"Meaning what?"

"Well, he writes books."

"No!"

"It's true. He's even had some glowing reviews in the press."

Haj Thobane's eyes are now as wide open as a hippo's nostrils as it sinks into the mud. His esteem drives him to get up and shake my hand.

"A cop who writes: how revolutionary!"

"Speaking of revolutions," the director notes judiciously, "Sy Brahim is a former *mujahid.*"*

This is too much for Haj Thobane. Literally captivated, he praises me to the heavens. If he could do it on demand, he would willingly shed a tear or two to show how proud and happy he is to clasp a *maquisard*** to his bosom—a hero, that is, a real one, even if he hasn't been as successful in business as the All Saints*** pensioners. I try to take his adoration with a pinch of salt as he bruises my back with his enthusiastic back-slapping. Every now and then, of course, I find myself flirting with comfortable illusions, but never to the point of believing that a *zaïm* of Haj Thobane's caliber might hold me in his arms purely to congratulate me. Or rather, I am certain he is weighing me up to see which pocket—his jacket pocket or his pants pocket—he will have to put me in.

"It's wonderful," he breathes. "The miracle of our glorious revolution is brought to life in this man, who has managed, despite the incompatibility of the two vocations, to combine his job as a cop with his talent for poetry. It's certainly the first time I've witnessed an alignment of this kind. I don't think it could possibly happen anywhere else. A novelist superintendent! Really, it's…it's—"

---

* *Mujahid* (plural *mujahideen*): freedom fighter, usually with religious (Islamic) connotations.

** *Maquisard*: member of the *maquis*, the underground resistance against French colonial rule.

*** On 1 November 1954 (All Saints' Day), the FLN organized a series of coordinated attacks across Algeria. The FLN militias were few in number and poorly armed, and only seven people were killed, but these attacks (sometimes called *Toussaint rouge*, or Red All Saints' Day) marked the beginning of the war of independence. (Summarized from Martin Evans and John Phillips, *Algeria: Anger of the Dispossessed*, New Haven and London: Yale University Press, 2007.)

"Unnatural?" I suggest.

The director bursts out laughing, partly to cover up my gaffe and partly to beg me not to spoil the solemnity of the moment. I know the very important fact that he has encountered a number of financial obstacles in the construction of his villa, and I'm guessing that the billionaire's charity is entirely dependent on my courtesy.

Haj Thobane runs out of breath at last, to my great relief. He falls back into the sofa, crosses his legs and rests his hands on his knees. His eyes, which have been sparkling, go dead and his features reassume their usual rapacious cast. I understand that the overture is finished, and that it is time to move on to serious matters.

"Well, here's the thing," he begins, his methodical approach reminiscent of a killer whale circling its prey. "I'm sorry to disturb you so early in the day, Mr. Brahim, but it's about an officer of your acquaintance—"

"I don't know any army officers," I tell him without beating about the bush, "in case you're hoping I'll intervene in favor of some protégé of yours, nor any Customs officers, in case you've got some containers held up in port...."

My excessive zeal shocks the boss, who almost swallows his false teeth. Haj Thobane, for his part, is flabbergasted by my inappropriate behavior. He looks questioningly at the boss, as if to ask whether I'm perhaps not quite right in the head, and then he puts on his demi-god expression again, with the aim of crushing me with his displeasure.

"I find you rather impulsive, Mr. Brahim Llob. That's unwise, in someone as inexperienced as you. Do you seriously think I would come to a mere superintendent of police like you if I had a problem in the army or Customs? I am Haj Thobane; I can summon any government minister I want, my little friend, and he'll come, in his pajamas. Immediately. Just by snapping my fingers...."

When you attach a lot of weight to figures, I suppose you are not obliged to weigh your words.

He points his index finger at me:

"You have a misguided view of your own importance, Mr. Llob. Your wine needs to be watered a little."

"I'm a Muslim."

"In that case, you need some ambergris in the water you use for your ablutions. I haven't come here to ask for your services. Strictly between you and me, I'd need a microscope to find you. It's just that a certain officer in *your* service keeps wreaking havoc in my restaurants...." He pulls in his horns a little. "If it were up to me, I'd have taken him by the ear and thrown him in the trash, making sure I didn't get my hands dirty. We did some research, and found out that he's a police lieutenant working out of Headquarters. Since I'm a good friend of your director's, Mr. Llob, and since I wouldn't want some wretched police officer to spoil a ten-year friendship, I thought it best to come over here to clear up the misunderstanding in a friendly and discreet manner."

The boss is as red as a peony. He's been caught on the hop, and he doesn't know whether to throw himself at me or at his guest's feet to beg him to stay a little longer. Haj Thobane won't stay one more minute. He pushes the armchair back and, with the veins in his neck bulging and writhing like earthworms, strides over to the door.

Once in the centre of the room, he turns on his heel and points his index finger at me again.

"Tell your lieutenant not to come within spitting distance of me, Superintendent Llob. I can dissolve cockroaches like him faster than grains of salt. Above all, tell him that his pig's badge counts for nothing in my establishments and that, next time, I'll use it to shoot him down in flames."

The boss tries to retrieve the situation. Too late: the nabob goes out into the corridor and is swallowed up by the elevator, still waving at his boot-licker to signal that he should not accompany him. The grilles slide shut and the cabinet hides him from view. The boss stands there looking sick for some time, his head in his hands and his jaw jutting out. He mutters a string of curses and turns to me. Suddenly, his nostrils and eyebrows combine to recreate the howl of a wounded animal: "It's unspeakable, what you just did."

Who does he think he's talking to? But I try to keep my cool.

He gulps to control his breathing, comes back toward me and starts murmuring, his voice rising gradually, syllable by syllable, until it's a frightful yapping sound: "I should have trusted my instincts and kept you out of our conversation. I knew you were full of yourself, but I didn't know you were the king of the assholes. What's got into you, Superintendent? You showed the most deplorable stupidity. Silence! I don't want you to utter one more pig-headed word. If you think you're going to spoil things with my friends, you're barking up the wrong tree. *My* friends have good sense. That's the first thing. Second: you're going to call that simpleton Lino into your office and you're going to pull his ears until his nose disappears into his face. I've been hearing the echoes of his scandalous goings-on for quite some time. What's worse, he uses his police lieutenant's stripes to call attention to his mischief wherever he shows up and, consequently, he's dragging the force, the entire force, through the mud."

"Director—"

"Stop right there! I know what goes on at Headquarters, Superintendent, and what gets cooked up outside these walls too. I get discreet reports on every action, every gesture. That cretin Lino's problems are on their way to becoming a major scandal. I don't intend to enter into the details. Instead, I order you to shut him down, im-med-iate-ly."

"Am I to understand that I'm responsible for his extra-curricular activities?"

"Certainly."

"I don't agree. Lieutenant Lino is an adult. His private life is his business."

"Not when he waves his policeman's badge about the place."

I lower my head, drained. "I'll see what I can do, Director," I growl, just so that I can take my leave.

"And another thing: tell your young pigeon that the turtle dove he's showing off might help him play to the gallery, but if I were in his shoes I'd be careful of the song I'm singing. She's going to pluck him bare. After that, he won't be able to puff out his chest without covering himself in ridicule."

"I understand, Director."

"As for you, Superintendent, the next time you make a spectacle of yourself in front of a guest of mine, I swear I'll...I'll..."

A fit of coughing racks his throat and he bends double. With his face flushed and one hand to his neck, he dismisses me with a gesture and staggers over toward a flask of mineral water.

I make myself scarce before he grabs me with his paws.

Five minutes later, Bliss invades my office with the bogus levity of a magic spell hunting for a susceptible spirit. He scratches his chin, pretending to be interested in the ceiling, and states, disingenuously, "I thought I heard a certain Mr. Hyde prowling around on the third floor."

"Who's this Mr. Hyde?"

"Someone who makes people yell wherever he appears. I was with the boss's secretary when I heard shouting. I asked the secretary if there was a crisis somewhere; she answered that she didn't know of one. I glanced into the corridor and saw Haj Thobane losing it. He was screaming like you seldom hear."

"Maybe he caught a pubic hair in his zipper."

"He wouldn't have screamed so loud. Besides, there was a round guy in front of him. I'm sure Haj had it in for him."

"In what way was he round, this guy?"

"Well, enough to stop good cops maintaining good relations with the better class of people."

Now I see what he's getting at.

I put my pencil down on my blotter and growl, "What do you want, you maggot?"

He pinches his chin with his fingers, looking for the right words, then looks me in the eye, hoping I'll look away.

"It's not often that manna from heaven comes and visits us, Llob. I think it's unfair that a malcontent should blow his colleagues' ambitions sky high just because he got out of bed on the wrong side. We're sitting pretty, here at Headquarters. We look good, and that helps keep our slates clear. If you're diabetic, you're entitled to your quota of insulin free of charge. But, if you don't mind, let the rest of us enjoy our sugar in peace."

We have violated the territorial integrity of every cabaret on the waterfront, causing apoplexy among the sleek herds in the cattle markets of

Greater Algiers. At about eleven o'clock in the evening we get to the Blue Sultanate, a protected hunting ground built on a bluff overlooking the sea. I ask Inspector Serdj to wait for me in the car and climb the streaked marble staircase leading to this prestigious establishment.

The dolled-up eunuch on duty at the entrance is a hair's breadth from keeling over with indignation. Each step I climb seems as though it will deliver the fatal blow. When I arrive at his level, he tries to block my way like a halberdier: "Are you sure you know the way, *monsieur?*"

"Not exactly, Boo-Boo, but I'll get there."

I show him the holster for my nine-millimeter Beretta, thrust him aside like a curtain and cross the lobby with the courage of a bear prowling through a camp full of boy scouts. A few painted tarts gulp with terror and rush for shelter. I ignore them and continue on my trajectory until I reach a heavenly courtyard peopled with magnificent couples parading their charms around a swimming pool.

A patrician turd starts when he finds me beside him. He looks at me, then at the sky, trying to work out which planet I've dropped from.

"Lovely evening," I purr at him.

"Isn't it just?" he says, choking, as he escapes, probably to alert the decontamination unit.

I adjust an imaginary tie and glance around at this rich man's *milieu*. Our turtle doves are there, cuddling in a cozy corner, with their backs to the world. I've come across a few sirens within the borders of my country, I've been dazzled several times by Kabylia's muses, but the *houri* smiling there on the terrace of the Blue Sultanate seems to illuminate the belvedere all by herself, better than any sacred flame. She is so beautiful, with her mane of midnight-black hair and her sparkling eyes, that I don't understand why the chair she's occupying like a throne doesn't burst into flames.

No! I won't disturb them. They're so delightful, and seem so happy. Even if Lino does look like a shadow puppet beside his companion, I can't remember seeing him so fresh, relaxed and contented. I watch them for a moment, surprised to find myself smiling when they laugh and crossing my fingers when their hands join, moved, almost ashamed at having sullied the realm of their idyll with my unclean shoes.

Careful to avoid being noticed, I retrace my steps without a sound and hurry to get back to Serdj in the car.

Chapter six

Every October 31st for the last two decades, come rain or shine, I pack Mina and the kids into my car and head for my village. Even when I'm on call, I arrange for a replacement. Nothing on earth would make me miss the chance to mark the anniversary of the outbreak of the revolution among my own people. Every November 1st, I meet up with my old companions in arms at Ighider. They arrive from the four corners of the world, some of them at the wheels of big cars, some of them aboard clapped-out jalopies, and gather in the courtyard of the village patriarch. After the Homeric embraces and the traditional glasses of tea, we file through the village and across the fields to place a huge wreath at the foot of the martyrs' memorial. There we observe a minute's silence in memory of those who are not with us, after which several of us find it difficult to raise our heads. Then the *imam* raises the *fatiha*,* and everyone returns to the patriarch's home to honor a roasted sheep.

I think November 1st is still the most edifying day of the year

---

* *Sura al-fatiha*: opening chapter of the Qur'an, recited at the start of each unit of prayer.

for the village. Even Da Achour, who hardly ever leaves his little back-water because he is too obese, manages to join us. We dig up the dead years, the epic tales of the *maquis*, the napalm bombs and the buried towns; we praise the charisma of this *mujahid*, the patriotism of that tribe; we remember those who paid with their lives for the freedom our leaders are now trying to usurp; we sigh as we recall the ideals we have dumped on the scrap-heap, at the promises we have hurriedly forgotten; we take stock of the affronts that have become our silence, our resignation; we complain about our offspring, who have been left at the mercy of uncertainty and then, just as we start flirting with apostasy, we get a grip on ourselves. Together, hand in hand, we give each other support and promise to "carry on the struggle" to the end. In this way, the tribe reconnects with its ancestral commitments and is born again from its ashes, like a magnificent salamander. Within twenty-four hours, I regain my *dignity*. That's why I never miss this rendezvous, this indispensable absolution.

That's also, and above all, why I'm on the point of imploding on this morning of November 1st in the year of our presidential grace, as I sit fretfully in my car in front of the prison at Serkadji, waiting for a sick, murderous piece of garbage to re-enter society because a committee of sons of bitches of questionable competence believes indulgence and demagoguery are the trump cards when it comes to reintegration, that the kinder you are to an alligator, the more likely you are to tame him.

A light rain weeps onto the city, and a limping wind batters its face against the wailing walls that our ramparts have become. A thin mist hangs its dirty laundry out at the corner of the street. It's as if all the world's depression has arranged to gather in our country, to drain our morale. Since it's a public holiday, few are tempted to swap the fetid warmth of their beds for the sobering cold of the side-walks with their closed-up shops and their mutinous potholes. Apart from the warder on duty in front of the gate of the prison, pitifully solemn and still as a lamppost waiting for a dog to lift its leg against it, there isn't even the shadow of a soul about. It's only 6:42, and the morning is already regretting its decision to venture into this squalid neighborhood, where even the alley cats are observing a truce. If it weren't for the crackling of the drizzle on the burst garbage bags, you would hear the devil snoring.

Lulled by such monotony, my vision begins to blur, and soon I can't distinguish the condensation on my windshield from the mist outside, which is overcoming my thoughts. Little by little, my eyelids wind down like steel shutters and my limbs go numb. Somewhere between Mina and Morpheus, I nod off.

The throbbing of a motor makes me sit up; I notice that my cigarette has spread its ash all over my crotch and that Inspector Serdj has worn out his fingers drumming on the steering wheel.

According to the official statement, the lucky beneficiaries of the president's amnesty are free from midnight on. It will soon be seven o'clock, and the gate of the fortress refuses to spit anything out. Serdj is not happy. The night was harsh, icy. Since his seat is all caved in, Serdj ended up slumped against the door, his mouth bigger than his snores. I felt sorry for him. I could have spared him this ordeal, but I wouldn't have been able to track Lino on my own.

"I'm going to get some coffee, Superintendent. Would you like yours with a croissant or some bread and butter?"

"The little birdies will come out soon."

Serdj checks his watch and purses his lips shiftily, "We've got a good hour ahead of us."

"Why's that?"

"The prisoners will be released at eight o'clock sharp."

I start. "How do you know?"

"I called the duty officer yesterday. They said it was unwise to open the prison floodgates during peak crime hours, that they had to wait until morning."

"What are you talking about? And why didn't you say anything?"

"I thought you knew."

"You think spending the entire night in a disgusting crock like this is my idea of fun?"

Serdj is embarrassed. He wrinkles his nose and whimpers, "I thought you had something in mind, Superintendent."

"You think too much, Inspector. In a cop, that's worrying."

The coffee tastes of dishwater, but it helps me order my

thoughts. The warder on duty opposite us has vanished. A group of ghosts appears from somewhere, wreathed in veils that might once have been white. These are the women: mothers or wives who have come to the prison gate to collect their beloved inmates. Some of them have brought their kids, puffy-eyed with sleep. They stay close to the walls, looking nowhere in particular, and end up squatting down on either side of the sentry-box. Some men arrive too; they cluster together as far as possible from the women and watch for the first of the freed men, each with one foot propped against the railing, chins pinched between thumb and forefinger. A strange silence, the product of deep shame, falls on the street. Then, less than thirty minutes later, a monstrous caravan invades the square. A van tries to make its way through the crush, maneuvering fit to twist its chassis; this is the television crew, here to cover the occasion. A strong-looking individual jumps down onto the tarmac, camera on his shoulder, and is swiftly followed by a disheveled amazon, complete with visible microphone to show that she's there to work, not to be beaten up by the jailers. The strong individual switches on his camera and sweeps over the assembly of poor bastards, pausing on an old man whom the presenter corners with stupid questions about the presidential amnesty. The old man looks around, not knowing what to say. An old woman pushes him aside to get into the picture, grabs the microphone from the reporter and launches into a long diatribe. She talks about the years she has had to spend without her kid, the lowly and ignominious jobs she has had to do in order not to starve to death, and her a war invalid. The reporter points out that the president has been as generous as a pharaoh. The old woman concedes this on the spot and immediately, hands joined in prayer, begs God to direct the totality of his beneficence toward the Father of the Nation. Nodding delightedly, the journalist encourages her to continue in the same vein. Behind her, there is a loud creak; everyone freezes. The gate yawns open, closes again, then opens with a bang. The first of the freed men appear. Strangely, no one goes to meet them. The reporter takes advantage of this hesitation to pounce on one of the ex-prisoners, a man with the cowl-like beard of an ascetic, who is happy to play the question and answer game like a true scholar. He declares that he is relieved once again to see his relatives, his friends, the streets of his town, the mosque, that God has answered his prayers, that from now on he will serve Him and never disappoint Him. As for the presidential amnesty, he adds that it is God that places goodness in the heart of men, and that the president has no merit except that he does not insist on straying from the true path. The reporter doesn't appreciate this; she tells the cameraman to stop recording. As soon as the interview is over, the families fall upon their loved ones. Children throw themselves onto their fathers' necks, old people into the arms of their hooligans; the women are more restrained and just sob.

Serdj watches the freed men, his eyes jumping from the photo Professor Allouche gave us to the unkempt faces parading in the prison forecourt. SNP appears, finally, wrapped up in a spotless *kamis*. He is the size of a fairground strongman, with a solid face pierced by two expressionless eyes. He positions himself to one side, so as not to block the gate, and waits with his arms folded over his chest. The crowd begins to disperse; the potholes in the road are exposed again. The television van leaves, followed by clusters of journalists. Soon, all that remains is a small group of somewhat disoriented freed men on the sidewalk. A black car draws up in front of the prison gate; a door opens. SNP jumps into the back seat, where someone is waiting for him.

"Follow them," I shout to Serdj.

Standing in front of the window, I am pretending to look at the smog-covered city. In fact, I am spying on Lino's reflection in the glass. The lieutenant, who has his hands in his pockets and his mouth twisted in a scowl, seems uncomfortable. He is wearing a genuine suede jacket and a satin shirt, unbuttoned enough to show an impressive gigolo-type chain gleaming on the cushion of his chest. His tight trousers are held up by a gold belt, and his freshly polished shoes sparkle like a thousand stars. Even with my blocked nose, I know he has emptied a bottle of cologne over his body.

Ever since he took up with his siren, Lino has been more and more irritating. What really gets my goat is that I have noticeably lost authority at Headquarters because I can't impose it on my closest collaborator.

I take a deliberate interest in the decaying alleyways to see how long my little scamp can hold out. I know him; his convictions have no depth, and no amount of strutting about like a turkey-cock will convince me he is ready for a fight.

Lino can feel me watching him. He tries to keep his mouth scowling and his eyebrows raised. Indifference having failed, he decides to remove his paws from his pockets and puts them on his hips.

"Would you mind telling me why I have to hang around in this zoo, Superintendent?"

I run my finger round my shirt-collar to show him how unimportant he is. The lieutenant shakes his head, puffs out his cheeks and sighs. He puts his hands in his pockets again.

Defeated, he comes all the way up to my desk. "Am I allowed to know what you've got against me, Superintendent Brahim Llob?"

At length, I turn to face him, an admonishing finger in the air:

"You can save the pretentious country-bumpkin act for the maitre d', okay? When you're in the wrong, if you have the slightest sense of duty, you ask forgiveness."

"What have I done now?" he asks, the hypocrite.

My finger trembles in the face of such exasperating imbecility, but I hold back.

"I know I'm absent from time to time," he admits, "but it's no big deal. Nobody at Headquarters works normal hours."

In an effort to keep my temper, I pull a sheet of paper out from under the blotter and push it toward him.

"In the last twenty-five days you've been absent seventeen times; you've had someone stand in for you on desk duty five times; you've gone AWOL five times while on duty; you've never accounted for your absences and you haven't once seen fit to provide an excuse for your lateness. True, Headquarters isn't a prison. But Headquarters has a director, and it's not me. I run an investigation division, and I have no intention of being treated like an ornament. I am your superior, your boss, your big cheese."

Lino sniggers audibly at this.

"And I expect you to account for your absences and let me

know where you are at all times when you're taking it easy. If you think that's too much to ask, you know what you can do."

"And what can I do?"

"One sheet of A4 and a ballpoint pen: you write a letter of resignation."

"I don't plan on interrupting my career when things are going so well."

"In that case, follow the rules."

Lino shakes his head. Smooth as ever, he makes to press his fingers to his temples, as if harassed, using the opportunity to search for a plausible excuse, and groans, "Why the hell doesn't anyone make the effort to understand me?"

He looks up at me pitiably. "I can understand other people giving me a hard time. But not you, Super.... Don't you understand that I'm experiencing the most wonderful period in my whole crappy life? I'm entitled to a bit of leeway, if only for that reason."

"That's no excuse. You're a cop, you've got obligations."

"It'll pass, Super. I'll go back to normal life. Right now, it's like I've been catapulted into a fairy tale. I feel as if I'm walking among the clouds."

"There are holes in the clouds."

"So what?"

"In that case, you can choose: the clouds or the street."

The lieutenant is aghast. His nostrils are dilated and his eyes are blazing.

"I'm suffering here, Super."

"I can't help that."

Faced with my obduracy, he persists, pleading, "I'm in love, for crying out loud! I've met my soulmate. I feel fulfilled, happy; I'm living in a dream, a wonderful dream."

"So wonderful you can't see the line of your creditors stretching out like a tapeworm."

At that, he stiffens. Rage fills his suddenly distorted features. He trembles from head to foot, fingers twitching, and summons all his strength so as not to explode in my face.

"I see the gossip-mongers have found a nice topic of conversation. You want to hear my side of it, Super? They're just jealous. They envy me my happiness. They can't stand it. As for the creditors, I'll pay them back soon. And another thing: I'm no sucker. Yes, I'm spending a bit of cash, but that's just so I can look good. I don't pay a thing, not a single bill. The restaurants, the clubs, the outings, she's the one who pays. She's loaded, my girl is. It's not the shitty cop's salary she's after; it's not even the cop; it's the man behind it. She's found her Mr. Right. And she attends to his every need. You see this signet ring? Know how much it cost? An arm and a leg. She gave it to me. And this solid gold chain, big Paris designer; know how much that cost? The skin off your ass. She gave it to me. And this Rolex watch: know how much that cost—"

"It could cost the hairs off my ass and I wouldn't get a hard-on. This isn't about bills, not at all; this is about a police lieutenant who's showing lamentably poor judgment. So you're following your perfect love, I'm happy for you. But to go from that to thinking you're the only person in the world, that's unforgivable. You have an office, work to do; you carry out your duties, period, end of story. As for the rest, you have your free time; you can use it any way you like."

"I—"

"That's enough, Lieutenant Lino. From now on, I want to find you in your office during working hours. As for now, get out!"

Lino stands there looking sick for a minute, at which point he realizes how futile his appeal has been. He wipes back his forelock, turns on his heel and leaves the office, slamming the door so hard behind him that Baya screams in the room next door.

Inspector Serdj arrives just as Lino is leaving. The turbulence has disarranged his hair, and he stays in the doorway with his notebook against his chest, not sure whether to come in now or come back later. I wait long enough to digest the lieutenant's effrontery, and then I offer him a chair. The inspector sits down, making himself as small as possible. His respect for me is so close to fear that I can't always work him out. He moves his chair forward with a screech that makes his nose pucker, puts his pad on the table and starts checking his notes to give me time to calm down.

"Well?" I burst out.

He scratches his temple, disoriented, for five seconds, then says, "We're short of men, Superintendent. Lieutenant Chater's section is on a training course. We've drawn on other sections, including Traffic and some of the new recruits. It's a big job. We can't manage non-stop surveillance of SNP's house. I've put three of our informers on the case, of course. They pretend to be selling peanuts or cigarettes, but once night falls they have to make themselves scarce so as not to arouse suspicion. Our surveillance teams consist of ten men, two of which are detectives. After a week, they're exhausted. The normal shift is eight hours, and there's no rest period because they go back to their posts as soon as they've finished their guard duty."

"What does this all mean? We drop it?"

"I'm just telling you our problems, Superintendent, in broad outline."

"I'm not satisfied. You can find more men. You have only to glance down the corridors of that tower of assholes at Headquarters. They're all twiddling their thumbs while we can't even pull in a few street peddlers."

"The other section heads won't cooperate. They say they need a written order, signed by the director."

"Fine, we'll just get along without their damn help."

"With what?"

"That's your problem, Inspector."

Serdj bows his head. I see his defeated neck, with its mat of writhing white hairs. It's the most pathetic neck I have ever had to examine.

"I'll see what I can do, Superintendent."

I grunt in approval and request a complete status report on the maniac.

"He hasn't come out of his hole once," the inspector says, "not even into the courtyard. Ever since he double-locked himself in, he avoids going near the windows."

"Is there anyone with him?"

"We haven't seen anyone."

"How does he live, for crying out loud? He has to eat, buy food somewhere. Are you sure he's alive? Maybe he's croaked while your men were contemplating their navels."

"He's not dead, Superintendent. He doesn't go near the windows, but we've seen him praying, through our binoculars. One time, the second day of his release, the big black car turned up. It didn't stay in the road. It went into the garage and came out again thirty minutes later. There were two men inside. We couldn't see much."

"That's why you have to get off your ass and collect as much information as you can about this psychopathic bastard."

"I managed to get a copy of his file. The tabloids used to call him The Dermatologist."

"Was he really a dermatologist?"

"Literally and figuratively: he bumps off his victims, then he skins them like rabbits. And not with a knife or a wire brush; with his hands, with his bare hands! Apart from that, the guy's an enigma. No relatives, no friends, nothing."

"And yet he was tried and convicted...."

"It looks like everything was rushed. On the face of it, neither the police nor the courts wanted to spend any time on the case. A man turns himself in and confesses to some murders that nobody checks. He's immediately hauled up in court. Condemned to life, locked up. Case closed. Good work was patchy in those days, but in this case they really went too far. There are only a few sheets collected in the file, with unusually worthless statements. They didn't even bother to check the defendant's real identity."

"And the house?"

"It belongs to a certain Khaled Bachir, a rich livestock dealer who's also a professional altruist. Before it housed SNP, it was a guest-house for the city's *imams*. The owner placed it at the mosque's disposal."

I lean my head against the back of my chair and try to order my ideas. I wonder whether Professor Allouche hasn't made a mountain out of a molehill.

I draw a circle on my blotter with the stump of a pencil, then two tiny circles inside it, then two semi-circles on either side of the first circle. I realize I'm not getting anywhere, put the pencil down, put my fingers together under my chin and look at the inspector.

"What do you think of all this, Serdj?"

"I don't know, Superintendent."

I reach out with my arm, unhook my jacket from its nail and hurry to set sail.

Chapter seven

At home, it's business as usual. Mohamed went to bed before sundown. Apparently he ran around all day looking for a decent job. My other kids are sulking in their bedrooms. Mina and Nadia are absorbed in gluey emanations from some cooking pots. I stroll as far as the living room, undo my shoelaces and take off my shoes. The smell of suffering big toes quickly fills the room. I sink into the sofa and click the remote. My old Sonelec television takes an age to warm up. It offers me a fatuous documentary on the steelworks at El Hadjar, flagship of the socialist project, Algerian-style, built on a foundation of triumphalist slogans and kickbacks from all sides. My children resent the fact that I refuse to install a satellite dish. The foreign channels are certainly tempting, but what with the gratuitous obscenities that spew out from the studios and the nudity that seems central to the film-maker's art, it's impossible to watch them as a family. Since I can't afford to buy a second television, I play the rigid and stubborn zealot.

Mina comes in with coffee and a plate loaded with cakes. She serves me, then sits down on a threadbare footstool in front of me; she gazes at me protectively, with the eyes of a devoted wife.

"Would you like me to run you a bath?"

"Is there water in the tap?"

"No, but I set two canisters aside for you."

"It's not worth wasting our supply of drinking water. Besides, I had a shower last week."

Then, prickly as a rash, I trace her thoughts back to their source and demand, "Why do you want me to take a bath? Do you think I'm starting to smell?"

She beats her breast, offended: "Brahim, where do you get these ideas?"

She seems sincere.

In order to get myself out of a hole, I make a suggestion: "What do you say we go out this evening? We could go down to the waterfront and look at the boats, or to Rue Larbi Ben M'hidi to drool at the shop windows. I need a change of scene."

"Just you and me?"

"The children are old enough to look after themselves. It won't be for long. I want to buy you a *merguez* sandwich, or a big sorbet at Ice Krim."

Mina grabs my hands. "Just give me time to put on my face and change my dress, and I'm all yours."

"Try not to put on too much lipstick. You know how I behave when people look at you too closely."

"You old flatterer, I'm too old to catch a passerby's eye."

She stands up and goes off to make herself into a beauty once again.

I have just swallowed my coffee when someone knocks at the door. It's Fouroulou, a kid who lives on the sixth floor. He flicks his thumb over his shoulder and tells me that some fat, gray-haired towelhead wants to speak me in front of the building.

The gentleman awaiting me in his car is one of a species of giant toad that is very fashionable in our country in these lean times. The kind that shits out ten kilos of green stuff for every kilo he swallows. Unlike Jean de La Fontaine's frog, he has managed his transformation into an ox very well. He starts with a huge calf-like head, white and hairless, like the ones French butchers display in their windows and proceeds, via a goiter, to a gut that could accommodate two airbags, a medicine-ball and, with a bit of good will, a big pack of floormats. Despite the dark glasses hiding his face like the windshield of an official car, despite his brand new Italian suit and the gleaming Mercedes that he drives with the grace of a hippopotamus jammed into a fishtank, despite the smiling lovely in the passenger seat, he can't help looking like a malodorous *nouveau-riche* clod. But he's loaded, the bastard, and he doesn't hide it.

Without getting out of the car, he winds the electric window down and offers me his jewel-encrusted hand like a sultan receiving the allegiance of his court. "I hope I'm not disturbing you," he bellows, hypocritically.

"You would disturb a rat in its tomb."

His fat belly shakes with a short laugh, which leaves him out of breath.

"Dear Brahim, always as polite as a fart in a yoga class."

"That proves the world hasn't changed."

"Are you sure?"

"You're not going to make me believe you're not interested in slime any more."

He turns to his companion to make sure she isn't shocked by my words, says a few words to her, opens the door and gets out, moving me away from his inamorata. "You should watch your language, Brahim."

"Social Security doesn't cover that kind of therapy. Why have you come here to spoil my evening, Hadj Salem? You don't think your friend the director persecutes me enough?"

Hadj Salem and I were part of the same intake. He had chosen to be a cop so as to be behind the law, well placed to screw it up the ass. But he was worse than useless when it came to studying, and at the end of our training at the police academy, his pitiful grades and his questionable proclivities on the job had made it impossible for him to be put on active service without causing a disaster. He was posted to a sub-office, and his duties were restricted to filing invoices and huge depositions in the basement archives. And there, in the apt shadows of the box-rooms, which soon wrought their influence on

75

his murky plans, he learned to fiddle the books, then to work on a grander scale, and discovered a vocation that seduced every corrupt boss and every bent trainee in his section: he became the go-to man for tricky situations. His talents as a failed cop steered him away from tracking criminals and toward keeping track of personal appetites. His inspector's stripes made his influence-peddling easier. He was much more often seen in the homes of crooked mayors or in dubious bars than hunched over his magnifying glass, following the tracks of a lowlife. Bit by bit, he began to know interesting people, to penetrate their little secrets and to intervene, here and there, to file away an explosive dossier or arrange for a piece of evidence to disappear. Once he had built up a little capital, he got into real estate to launder his dirty money. When he was arrested for the first time, he got the benefit of the doubt. In return, he began greasing his superiors' palms, who, whether through gratitude or venality, turned a blind eye to his activities. His reputation as a Midas reached the ears of the upper echelons. The movers and shakers in the police force found him discreet and effective, an excellent negotiator, and entrusted him with their little sidelines. Within a decade, he had managed to enrich every single influential member of the Ministry of the Interior, and climbed the ladder as quick as a rat. He was made superintendent, then chief superintendent; when he joined the minister's private staff it was as a wide-ranging adviser, an expert in skullduggery of all kinds. Today, Hadj Salem controls a security set-up like a nervous system, and a sprawling fortune with tentacles spreading beyond the borders of the country.

He takes out a pack of American cigarettes and offers me one. "They're genuine Marlboros, bought in Paris."

"No, thanks. They seriously damage your health."

"Have you given up smoking?"

"Not necessarily, but my Algerian cigarettes don't carry a health warning."

Amused, he barks out a laugh, lights a solid-gold lighter and blows smoke in my face. Then he puts on a solemn and embarrassed face: "Brahim, I've come to talk to you as a brother."

"I didn't know my mother had other lovers."

"Put your sarcasm away alongside your false teeth, please, and try to be agreeable. I have a friend who's worried. He's on the horns of a dilemma. He loves cops, and he would hate to wreck any of their careers for a trifle. He's a remarkable guy, very generous, very objective. He's very friendly with our bosses. And he doesn't understand why some wretched sucking piglet is creating trouble for him. He came to see me in my office this morning. His story broke my heart, I tell you. I felt so bad for him, and so ashamed of our institution that if the earth had opened up in front of me I would have thrown myself right in. While we, the senior officers of the force, do everything we can to restore the prestige of our profession, certain little flatfeet, only just promoted off the beat, spit in our soup and drag the minister through the mud. I asked my friend why he didn't go straight to the minister, who's a friend of his. Listen to this: this special man told me he didn't want to blow a young officer's career sky high just because he got a little above his station. It brought tears to my eyes, *wallah laadim.** And yet he's a very powerful person. He has only to snap his fingers for the toughest among us to be reduced to a pulp. But no! He won't abuse his notoriety. He just wants someone to have a word with the black sheep...."

"I suppose your Good Samaritan is Haj Thobane."

"Bullseye."

"And the indiscreet officer is Lino."

"I can't hide anything from you."

"That's because shame doesn't offend anyone any more, Hadj."

"That's exactly what I told our friend Haj Thobane."

Slippery as an eel!

"Have I said something wrong, Brahim?"

I nod, despairingly. "The fat in your belly has invaded your brain."

He reddens. His jowls flap like an elephant's ears. He sighs hard enough to fill a sail and roars, "You see? You refuse to listen to reason. With you, there's always a catch. I come as a friend, you greet me like an undesirable. I tell you about a misunderstanding, you

---

* *Wallah laadim*: I swear to Allah.

turn it into a dialogue of the deaf. I try to be civilized, you exploit it to be unpleasant."

"May I know why you came to see me?"

"To put an end to your lieutenant's indiscretions…if you still care about him."

"I set him straight this afternoon."

He removes his glasses to look at me, looks for the trap, doesn't see one anywhere. His jowls are suffused with sudden happiness.

"You've talked to him?"

"I was firm with him."

"And what's he going to do? I mean, does he intend to give Nedjma up?"

"Nedjma who?"

"The girl he's going out with."

"Her name is Nedjma?"

"That's of no importance. The main thing is that your lieutenant turns over a new leaf and goes sniffing around elsewhere. We're certainly not going to let subordinates compromise our integrity."

I gesture to him to move his imperialist cigarette away, because it's bothering my eyes, and explain to him calmly, "I told the lieutenant that from now on he would be in his office on time, that I wouldn't tolerate any unauthorized absences and that I refused to let him step on my toes."

"Excellent. Do you think he heard you?"

"Certainly!"

"That's wonderful. I'll go and reassure Haj Thobane right away."

"Wait, Hadj. I set the lieutenant straight, not the lover boy."

He frowns and stubs out his cigarette on the wall of my building. His hand is shaking; his lips are quivering in a disagreeable manner.

"What does this nonsense mean?"

"The lieutenant will be at work on time. The rest, his evenings, his weekends, his whores, that's his private life. He's old enough to take care of himself."

"I fear your little runt may not be man enough. Haj will swat him like a fly."

"That's not my problem."

"Yes it is: it will be your fault. You won't have done anything to dissuade your young pup. And it will rebound on you: one way or another, you'll be tainted by the scandal. I remind you that Haj Thobane's reach is long. He's a great revolutionary."

"Let him make a nice sugarloaf out of his revolution and sit on it. This is between him and Lino. I want nothing more to do with it."

"How dare you speak like that about one of our bravest *mujahedin*?"

"He's yours, not mine. As far as I'm concerned, he's just a fat, stupid, hypocritical zealot who finds stealing as easy as breathing and doesn't deserve any more consideration than a goat-fucker with his dick caught in a ram's teeth."

"Oh!" says Hadji, indignantly.

He retreats to his Mercedes, his face distorted, stares at me hard for ten seconds, then jumps into his car and leaves with a screech of tires.

"That's right, you fat bastard," I growl. "Get out of here and don't come and pollute the oxygen in my home again."

Mina is resplendent. She has donned the dress I bought her recently, which is to say three years ago, a touch of mascara to tame her bewitching eyes and an imperceptible coat of powder on her cheeks. She's as beautiful as can be. But the moment I come in and she sees my face, she understands that the evening has been spoiled. She turns off her enthusiasm philosophically, just as you might withdraw a complaint, turns on her heel and goes back into her room to put on her apron.

"Where are you going?" I ask.

"Er, I'm getting changed."

"Why?"

"Someone's got you annoyed again...."

"Someone got me annoyed, that's for sure. But we're not going to let someone so contemptible bother us."

I offer her my arm.

Still Mina hesitates. Then, when she sees my smile being reborn, like a beatific baby, she slips her hand around my elbow and follows me outside. Tonight, Mina and I are going to have a good time like there's no tomorrow.

I get to the office at about eight fifteen. Lino is already there, shirt-sleeves rolled up to his shoulders and pencil in hand. He is hunched over a pile of pending files and he's "working." When he sees me show up, he looks ostentatiously up at the clock on the wall.

"It's always fast," I growl, so he knows what I think of him.

Lino chuckles, goes back to his paperwork and pretends to ignore me. He has a still-steaming cup of coffee next to his typewriter, a magnificent tortoise-shell ashtray within reach and a cigarette-end in the process of giving up the ghost inch by inch. Which proves he's been there at least twenty minutes. Lino smokes three cigarettes an hour. I chuckle back, and send the watchman off to get me a coffee.

The lieutenant and I play a first set, then another, then a third. He refuses to look up from his files; I forbid myself to make the first move. When the watchman comes back, and after a good brown ciga-rette that tastes of cat hairs, I ring for Baya and have her sit down in front of me. She obeys, opening her diary to today.

"Take a memo," I say.

"Ready when you are, Superintendent."

"Subject: absences."

My blow hits home: it makes Lino's forelock quiver. He recov-ers quickly and buries himself in his papers.

I dictate the memo to my secretary, speaking clearly and insist-ing on correct wording. Satisfied with the arrangement of my brief and to-the-point phrases, my judicious commas and the firmness of my summing-up, I conclude:

"I'd like this memo pinned up everywhere, even in the toilets. That way no one can say he didn't know about it."

Baya glances at the lieutenant. He returns the look, to tell her I don't scare him and that he'll respect my memo about as much as a Kleenex.

I signal to Baya that I'm already tired of her presence; she scrunches up her nose and stands up with the diary pressed to her breasts.

Lino deliberately slams his files down on the table, one after the other. He's telling me that the cases they contain are now solved. I can tell, from the speed with which he's turning the pages, that his mind is elsewhere. At about nine o'clock, he pushes the remaining paperwork to one side and presses his thumbs to his temples. Twice, his hand reaches over to the telephone and then beats a retreat. He sighs, coughs, gets out a newspaper, tries the crossword, has a go at a cartoon, altering the drawing and then scratching it out; his jaws grind like pulleys in his tense face. In order to wind him up even more, I put my feet on my desk and point the soles of my ancient shoes in his direction. The silence in the room is replete with suppressed hatred.

A car passes by on the road, and it inspires the kind of idiotic idea that enters the head of a mayor who can't wait to pile yet another irritation onto his rudderless citizens' plates. Lino surrenders; he grabs the receiver and dials a number, hiding the telephone with his arm. His face tenses up even more, then glows with pleasure when someone picks up at the other end.

"You're not missing me any more, darling? …Well, you haven't called me…." (He looks at his watch.) "Nine thirty-two exactly…. Oh! I completely forgot that you never get up before noon."

Lino, in trying to impress me by calling his sweetheart, realizes he has put his foot in it. Even if I called Mina at three o'clock in the morning, she would never hang up on me in a million years. He puts down the receiver, picks up his pen and starts mutilating the pictures in the paper, one by one.

Suddenly, the furious clacking of a pair of stilettos echoes down the corridor. The lieutenant pricks up his ears like an animal in heat, sensing the presence of a female. The clattering gets louder and nearer, veers off and enters Baya's office. Metal chairs are pushed roughly aside. I hear my secretary shouting, "Hey! This is a private office." A penetrating voice replies, "I know!" And my door is abruptly thrown open, despite Baya's bravado. A woman strides toward me and sullies her cheerleader's fist on my files.

"Are you Superintendent Llob?"

I don't like her manners much, and yet I restrain myself. The woman interests me. She's a type that sets me on my mettle. She reminds me of my young days as a militant FLN member. Cybernetic energy whirls around her. The strength of her hands, the steeliness of her gaze, the severity of her hairdo fascinate me. This little slip of a woman, cinched up in an austere business suit, with her syndicalist glasses and her high forehead, is a veritable bomb in disguise. I know Algerian women; they're complicated. So when one of them makes it crystal clear that she intends to blow a gasket, it's foolish to stand in her way. So I relax in my chair, rest my hands on my belly and just look at her. She is magnificent; and her fury is enchanting in its own right. Lino is under her spell too, except that he can't help looking down.

"Are you?" she demands, pointing her finger at me.

"To whom do I have the honor...?"

"Justice."

"I don't see her blindfold."

"You're obviously the one wearing it, since you can't see where you're putting your feet. I won't beat about the bush. This is your last warning. If you don't, within the next thirty minutes, call off the ludicrous harassment operation you've set up around my client, I'll have you up before the court so fast your belly will bang up against your spine. I remind you that Mr. SNP was the subject of a presidential pardon. Nothing gives you the authority to contest or undermine that order, Superintendent. For the moment, I've decided to come to you directly, to warn you to guard against overzealousness. Next time I'll skip that step, and you'll be hearing from *Maître* Wahiba."

Upon which she turns round and leaves as she came. In a gust of wind.

"Well, well, well!" says Lino.

Chapter eight

Monique has invited us to dinner. She was very persistent. I told her she needn't go to the trouble. The truth is that I was exhausted and wanted to plant myself in front of the television to watch the JSK–Olympique El Khroub match, one of the qualifying rounds in the Algerian Cup. Monique reminded me that there was a television at her house and that it would make Mohand happy to be able to talk with me. I dithered indecisively for a minute and then, once my Alsatian friend started listing the provincial specialties she was cooking up, I gave in to temptation.

Mina didn't want to go out either. She pretended to have a migraine in order to escape. I pointed out to her that if she wanted to put a little money aside, this would be a good opportunity. The last time we shook out our piggy bank, we first had to remove all the cobwebs encasing it. Mina weighed up the pros and cons and then, sensibly, put on her dress and hurried to catch me up on the stairs.

We jumped into our rustbucket and went to buy some pastries from the cheapest baker in the area so that we wouldn't arrive at our hosts' empty-handed. It was still daylight, so we decided to go for a walk in the city to build up an appetite and, in one evening, store up something to digest until the next elections.

Algiers takes each day as it comes. She is a city without much coherence to her ideas, but, like a tortured man on the day before his execution, she tries to take advantage of the rare moments of respite granted by her *jinns*. She seems to avoid looking herself in the face. Perhaps because there's nothing to see. In any case, people don't care. Rue Larbi Ben M'hidi is teeming with peasants who have traveled from distant parts to bribe wicked and greedy clerks. Young toughs strut up and down the sidewalks, their shirts open to show off solid gold chains; they think of themselves as shop windows and are unhappy if young women don't stop to admire them. Others, less rich, show off their downy chests, forgetting that the bones protruding visibly from their starved bellies considerably reduce their chances of seducing some fortune-teller in need of lubrication. Mina smiles, amused by their performance. It must bring back a flood of memories for her. When I was twenty, I was more daring. If you wanted to get into the pants of a supposedly virtuous woman in those days, you had first to put up with her prayers, because the honor of the tribe was at stake. I remember that the first neighbor I attempted in my aunt's laundry was twenty-five years older than me. She was so hairy she couldn't stop sneezing every time my finger managed to break through to solid flesh. And by the time I had pulled down my underwear she had perked up so fast I didn't know where I stood any more. When I tell Mina this story, it makes her so sad that she regrets having hesitated for so long before accepting me as her husband. But those days are long gone. Passions are misdirected and dreams are manufactured elsewhere. Algiers hasn't completely lost her soul; and yet, wherever your gaze washes up, you see that things aren't going well. You can't wait to get down to the sea front; once there, you have only one fixed idea: to get home as quickly as possible. The sparkle that used to inspire you once upon a time now suddenly worries you. All the little details that used to add a shine to the city's charm have fled. The cafés are like animals' dens, the movie theaters are sealed shut, the parks and esplanades are falling apart under the burden of their humiliation; there's nothing for a poor man to do but pace up and down the pitted roadways all day long, his ears assailed by vulgar obscenities, his nostrils tormented by the stench of cheap eateries. You can't sit down at a table without some malcontent drowning you in his shadow; you can't lean over a sea wall without being tempted to throw yourself into the abyss. El Bahja* is sick. She no longer bothers to hide the withering of her sense of decency. Her pain is blatant, her suffering knows no bounds. Everywhere, slovenly cops harass their people, except when there's a riot and immense crowds gather in public places. An inexplicable sickness is perverting people's minds. Invective passes for bravery, and blasphemy seems seismically significant. These symptoms are unmistakable; warning signs that tell you nothing of value. No one has yet touched on the essential, that's for sure; and yet no one, university graduate or railroad worker, psychic or pig stubborn, clever or cretinous, understands why, in a country where there is enough to eat and drink for everyone, great or small, the people are starving; no one can explain why, beneath the torrent of light pouring down from Algeria's good old sun, the fundamentalists are inching ahead, good people are pulling down walls and the young are seeking the terrible darkness of despair in shadowy doorways.

Mina considers all this without saying a word. Her gaze is veiled. There's no doubt about it: the country is well and truly caving in on itself. Good will is being shattered on the ramparts of deranged appetites, asceticism is taking hold among the militants, and the most recent graduates are demanding, loud and clear, a slice of the cake they're not even close to catching a glimpse of any day soon. One of these days, without warning, the powderkeg will take even the most alert by surprise. The collapse is likely to be on a grand scale, the damage irreversible.

To cheer my companion up, I nudge her affectionately in the side and whisper, "Do you remember Algiers during the *baraka*** years?"

---

*   El Bahja (The White): nickname for Algiers, because of her white buildings.
**   *Baraka*: in Arabic: the blessing of Allah, the greater good; in French: arising from the French colonization of Algeria, good luck.

"I try not to stir up the past too much," she sighs.

"These are the same streets, the same people, the same light. What is it that's changed?"

"People's mentality."

"Mentality?"

"Before, people shared everything."

"They didn't have much, though."

"But there was love."

"You think we're unhappy because there's no love any more?"

"That's what I think. When the colonizers left, we lost sight of one another. We tried so hard to reach for the stars, and hang the cost, that we gave up the most important thing: generosity. Men are like elephants, Brahim. One step outside the group, and they're lost. We've become selfish. We've lost our moorings. We think we're keeping our distance from other people; in fact, we're drifting. As we isolate ourselves, we expose our flanks so that the slightest buffet goes through us like a fatal thrust. Because we've chosen to act alone, we're falling apart. We'll shout ourselves hoarse, but no one will come to our aid because everyone's listening to his own siren song."

"Well, you've got more on your mind than household worries. Where did you learn to talk like that?"

"Darning your socks."

"You should have tried your luck at university while you still could."

"Impossible. While I was still in high school, there was this cool young man who used to wait for me on the sidewalk when class let out every day. He would stick close beside me and whisper sweet nothings all the way to my home. Because he was in the police force, he thought he could do what he liked. He used to tell me about an apartment he had all to himself on the third floor, with lots of windows, any number of rugs and a nice fridge. He said it was a little bit of paradise; that the sun, before giving up the ghost in the evening, would throw its rays into the room at the end of the corridor, a bedroom as big as an empire, with a brand-new mirrored wardrobe, a bed decorated with embroidered pillows and covered with silk sheets, beneath which the most beautiful children in the world would be conceived."

"He was quite the charmer, this cop, you must admit, because you used to recite his patter by heart instead of revising your coursework the day before your exams."

"He wasn't a charmer so much as a fakir, but my father, who was deaf in one ear, was happy to lend him the other one rather than listen to me."

I slap my knee and burst out laughing.

I often wonder what would have become of me if Mina hadn't married me. She's more than my wife; she's my personal guiding star. Just having her beside me fills me with incredible confidence. I love her like crazy but, in a land where the forbidden is in contention with the *harem* for the palpitations of our hearts, I would be even crazier to tell her so.

The old building Monique lives in is at the back of a square furnished with ruined benches. On one side, aggressively ugly buildings block its view of the sea. On the other, the austere walls of a school look at it respectfully. Caught in a vise between the wretchedness of one and the hullabaloo of the other, it tries to keep a cool head. Unlike the surrounding slums, it has been given a coat of paint on the front façade, has an entrance that inspires trust and staircases with lighting and a still-functioning elevator, all of which, amid the general decay, is something of a miracle. The stairs are clean and the walls, though touched with damp, have no graffiti. We are among well-brought-up people.

We get to the fifth floor without difficulty. Monique's apartment is on the left. There is a doormat for the use of yokels. Mina, with a slight moue, takes in the respectability of the landing, because the neighbors where she lives don't leave anything lying around: they grab everything, even trashcans and half-crushed cigarette ends.

I ring the doorbell.

A lock clicks and the door opens to reveal Mohand, looking pathetic in his working-class scholar's suit.

"Did you get lost?" he gulps, looking at his watch.

"Just a flat tire. Unfortunately, the repair man had his arm in plaster."

"Very inconvenient, I don't doubt."

"Are you going to let us in?"

"Oh! I'm sorry," he blurts out, turning aside.

Mina goes first. I'm beside her. The inside of the place looks like a bookshop. Books everywhere, on shelves, on chairs, in corners. Over the fireplace, a portrait of the writer Kateb Yacine flirts with a painting by Issiakhem: then, amid a shambles of statues and a vague air of dilapidation: books, manuscripts and more books.

Mohand takes our box of cakes off our hands and offers us a threadbare sofa beneath the window.

"The match hasn't started yet," he reassures me.

"So much the better. Where's your big cow?"

"I'm in here," Monique bellows from the kitchen. "I'll be with you in a couple of minutes."

Mina glances at me disapprovingly before sitting down. I wink at her to tell her to put her complexes back in their box. I've come to Monique's mainly to relax, after all.

Mohand comes back with a wicker chair, sits himself in a corner and folds his arms across his chest, like a well-behaved schoolboy waiting for his meal. There's no chance of fun with him around. He can spend hours in silence, slumped in a chair, with his eyes staring into space and his mind elsewhere. I wouldn't want to end up on a desert island with him for anything. He can't go to bed without something to read in front of his nose, and spiteful gossip has it that he only puts his hand on Monique's pussy to wet his finger so he can turn the pages.

"Are you really interested in football?" I ask him.

"What do you think?"

"Is there anything else you've been keeping from me?"

"That depends what you want to see," he says, without irony.

"Have I ever told you the story of the gravedigger who wanted to become a caver?"

"I don't think so."

"With your wife's agreement, I'll save it for dessert."

"Great."

I look him over for a moment. His lips are like healed-up wounds, his enthusiasm like the flu. It's going to be hard to support my team with him around.

I don't even have time to take off my cardigan before the telephone intervenes. Mohand answers. He says hello as you might say "Your Lordship," listens, forces out a commonplace courtesy and looks up at me. "Very well, *monsieur*, I'll hand you over to him."

He passes me the receiver.

When I recognize Inspector Serdj's shrill voice at the end of the line, my heart misses a beat.

"Can't I breathe easy for one minute any more?"

"I'm very sorry, Superintendent. I called your home first. Your son gave me this number."

"What's it about this time?"

"One of our men, who was watching our friend's house, has been attacked. I've called an ambulance and it'll be there in ten minutes."

"Is it serious?"

"I preferred not to take any chances."

"Okay, I'm on my way."

Mina tries to object. My somber expression freezes her. Mohand is upset, but keeps his feelings to himself.

"I have to go," I explain to them. "One of my men has been roughed up. I mounted this operation without the backing of my superiors. An initiative that might turn nasty."

Monique comes back in. She has tidied up her hair and put on some lipstick. Her breasts jiggle frantically beneath her bouncer's shirt.

"Leaving already?"

"Duty calls."

"Can't you get anyone to take your place? Look what I've done to my face for your ghost-writer's sake."

"It's imperative that I be on the spot to stop this matter leaking out. It's very serious. I promise to be back before half-time."

* * *

The ambulance is already there. The flashing lights machine-gun the narrow street with splashes of bluish light. It is dark, and the only street light in the place gave up the ghost long ago. Two police cars are parked arrogantly on the sidewalk while the ambulance attendants finish strapping up the wounded man. Inspector Serdj seems embarrassed:

"It's bad," he says, without beating about the bush.

I lean over the stretcher. The unfortunate victim seems completely rigid. Although his eyes are open, he doesn't seem to know what's going on. A brace has been placed around his neck and his head has been wrapped up in a thick, turban-like bandage.

"Which one's the doctor?" I ask.

"Me," a youngster replies, fiddling with his stethoscope.

"How's he doing?"

"I need to do some x-rays. First off, the blow to the head is nasty. The compression of his vertebrae was certainly caused by the impact. There's no serious bleeding, but there is major swelling."

"Has he said anything?"

"No. May I take him away, Superintendent? The quicker we get him to the hospital the better our chances of fixing him up. I can't rule out internal hemorrhage."

"Thank you, Doctor. I'm relying on you to get him back on his feet."

The ambulance leaves immediately, sirens wailing.

I turn to Serdj.

"I told you to put two men on watch at a time," I begin, playing the blame game.

"There *were* two of them."

The coldness of his tone brings me up short. I change tack: "Talk to me...."

"They had been on duty about four hours. One of them went to get some coffee nearby. When he got back, he found the door open and his partner slumped over the steering wheel with his neck twisted."

"I wasn't gone long," the survivor says. "Five, maybe ten minutes. The café's right there, at the bend in the road. I came back quickly and found Mourad with his face on the dashboard. I asked the lady in the house opposite if she'd seen anything. She didn't notice anything. I ran to the corner, over there; no one. I checked whether anything had been stolen from the vehicle. Nothing had been touched. Not even Mourad's piece, which was in the glove compartment."

"All right," I say to calm him down. "Let's get out of here. We'll talk about this first thing tomorrow, in my office. You too, Serdj, go back with your team. It goes without saying that this never happened. As for the injured man, send one of his friends to guard him at the hospital."

Serdj waits until the first police car has gone before he says confidingly, "If Headquarters ever finds out about this, we've had it."

"*I've* had it. I started this and I'm not in the habit of lying low when the shit starts to fly."

"That's not what I meant, Superintendent."

"Go home, Serdj."

"What are you going to do?"

"I'm going to have a chat with our assault ghost."

"That's a very bad idea. There's nothing to prove it was him. Besides, he might lodge a complaint against us, and then everyone would know what we've been up to. Not just Headquarters, Superintendent. The *wilaya*,* the ministry and…the president. I think we've messed things up enough. Now let's clear out. I knew from the start this would turn out badly."

"Go home, Serdj, and try to sleep."

The inspector realizes a tank wouldn't hold me back. He nods, more frustrated than ever, and points to a villa behind a low wire-mesh fence.

I ring the doorbell.

Two minutes later, I do it again.

A built-in intercom by the gate crackles. I introduce myself. There is a click at the level of the lock, and the gate gives way.

I cross a small paved courtyard, go up three stairs to the entrance, push open an oak door and find myself in a large, bare,

---

* *Wilaya*: province

poorly lit hall. Something moves at the end of the room. It is SNP, wearing a safari suit and a skullcap, his beard like a fan. He looks like someone out of a Phoenician inscription. He is sitting on a mat, like a fakir, hands on his knees, body upright, and resembles a heap of rags left behind at the docks. A streak of rage suddenly courses through my whole being, as it does every time I find myself in front of a murderer who is arrogant and proud of it.

Flicking my thumb over my shoulder, I growl, "Was it you who beat up my officer?"

SNP allows himself a contemptuous smile. His eyes glide over me like the shadow of a bird of prey, sending shivers down my spine.

After an interminable pause for reflection, he says, "I knew the police produced second-rate minds, but I didn't think their enquiries were so disconcertingly simple-minded."

His voice seems to come from deep underground.

"Very well," I concede. "I'll ask my question in a more intelligent way: are you the bastard who injured the young cop who was on watch outside?"

"Get out, Superintendent."

There is no anger in his demand.

"And do you know who I am?"

"Don't be a fool. Go away."

His self-assurance makes me feel disagreeable. He is trying to push me to my limits, and I have to struggle not to join in his game.

"I'm going to say one thing to you, you piece of scum. You can send in your lawyers, your guardian angels, your damned souls and every presidential committee in the land, but I won't be deterred for one second. I'm going to ride your ass so hard there'll be no skin left on your buttocks."

"Do as you wish, Superintendent, but don't tell me about it. I haven't asked anything of you. Now leave me."

I lower my head, a couple of heartbeats from apoplexy.

I point my finger at him threateningly: "A common criminal like you needs to watch his step."

With this, I feel I have happened on a small chink in the guru's armor. For his beard trembles and his eyes flash.

He collects himself immediately, his neck stiffens and he decides not to address any further words to me. For my part, I feel I've seen enough of him. I turn on my heel and am about to leave when his voice pounces on me: "What gives you the right to talk about 'common criminals,' Superintendent?" he says, suddenly switching to the familiar *tu* form. "Your bravery, your integrity, or maybe just one of many ways to earn a crust? Just because you're a cop, do you think that automatically puts you on the same side as widows and orphans? Like hell! You're nothing more than a vulgar slave of the civil service who has to get up early in the morning if he doesn't want to be the boss's doormat. You've got no more respect for the poor taxpayer than a circus horse does for the audience. They're all just roles, handed out arbitrarily and irrevocably. Everyone conforms, period. The end."

I go on walking toward the exit.

His voice pursues me across the empty courtyard: "It's really not worth making a song and dance about it. We're all as bad as each other. There are the same criminal impulses in you as there are in any predator, Superintendent. You track your prey in the exercise of your duty; I track mine in the fulfillment of my vocation. That makes you a hero; it makes me a master."

I reach the gate.

His voice rises an octave, grabs me by the collar and breathes down the nape of my neck: "Life and death, Good and Evil, chance and fate, they're all the same; foolish theories that strive to take the place of destiny; commonplaces substituting for genuine inquiry. And so the wheel turns, sweeping millions of clones into the mix, links in the chain, complicit in the drama like the fingers of the hand gripping the murder weapon. Who are we, Superintendent? Nothing but creatures subject, whether they will it or not, to that sovereign and immutable breaker that is fate; nothing but pawns on the Lord's chessboard. You yourself must have wished to be someone else, a leading light, a commander, an idol, perhaps Croesus himself. Alas! We are not in possession of the script written for us by destiny, but we try to follow it. Later on, we'll say we're proud to be this or that puppet.... Bullshit! We have no merit, and nor do we have any fault. That's how cunningly God made the earth. Why? Who dares ask Him? All I know is that God is free to make any changes He wants to. If He doesn't lift His little finger, it's because He has His reasons. What affair is it of mine?"

I turn round and stare at him for a moment.

His smile has disappeared.

I don't know the real value of this first confession, but at this stage it's something rather than nothing.

Chapter nine

Hocine El-Ouahch, a.k.a. the Sphinx, never attended an educational establishment. He learned on the job and firmly believes that experts are forged on the street—hence his horror of those pompous windbags known as graduates. As far as he's concerned, it's not the head that makes a man but the hands. If we speak of skill in terms of a safe pair of hands, it's because everything depends on the hands and anything can be overcome with the strength of the fist. The proof is that he worked as an explosives expert during the war of liberation, without opening a manual, and blew up so many tracks and bridges that the Algerian railroad network hasn't recovered to this day. At independence, he accepted the rank of corporal in an engineering unit and spent most of his time swaggering about his *douar* with a Bastos cigarette clamped to his lip, a studded belt slung over his shoulder, and an unbuttoned tunic exposing the belly of a peevish and belligerent drunk. In those days, when loose women were not exactly plentiful on the streets, soldiers made do with brothels, where doses of clap and crabs were handed out in industrial quantities. Hocine wasn't very particular. He got on well with the madam, occasionally helping her deal with soldiers suffering from premature ejaculation who accused the girls of malpractice. It was a great life. During the day, he would kick ass among the potato-peelers; in the evening, he would booze it up at the Caméléa, courtesy of the innocents who would listen to him tell how he personally defeated the French paras, single-handed and without orders from above. Then his battalion started to take delivery of more sophisticated materiel, and things began to get complicated. It was no longer enough to put together explosive devices and set them off when an enemy truck went by. The Soviet instructors flourished books full of distressing mumbo-jumbo and insisted on the absolute necessity of following the instructions in them. Hocine couldn't follow. He had been superseded. He was sent on a refresher course in a specialist institution. There, his neurons were worn out by sophisticated formulae and esoteric calculations and he had to drop out, hand in his kitbag, helmet and boots, and try his luck as a civilian.

He was by turns a mechanic, a delivery man and a pawnbroker before renting a trawler. He was locked up for illegal use of dynamite during his fishing trips. The alarming conditions of his detention reached the ear of his former commander in the *maquis*—now an interim god—who intervened double-quick, lighting a fire under the governor of the jail and telling anyone who would listen that throwing a hero of the revolution in the slammer was the height of ingratitude, a disgrace. Hocine El-Ouahch was freed on the spot. He immediately joined the police, to get revenge on his jailers. He was first seen in the late 1960s, blowing his whistle at the cart-drivers in the Place du Premier Mai, then beating up Mouloudia fans on their way into the Bologhine stadium. His reputation for strong-arm tactics spread quickly in the underworld. He was a cop by day and a pimp by night, and his schemes did very well, in full view of everyone and with no objections from anyone. Within the police force, *esprit de corps* trumped all other considerations. Hocine was inspired to work twice as hard. And he showed much talent. He knew how far he could go, he never overstepped the mark, and he was careful not to hunt in anyone else's territory.

One morning, out of the blue, it turned out that he had been sworn in as the driver of a senior official of the nation—one famous for his verbal attacks on the Political Bureau—who bowed out in such a suspicious manner that several nabobs decided it would be wise to drive their official cars themselves. It must be said that events of this kind were almost a regular feature of society during this period of revolutionary adjustment: after the brain drain came the flight of capital, and a large number of apparatchiks, both honest toilers and high flyers, opted to make themselves scarce before being caught up in a net of conspiracies. The many departures left vacant posts, and the opportunists helped themselves. This is how Hocine El-Ouahch, a.k.a. the Sphinx, came to be squatting in the Bureau of Investigation after the tragic disappearance of its director. Strangely, no bailiffs turned up to remove him. In fact, Hocine El-Ouahch was the best applicant for the post in the nation's black market. The upper echelons were involved in speculative investments on all sides, so what better way to ensure the success of their little ventures than to allocate Investigation to a zealous cretin and outstanding wheeler-dealer rolled into one? Hocine wasn't stupid, he was just illiterate. He played the game to the hilt, signing off false invoices, closed cases, dead dossiers, backdated reports, rigged statements, etc., with enthusiasm and to the great satisfaction of his superiors. From one day to the next, he couldn't move without an entourage of fire-breathing courtesans. He became very rich, which meant absolution of his sins, as far as he was concerned, and very influential, which raised him to the level of a local divinity. Today, Hocine El-Ouahch is a *zaïm* in the fullest sense of the word. He still can't read a newspaper, but every time a graduate of one of the elite colleges lays out his degrees in the hope of benefiting from at least a minimum of consideration, Hocine immediately pulls the rug from under his feet by lifting his jacket and showing off his war wounds, and by working his way through the hypocritical rosary of his countless feats of arms, without which Algeria would still be under the French yoke today.

Which shows how history is sometimes the worst enemy of the future!

Personally, I've had no dealings with the Sphinx. We've known each other for years and our relationship is unremarkable. That doesn't mean I have any respect for him; I just think I have no cause to blush under the disapproval of my colleagues. As far as I'm concerned, the Sphinx has a cannonball where his skull should be and I have no reason to expect any great show of intelligence from him. That's why, when I spotted his name among the members of the president's committee on pardons, my Adam's apple almost leaped out of my mouth. First I asked Serdj if it was really Hocine El-Ouahch, a.k.a. the Sphinx. Serdj telephoned right and left and came back to confirm that it was. I spent the rest of the afternoon failing to understand what the hell a saddled-up donkey was doing in the middle of a team of respected psychiatrists. That night, I couldn't sleep a wink. In the morning, unable to reconcile myself with the idea that the country could be up the creek because an ignoramus was chairing a panel of intellectuals, I decided to go and see him in person. Who knows? Perhaps he had changed.

I arrive at the Bureau of Investigation on the stroke of nine thirty. I have been warned that the Sphinx doesn't really wake up until he's had ten good cups of coffee and three furious rows. So I take my time. I munch on a croissant in a seedy café, skim through the newspaper, where the news isn't new, and then, once I've finished my second cigarette, I get down to business. The administrative block under Hocine El-Ouahch's control looks like a haunted castle. Not a flunkey to be seen in the corridors. Every functionary is buried in his paperwork, pretending not to be there. In the heavy silence, all you can hear is the occasional clearing of the Sphinx's throat, which has the effect of burying his underlings even deeper behind their type-writers. And yet these sheep, pitiful beasts of burden that they are, metamorphose into vile animals as soon as they are let loose on the poor taxpayer. Suddenly their vampire's fangs and their demon's horns are rivals in aggression, so nightmarish that even the most powerful flamethrower cannot save their souls.

Ghali Saad, the permanent secretary of the Bureau of Investi-gation, is waiting for me on the threshold of his sanctuary, his smile radiant and his eyes sparkling. I've never liked his kind. Every time our paths cross, the iron enters my soul and shivers run up and down my spine. I knew him when he was a ballboy at the tennis courts. How did he get to the level of the Sphinx, and so quickly? Even he doesn't know the answer. In Algeria, the door to salvation is as unexpected as the trapdoor from which there is no return. It's all about *baraka*. Either you have it or you'll never have it. Ghali Saad must be related to Aladdin's genie: wherever he puts his finger he finds a nugget of gold. He is successful in everything: women, cars, raffles, investments, connections, banana skins; in short, he was born under a lucky star, and nature hasn't neglected him either. Ghali is tall and dark, handsome as an Olympian, very courteous and irresistibly gallant. At official receptions, the guests have eyes only for his elegance. His smile works miracles, his wink wreaks destruction. Admired by all men, dreamed of by all women, malicious gossip has it that his wardrobe contains the knickers of the finest ladies in Algiers as well as a few Y-fronts, size XXL.

"This is a blessed day," he cries, spreading his arms wide to welcome me.

"Don't talk nonsense," I reply.

"It's not every day you see a monument of integrity bringing his uprightness in here. Your odor of sanctity will purify the place. In fact, I've just been informed that our much-loved minister is getting out of hospital this afternoon, on his own two feet, without crutches."

"Do you think I'm after something? Because if so I'll have to turn my prayers back to front."

Ghali throws his head back with a laugh that's so refined I almost take it at face value.

"Delightfully incorrigible," he says, inviting me into his gilded cage.

Ghali's office is certainly one of the most flamboyant places in the Bureau. You can't describe it without being accused of being under the influence of hallucinogens. Fine paneling, crystal ware, velvet curtains, pale blue carpet and, on the walls, paintings borrowed from the National Museum without receipts and with no chance of being returned. The permanent secretary is aware that this splendor is fascinating to the distinguished visitors that pass this way. He says nothing, but the décor speaks for itself. Studying my reaction, he steers me politely toward an armchair that would relax the backside of the most constipated of dowagers.

"I'm in a hurry," I say.

"There's no rush. You can have a cup of coffee with me. Mr. El-Ouahch is on the telephone with the president's office. As soon as the red light on the wall turns green, he'll be all yours. He'll be pleased to see you. He's got a lot of respect for you."

"You'll give me a complex."

Ghali sits on the edge of his desk, like a Hollywood god posing on a rocky outcrop, rests his manicured hands on his knees and looks down on me magnificently.

"There's a group of superintendents going to Bulgaria for some training. The list is still open. If you want, I can whisper a word in the Foreign Section's ear."

"I'm happy near my kids."

"Think before you talk such nonsense. We're not talking about an expedition up the Amazon. From the financial point of view, it's a real windfall. Nine months in a school with an excellent reputation. The stipend, in cash, will easily buy you two cars when you get back. You could even start a small business. How long till you retire?"

"I'm not planning to hand in my badge just yet."

"Brahim, you're not getting any younger. There's a compulsory retirement age now. One day, you're going to get some unwelcome news in the mail. Unwelcome because you make the mistake of not planning for it. If you ask me, you should jump at any opportunity that presents itself. Bulgaria's a beautiful country. The people are marvelous and living is cheap for a trainee being paid in dollars. Nine months will pass quickly. But they're highly lucrative."

"I don't speak Bulgarian."

"Who said anything about languages, Brahim? We're talking about cash."

"I cede my place to someone younger."

"The young have the future ahead of them. The old should enjoy a warrior's rest. You've been struggling for decades, Brahim. I'm among those who think you deserve all the respect in the world. I value your uprightness, your commitment, your patriotism and your probity. Really, cops of your caliber are a rare commodity these days. I'd be delighted to be helpful in some way."

"You're too kind."

"I mean it."

I stare at him calmly. He doesn't turn away, to prove his good faith. At that precise moment, a magnificent young woman in a magnificent outfit appears, languidly bearing a glittering tray. She's wearing several layers of make-up, and her blouse shows off breasts so proud that my sense of decency is automatically rendered null and void. She places a porcelain cup in front of me and pours two fingers of coffee into it with infinite delicacy. Ghali thanks her, putting his hand over his cup, and dismisses her. Before leaving, she looks right into my pupils, so deeply that something stirs at the center of my being.

"Her name is Noria," Ghali tells me. "She comes to us from the Sorbonne. The panel gave her her doctorate with their heartiest congratulations."

"I didn't know the Bureau required a postgraduate degree to operate a coffeepot."

Ghali realizes his mistake. He wipes his crimson face and clears his throat. I am about to administer the coup de grâce when the light on the wall turns green. Saved by the bell, the playboy swiftly gets rid of me by announcing me to his leader.

The Sphinx doesn't get up to greet me. He even seems bored at my visit. His conversation with the president's office seems to have stuck in his throat. He looks searchingly at the receiver for a long time, frowning. I use the opportunity to examine him up close. I'll never get used to his profile. Hocine El-Ouahch doesn't have a single millimeter of nose. It's as if a mischievous draught slammed the door of a safe in his face when he was a baby. You could put a spirit level on his face and the bubble of air would settle immediately at dead center. He isn't called the Sphinx by chance. His ugliness would normally be intolerable. To mitigate the disharmony of his features, he sports an enormous moustache, whose effect is magnified by a shyster's beard that would make a brothel-keeper's pubis blench with envy. But the most shocking thing of all about our Mediterranean yeti is his hands, hairy and repellent as giant tarantulas. He is holding them clasped together, like a secret policeman about to beat a suspect to a pulp.

"Good old Brahim Llob, as hard to shake off as crabs," he

sneers, after a quick glance at the clock. "You can't look up without finding him in your sights."

"Just goes to show I'm a genuine Algerian."

He considers my words for five seconds, not getting it, then starts the discussion up again. "Meaning what?" he says, cautiously.

I explain: "The characteristic of an Algerian is that he doesn't go unnoticed: he either fascinates or he makes a fool of himself."

"The trouble is that you go too far: you make a spectacle of yourself."

"You think so?"

"Going by what I've just heard, yes."

"And what are people saying about me?"

"You name it. Have you had anything to do with a certain *Maître* Wahiba lately?"

"She came to my office and bent my ear a few days ago."

"You'd better watch out. That woman is nitroglycerine. Wherever she drips, the damage is catastrophic. Guess who was on the line three minutes ago? The president's chief of staff. They're sleeping together. She had to wait for him to come back to bed before she could turn him against you. It obviously worked. He tried to reach you at your office. They said you were here. I had to pull out all the stops to calm him down. He told me to warn you about your overzealousness. He'll let it pass this time. Go astray one more time and you'll be publicly quartered."

He notices, finally, that I am standing in the middle of the room, swallows, and invites me to sit down on a padded chair. I lower myself onto the seat and cross my legs, scowling.

Hocine gathers himself together.

He fiddles with some beads, twirls them around his index finger and thinks.

"Do you enjoy trouble that much, Brahim?"

"I try to earn my salary."

He puts his beads down, strokes his beard and examines me shrewdly. "Why did you come here, Superintendent?"

His tone is businesslike.

"I fear that a public menace may have benefited from a presidential amnesty."

"So what?"

"I've been trying to work out what's wrong with this story for weeks. But who can I ask? And then, suddenly, I realize that a colleague was on the presidential committee. So I came to see to what extent he could enlighten me."

"Good God!" he sighs, exasperated.

He clasps his head in his hands, shakes his beard and then, after a silent curse, confesses, "Your case pains me, Brahim. It's crazy, but it hurts to see a former *maquisard*, a hero of the greatest revolution the century has seen, aging so badly."

"Only wine gets better with age."

"Whatever you do, don't feel you have to have an answer to everything."

"I can't help it."

"And you're a wit, what's more. I'll enlighten your little firefly's tail, Superintendent. That's what you want, right? Your problem is *you*. You can't bear yourself any more. You pick fights in the hope that someone will shut your mouth for good and all. The other problem is that no one can be bothered to give you a good hiding. People have better things to do. For goodness' sake!" he rages, stirring up the air with his beads, "wake up! The sun's shining, there are parties in the streets, gardens on every corner. Kids are having fun, grannies are getting their fixes at the perfume counters, young people are swarming about in the high schools and girls are pretty as golden sequins. Do you see what I'm getting at? The war's over. The enemy's gone away. The country's doing great. No murders, no attacks, no kidnappings; everything's hunky-dory. Maybe that reassures the people, but unfortunately it bores Superintendent Llob, born to do battle, or to make mountains out of molehills. There's the rub: your dissatisfaction. Since you don't have any cases to investigate, you hunt down your own unhappiness. And you tread on everyone else's toes while you're about it. Work it out: it's not the answer. You're not just failing to whip up a storm, you're also making something out of nothing. If you want some advice from a friend, take a few days' leave and reward yourself with a cure at the spa at Hammam Rabbi. There's nothing wrong with our story. If the committee decided to grant a presidential pardon to a prisoner, it's because he deserves it. The experts are eminent scientists, very thorough. And I was there to supervise their work. The intellectuals have their knowledge, but I have my experience. I understand the human factor better than anyone. I've been commanding men for decades, training and retraining all kinds of people."

"I've been a cop for decades, too. It's not boredom that's kicking my backside, it's intuition. I'm sure I've put my finger on something, and I refuse to give up."

Hocine the Sphinx is hurt. My obstinacy upsets him. He spreads his arms resignedly and growls, "Do what you like."

"I need to have a look at his file."

"Who are you talking about, exactly?"

"SNP."

He frowns. "Are you sure his case came before *my* committee?"

"May I go to hell if I'm lying."

He frowns again and tries to remember. He comes up empty-handed and his mouth softens. "Doesn't ring a bell."

"SNP, a.k.a. the Dermatologist. In prison since 1971. For a series of horrific murders—"

"Don't go on, I've heard enough. My committee studied one thousand, three hundred and fifty-seven files. One by one. With the highest integrity. There was no external pressure and no decisions were taken lightly. If your suspect was released, it's because we felt he was perfectly capable of going back into society and making a new life. You say he's been inside since 1971. That's seventeen years. When you've spent a slice of your life like that behind bars, you don't have any more secrets from your keepers. Therefore, if the prison authorities recommended him for release, and if the experts supported the recommendation, it means the prisoner has the right to a second chance. There are no hidden depths, Brahim. In fact, there's no water in the river. You're building fantasies around a poor bastard who wants only to start afresh."

"Maybe. I'm not asking the earth, I just want to have a glance at his file. The little information I've been able to gather about him is too meager to draw a worthwhile identikit picture of him."

"I don't have any such file in my offices."

"Maybe you could point me in the right direction—"

"I don't have anything to point to," he cuts in. "Are you trying to start a second-guessing operation or what?"

"I'm trying to stop a murderer from butchering innocent people."

"First, wait for him to do something before you read him his constitutional rights. There's no law that permits us to throw a man in the hole just because we don't like the way he looks."

"Well, the law needs to take a good look at itself."

The Sphinx starts. He grimaces in disappointment and growls, "You're completely mad. And I have no intention of setting up another committee of experts to look into your case. You're obviously in the grip of a nasty mental cold, and by all appearances you have no desire to get better. I've given you ten minutes of my time. I've even been nice. Now, if you don't mind, I have some phone calls to make."

I stand up.

He's already reaching for the receiver.

When I get to the door, he says, "By the way, your Lieutenant Lino: are you sure he's right in the head?"

"He's got a nice face, and that's enough for him."

"In that case, why can't he find some other piece of skirt?"

"He's already got one."

"Exactly, but it's not his size."

"Just as long as he's getting inside it."

"If I were him, I'd run a mile."

"It's difficult to stay upright sitting on your backside."

"It's better than getting yourself screwed."

I turn round and look him up and down. "Who knows? Maybe the lieutenant's gay."

My combativeness takes him aback. He is not accustomed to people facing up to him, and it irritates him to the point of breathlessness. The Sphinx is well known for it. One word out of place, and his interlocutor is removed from the ranks. He has wrecked a bunch of households and brought on depression in worthy officers who made the mistake of thinking it was their duty as citizens and professionals to point out where Hocine El-Ouahch is going wrong.

He puts the phone down and looks at me. His intimidating eyes fill with blackness.

He mutters, "I hope you know what you're doing."

I can hear his jaws grinding.

I look at him for a good three seconds, then say, "I certainly know what I need to do next: stock up on toilet paper immediately, because this story is starting to give me the shits."

Chapter ten

In Algiers, all you have to do to go from one century to another is cross the street. And when it falls to you to leave the city, try not to be surprised if your car occasionally turns into a time machine. Which is why I didn't jump for joy when Professor Allouche suggested I leave the din of Bab El Oued behind and take a trip over his way. I told him that setting foot in his purgatory was out of the question, as far as I was concerned. He replied that I was under no obligation and arranged a rendezvous at the Café Lassifa, in an ancient hamlet two kilometers from the asylum.

I had to ask the way three times before I came upon a moldering *douar* behind a hilly excrescence where you wouldn't even take your worst enemy to finish him off. The place looks like the asshole of the world. A sense of bottomless despair rises in your throat the moment you arrive. It really is utterly without significance. A few hovels clustered around livestock enclosures, crooked alleyways, the stench of open sewers, and a feeling of immense mental decay. If the people here haven't climbed aboard the revolutionary train, it's because it never came anywhere near them. Once the settlers left, nobody took any interest in the fate of the indigenous people. The

world carries on elsewhere, and the exodus from the countryside has
contributed considerably to keeping this settlement barren and stag-
nant. The stubborn few who have refused to take flight go on mull-
ing over their remaining convictions, playing a waiting game with
no future. They take promises at face value, and survive on illusions
and dubious water. It's called naivety; its continued survival is not the
result of ineffective cures but of a fierce preference for divine assistance. The official speeches are certainly forceful; and yet, despite the
blatant demagoguery and the lessons offered by disappointment, the
common people refuse to admit that the elite might be making fools
of them. Some people just think like that; it's distressing enough to
make you want to throw yourself off a cliff but your sacrifice won't
change the problem one bit.

I spit under my shirt superstitiously before driving my car into
the godforsaken place. From the doorways of shacks on both sides,
gatherings of old men near the end of their days watch me go by as
if I were an unexpected thought going through their heads. I give a
small wave of greeting; my gesture intrigues them even more.

The main square is depressing, no more than a clay tongue
bounded by sidewalks half buried in mud. Apart from the skeleton of
an old van and the chassis of a tractor, which look like wreckage left
behind by some wandering cataclysm, you would swear that civilization had made it a point of honor not to hang about here.

The Café Lassifa is next to a grocer's shop guarded by a herd of
half-starved cats. The kid standing in for his father at the cash register
is bored to death. Not a customer in sight. The establishment itself
is besieged by an intimidating mass of crushingly under-employed
teenagers. They have been there since the dawn of time, staring at
the building on the other side of the street and keeping an eye out
for the Mehdi that is spoken of by the prophets, who will come and
lay waste the chaos of the doubters.

I put one foot on the ground.

Check the surrounding area.

A miraculously intact poster on the wall plugs some crook for
the post of village headman. There aren't any other potential can-
didates, or else their posters have been torn down. I understand, a

little, why the village is so ill-starred. But it's not the poverty of a fine and courageous people, betrayed by their patron saints, that pains me. This time, without a doubt, my esteemed psychiatrist is proving, once and for all, that he has little reason to envy his patients. You would have to be soft in the head to choose a spot as traumatic as this for a meeting place.

The professor is leaning on his elbows on the counter, absorbed in the café owner's stories. He is still wearing his white coat, but he has kept his slippers on. With his cheeks cupped in his hands, he is listening to the poor man's sob stories. There are two peasants in turbans sitting sympathetically beside him, silently praying that someone will remember their orders.

The café owner lifts his head and sees me in the middle of the room. He immediately identifies the cop lurking behind my placid family-man front and starts polishing the surfaces around him.

Next, the professor sees me and says, "Ah!" as if he had not expected to see me there. And then he glances at his watch to check whether I'm on time.

"For once, you're just in time."

"That depends for what."

"Do you have time for a cup of coffee?"

"I've only just got over a bout of dysentery."

"What does that mean? What are you insinuating?" a voice roars behind my back.

I turn round.

An old peasant is sitting in a wicker throne beneath a ragged hole pretending to be a skylight. He is draped in a brightly colored robe, his cheeks are rosy and his beard well tended. A club rests on his knees like a scepter. This must be the master of the house.

Seeing that I don't say anything, he reopens the debate: "Have you tasted my coffee?"

"I'm flat broke," I say to get out of a tight corner, because I can see that I have before me an authentic Bedouin of the old school, proud and prickly, fist on the alert, ready to smash your face in for a word in the wrong place.

"So go do your shopping somewhere else."

I calm him down with one hand, grab the professor with the other and rush out of the place.

The old man's voice follows me into the street: "Just because they come from the city, they think they're colonials. Did he even give my coffee a try?"

"No, Haj," the customers reply in chorus.

And the old man goes on, sententiously, "In my day, you'd wipe out a whole tribe for less than that."

"Quite right, Haj...."

*   *   *

Once back in my rusty wreck of a car, I hurry toward the exit from the village.

"You could have found us a better place to land up," I say to my passenger.

The professor watches a young shepherd running after a stray sheep, pursing his lips, then admits, "I haven't set foot in a town for four years."

"Maybe today was the time to do it."

He sighs, and his translucent hand clenches into a fist.

"You can't see what's coming, in your vile and chaotic city. Too much noise, too much hustle-bustle. You're caught up in the tide of days and worries, and it's more than you can manage to find sense in what's passing you by. Here in the country, you don't need a degree to guess where the beaten paths lead. The things I learn, every day that God gives me, break my heart. All I have to do is look up at a young man sitting on the sidewalk, glance inside a housewife's shopping basket, watch a poor wretch losing himself in the bottom of a coffee cup for two seconds to understand what they've all got in their heads. I'm worried, Brahim."

"You should talk to one of your colleagues."

He wipes his face with a piece of tissue paper. His eyes are filled with tears.

"That's what some senior people think too. They lock me away in an asylum and think the case is closed...that's not the way things work. You can't hope to keep your distance by ignoring the drama.

You yourself used to like to say that if you turn your back on misfortune long enough, misfortune starts in on you in the end."

A gully filled with water blocks my way and I have to swerve to the right. I mount the embankment, hit a large rock and bounce back onto the road, spraying muddy water all over the hood.

"The people you saw in the *douar* are neither beggars nor condemned men," he goes on. "They are normal men, who used to dream of a decent life. They've made the best of things for years, convinced that one day they'll find a sliver of the sun that's been taken away from them. A decade ago, I used to go there at weekends to see them let off steam without inhibitions. They were happy, and their laughter echoed for miles around. I didn't even need to introduce myself. They called me *Hakim*,* and had a religious awe for me. They weren't rich, but that didn't stop them inviting me to some memorable feasts. In those days, it was considered dishonorable to let a stranger pass by in the street without offering him hospitality. Well, nowadays, the looks that follow a stranger have changed. And so have the people. Any intrusion on their privacy is seen as a violation. So they shut themselves away behind their silence and their hostility, to retain the few crumbs of self-respect they still have. And there, locked up in their unhappiness, they ask themselves alarming questions. What have they done to deserve to fall so low? Where did they fall down, which saint did they offend? The more they don't find answers, the less they can keep their heads screwed on. They're losing their equilibrium. Very soon, they're going to go looking for an explanation in hell. Once they've taken that step, I can't see how anyone will be able to silence them. Algeria will then experience a nightmare of the most absolute horror."

"There's no cause for alarm, Professor. We're just going through a bad patch, that's all."

"You know very well that's not true."

I finally get back onto the tarmac. My car is on its mettle again and starts devouring the kilometers the way a starving man eats a country soup.

---

*   *Hakim*: Wise man, a title given to country doctors by the indigenous people.

I tell my killjoy, "I was born in a worse place than your *douar* and I've got the scars to prove it. They're what keep me on the straight and narrow."

"Can I take those words to the bank?"

"I don't have any more checks."

"In that case, I don't take back a word I've said."

"If that makes you happy. Now, may I know why you've taken me away from my 'vile and chaotic' city?"

"Take a left at the next exit."

A strip of asphalt leads us through the undergrowth. The sun plays hide and seek among the leaves. The cool under the trees is like a hymn to tranquility. Far off, beyond the hilltops, a flock of birds is bidding the area farewell before their great journey. The professor abandons himself to his dreams. His face is suddenly relaxed; freed of their pain, his eyes shine with a distant light again.

The path slips across the middle of a fallow field, skirts a small hill and straightens before crawling on its belly right into a farm framed by cypresses. A pack of baying dogs appears from behind a hedge and escorts us to the door, where a ragged old man has just finished tinkering with a wheelbarrow.

I park my car under a tree.

The professor gets out first, to announce our arrival, then comes back to fetch me.

A solid-looking type is waiting at the entrance to a garden. He asks us to follow him, then disappears, leaving us alone in the midst of the greenery.

"Isn't it a beautiful day?" says a man I hadn't noticed, buried in a forest of roses.

He is crouched behind his flowers, as if in ambush, with a straw hat pulled down almost over his ears. His denim overalls are brand new and his boots, though spattered with mud, gleam shamelessly. I deduce that I am looking at a hobby gardener who would do better to go back to his nabob's bed instead of stubbornly shredding his fingers on rose thorns. A glance at his shirt collar, spotlessly white, at the dazzling pallor of his neck, at his haircut, confirms this conclusion. The man is probably trying to create an impression, but he doesn't succeed. His posture and his way of tending the plants speak of a pampered mammal who has been brought up to look down on physical effort and manual labor; the kind of man of leisure who has everything, who can't move from one place to another within his palace except in a wheelchair and can't want something without tinkling a bell at his elbow; in short, a petty aristocrat surrounded by sycophants and flunkeys, for whom picking up a handkerchief or wiping his glasses is a lowly and demeaning gesture.

He puts his shears in a toolbag, takes off a glove and stands up to shake our hands.

"The *hakim* has often spoken of you, Superintendent Llob."

I frown. The man's face seems familiar, but I can't place him. He's a small fellow with chiseled features and grizzled temples. He must be sixty-odd years old, and there must be good reasons why his expression is so alert and fierce. The hand he offers me is scarcely bigger than a child's, yet its grip bites as fiercely as an embossing tool.

He shows us to some wicker chairs beneath a eucalyptus. Obsequiously. A typewriter shares a table with a basket overflowing with sheets of typescript. It feels like a poet's home, and I'm almost embarrassed to disturb him.

"So how are the Memoirs going?" says the professor, sitting down in the shade.

"They're coming along, bit by bit. Will you have something to drink?"

"A squeezed orange for me."

"And you, Superintendent?"

"A fruit juice."

Our host turns toward a hut.

"Bring us some fruit juice, Joe."

The solid-looking type from before reappears with a tray bearing glasses and dried fruit and nuts. He serves us and withdraws.

"His name is Joe?" asks the professor.

"He loves being called that. He went to Chicago once and never got over it. Once upon a time, he boxed like a god and dreamed of becoming world champion. Then he went up against someone better than him. His manager begged him to throw in the sponge. Joe refused. He went the full distance. When he left the ring, he left a good part of his reason on the canvas. Sometimes, he puts on his tracksuit in the evening and disappears into the forest for days on end. Then, one morning, he comes back and can't remember where he's been. He's not all there, but he's a good lad. When the roof of my shack is threatening to call it quits, he's the one that fixes it. He doesn't bother me. I don't see why I should have to do without him."

Then, turning to me: "Have you been in the police long, Superintendent?"

"Since independence."

"Don't you get sick of it?"

"I've seen worse in other places."

He nods.

The professor lifts his glass to his lips, empties it in one go and then pounces on the roasted almonds. We listen to him chew voraciously for three long minutes, after which I clear my throat and venture, "The professor hasn't told me anything about you, Mr...?"

"What?" cries Allouche. "You don't recognize him?"

And that's when it comes to me. Good heavens, what was I thinking? He's aged, to be sure—not unreasonable—but not to recognize him at all? I'm the one who should be worrying.

"Mr. Chérif Wadah, the African Che?"

"Chérif, that's fine. As for Che, I don't think I deserve it. Sit down, Superintendent. We don't stand on protocol or *salamalek** here. We're among friends, and so much the better."

"I'm a little puzzled."

"Nothing to worry about. Strictly between us, I don't mind. If I've chosen to isolate myself, it's so that I can have the time to look myself in the eye, without an escort and without allies. Just me, facing up to what I think I am. You can't reabsorb your essence until you can take yourself away from the eyes of other people. Flattery is just as dangerous as enmity. Here, in my place, I escape interpretation.

---

* *salamalek*: contraction of *as-salaamu alaikum* (peace be with you), the standard Arabic greeting.

I'm in front of my self and I confront it without holding back. It's a must for someone like me, who has benefited from exaggerated respect before being subjected to unimaginable cruelty, to ask himself a lot of questions and answer them alone. The world is no longer what it used to be. Human beings, in particular, have strayed in many respects. Myself included. Am I the same person I used to be? If so, to what extent and for what purpose? Our doubts surround us, like armies of ghosts. Which of our commitments have we lived up to, and where have we led the nation? Why does the dawn bugle startle us instead of launching us into the conquest of the day, as it used to do? Where did we fail? Because we obviously have failed. Nowadays, it's almost shameful to have been a *zaïm*. You have only to look at how our heroes behave. They've turned the page of the revolution so that they can turn their coats more easily. They stand up straight every morning, insults to the memory of the Departed; every evening, they lie down like dogs on the mattress of their promises. I puke whenever I think about it."

"That's the subject of the book he's writing," Allouche feels he has to warn me. "He's going to settle scores with them, those over-privileged monkeys."

"When a revolutionary wants to settle scores, he doesn't write, he shoots."

Che's voice is calm, but firm enough to put the professor in his place. A pall of lead falls over us. Allouche swallows, but can't get rid of the piece of almond stuck in his throat.

The old *maquisard* is angry, but doesn't show it. He examines his nails slowly, his lips pressed firmly together and his gaze opaque.

Then, as if nothing had happened, he turns back to me. "You were saying, Superintendent?"

"I was listening to you, *monsieur*."

He frowns. He scratches a mark on the table with his thumbnail, methodically, laboriously.

After an interminable period of meditation, he lifts his chin again and confesses, "I've lost the thread. What were we talking about?"

"Commitment, *monsieur*."

His lower lip quivers. That hasn't got him any further.

He stands up and holds out his hand. "Delighted to meet you, Superintendent Brahim Llob."

"Me too, *monsieur.*"

"I appreciate your honesty."

"Thank you, *monsieur.*"

He takes a step back and, without so much as looking at the professor, goes back to his roses and forgets all about us.

Joe is already there to lead us away.

In the car, as we leave the farm behind us, I notice that my passenger is pale.

"I didn't understand that," I say.

He squirms in the passenger seat, embarrassed.

"He's unpredictable, you see," he tells me. "Sometimes he's so gracious. Other times, he digs in behind his ambiguities and everything seems hostile to him."

I wait until I have negotiated a pothole and then grumble, "Why did you take me to his house?"

"I heard you were going round in circles, that your investigation into SNP was getting nowhere. The other day, during a conversation about nothing in particular, I told Chérif the story of our friend. We were talking about the president's clumsiness, and we got round to this amnesty, which has thrown thousands of lowlifes onto the street. I told him I utterly disapproved of this measure and, for the sake of argument, I mentioned SNP and the threat he represented. Sy Chérif listened carefully and then admitted that the boy's story was not unknown to him."

"In what way?"

"I don't know. He was going to tell us more today."

"And you put your foot in it."

"I'm sorry."

I close the window, turn on the radio and don't say another word to him.

Chapter eleven

I've got good news for you, Llob," Inspector Bliss announces at the other end of the line.

"Surely you're not calling me from beyond the grave?"

"As far as that's concerned, you can keep on whistling. I'll be the one digging your grave. Free. I'll do it for pleasure."

"I assume the boss is sitting beside you."

"You're right. You know very well that without his close protection you would have chewed my balls off."

His insolence makes me feel sick. But I overcome the urge, knowing that one day he'll get his comeuppance. On that day, it will be his party, and I won't give him a present. Little bootlickers of his ilk are legion. They think they'll enjoy their bosses' *baraka* for all time and so push their abuses to breaking point. Then, one evening, they realize that nothing really lasts for common mortals. The blow to their heads will be enough to shift the earth off its course.

"Are you still there, Llob?"

"Like all ghosts, Fido. What do you want?"

"There's been a punch-up at the Blue Sultanate."

"You call that excellent news?"

"Well, ever since you've been getting on our tits with your depression. Isn't this what you were waiting for to get your ass moving again?"

I hang up. Bliss is on form, and I'm not. Exchanging banter with him would just confirm his status as a bastard. I know him: the slightest hint of weakness and he throws himself on his victim like a hyena on a dying lion.

I pick myself up from my chair and go into my bedroom to get changed.

Mina joins me, intrigued. "What's going on?"

"Duty calls."

"At eleven o'clock at night?"

"Duty is shameless, darling. No one ruins your life quite like it. The trouble is that no fool can ignore it. Bring me my sweater, will you?"

A flash of lightning streaks across the sky as I drive my car out of the garage. Within a few minutes, large clouds arrive over the city, their asses kicked by gusts of wind. The first drops of rain on my windshield look like constellations being born in the glare of the streetlights. There are not many people in the streets. The shops have lowered their shutters, as have the diners and cafés. The sidewalks have been left to gangs of the aimless unemployed. I drive fast along the boulevards, racing through red lights just as they change.

I arrive at the Blue Sultanate. There are already two police cars on the scene, and a small crowd is gesticulating by the road. I recognize Sergeant Lazhar in the middle of the crush. He is taking notes in his notebook, paying exaggerated attention to the statements coming at him from all sides. I go toward him with my hands in my pockets to show that I'm the boss.

"Let's not stay outside, please," I say, to take control of the situation. "Apart from the owner of the establishment, I don't want to see anyone."

The manager pretends to be relieved when he finds out who I am. He gets the crowd to disperse and leads me deferentially to his office.

"We came close to disaster," he says right away, delicately wiping his face with a silk handkerchief. "He took out his gun, Superintendent. When the women saw the weapon, they started screaming and tables got overturned. Some people threw themselves on their stomachs and others dived into the swimming pool. Indescribable. People were running about in all directions. Can you imagine, Superintendent? Respectable people had come here to spend a little time with us, and with no warning, horror.... That officer went too far. He has no idea what's going to hit him. We only accept well-known officials, businessmen, leaders of the regime; people who are the opposite of aggressive, who won't forgive someone who comes and disturbs their peace and quiet. The Blue Sultanate is their miniature universe. Very exclusive and very expensive, to keep undesirables out. And then bang! Right in the middle of the show, a police officer starts making a spectacle of his own. I'm ashamed," he confides, shifting his weight. "If you had only seen how embarrassed I was. If the earth had opened up, I would have jumped in without hesitation. Good God! What a scandal. No one will have anything to do with my establishment from now on. I think I'm going to die...."

He is quite done in, the manager is. Like a dowager duchess discovering a black crumb in her brioche. I've half a mind to offer him my shoulder to sob on.

"Have a seat and try to calm down," I advise him.

He collapses into an armchair, dabbing at the corners of his mouth with his handkerchief.

"Please forgive my emotion, Superintendent. This is the first time I've witnessed such deplorable behavior in a place considered to be the most high-class in the country. There are places for hooligans and places for the cream of society. I think it's unforgivable to enter an environment other than the one that's appropriate for your social class."

"You're right," says Sergeant Lazhar hesitantly, to make his presence felt.

I silence him with a gesture and ask him to make himself scarce. The sergeant feels he's been insulted. He grumbles with resentment and leaves, protesting, for the corridor. I close the door behind him and ask the manager to air his dirty laundry.

"Perhaps you could start at the beginning?"

The manager gulps, not sure where to start, then, still wiping the corners of his mouth, which is as vicious as a moray eel's, he starts squeaking, "From the first moment I saw him, I sensed an obvious absence of class. His clothes were clean, but no more. Thrift-shop stuff, a mixture of parroting and naivety. The kind of handsome lad from the most deprived fringes of society who struggles to climb the ladder on the strength of his pretty face, if you get my meaning. I was against his membership of the club. We're very particular at the Blue Sultanate. Our customers are selected with extreme care. Even *nouveau-riches* aren't admitted. A fortune isn't enough, on its own. Our vocation here is to protect the great families against the dangerous disorder and disrespect of *arrivistes*. Alas! Our friend was a police officer. And we respect our institutions religiously, Superintendent."

I cover my mouth with my hand, to hide a yawn that threatens to tear my face in half. The manager is shocked by my bad manners, but his respect for institutions is obviously stronger than his desire to re-educate me.

"I'm sorry," I say. "After midnight I start thinking I'm a hippopotamus. Perhaps you could get straight to the point: who is this officer? Why did he take out his weapon? Where is he now?"

He asks me to wait with a motion of his index finger, and presses a button. A flunkey in a dinner jacket appears, his bowtie undone, his shirt-collar soiled and his face hidden behind a blood-soaked cloth.

"Mr. Tahar is our maitre d'. He can tell you what happened better than I."

"Go ahead, Mr. Tahar."

The maitre d' understands that I'm not going to sympathize with his suffering. He pulls the cloth away from his mutilated nose, notices that his injury leaves me cold, and gets on with the serious business.

"The lieutenant arrived at about eight o'clock, with his fiancée. They had reserved table sixty-nine, which I had personally arranged. The lieutenant wanted to celebrate his companion's birthday properly. He was very happy with the table decorations. They dined like

Yasmina Khadra

lovers, very absorbed in each other. At about ten o'clock, he made
a sign to me. It was a signal we had agreed on the night before. His
fiancée wasn't supposed to notice anything. He wanted to surprise
her. We turned out the lights and pushed the cake up to their table,
to the accompaniment of applause from the staff. It was a magnificent giant cake, made by the most famous pâtissier in Greater Algiers.
The fiancée got very emotional. Especially when their neighbors
started clapping too. They cut the cake with great ceremony. When
the lights came on again, the two turtle doves' smiles vanished. Mr.
Haj Thobane was standing in the doorway of the restaurant. Proud
as a god. Leaning slightly on his mahogany cane. He looked at the
lieutenant's fiancée in a very touching way. An extraordinary silence
had come over the room. All movement had stopped. Everyone knew
that something remarkable was going to happen. The two turtle doves
were ill at ease. The looked at each other as though the end of the
world was knocking at the door of their idyll. At that moment, Mr.
Haj Thobane spread his arms, which, in the general bewilderment,
seemed broader than the horizon. I don't know what can have happened. We were in a sort of trance. The lieutenant's fiancée dropped
her piece of cake and, as if pulled by some irresistible force, tore free
of her fiancé's hand as he tried to hold her back, ran to Haj Thobane
and fell into his arms. It was so incredible that no one knew whether
to clap or sympathize. Haj Thobane hugged the young woman for
a long time, and then they went out, arm in arm, to a big car that
was waiting in the courtyard. After they left, it was as if we had been
turned to stone. Our customers didn't dare to continue their meals.
Everyone was looking at the police officer. No one would have taken
his place for all the gold in the world. Even he didn't know what
had just hit him. He was groggy and almost keeled over, but went
on staring stupidly at the door through which his fiancée had disappeared. We waited an eternity for him to react. He collapsed into his
chair and clutched his head in his hands. We chose that moment to
start the orchestra up again; but it was too embarrassing to behave
as though nothing had happened.... The lieutenant didn't lift his
head again. He emptied glass after glass, bottle after bottle. Once he
was drunk, he stood himself in the middle of the room and started

calling the customers dirty bourgeois, jumped-up peasants. We tried to calm him down but everything we tried just wound him up even tighter. When he hit me, my staff surrounded him and led him outside. Somehow, he got away from them and came back in, spreading mayhem in the room with his gun. An explosion would have caused less terror. It was panic, a nightmare. Then the lieutenant seemed to realize what he was unleashing around him. Without putting his weapon away, he called us well-heeled assholes and hypocrites and staggered off somewhere or other."

I am so stunned by what I have just heard that I feel my knees give way under me and I fall into a chair.

What a fine mess you've got yourself into, Lieutenant Lino!

I looked for him all night, calling out every available patrol across the city. Police stations were alerted and bars were searched with fine-tooth combs. Lino has vanished. My anxiety increases tenfold when the lieutenant shows no sign of appearing the next day. Awful possibilities float around in my head. Algeria's young suffer blatantly from affective disorder, and the lieutenant, though thirty years old, is still an adolescent, emotionally speaking, so he's quite capable of putting a bullet in his head, especially after the massive humiliation he experienced yesterday, or of throwing himself off a tower without a parachute.

I send men into hospitals and morgues, my veins freezing every time the telephone rings. Toward evening, my sleuths come back empty-handed, tails between their legs.

Lino hasn't gone home either. Nobody has seen him anywhere.

I stay in the office late into the night, stirring my coffee with shaking hands and praying to the patron saints of the city. Nothing.

The next day, I report his disappearance to the boss, who thumps his desk and throws a tabloid newspaper in my face. The incident at the Blue Sultanate is on the front page.

"Your dog of a lieutenant is front-page news in all the papers this morning," he announces without preamble. "You must be very proud."

"I don't think so, sir."

He makes to tear his hair out, changes his mind and tries to keep his cool. His effort falls apart after a few snorts. His body suddenly expands, and he staggers back to his desk.

"Why, Brahim? What is he out to prove? What does he think he'll achieve? Bring thunderbolts down on my head?"

"I'm very sorry, sir."

He's in shirt sleeves, and his tie is undone. His wan face is furrowed with wrinkles. He's baffled by my stoicism. He was expecting me to get on my high horse, and thought he would be able to use that to unload his rage on me. Except that, well, I made sure I didn't play along and that has spoiled his plan.

"I told you to lock him up in a kennel, Brahim," he says, starting up again.

"That's true, sir."

"How are we going to manage this disaster, tell me that? What possessed him to go and make a spectacle of himself at the Blue Sultanate? It's a place even I wouldn't dare show myself. There are only nabobs and Medusas there. What will become of me now?"

"I don't know, sir."

"The top brass are beside themselves," he informs me, trembling. "I heard from the *wali** two minutes ago. I couldn't breathe while he was hauling me over the coals. The minister himself has ordered a disciplinary committee to be set up. They're going to hang him out to dry, and all of us with him."

"I understand, sir."

He nods, utterly defeated, then turns his back on me and asks me to get out of his sight.

Two days of searching, and not a trace of Lino.

Then, the next day...

I park my car at the corner of Rue Baba Arrouj, a constipated alleyway barely wide enough to let the winds of time pass through. Dilapidated buildings defecate on the sidewalk on both sides of the street. The area hasn't so much as glimpsed a street-cleaner since the period

* *Wali*: senior official at the head of a *wilaya*.

of student volunteerism in the 1970s. The stench from the potholes is so bad that you have to hack your way forward with a machete. A primitive food shack lurks behind a storefront, unsavory as a den of thieves. The boss is dozing on a chair in the doorway. The hotel is next door, hunkered down beneath its improbable sign. It says *The Oasis*: one is among friends and one can always dream.

A kid wearing a faded armband above his elbow appears from between two vans, club in hand. He's a lad of maybe twelve, slim as his chances in life. He's wearing ragged trousers and a holed sweater and carries a good bit of the country's poverty on his shoulders. Boys like him are legion. They haunt the streets all day long. Since they can't shine shoes—an activity considered demeaning and therefore banned by the apparatchiks—they try to earn a crust watching over parked cars, ready to make themselves scarce the moment a *képi** is spotted in the neighborhood.

"Shall I watch your car, *monsieur*?" he asks.

"Not worth it. It's booby-trapped."

The kid doesn't insist. He slips his stick under his arm and goes back to his watch post.

I climb the stairs to the hotel entrance, then turn round on the top step: "Hey, kid...."

The boy trots back like a puppy.

I toss him a coin and he catches it in mid-air.

"You're a prince, *monsieur*," he says gratefully.

I go into the hotel.

The receptionist is picking worms out of his nose behind the counter. His cubicle, which resembles a wrecked aquarium, doesn't seem to bother him. He looks up, disturbed by my intrusion, and stares at me is if I've emerged from a magic lamp.

I show him my badge. "Was it you who called?"

"That depends..."

"Police headquarters."

"Ah."

He checks my badge unhurriedly, then comes round the

---

* *Képi*: cap worn by soldiers and gendarmes.

counter to the front. He's a little man, twisted up like a couple of conjoined watermelons, with his belly at his knees and his behind at ankle level. Judging by his barking accent, I would say he is a Berber from the high mountains who was swept into Algiers in the spring thaw and can't find his way back up the hill.

It's a wretched dump, lost in a network of narrow corridors leading off moldering staircases—if tourists steer clear of us, it isn't because we're lacking in hospitality, it's just that they feel slighted by the inconveniences that come with it. We reach door number 46, at the end of a corridor on whose floor you wouldn't be surprised to find a Foreign Legion thumbprint, class of 1958. The receptionist shakes his bunch of keys with a mournful clinking sound, fiddles with the lock and pushes the door open. It's dark inside the room. I look for the switch. A harsh light fills the room. There's a man lying across the bed, arms folded and mouth open. A few bottles of whisky scattered on the floor suggest the scale of the damage.

"How long has he been here?"

"Three days. He arrived one evening and asked not to be disturbed."

"He's been here for three days, with no sign of life, and you weren't worried?"

"I'm a professional, Officer. In my profession, discretion is essential. If a customer says *do not disturb*, you don't disturb him."

I lean over the sleeping man, hold his wrist, and can't find a pulse, but Lino is still breathing. He has vomited all over himself and shat himself.

"This morning," the receptionist tells me, working out the consequences of his negligence, "I said, what's he doing, that guy in forty-six? He hasn't come out to eat since he arrived. He hasn't rung for anyone or used the phone. It isn't Sunni. Maybe he's gone off without my noticing. So I got worried; sometimes a bad customer takes advantage of a moment's inattention to do a runner without paying the bill. I had to check, so I came up to see what was going on. The client hadn't done a runner. He was in exactly the same place, in the condition you see now. I didn't want any trouble. I've always been straight with God and the police, *kho*. I searched his pockets to see who he was and found his badge—" His throat tightens as he asks me, "Do you think he's dead, *monsieur?*"

"Call an ambulance."

The receptionist clicks his heels and runs down the stairs making a noise like a cavalry charge.

Once alone, I crouch down to think, my finger to my temple. I start by looking for the lieutenant's weapon, find it in a drawer of the nightstand and slip it under my belt.

Then I take off my jacket, roll up the sleeves of my sweater and start changing my officer's underwear before the ambulance crew arrives.

Part two

Our wounds once opened in time's excuses,
dust and flowers look much the same.
Djamel Amrani

Chapter twelve

Lino woke up from his amorous misadventure like a farm girl who wakes up between two bales of hay after she's been taken advantage of: haggard, dirty, and humiliated.

Ever since he came back from sick leave, he's been lurking behind his desk, sullen and unapproachable, looking as though he has it in for the whole world, as if he holds us all responsible for his misfortune. He shows up at Headquarters with much more interest in picking fights with underlings than making himself useful, and he's well on his way to poisoning our existence.

I've tried a hundred times to reason with him, and a hundred times his finger has ordered me to stay in my corner, threatening to run me through from one side to the other. I suggested he stay home to take stock after his setback; he flung a sheaf of papers in my face and went to hide in the toilets until late that night.

I went to see a psychologist friend of mine; when he found out about it, Lino made a terrible scene in front of the staff at Headquarters and swore that if I went on interfering in his business he couldn't answer for my continued safety.

The way he was making a spectacle of himself worried me.

Lino is adrift—there doesn't seem to a leash up to the task of restraining him. He has taken to giving every big car he passes a kicking. If the driver complains, he hurls himself on him with every intention of tearing him to pieces. His circus act is obviously going to degenerate even further. But how to avoid the worst?

Serdj drags me out of bed to tell me the lieutenant is making a fool of himself in a swanky cabaret. When I arrive on the scene, I have to call in reinforcements to restore a semblance of calm. Among the people who have been attacked there are scions of wealthy families and ministers' call girls. I almost have to get down on my knees to persuade them not to make a complaint or call their sponsors.

I march Lino to the sea front to refresh him. He is drunk as a lord. While I am trying to preach at him, he shows complete indifference, giving me the finger and calling me a sad peasant, an ass-licker and a poor fool. My partner is in such bad shape he seems about ready for a straitjacket. Seeing him in this state, roaring with laughter and making a nuisance of himself to the whole city, doubled over on the slipway and vomiting up his bile, is unbearable. And I find myself cursing the Haj Thobanes of this world, their incendiary whores and a social hierarchy set up so that a poor wretch in our country can't touch even a likeness of happiness with the tip of his finger without getting electrocuted.

Lino is out of breath; I put him on a bench, facing the port, to recover. He throws his head back and frowns when he discovers the millions of stars in the sky. Perhaps he's looking for his own, because a foolish smile crinkles the corners of his mouth. His head droops and his chin drops gently into the folds of his neck. His shoulder twitches once, twice; then comes the stuttering sound of a sob, piercing my heart like a bullet.

I avoid laying a hand on him; he's in desperate need of a good cry in peace.

After blubbering for a few minutes, he wipes his face with his sleeve and, without warning, starts lancing the boil: "She used me...can you imagine? She dragged me around like a bundle of old clothes wherever people would notice her going by. All she wanted to do was get her lover's attention and make him jealous as a wild boar. And me, straight-up-and-down idiot that I am, I played right into her hands by showing off the whole time."

He looks up at me with red-rimmed eyes. "How could anyone play with people in that way, Brahim?"

"You're in a better position to know."

"I've been had, like the king of the assholes, right?"

"Anyone would have dived in, in your shoes."

He nods, sniffling, and looks over at the lights of the port.

"You can't imagine how much I loved her, Brahim; no, nobody can imagine. I was ready to sacrifice my life for her."

"That would have been a very bad idea, Lino. Sacrifice isn't about dying for someone or for a cause; I'd even say that that is the least reasonable act of all, without a doubt. Sacrifice, true sacrifice, is about continuing to love life *despite everything*."

Lino doesn't agree.

He wipes his nose with his fist again and says, "They've left us with nothing, those rich shits, nothing, not a crumb, not an illusion. They've stolen our history, our opportunities, our ambitions, our dreams, even our innocence. We don't even have the right to fail with dignity, Brahim. They've taken everything, including our misfortune."

"That's not true, Lino. That's the way life is; there are rich people and poor people, and each community only exists in relation to the other."

"Our unhappiness is because of those rich bastards."

"Some people think it's down to fate."

"And what the hell is fate?"

I sit down beside him on the bench. He doesn't push me away, nor does he move away himself. I sense that he is tired and resigned. His distress and rage are still engaged in a titanic struggle, but it's as if he's watching them from a distance, slightly puzzled. His labored breathing leaves him hanging, as it were. He obviously has no idea how to bring his suffering under control; so he waits.

A soothing silence surrounds us.

We watch a boat signaling in the entrance to the harbor.

The sea is black, like a bad mood.

"I hate those rich shits," he growls, clenching his jaws.

"All the more reason to ignore them."

"I don't *want* to ignore them."

"That's what you think now, but the truth is, you've got the wrong target. It's not their cash you loathe but your bad luck. You have to learn to rein in your envy."

He gets angry again. He leaps up from the bench and positions himself in front of me, his finger deadly as a gun. "I don't give a damn for your speeches. I couldn't care less about those lousy bourgeois, and your castrated old man's wisdom isn't about to lessen the contempt I feel for them. While we were singing the national anthem on parade with the scouts, they were getting fat on the taxpayer's back. Now they think they're so smart, they can do no wrong. I'm a cop, and I'm not going to worry either. The next nabob that falls into my hands can have his burial certificate before he's even had time to read his statement."

"Those people don't know what a cop is for. As far as they're concerned, he's just someone who controls the traffic, a funny little man who frightens off hooligans. Whatever you do, don't tread on their toes, because they'll run you over without even noticing you. I'm not saying this to make you angry. We're from different worlds, that's all. If I haven't been successful in my career, it's not for want of trying. I can't blame anyone but myself. We come into this world poor and naked. Then everyone makes his life as best he can. Just because you open your eyes in a hovel, it doesn't mean you can't close them in a palace. If you're born surrounded by coats of arms, it's not impossible that you'll die on the trash heap. To each his destiny. Traditionally, pride is supposed to have legitimacy. It would be right if a low profile was too. The mistake, the fatal mistake is to make others wear the hat that was made for you."

Lino's finger trembles. His face is racked by a series of grimaces, until finally he spits to one side to cut the conversation short. I watch him stagger off and know there's no point in running after him.

Bliss comes and defiles the rays of light pouring into my office. His nabob-like build seems ridiculous in the doorway, but it's enough to block out the daylight. With his hands in his pockets, he leans a shoulder against the wall and considers me for a moment.

"Are you sure everything's all right, Brahim?"

"Do I look like I'm complaining?"

"I saw you park your car just now. Your maneuver left something to be desired."

"My mind was on other things," I admitted.

He jerks himself upright and then, without taking his hands out of his pockets, he dares to take a step into my lair. Strangely, he seems embarrassed.

"I glanced at the mail this morning. I'm on the disciplinary committee that's been assigned your lieutenant's case."

"Isn't that what you wanted?"

"Don't talk nonsense. I'm very worried. Lino's a depressive. He won't be able to stand up to this extra ordeal. It's like putting a grenade in a cat's paws."

"When's the hearing?"

"Beginning of next week."

"You're right. He won't have recovered by then."

Bliss is now within spitting distance of my desk. He feigns interest in the portrait of the president hanging on my wall. Acting casual, he eases himself into a chair and crosses one leg over the other.

"I told the director it wasn't a good moment to beat Lino up. He agrees, but he doesn't see how he can postpone the disciplinary hearing. I suggested he extend Lino's sick leave, just to cut him some slack. He promised to think about it. It'll be difficult, given that the complainant isn't just anyone. I warned you. Your protégé was rubbing a rhinoceros up the wrong way. And he got himself flattened like a turd as a result."

"What's done is done."

"The trouble is that we haven't seen anything yet."

"What do you mean?"

"Me, nothing. I'm worried sick about Lino, that's all."

"Stop, you're breaking my heart."

Bliss takes his hands out of his pockets and raises them shoulder high. "I see you're as short-sighted as he is."

He stands up. "Does it ever occur to you to be polite once in a while?"

"Never with no-necks like you."
He grimaces, nods and leaves.
I hurry to shut the door behind him.

In the canteen, I notice that no one will sit at my table; I conclude that the look on my face would repel even my own mother. I don't touch my food and decide to get a change of air.

*   *   *

And what had to happen happens. It's about ten o'clock at night when I get a call from Headquarters. Thirty minutes later I show up at number 7 Chemin des Lilas. The street has been plunged into semi-darkness. An ambulance, two vans and at least seven police cars clutter the street. Curious onlookers, some of them in dressing-gowns, crowd the sidewalks and watch the commotion. A security cordon has been placed from one side of the street to the other. Plainclothes cops are moving about here and there, in search of clues. Four chalk circles on the ground mark where shell cases fell. Bliss, kneeling at the base of a switched-off street light with a stick in his hand, is conscientiously poking at a bunch of wild grass. He signals to a photographer to come over, and asks him to take some pictures of a footprint.

Serdj catches sight of me; he slips his notebook into his jacket pocket and comes over to say hello. His thumb points out a big car sitting in front of the entrance to the villa with its windshield shattered:

"Someone just killed Haj Thobane's driver. Three bullets in the face, two more in the neck and shoulder. The killer was behind this bush. It was probably him that put out the two street lights, so he could hide in the dark."

"When did it happen?"

"About forty-five minutes ago. Mr. Thobane was coming back from his office."

"Were there any witnesses?"

"Not so far."

"Have you questioned the neighbors?"

"Well, we've only just got here. If anyone saw anything, they're sure to come forward."

"Not always, Serdj, not always. Often you have to go out and get them. I want everyone in the neighborhood questioned, no exceptions."

"Will do, Superintendent."

I glance at the interior of the Mercedes. The man is in the passenger seat, his upper body slumped over the gear stick. A good part of his skull is gone, and his right arm and half his thigh are covered with blood. His eyes and mouth are wide open, as if he doesn't understand what has happened to him.

"Where is Mr. Thobane?"

"In his villa, with our director and some local officials. The news spread very quickly. We're expecting the minister of the interior any minute."

Bliss joins us, a shell case in a small plastic bag.

"Nine-millimeter Beretta," he says.

I leave my men to gather as much information as they can for the rest of the investigation and go into the villa. Mr. Thobane is sitting on his throne, stunned, white as a sheet. He's in a state of shock, his trembling hand holding a glass of scotch. The boss, who is standing beside him, is livid. He is waiting for me, arms folded over his chest, with a determined air. Hocine El-Ouahch, director of the Bureau of Investigation, stands a little to one side, chatting with his secretary, Ghali Saad; neither of them knows where to look.

"Ah! There you are at last," the boss greets me. "I've been trying to reach you for ages."

He can't help it. Any time he is overtaken by events, he comes down on a subordinate. I stay calm and ask what is going on.

"Someone shot Mr. Thobane's driver."

What an idiot!

"They were after Mr. Thobane," Ghali Saad explains.

Haj Thobane starts, as if brought to earth by the secretary's remark. He doesn't notice that he has spilled half his scotch over his suit.

Ghali Saad detaches himself from his boss and lays his hand on the intended victim's shoulder in solidarity.

"May I ask what makes you assume that, Mr. Saad?"

"It's not an assumption, Superintendent. It's what the evidence itself shows."

"That's right," the nabob confirms. "Now that I think about it, I'm the one who should be laid out on a stretcher right now. Normally, I don't drive. When we got to the basement of my office, we found the car had a flat. Poor Larbi hurt his wrist changing the tire, so I took the wheel. The killer wanted to do me in. He shot my driver by mistake."

"What did he look like?"

"Mr. Thobane isn't quite himself yet," the boss chides me.

"I'm perfectly clear in my mind," the nabob insists. "No common ruffian is about to make me lose my grip."

"That's not what I meant, Mr. Thobane."

"So shut your mouth. You seem to forget that I've just escaped an attempt on my life. Someone's after my hide. Do you understand?"

"Completely, *monsieur.*"

"That's what you think."

Haj Thobane's lips pull back in a ferocious grimace, as if he is about to eat the boss alive. The latter's head shrinks down into his shoulders: there's nowhere to hide. Opposite him, Hocine the Sphinx gestures to him to stay calm.

The nabob is shocked to find Ghali Saad's hand still on his shoulder.

"Get your paw off me, you. Just because some criminal loser has dared to cross swords with me, it doesn't mean everyone can treat me like a dishrag."

Ghali removes his hand and goes back to his boss.

"In any case, loser or not, he's had it," the nabob growls. "I'll find him in hell if that's where he goes. Where is that asshole of a minister?" he screams, hurling his glass at the wall. "Is he waiting for his mother to give birth to him or what?"

"He's on his way," stammers Ghali Saad in conciliation. "He'll show up before long."

"I want every police officer on this bastard's tail. I want his hide before the end of the day."

"I'll take care of it personally, Mr. Thobane," the Sphinx assures him. "Your attacker will be arrested within a few hours, you can count on me."

A door opens on the upper floor. Nedjma, the billionaire's little companion, comes out onto the landing. She is wrapped in a blood-red silk dress that makes the perfect curves of her siren body all too evident. Her glance barely touches us. The way she seems to float in the air, it's as if she's on a cloud.

"Was she with you?" I ask him.

Haj Thobane is not happy about the spectacle his beauty is offering us. He gives her a look; she delays visibly before going back into her room.

"I was alone with my driver. Just as I was about to go through the gate to my house, a lunatic leaped out from behind the bushes and started emptying his gun into Larbi. The first thing I saw was the windshield shattering. At first I thought I had hit a drunk or something. It was dark. The street light must have been sabotaged. My street is always well lit and there are never any power cuts around here; I make sure of that myself. It wasn't until Larbi's head fell onto my shoulder that I realized someone had been taking potshots at us. When I pushed him back I realized I couldn't do any more for him. That son of a whore didn't give him a chance."

"Can you describe the assailant?"

"It happened so fast. I can't even tell you whether he was tall or short. I just caught a glimpse of a shadow in the light from the gunshots. I tried to look at his face. He turned round to run away and I couldn't see his profile. His head was round and smooth, as if he was wearing a stocking or a hood. I could be wrong, I'm not sure of much, but within those few seconds that's what crossed my mind."

He turns his whole body toward the Sphinx, his eyes popping out of his head.

"What country are we in, Mr. Hocine?"

"We are in Algeria, Mr. Thobane."

"And since when have concealed firearms been in circulation in our country? To my knowledge, apart from the Boulefred case, which was all over the news in the nineteen sixties, not a single delinquent has been caught with a gun on him. Am I to understand that Colombia has arrived here?"

"There must be an explanation, Mr. Thobane."

"It's in your interest to provide me with one."

"You'll get one, *monsieur*."

Just then, the minister of the interior arrives, so flustered that his foot catches on the carpet and he almost ends up on the floor.

"I've just heard about this terrible catastrophe," he begins, throat on fire. "I hope you're not hurt. My God! It's beyond belief! Who would dare to attack Haj Thobane?"

"It's up to you to tell me, Réda. You and nobody else. Otherwise, I promise no one will ever hear of you again."

The minister is brought up short. If the sky had fallen on his head it wouldn't have caused him as much grief. His face goes red and then gray before darkening; and his Adam's apple, having scraped his gullet several times, jams in the exact middle of his neck. For a moment, as I watch him dither, I think he's going to faint.

Sickened by the sycophancy of one lot and the weakness of the other, I hurry to join my men in the street.

When I get home late that night, Mina is waiting for me in the living room, puffy-eyed. Lack of sleep, together with her domestic chores, are well on the way to wearing her out for good. But she is relieved to see me safe and sound.

"Is it true that a minister has been shot?"

"Do you know what time it is? Why aren't you in bed?"

"The attack was on the radio. Even the announcer's voice was shaking. What's this all about? Nobody's targeted a minister here since Khémisti."

"It was much more than a minister. It was almost a god. He's not dead, it was his driver that got killed."

Mina beats her breast, aghast. "My God! If they're going to amuse themselves by shooting at people, on top of all our other worries, which are getting worse by the day—"

"It's not the end of the world, Mina. Now go back to bed and be quiet. My head's threatening to explode."

Mina understands that I'm in a bad mood. She stands up, swaying.

"I'll go heat up your dinner."

"Don't bother. All I want to do is take a bath."

"Our area didn't get any water tonight."

"Again!"

Mina spreads her arms.

I hang my coat on the hook in an effort to remain calm. Once in bed, I empty my head and try to think through what happened this night. After a few pieces, the puzzle starts to weigh on my mind. Exhausted by the overtime, I put my hands behind my head and close my eyes. Mina stirs beside me, constantly forcing muffled creaks out of our ancient bed; I know she won't go to sleep before I do.

I'm up at six o'clock in the morning; not completely recovered from my insomnia, but determined to make the best possible use of my day. After a good sweet breakfast, I start by going over to number 7 Chemin des Lilas. I want to visit the scene of the crime with my mind clear; perhaps daylight will deliver up to me what the darkness of the night kept hidden. The previous night I noticed two neighbors, a young man and an old woman, who didn't stop looking meaningfully at each other every time a cop came anywhere near them. In my opinion, they certainly saw something.

It's going to be a dazzlingly bright day. Not a single damned cloud besmirches the clarity of the sky. Behind the hill, the sun promises to excel itself. It is Friday, and on this Muslim weekend, the streets are empty. The noise of my Zastava bounces self-importantly off the buildings, filling the morning silence with a certain boldness I can't quite answer for. I go through several neighborhoods without spotting a soul. Even the traffic lights are on flashing yellow. I get to Hydra in less than twenty minutes, without a glance at the opulent villas, which give off a sense of extreme beatitude. Here, people don't fuck, they take their pleasure. They are the best the Algerian bourgeoisie has been able to achieve, in the shadow of their mimosas and their untouchability. For a believer like me, to pass through these areas is to get an idea of the Eden that awaits us post mortem. I catch myself promising to remain honest, to carry out my five daily prayers punctually, never to talk ill of my neighbor, etc.

Chemin des Lilas soon puts paid to my daydreaming. I won't be able to inspect the scene of the crime with my mind clear; a crazy mob surrounds number 7, trampling the theatre of the drama underfoot and compromising my chances of coming upon an intact clue. Yesterday's two vans are still there. Other cars have shown up; some of them, the size of passenger ships, clog the sidewalk. A plainclothes cop orders me to turn back. I introduce myself; nothing to be done, there isn't so much as a pocket handkerchief where I can park my car. I decide to abandon my Zastava somehow and to continue on foot.

It is Superintendent Dine, from the security services' Communications Center—the equivalent of the FBI—who intercepts me. He was sipping a cup of coffee in his car when he spotted me. He opens the door and signals to me to come over. I notice that he's developed a gut and that his suit is somewhat sharper than the attire I've been used to seeing on him; I deduce that his new stripes are beginning to bear fruit.

"What are you looking for here?" he asks as he climbs out of his seat.

"I lost my morale somewhere around here last night. I came over to see if there was any chance of finding a few crumbs of it."

He bursts out laughing, like the great clown he is, and folds me in his arms.

"It's always a pleasure to see you again, Brahim. I ran into your Inspector Serdj just now and asked for news of you. He told me you went home five minutes before I arrived."

"You've been here since four o'clock this morning?"

"Everyone's been here for ever. The target was Haj Thobane, my friend. When bigshots of his caliber are attacked, the whole country's put on high alert. The minister has only just got started. He set up the plan personally. All services are on a war footing, and patrols are going over the city with a fine-tooth comb. Strictly between you and me, it's excellent practice. Since we've been twiddling our thumbs for so long, there's nothing like a good scare to shake us up. How about you? How are you doing?"

"As well as can be expected."

He grabs my elbow and steers me away from prying ears.

"What's going on here, Brahim?"

"I don't know."

"It's the first time a national god has been attacked like this."

"There's a first time for everything. Since Comms has been called in, I assume this is beyond Headquarters' expertise."

"Do you think Haj Thobane is about to entrust this business to small fry? Not only has Comms been mobilized, but the head of Investigation is inside the villa licking the *zaïm*'s boots. I saw him come out and lecture his men an hour ago; I'm not making it up. He's going through the worst quarter of an hour of his godawful career."

"I guess, judging by the forces that have been committed, that there's been some progress."

"It's not confirmed yet, but apparently a suspect is about to be taken in for questioning. The guys from Investigation found a woman's stocking not very far from here. They think it's the mask the killer wore during the attack. The shell cases found at the scene come from a nine-millimeter Beretta, just like the ones the police use."

"Are my men still here?"

"They've been dismissed. It's a state matter. We haven't had any definite orders yet, but it looks as if Comms will handle this, using the Bureau of Investigation's technical facilities."

"I assume I shouldn't hang about here for long."

"You don't have to any more."

"What luck!" I say, irritably. "I'll be able to say my prayers at the mosque this afternoon."

"You'll also be able to take as many naps as you like."

The atmosphere at Headquarters is the antithesis of the excitement reigning at Chemin des Lilas. A disagreeable calm oppresses the building. The officer on guard at the entrance to the establishment chooses to tie his shoelaces rather than salute me. In the corridors, no coming and going; it's Friday, of course, but there's no need to abuse it. The sound of my footsteps echoes down the corridors like distant gunshots. I wonder whether the place has perhaps been evacuated for fear of contamination.

I push open the first door I see. The underlings are still there, kicking their heels behind their typewriters.

"How's it going?"

"Fine, Superintendent. Why shouldn't it be?" someone answers.

Really? I close the door and head for my quarters, a little less stressed.

Baya is on leave, so a young trainee has taken her place. Because he's very ambitious, he's manically working on the crossword puzzles in the newspaper. When he sees me appear in front of him, he stretches out like a spring, almost knocking over the shelves behind him.

"Relax, son. You haven't really arrived here yet, and our budget doesn't even guarantee us a cup of coffee in the morning."

"I'm sorry, Superintendent."

I sense that he is a hair's breadth away from passing out, so I give him a smile designed to bring him to his senses, and change the subject:

"Any calls?"

"Nobody, sir…. The inspector from the third floor came looking for you."

I stop him right there and go into my office.

I don't even have time to open a couple of drawers before the director calls me. His voice is almost unrecognizable. "Come up quickly," he pants. It takes him three attempts to hang up the phone.

I find him behind his control center, jacket off, sleeves rolled up over his elbows, tie undone and head in hands. He has often spent sleepless nights in the office without losing his grip. This morning he seems absolutely lost. His hands run through his hair nervously and persistently, as if trying to make a tabula rasa of his scalp. At the far end of the room, standing at the French window with his fingers clasped behind his back, Bliss is looking at the city. His rigid pose makes the hairs rise on the back of my neck.

"Director," I say.

The boss seems to hear voices. He raises his head and looks around, dazed, then half-sees me through a fog. It takes him a while to recognize me; his movements are leaden.

His arms drop and his chin collapses onto the telephone.

"Are you unwell, Director?"

"And how!" snorts Bliss, without turning round.

"Will someone enlighten me?"

"You have only to do it yourself, Brahim Llob. Because there's a fire in the hole, a fire that's in danger of ruining everything we've built up over the years, and all our fine plans with it."

The director finally decides to gather himself together. He begins by wiping himself with his tie, takes a deep breath and asks me to sit down.

"Something terrible has happened, Brahim," he announces in a quavering voice. "Terrible, terrible, terrible. The worst is that it's happening to me. What have I done to God to deserve this, at my age, after an exemplary career?"

Bliss sees that the boss is not going to get to the point. He turns on his heel and comes closer.

"A suspect has just been arrested. It turns out that it's an officer from Headquarters."

"No," I say, panic-stricken.

"Yes. The guys from Investigation collared him an hour ago."

"It's impossible, there must be a misunderstanding. Lino would never do something like that."

"You see?" the director groans. "Even you haven't spared him. A police officer was mentioned and that was enough: you immediately put a name to him. I've been trying to persuade myself that there's been a misunderstanding since I heard, that none of my men would ever dare to drag the institution through the mud like this...and yet, and yet, Superintendent, it really is Lieutenant Lino, Criminal Investigation Division, who's just been locked up. Under suspicion of having made an attempt on the life of Haj Thobane and killing his driver."

I can hardly hear the director's trembling voice any more, nor can I control the shaking that is taking over my fingers, my cheeks, my guts, my spine. In a fraction of a second, darkness engulfs the room and then takes root in me. My throat is dry and my temples are pounding: I realize I am suffocating.

Bliss looks at me with contempt.

I feel as though I have shrunk at his very feet.

Chapter thirteen

The next day I ask to see Hocine the Sphinx; the duty officer at the Bureau of Investigation tells me he has an appointment out of the office. I fall back on his secretary, Ghali Saad; he hesitates a moment before inviting me to come by his office at a time that suits me. I go for around midday. I need to know that the entire staff will be in the canteen so that I can talk to Ghali without anyone disturbing us.

At 12:10, no irritants in the corridors, no stragglers in the offices, I arrive at the door to the office and knock on it; no answer. I wait thirty seconds and start again; nothing. Yet the receptionists told me Mr. Saad had not left the building. Besides, when Hocine El-Ouahch is out, his private secretary is forbidden to so much as stretch his legs on the landing. When I see that no one is coming, I decide to go in by myself. I turn the handle and glance into the room; nobody. Just as I am about to leave, a guttural cry issues from behind a hidden door, which I push gently. First I see a skirt and some lace panties on the ground, then a half-naked girl lying face down across a desk with her thighs generously parted and Ghali Saad, his erect phallus like a thermometer, taking her temperature.

Stunned by the sight, I hurry out to the corridor and wait for someone to whistle for me.

Five minutes later, the girl comes out of the office and disappears down a corridor. I consider it wise to wait another five minutes before announcing myself.

Refreshed by the physical exercise he has just taken, Ghali receives me with a certain self-satisfaction.

"I'm sorry about Headquarters," he says. "This episode will harm its reputation for a long time. Heads will roll, that's for sure; and that's just for starters.... I hear your director has been on a continuous drip since your lieutenant was arrested. I feel bad for him. He's a good lad, he really doesn't deserve this."

"It's all an unfortunate misunderstanding."

"That's not what most people think."

"It's nonsense."

"Be careful, Brahim, the case is being handled by our finest detectives."

"It doesn't make sense."

Ghali asks me to stay calm and sits down on the corner of his desk. He sucks in his lips and juts out his chin in thought, then says, "I won't hide it from you—he was a suspect from the start."

"Really?"

"Everything led to him. Your lieutenant is a bad loser. He never got over the defeat in love that he suffered with Nedjma, Thobane's little friend. All the witness statements agree, they converge on him and condemn him. Back at the Blue Sultanate, he drew his gun and threatened the restaurant's staff and customers. After that scandalous incident, he went and got himself blind drunk, to the point that he ended up in hospital. Detox obviously didn't achieve anything. As soon as he's back on his feet, our friend dives into the club scene. When he's not starting brawls, he's being picked up from the gutter like a bum. The various reports we've had suggest a man who's depressive and unpredictable."

"It was just anger, poorly digested disappointment. I know him, he's a loudmouth, but no worse. He shouts loud because he can't go where his shouting takes him. He's not a criminal—"

"He wasn't far off, whatever you say. If you ask me, he was absolutely furious at Thobane. The situation never stopped working on him, and his drunken foolery betrayed his intentions. He was going to screw up in the end, it was obvious."

"Just don't bury him right away, okay? To hear you talk, there's no need for a court case before he's lined up in front of a firing squad."

He stands up to signal that he's granted me more time than he had to.

I refuse to give up. "I must speak to him. Where is he? Where have they locked him up?"

"I'm afraid that's impossible, Brahim. The lieutenant is being questioned at the highest levels of the hierarchy."

"I won't allow him to be abused. There's been a misunderstanding. I know it doesn't look good for him, but Haj Thobane has other enemies."

"I agree completely, except that none of them left their prints behind. Your lieutenant did."

I frown. "What do you mean?"

Ghali puts his hand on my shoulder and pushes me gently toward the door.

"Of the five shell cases found at the scene, three couldn't be used for various reasons, but two were clean. Lieutenant Lino's fingerprints were found on them."

Again, for the second time in twenty-four hours, I feel as though the sky—the whole sky, with its storms, its prayers, its comets and its space probes—is falling in on my head.

I park my heap in a corner and go for a crowd-bath in the Place des Trois-Horloges. The weather is pleasant and people are crowding into the cafés. I have often wondered what the country would be like if, on a sudden impulse, a *fatwa* or a presidential decree decided to board up our cafés. There was a time when you would have found, here and there, cinemas, theaters, a crowd gathered around a snake oil salesman or an acrobat; it wasn't necessarily happiness, but it was good. You could pick up a joke, a short quarter of an hour of escapism and, that evening, when you got back to your slum you didn't feel as though you had come back empty-handed. Nowadays, apart from the café, where you just stare at each other so you don't have to look at yourselves, you're oppressed by the same feeling of emptiness wherever you go. You can fix up your expression at each shop window all you like, and try to believe the faces filing past aren't the same ones they've always been, but there's no way to shake off your dissatisfaction. You walk through the city and the city hides herself away, isolating you even further; you're as alone in the crowd as a dead gnat at the bottom of an ant heap.

I can't shake off the feeling of helplessness that clings to me, and I'm surprised to find myself driving at breakneck speed down the Moutonnière. I can't remember how I escaped the hubbub of Bab El Oued, nor how I tore loose of the frantic rush-hour traffic. In Algiers, nine o'clock in the morning is already rush hour. The city vibrates so constantly with the sound of car horns and arguments it's as if everyone works in his car.

The open window allows gusts of wind to blow in my face, slowly bringing me back to my senses. I start by working out where I am. I'm coming from the east, as if I were returning from the airport. Where have I been? I don't have the faintest idea. The sea is calm and Algiers, wallowing in its bay, broods over its deprivation. I take advantage of a general slowing down to pull over to the hard shoulder, find a place to park and go down to stretch out in the sun, then I walk on the moist sand of the beach, shoes in hand, taking care not to cut my feet on shards of glass. There are a few unemployed men scattered here and there, some of them noisy, others lost in thought. The stench of the boulevards contaminates their souls, and they come here to walk off their bitterness. Two kids in the shadow of a ruin, scarcely out of their hiccups, are sniffing all kinds of filth just to keep their heads above water. On the scrapheap at twelve years of age, they don't expect anything from life or the sandman any more. Since cops don't venture into the area, they spend their time sniffing glue and poisoning themselves with unimaginable concoctions, hoping the more quickly to wear out the moorings that prevent them from reaching nirvana.

I take up a position on a dune, light a cigarette and look out to the horizon. In the distance, ships patiently wait for the big fish that will take their anchors for bait. Seagulls dart over the waves, like flickering facial expressions. I lean back on my elbow and abandon myself to despair.

The boss still doesn't look too good. A weeping willow would be more attractive. Behind his desk, stunned, with packets of medicine within reach, he's leaking everywhere. He's taken up smoking again. Normally, when having a post-prandial rest, he would indulge in the occasional fat cigar, preferably a Havana, to fit in with his status as a privileged pensioner of the republic. This evening, he's sucking on untipped laborers' cigarettes. Probably to get ready for the hard times visible on his horizon. He already sees himself fired, all doors closed to him, his credit cards confiscated. It's hard to walk on the ground when you've spent your life swaggering about in the clouds. I almost feel sorry for him.

In Algeria, when the trapdoor opens on your empire, there's no abyss as dark as your night. The boss knows this. He's seen colleagues slide down the ladder and end up shambling old men after years of privilege. He can see himself going the same way, dethroned, no armor-plating and no friends—for one's friends have a disastrous tendency to vanish like snowflakes as soon as one's descent into hell is announced. This is wearing him down, filling his guts, rising in his gorge. He can't bear anyone looking at him any more, nor can he stand their silence; he can't stand himself any more.

He has taken off his shirt and is wearing only an undershirt soaked with cold sweat. Graying hairs stick up on his shoulders. His eyes are pouched, his mouth tight; his face looks like a death mask.

Other section heads are there to help him in his misfortune. Bachire, from the forensic science lab, an *éminence grise* who spends most of his time in the basement of Headquarters, working like a negro. It's the first time I've seen him on the third floor. Even he doesn't know what he's doing on this level of the building. Disoriented, he huddles in his chair and pretends to be elsewhere. Beside him, Lieutenant Chater, head of the Flying Squad, is contemplating a painting signed Denis Martinez. He makes a small gesture at me before disappearing behind his moustache. Opposite them, visibly bored, Ghaouti the computer expert is marinating in his questions. And then, somewhat apart from the rest, Bliss is examining his fingernails.

"How long is the wake going to last?" I ask, disgusted.

The boss stubs out his cigarette in the ashtray. He doesn't seem to have heard me.

"Did you get permission for me to see Lino?"

"Sit down, Brahim."

"Did you get it, yes or no?"

"What for?"

"I want to talk to him. He's the only one who can clear this thing up."

Bliss raises his eyebrows.

The boss fishes out another cigarette, twirls it absent-mindedly in his fingers a few times, then jams it between his lips. Ghaouti gets up to offer his lighter. The boss breathes in interminably and blows the smoke out through his nostrils; his eyes fall on me.

"What does ballistics say?"

Bliss jerks himself upright. With his hands in his pockets, he goes round me to position himself beside the director. He says, "Ballistics wants to get its hands on the murder weapon before committing itself. Our lieutenant says he lost his gun. He doesn't remember where he lost or mislaid it. His home has been searched; nothing."

He takes advantage of my state of shock to deliver the coup de grâce: "Too many coincidences stretch chance, Llob. Lino isn't leaving us any room for maneuver so that we can get him out of the hole he's dug himself. The only thing he can do is make a confession and let us all go home. He doesn't even have an alibi. It's really bad luck. On the night of the attack, the lieutenant is out for the count. He says he's tying one on in town. Where? Which bar? He doesn't remember. He says he lost his gun. Where? When? The cat's got his tongue. I went to Bab El Oued myself, hoping to find some insomniac who saw him in the area on the night of the attack. There's not even an alleycat willing to vouch for him. This business is too fuzzy to clear Lino of suspicion. His file is thick enough to send him to the firing squad."

I go to Soustara with Serdj, to the home of Sid Ali, a cop turned res-
taurateur. Colleagues come here from time to time to have a quiet
drink in his back room, safe from tattle-tales. Since Lino knows the
place, I've convinced myself I have to start here; maybe we'll find
him an alibi.

Sid Ali spreads his whale's fins in welcome. He slaps his fat
slobbery lips to my cheeks. "What happens when a cop is offered
roast pig?"

"I don't know."

"He drools tears!"

Seeing that his little joke leaves me cold, he raises his eyebrows
in consternation. "If you've lost your sense of humor, Brahim, things
must be really bad."

"I'm at a loss, if you want the truth," I confess. "You haven't
seen Lino lately, have you?"

Sid Ali pinches his temples between his thumb and index
finger to remember. His broom-like moustache quivers beneath his
nose for five seconds. I'm hanging on his lips the way a shipwrecked
sailor clings to a piece of wreckage, praying for his expression to light
up; to my great disappointment, Sid Ali shakes his head, racking my
despair up a notch.

"It's very important," I say encouragingly.

"I haven't seen him for weeks. What's up with him? Has he
dropped out of sight?"

"He's in the shit, and I need to know exactly where he's been
these last few days, with whom and, most of all, what he got up to
between Thursday night and Friday morning."

"I don't like the way you're giving me this all of a sudden, Brahim. I hope it's just a lover's tiff."

"It's worse than desertion, but I'm not here to discuss the matter in depth. I have to know where he's been the last few days. You
don't have the slightest idea? He used to come here and raise a glass
occasionally."

"Only when he was broke. His tab is full to the rim. Ever since
I reminded him he owed me some dough he hasn't dared come back.
But I know a joint he used to go to from time to time. The wine is

less watered down over there, and girls are allowed, which isn't the case here."

Serdj gets out his notebook to write it down.

"Is it far?"

"Maybe ten blocks, opposite the old soft-drinks factory. You take a left at the rotary, follow the old avenue and then, when you get to the factory, you take a right. The street's called Frères-Mourad."

The Impasse Frères-Mourad resembles its history, filthy from start to finish. The road is wide, paved with ancient flagstones, with high sidewalks and cracked façades. The houses go back to the Ottoman era, squat and gloomy beneath dilapidated roofs. The bar is in a dead end, lurking behind a faded sign on which, with a bit of effort, it is possible to decipher *The Black Cat*. During the reign of the *dey*,* it was a *hammam*** where Turkish dignitaries came to slim down. The day after the July 1830 invasion, French soldiers, drunk on their triumph, requisitioned it and turned it into a field brothel. It enjoyed a long career as a house of pleasure, with plenty of orgies, crimes of passion and syphilitic declines before the FLN closed it down with machine-guns during the Battle of Algiers. It stayed that way until the late 1960s, when an old prostitute took it in hand. After a series of murders, the place was closed down again. Nowadays, it's a low dive, mournful as its customers, with a bar that looks like a trench and corners freighted with darkness.

It's closed during the day, so I wait until evening before going over there. As a precaution, Serdj comes with me. Venturing there alone—a dead-end street after nightfall—would give some evil ideas to the winos that have been turned away.

The giant standing guard at the door nurses a permanently gestating grudge; his fist would lash out at the slightest false move. My badge doesn't impress him at all. He steps aside reluctantly and lets us in.

Serdj can't conceal his unease. The place inspires extreme

---

* *Dey*: title given to the rulers of the Regency of Algiers under the Ottoman Empire.
** *Hammam*: Turkish bathhouse.

distrust. A dozen men are scattered around the room, some in the company of dubious girls, others happy to carry on conversations with their own hallucinations. An old man in a coverall is playing with his hands and giggling to himself. When he sees us coming in, he opens his toothless mouth wide and gives us the finger. At the bar, an enormous African is leaning over a glass, his shoulders like ramparts.

The barman polishes the counter, a stick of liquorice between his teeth.

"The house doesn't give credit," he warns, as soon as he recognizes my badge.

"That's good, I'm trying to give it up."

Serdj intervenes so that things don't turn sour too quickly: "A colleague of ours, Lieutenant Lino, is a regular at your establishment. We want to know if he's come in here for a drink in the last few days."

The barman hangs his cloth up somewhere and, ignoring us magnificently, goes off to talk to another customer at the end of the bar. Serdj joins him, calm and polite: "He's tall, dark-haired, quite a good-looking lad, and he dresses very fashionably."

The barman goes on talking with his customer. His nonchalance infuriates me. When he comes back to get a bottle, I grip him by the throat and pull him toward me.

"We're talking to you, asshole."

Completely unmoved by my assault, he looks at me disdainfully and says, "There's a shortage of irons in the land, *kho.*"

"So?"

"So, your filthy great mitts are creasing up the collar of my best shirt."

I can tell from his expression that I'm not going to get anything out of him. I push him back into his shelves. Just then, the big African raises his carcass and turns threateningly in my direction.

"What's your game, fool?"

"Leave it, Moussa," says the barman. "It's just a bastard of a cop."

But Moussa goes on, more and more in my face, "A bastard of a cop? Where'm I, down at the station?"

"You're at home," the toothless old man informs him, "at The Black Cat. It's the bastard of a cop who's not at home."

Moussa looks down at me from his monstrous height. His nauseating breath pours down on me and threatens to drown me. "You've got no business here, hey! You piece-of-shit pig. Are people writing about our rage on walls around the republic? Are people demonstrating in the streets, mounting hunger strikes, criticizing the rotten system that rules over us?"

"We're just having a drink, not bothering anyone," says the old man. "We're not hurting anyone."

"So why's he come here to bother us, this piece-of-shit pig? Why can't he let us drink in peace?"

"Leave it, Moussa," says the barman, not really meaning it.

Moussa sways. His arm points at the door. "Beat it!"

With his other arm, he grabs me by the scruff of the neck and prepares to fling me across the room. So I turn on my heel, throwing him slightly off balance, step back and kick him between the legs as hard as I can. Surprised, at first, by the effectiveness of this maneuver, the ebony giant stares at me with big round eyes, grabs his crotch with both hands and collapses to his knees, grimacing with unbearable pain. "The bastard," he bellows. "He's burst my balls!"

"Sorry," I say. "I thought they were made of bronze."

Superintendent Dine's answering machine is on. He hasn't come in yet, his secretary tells me in a monotone. He's at work, states his wife. In short, he's avoiding me. But I'm not one to give up easily. I know the man; he has his habits, and it's thanks to them that I manage to run him to earth. Dine likes a drink. In the evening, before he goes home to his little family, he goes to the Lotus and has two or three beers. I catch him at the bar, sucking up the foam from his drink. He is dismayed to find me at his shoulder.

"Is somebody on your tail or something?"

"It's the job, Brahim. My secretary passed on your messages."

"You could have called me back."

"I didn't dare."

He picks up his glass and leads me to a discreet corner at the end of the room.

"Why didn't you dare?"

"No need to beat about the bush. Right now, you won't find anyone. Everyone's gone to ground, you see. If you want my advice, let things run their course. I know how much Lino means to you, but to them, he doesn't count for much. Nor do people who want to prove the contrary. This business stinks. If you don't know where to start, it's because it's scarier than a nest of vipers. Dip a finger in and your whole arm will be gone forever. We're old friends; we've been through some rough times, touched bottom together and had a very few successes. This time, it's different. We're talking about Haj Thobane, and that's not a walk in the park."

"He's not God Almighty."

"God Almighty is merciful and compassionate, Brahim. Haj Thobane has never forgiven anything."

I look him right in the eye. He turns away and tries to drown himself in his glass, such is his confusion.

"As far as I'm concerned, he's just a cretin with balls."

"I'm sorry I don't share your cavalier attitude. I shit my pants just thinking of him, if you want to know what I think."

"My own thoughts are enough for me."

Dine stops fiddling with his glass and looks at me. "What do you want, Brahim?"

"To get my lieutenant back."

"How?"

"He's been transferred to Comms headquarters."

His jaw clenches violently, almost closing one eye. "Do you want me killed?"

"I want to speak to my partner. Do what you have to do to get me to him. I promise I won't be long."

He gulps, looks around to make sure no one has heard me and starts up again, nostrils quivering, "What you're asking is sheer madness. First, Lino isn't in our building; then, even if he were, I wouldn't take you to him. It's not good for you and it's not good for me. Let me remind you that your lieutenant attacked—"

"He's innocent," I interrupt.

"Haj Thobane is sure he's got his hooks into his 'bastard.'"

"I don't give a shit."

"You're the only one."

"I tell you he's just a cretin with balls. There's such a thing as the law in this country. And official procedures too."

Dine is flabbergasted. He takes a deep breath to recover his senses, then he leans over toward me and shouts, "What law are you talking about, and what procedures?"

His yell crashes off the walls and creates an immense silence in the room. The customers, as one, turn to look at us.

Dine adjusts his tie, passes a trembling hand through his hair and waits for the hubbub gradually to rise in the bar before he says in a low voice, "You don't teach the executioner to hide his face, Brahim; and I'm not going to try to teach you that lesson. You know very well how this country works. Our brilliant careers can be blown sky high in the blink of an eye; life itself can depend on 'a phone call.' What are you talking about? There's no charter, no constitution, no law, no equity; if justice wears a blindfold here, it's because she doesn't have the courage to look herself in the eye. We don't serve a country, we serve men. We're dependent on their changing moods and we adapt ourselves to their pleasure. I'm as panic-stricken as you, I'm worried sick about Lino. But, dammit! He's not even defending himself. I know tougher nuts than him who haven't survived criticism from the upper echelons. And they hadn't killed or attempted to kill a big cheese; they had just tried to carry out their duties correctly. Because they showed a zeal the hierarchy considered offensive, they were fucked upside down and sideways. Lino, though: he has committed sacrilege. He helps himself to a god's little whore, then plays the cowboy on the big shots' turf and refuses to play ball. Result: he's had it. As for you, Brahim, you won't put one over on Haj Thobane by puffing yourself up like a balloon. He's a *zaïm*; whether you like it or not, he's someone who can make the rain fall and the sun shine at will. If he tells us a pack of lies about his past as a Great Revolutionary and looks us in the eye while he's doing it, that doesn't make him a cretin with balls; it means that many of us aren't much better than him when it comes to morality."

Dine is right. One day, perhaps, Haj Thobane will suffer a stroke or choke on a bone, and a large number of people will turn out at his grave, crying that History should never slack off on her heroes. We'll see them transformed into fully paid-up hagiographers and embalmers, willing to be buried alive in the same sarcophagus as our pharaonic creation. And then, once the lid has been closed, we'll finally understand why a land as noble as Algeria isn't nearly out of the woods yet.

I try to find a glimmer of hope in Dine's eyes. He looks away. I understand that my presence by his side is a serious embarrassment to him and that I therefore can't rely on him.

Chapter fourteen

The redhead says the suspect produced a gun and attacked
Thobane. Except that the latter wasn't Thobane but a junior Comms
officer in disguise. The suspect hadn't gone ten meters before he was
pinned down by spotlights. "Police!" they shouted through a mega
phone. "You're surrounded. Put your weapon on the ground and
lie face-down on the ground." Taken by surprise, the suspect took a
shot at one of the spotlights before being hit in the leg by the fake
Thobane. While trying to escape, he came face to face with the redhead. "It was him or me," the redhead said. "When I saw him aim
his gun at me, I fired."

When I got to the scene, Comms's excellent sleuths were still
patting each other on the back, very proud of their coup. I found this
odd. It took me ten, fifteen minutes to get there. I thought I was the
first idle spectator to show up, after the people who were in the restaurant, who were now moving about on the stairs and keeping their
distance, frightened by the volley of shots. A panoramic glance around
the theater of operations was enough to convince me of the flimsy
staging—it stank of a cheap set-up, of going through the motions;
furthermore, the ambulance is on the scene, which proves it was there

well ahead of time. I went over to the corpse. His head has more or less exploded and he is clutching a nine-millimeter Beretta in his fist.

It's after midnight, and I ask myself what they're waiting for to seal off the parking lot and proceed to the forensic examination. The team looks to be in no hurry to get down to business; as for the ambulance crew, they're calmly smoking cigarettes inside the ambulance, with their doors wide open.

I remain standing in front of the stiff, with my hands in my pockets. A second panoramic glance confirms that our suspect really chose the worst possible place to exhibit himself. The hoarding he crouched behind is barely high enough to hide a child. As for the spotlights arranged around the parking lot, a blind man would have noticed them. I don't know why this business doesn't succeed in making me angry. Sure, I've always been jealous of Comms's brilliant success rate, but I'm sure that has nothing to do with this.

"Hi, Llob," Captain Youcef whispers in my ear.

"Nice collar," I say.

"Too right. Were you in the restaurant?"

"I was nearby."

"And you came to congratulate us?"

"It's good work. Just like in training."

Captain Youcef raises an eyebrow, sensing an insinuation of some kind. He's an efficient guy, even formidable. He worked in the Bureau of Investigation for many years during the cold war with Morocco until he put his foot in it in France during the elimination of a dissident. His name was printed in a Paris newspaper, which forced him into hiding somewhere in the East. Once things had calmed down, he came back to haunt the basement of Comms. He takes care of the kind of sensitive matters that irritate the upper echelons from time to time.

We have known each other since the business with the three French spies who tried to blow up the party newspaper in the 1970s. I was still an inspector then, and he was a young officer with shining eyes and a tortured soul, the image of the blows he had suffered. I was leading the inquiry into the death of a madam. The three spies—two

Algerians and a *pied-noir**—had chosen her house as their residence. Thus it was that at a critical juncture in my investigation, I had to hand over to the officer. The affair went beyond the criminal and was well on its way to becoming a diplomatic crisis. Youcef managed to trap these enemies of the revolution. Since they don't hand out medals in our country, he was sent to Europe as a reward. After being expelled from Germany for flirting with a western terrorist group, he landed up in Paris two years later. There, a dissident was making trouble for the regime, stirring up shit for the FLN nomenklatura on the television screens and newspapers all over France. He was making a lot of noise, preventing our *zaïms* from jumping their whores in peace, so Youcef was given the task of silencing him. Youcef's mistake was to get a hood from the slums to do the dirty work: this hired killer couldn't keep his mouth shut around indiscreet ears—he confided in his girlfriend, who wasn't impressed and turned him in, after arranging a romp for him with a rival. Youcef hasn't set foot in the motherland since.

"Can you tell me who the guy asleep on the tarmac is?"

"You're not welcome, Llob. Not only do we have nothing to say but also, it's none of your business. Only Comms and the Bureau are authorized to be here. Do me a favor and get in that wreck of yours and get lost, with your mirror folded away. The Sphinx is about to show up. He was in seventh heaven when we told him the news. If he finds you here, it'll spoil his evening, and we won't get our lump of sugar because of you."

I pace up and down to keep warm.

"Did you see his gun?" I ask. "Isn't it a nine-millimeter Beretta?"

"You don't miss much, do you."

"He's wearing a sweatsuit and a nylon top with no pockets."

"So?"

"It's not very practical for lugging a gun around."

"Maybe he kept it hidden somewhere around here."

---

* *Pied-noir* (blackfoot): French citizen born in Algeria.

"Maybe…but I don't see his flashlight either. The redhead said he saw him shine a flashlight on the Mercedes."

"We haven't finished our work yet."

"I thought as much. Obviously, you were hot on his heels. The trap was sprung in exactly the right place, it seems."

"You obviously need to go through training again, at Headquarters."

"I'm too old to be emptying my inkpot onto my blotter."

"You should hang up your hat, Llob. Things don't work the way they used to. We don't live in the trees, nor in caves."

I smile to show I believe in fair play and then, innocently, I start right in again: "Are you really not going to tell me who he is?"

I think I've had an effect, because he admits, out of the corner of his mouth:

"We don't know yet. For the last five days, we've been getting reports of a mysterious figure showing up wherever Mr. Thobane goes, but the security cordon around our subject was keeping the stalker beyond our reach. Every time we showed any interest in him, he vanished. So we thought up a little drama to suck him in. Adjutant Kader agreed to play the part of Mr. Thobane. We came to the Marhaba restaurant three times to see what would happen, reducing the escort perceptibly. The fish took the bait this evening. Now that we have the body, we won't take long to put a name to it. After which it'll be child's play."

"Thrilling. I bet a masterful haul like that must be worth a whole heap of sugarlumps, at the very least. Do you think this might have anything to do with the attack on Thursday? Because, just think, I've got an officer who must be feeling bad in that place of yours, and it would give me a real lift to find he's there for no reason."

Youcef folds his arms across his chest, looking like a locksmith who doesn't understand why none of his keys is opening the door. His lips squirm around a sick-looking grimace.

"You are exasperating, Llob, like all assholes who don't know they're assholes. Pack your bags and leave before the Sphinx arrives. He's spent the week vomiting with terror; he'd come close to spitting out his guts if he caught sight of the expression on your face."

I lift my arms in surrender and go back to my car.

In an apartment block not far from Headquarters, there's a café I use occasionally for decompression purposes. The clientele consists mostly of old men on their last legs, and the waiter is so slow on the uptake that he doesn't remember the morning's orders until the end of the evening. It's a depressing place, with moldering furnishings and blocked-up toilets, but its terrace provides a very interesting perspective on the regression taking place on the marginalized fringes of society. Two decades ago, the street was flourishing—the shopkeepers were elbowing one another aside, the butchers were besieged and housewives sagged beneath the weight of their shopping baskets. Today, apart from a grocery with a crumbling façade and an unsavory-looking dairy, recognizable by the creamy tentacles branching out on the surface of the road, business has slowed to a crawl and ill-fed purses can't keep up. The few passers-by one sees here and there look even hungrier than they are; their world is getting poorer faster than their efforts, and their tomorrows have gone off for another facelift. I used to come here a lot at the beginning of my career. In those days, at Headquarters, coffee was only served to the director and his guests; as for the small fry like me, we weren't even entitled to a glass of water. We ate garbage in the canteen, and we often wondered if we weren't actually in jail, with the result that any time the duty officer turned his back we would dive into the greasy spoon next door. I didn't like greasy spoons. I thought I deserved better. With my buttocks well shaped by my jeans and my cowboy shirt opened wide over my blond down, I would skip lunch and come over here to show off my muscles and hunt for virgins to deflower. People could see that I was just showing off and hardly held it against me. In those days, high spirits were enough in themselves to make a party; everyone, young and old, took pleasure in them. But I knew my limits. When I realized that my act was getting close to crude exhibitionism, I would retire into the nearest café, order a strong black coffee and never pay for it. Every time I reached into my pocket and asked for the bill, the owner would wave his hand to say no, explaining that an anonymous person had already taken care of it. Ah! Dzaïr,* my home, how you

---

*   *Dzaïr*: Algeria (Arabic).

have changed! We were a true tribe, and we didn't need alliances to be close to each other. People respected each other, I would even say they were fond of each other, and their generosity was often ahead of their thoughts. It was so…

"Superintendent."

Inspector Serdj is standing in front of me, hiding my ray of sunlight and spoiling my few moments of respite. His expression doesn't improve things.

"Now what?"

"There's been some news."

"Go on."

"Not here, Superintendent. Do you mind if we go stretch our legs?"

I toss a couple of coins on the table and follow him. We walk in silence as far as the avenue and then he tells me, "The Comms guys killed a suspect yesterday."

"I heard."

His eyebrows almost disappear.

"I was in the neighborhood when I heard shots," I explain. "I headed for the scene without asking too many questions."

"Did they tell you who he was, the armed man?"

"I hope you're going to enlighten me."

Serdj scratches his temple and then hurls his thunderbolt: "SNP."

"What?"

"He was identified this morning."

I don't know what got into me. I left the inspector right there and ran for my car like a madman.

"Mr. El-Ouahch isn't seeing anyone right now," says Ghali Saad, irritated at my arrival in his kingdom without an entry visa. "Haj Thobane is with him. They are both in bad moods. Yesterday evening, a suspect was killed by our men. If you can believe it, it was a man condemned to life imprisonment who had just been granted a presidential pardon, less than a month ago. What's going on in the office next door is like a nightmare. Thobane has come here demanding an explanation from the boss, since he chaired the committee responsible for the recent releases."

I look at the padded door as if trying to pierce it. Ten drums are beating full blast in my temples.

Ghali Saad watches my fury but isn't overly disturbed. He is sitting behind his desk with his fingers interlocked on the blotter, fully in control of his nerves. His blue eyes hold my gaze dispassionately.

"It's true that things couldn't get much worse," he admits. "But that doesn't mean we can allow ourselves to be distracted. On the contrary, we must keep cool heads if we want to keep them on our shoulders. I can assure you I'm not losing any sleep over this business. Yesterday, I was dragged out of bed at two o'clock in the morning and spent the rest of the night waiting around in this chair. I'm exhausted. And this morning, as soon as our friend was identified, the sky fell in on the Bureau. First, the minister. He was here before the security guard. I don't need to tell you. Then the boss, tearing his hair out. When Thobane showed up, I thought I was witnessing the end of the world. If you want some advice, Llob, go back to your post and pray with all the fervor you possess. Because it won't be long before you're thrown in the pot too. There's a report that says you set up a surveillance operation around the convict in question as soon as he came out of jail, without authorization or special instructions. Without even asking your superiors. Why? I imagine you have a solid answer to justify this foolish initiative. If you don't, you'll find yourself in the same place as your lieutenant: in the dock. And no one will invite you into their living room. Not even your kids and your friends. Given the schizophrenic atmosphere, any protest you make will be interpreted as sheer insubordination, and the sword of Damocles will be waiting to settle the argument once and for all. In short, Superintendent, you're in the shit up to your ears."

A cold sweat makes its presence felt on my back. I hadn't planned for this eventuality, not for a second, not for a fraction of a second. I was so busy having nightmares about the fate awaiting Lino that I had completely lost sight of the possibility that something like this might happen. The beginnings of panic take hold in the pit of my stomach. My hand grips the chair of its own accord.

"What is this crap?" I hear myself muttering.

"The noose is tightening, Llob. The Beretta they found on the murderer really is your lieutenant's. To put you fully in the picture, here's where things stand: Lino couldn't stomach his defeat with Nedjma and was trying to retrieve his honor with Thobane's blood. He needed a killer. He had one in mind: SNP, a psychopathic killer. He must have got to know him a bit better when he was following him around, with your blessing, and suggested a deal. SNP was just waiting for an opportunity to get back in his element. Lino lends him his gun for the dirty work. Things go wrong, hello trouble."

This time, my hand isn't up to supporting me. I fall into the chair and fumble frantically in my pockets for my cigarettes. Ghali takes the trouble to stir himself and offers me his lighter.

He confides, "As far as the idiotic surveillance operation around the suspect's home is concerned, the boss doesn't know anything yet, and nor do Thobane and the minister. The report is in my drawer."

I look up at him like a beaten dog. "I don't understand."

"I've got a lot of respect for you, Brahim. I know you don't have anything to do with this nonsense. As for your lieutenant, he'll just have to find his own way out."

"What do you mean, 'the report is in my drawer'?"

"I mean I don't intend to show it to the boss. Not immediately, at any rate. It would only make an already explosive situation even worse. I've decided to delay things, to offer you some room for maneuver and a breath of oxygen."

"You would do that for me?"

"Who do you take me for?"

My throat is dry, and the rancid taste of my cigarette is ravaging my palate. "I'll pay you back, Ghali."

"I don't think you have the means, Superintendent. Just make it your business to get something out of the reprieve I'm giving you. Honest as you are, I'm not doing this because of your looks. I'm acting as I am to preserve your director's excellent reputation. I hear he was taken to hospital this morning. The latest twists and turns in this affair have taken their toll on him. It's mainly for his sake that I'm taking the risk of burying the report. Now beat it. It won't be

166

long before our two ogres will take their leave of each other. If they catch you in that chair, they'll eat you alive, and me along with you."

I nod and stand up.

Despite the load Ghali Saad has taken off my shoulders, I find it difficult to cheer up.

"Ghali," I say, "if you want me to get something out of the reprieve you've given me, you'll have to do me one more favor."

"What?"

"Fix an interview with my lieutenant."

With his fingers still interlocked, he shakes his chin imperceptibly. "I can't get involved in your business, Brahim."

"Five minutes, that's all."

"I'm fond of my privileges."

"Without his side of the story, I'm helpless."

"Don't insist."

At about one o'clock in the morning, Mina shakes me to warn me that the telephone is threatening to rouse our neighbors to insurrection. My hand knocks a few bits and pieces over on the nightstand before picking up the receiver.

"Hello?" I say.

"It's Ghali. Am I disturbing you?"

"That depends what you're about to tell me."

A silence at the other end of the line, then the determined voice of the secretary of the Bureau of Investigation: "I don't know what I'm getting into, but I'll see what I can do about getting you an interview with your lieutenant."

This wakes me right up.

Ghali hangs up before I have time to thank him.

Someone has taken my spot in the parking lot at Headquarters; at first, I considered blocking him in, but since the car is a top-of-the-range model, I decide I don't need to bring any more problems with influential nabobs down on my head. I drive round and round looking for an empty space and finally, enraged, come back to block the big car in, ready to have it out with Azraïn himself. And I find a police car has got itself stuck in a pothole right in the middle of the lot. With his tunic open over his gluttonous belly, the driver is kicking the trapped wheel, visibly out of options. His colleagues are standing around watching; not a single one deigns to offer him any help, which annoys him not a little. He is sweating, with saliva frothing at the corners of his mouth, and watching him use up so much effort makes me want to hand in my chips.

I hurry back to my office.

The usual frenzy of a police station has given way to a strange kind of calm. Officers stop talking as I go by.

I stop first at Serdj's office to ask after the boss. Serdj informs me that the director has had an anxiety attack and is under observation in the military hospital at Aïn Naadja. I suggest he sends some flowers and a box of imported candy; there's nothing to lose.

Baya puts the telephone down in a hurry when she hears me coming. She smoothes her skirt and then forces a smile that's difficult to read.

"Superintendent Dine has called three times."

"Did he say why?"

"No, but he promised to call back."

"Get him on line two for me."

"Right away, sir."

The phone rings just as I'm hanging my jacket on the back of my chair. Dine flies off the handle when he hears my voice. He begins by asking where I've been, as if I've missed the chance of a lifetime, then calms down and asks me to meet him at 66, Rue des Soviets. Alone, he insists.

And there he is, waiting for me at the appointed place, sitting on the hood of his car with his arms folded. He is alone, too. From the joy shining in his face I guess that he has great tidings to impart.

"Leave your car here," he says. "I'll drive."

He opens the door and helps me into my seat with exaggerated politeness, then jumps behind the wheel and starts the car.

"Where are we going?"

"I've managed to get one of the bigwigs to see sense. It wasn't easy, but the result is great: we have permission to go and see our friend Lino."

Liar!

Dine is a great guy; getting involved in toxic affairs is not his style. This seeing sense stuff isn't like him. He's just following orders. Ghali Saad has kept his word. How did he set the wheels turning? That's his problem, not mine. If Dine wants to get some personal satisfaction out of it, I don't see any harm. I'm so happy finally to be able to see my lieutenant that I pretend to feel indebted.

"I knew I could count on you."

"We've got to stick together. These are treacherous times."

"You're right."

We cross half the city, taking one tortuous alleyway after another. For a moment I think my guide is trying to cover his tracks so that I won't be able to retrace them. He might just as well blindfold me while he's about it. It's no big deal. I'm so excited about locating Lino that I avoid spoiling my pleasure. Half an hour later we plunge into a forested area bristling with tall fences, some of them topped with barbed wire. Not a hiker on the paths. A silence filled with questions crushes the place. Dine turns down a shaded road and drives up to a gate that slides open gradually as we approach. We are greeted by a courtyard ringing with birdsong. One might be tempted to think it was some Eden-like clearing, were it not for the body-builder with the swinging arms and the face barricaded away behind dark glasses waiting for us beside a crumbling fountain, like an executioner resolutely awaiting his prey.

"End of the line," Dine warns me. "All change."

The body-builder doesn't come and meet us. He doesn't even make a move, though I can feel him looking me up and down with x-ray eyes, going over both my subconscious thoughts and my surface obsessions with a fine-tooth comb. His tailor-made black suit is brand new, but the carnivorous leer stretched over his salivating fangs makes him look like a rabid hound straining at the leash.

I'm overcome with a sick feeling; I get out a handkerchief and wipe my temples.

The guardian of the Temple contents himself with opening the door behind him with nary a *salamalek* or a grumble. He lets us past him, shuts the door and leads us along a sinister corridor. On both sides, low cells, plunged in darkness. No tenants, just barred rat-holes that send a chill down the spine. Further on, a soiled staircase plunges down to a horrifying lower level where further cells molder beneath thick layers of saltpeter. A penetrating stench irritates my eyes and throat. There are no skylights and no air vents, just stone walls sweating fetid secretions, with the feeling that one is wandering somewhere among the insalubrious mists of purgatory without the slightest chance of escaping unharmed.

The ice on my back spreads, setting off my rheumatism.

The body-builder fiddles with the lock on a kind of junk-room, shoots two bolts, and switches on a ceiling lamp. Something moves in the interior of the hole; a human shape huddled on the ground. It's my Lino. Or at least what's left of him. His face is completely distorted, his eyes puffy with huge purple bruises and his lips smashed: a horror.

"They brought him here like that," the gorilla says. "Nobody here has gone near him since he was admitted."

Rage floods into me from all sides, but I keep my cool. Making a scene, or letting slip my intentions, is out of the question; I'm in enemy territory.

I kneel down beside my partner and slowly pull back the thin, greasy blanket in which he has wrapped himself in search of a tiny bit of warmth. His shirt and undershirt have been taken away, leaving just jailbird's trousers from which his feet, bare and filthy, protrude. It's a sight fit to make a stone weep. His scrawny body is striped with blackish welts—the result of blows from a night-stick or a whip—and, here and there, wide, pus-covered abrasions. It's as if he's been swallowed up and spat out by a garbage-compressor.

Lino doesn't know it's me. He tries, in vain, to open his eyes. His nostrils are blocked by clumps of clotted blood. He lifts a crushed hand but can't manage to get it as far as me; I seize it and press it to my chest.

"It's me. You see? I've found you at last."

I feel a wave of shock pass through the lieutenant from head to toe. He tries to move a bit more; his breath runs out and he gives in to his pain. For a moment, he tries to smile to show how happy he is to see me, but the wounds in his mouth immediately start to bleed.

"You're too messed up, my friend. Save your strength."

Dine is struck dumb. He must have been expecting something like this, but what he is seeing surpasses understanding.

I gesture with my head, asking him to leave me alone with my officer.

"I'll be down the hall," he mutters as he leaves.

The ape doesn't move, however.

"I'm not going to steal him," I say.

He thinks for three seconds, accentuates his leer and then, evidently encouraged by Dine, agrees to disappear from my sight.

"They did a good job on me, eh, Super?" Lino croaks.

"They didn't hold back."

His police officer's stripes didn't do him any good. Minister or porter, power behind the throne or obscure middle manager, he who ends up in the jails of the secret police of Algeria will be conscientiously torn to shreds. His dignity will be confiscated so that he may be better prepared for the worst, and he will be dragged through the mud until death ensues. If he manages to pull through, by some miracle, he will go back to free air only in order to give those who are tempted to get up to mischief with the regime something to think about.

"What day is it?" the martyr asks shakily.

"Almost the Lord's day."

He shuffles around to get on his backside, but tires quickly and curls up on the mattress. I put my arm around his waist and lift him carefully; his breath struggles to make headway through his groans, and his tortured grimaces add a biblical hideousness to his facial deformities.

"I should have squashed them between my paws like a carbuncle."

"Take it easy."

Rage makes his wounds tremble. He pulls his head down between his shoulders and starts sobbing. If the ape had come back at that moment to see what was going on, I would have gouged his eyes out with toothpicks. But nobody comes to bother us.

"I'll get you out of here, Lino."

"I can't take it much longer."

"Yes you can. You won't let me down."

A fit of coughing overcomes him.

His hand searches for me and grips my wrist.

"I'm in the shit," I confess to him. "You have to help me. I want to know what happened to you that night. Where you were, what the hell you did that evening and how you lost your gun. You must remember some detail, however small, something that might lead us somewhere. Is it true you were in a bar on Thursday night? You were drunk as a lord when they arrested you."

"Is it true they've shot the suspect?"

"It's true."

"Maybe it's a bluff."

"I was there and I saw him, shot at point-blank range. I didn't recognize him there and then because he didn't have a beard any more and he had cut his hair, but the identification is definite. It was SNP."

"I never came across the guy. Every time it was my turn to do surveillance duty, I fixed things with my colleagues and ran off to see Nedjma."

"It's your service revolver that was found on him, the same one that was used in the attempt on Thobane and which killed his driver. You must remember how you lost it."

His fingers clamber up my arm, looking for something to hold on to. He's trying to gain time, and I dissuade him.

"I won't get permission to see you again, Lino. So we won't have a chance to think it over calmly, what happened to you that night. It's now or never to refresh your memory."

Lino nods. A thread of blood oozes from an abscess on his temple and runs down his cheek. "I haven't stopped thinking about that day, Brahim. Ever since they threw me in the hole I've done nothing else. I know that a single spark could shed light on this whole business."

He shakes his chin in desperation. "I'm sorry, it's a black hole."

The ape comes back, looking ostentatiously at the dial of his watch. I stand up. Lino realizes it's the end of the visit. He clutches my arm. What I see in his expression pierces me like a dagger. His lips quiver among the cuts, trying to say something and then, aware of the extent of my distress, he changes his mind and sinks into his corner with his eyes to the floor.

Chapter fifteen

I think he was drugged," says Serdj, taking a drag from his cigarette. "How do you expect him to remember anything after what he's been through? He was already groggy when he was handed over to his torturers. I'm sure they didn't even give him time to understand what was happening to him. What with the blows to the head he's had and the humiliations he's suffered, it's not surprising he doesn't even remember his own name."

I contemplate my cup without saying anything.

We are on the terrace of a café in Belcourt, far from family and colleagues, drawing up the balance sheet of our theoretical investigation, then drawing it up again, over a glass of dishwater.

Serdj stubs out his cigarette in the ashtray.

He's exhausted.

For the last six days, we have each been separately racing about, looking for some providential witness who might inject hope back into our investigation; not a thing. Serdj has scoured a hundred low dives showing Lino's photo around; not a single barman, not a single drunkard, not a single prostitute so much as frowned. For my part, I went back to square one to re-establish the chronology of events.

Two of Haj Thobane's neighbors, an old lady and a young crooner, told me that the man lurking in wait for the *zaïm* to get back near number 7 Chemin des Lilas was carrying a walkie-talkie. Five minutes before the victim arrived, they heard the crackle of a receiver and a few unintelligible instructions, which implies that the shooter had at least one accomplice. Far from cheering me up, this possibility knocks me sideways. Until now, my affection for Lino and my fear that I won't be able to get him out of the hole he's dug himself into haven't been much help. My emotions have had the upper hand over my objectivity and have been changing the way I approach things. Then, one night, I got a grip on myself. If I wanted to move forward, I had to put my worries aside and look at things with a bit more rigor. I'm a cop, and a cop follows logic: what if Lino *was* into this mess up to his neck? What if he really did give in to his hatred and jealousy? After all, why not? He isn't cooperating, but hides behind a wall of dubious amnesia, he knew about SNP, his weapon is the main piece of incriminating evidence, he has a motive and no alibi.... It's sad to arrive at this hypothesis, but from a professional point of view it makes the puzzle less chaotic. Lino wasn't sober when it happened. Maybe, in the end, he took his own threats seriously. Approached from this angle, the story stops contradicting itself and can be judged on its merits. If you move away, the haze comes back and you don't know where you are any more. The only thing that bothers me is that botched set-up at the Marhaba parking lot. Why was SNP eliminated? He was caught like a rat in a trap; he could have been handcuffed. Was it to put an end to a scandal that no one wanted, especially Haj Thobane, who was suing the newspapers that exposed the affair, according to my latest information? This kind of thing is common in our country. Any gossip that might prejudice the smooth progress of the revolution is nipped in the bud. In the current state of political dereliction, a rumor quickly takes on the proportions of a cataclysm. Thus the regime owes its longevity entirely to keeping the common folk in a state of lethargy....

I went back to Professor Allouche twice. I needed to study SNP more closely. Allouche played me some more tapes without helping me to understand his personality any better. His identity was diffused through a thousand fantasies. His file was as meager as a dunce's copy-book. Without connections or a past, he remained an enigma.

"Anything else?" the waiter asks, tray in hand.

I look at Serdj. "Not for me," he says.

"Nothing for me either."

The waiter stays where he is, an irritated expression on his lips.

"What?" I ask.

"Well, you've been here two hours and you've only ordered one thing."

"So?"

"So, if all our customers did the same we'd go bust."

Serdj pushes his chair back. "You're right. We're leaving."

I pay and stand up. Once upon a time, this kind of rudeness would have made me blow my top. If I've calmed down since, it only proves that I'm going downhill.

Serdj offers to drop me off at my home. My watch says 15:38 and I don't know what to do at home, so I ask him to drive me back to the office.

I find Baya powdering her face behind a pile of pending files. She is dismayed because she was getting ready to slip out early. She puts her bag back on the ground and delays the organization of her evening till later. As it happens, I keep her in the office until late in the afternoon. Before, this would have upset her planned debauchery and would have put her in a bad mood for several days, but ever since Lino has been languishing in the underground jails of the Bureau of Investigation and Comms, she has been ready to give up the assignation of her life for the sake of making herself useful.

"You can go if you like."

"I'm in no hurry."

"Is it the albino I caught a glimpse of the other night?"

She shifts about shyly. "He's not an albino, he's just got red hair."

"Lucky you. Apparently they're raging stallions, those redheads. That's why they've got those flaming locks."

Her smile fades into the redness of her cheeks and her eyes

sink to the tiled floor. "It's early days, Superintendent. We don't really know each other yet. I'm not going to embark on that sort of thing, you know; I'm not sucking my thumb any more."

"There's more to it than your thumb."

Baya flares right up. Although she puts on the outraged innocent act at my words, I know she loves it when I talk to her like this from time to time; her fantasies are all the better for it.

"Anything to report?"

Without looking up, she tells me that Professor Allouche is trying to get hold of me.

"Get him for me and then go home. I don't need you this evening."

She nods.

The professor is all worked up.

For a moment, I think he's going to materialize through the receiver.

"Pay attention," he warns. "It's not enough for a feast; but it's something to keep the wolf from the door."

"My mouth's watering already. What's on the menu?"

"Not on the telephone, Brahim. Can you come to my place around six? I've got someone who might interest you."

"Why not immediately?"

"The person isn't available right now."

"All right. Can't we meet somewhere less depressing? Your empire of defectives stops me concentrating."

"I promise you we'll be better off there than anywhere else. It's very, very important."

I arrive at the asylum at dusk. Large and ominous clouds are battling it out over the huts. The avenues are deserted and the parking lot is empty. A strange wind gusts intermittently, tweaking at the shrubs and then disappearing into the darkness without warning. Lights here and there, yellowish and bleak as fast-day faces, show occupied rooms. In the distance, a long scream rings out, quickly cut short by orders in the form of obscenities; calm immediately takes control again.

Professor Allouche is not alone in his office. A woman is waiting impatiently in a chair, clutching a cardboard file to her chest. She is a brunette, beautiful and aware of it, with enormous eyes, generous lips and a magnificent beauty spot adorning her cheekbone. Her thirty-five or forty years lend a maturity to her refined appearance that is more likely to bring on salivation than reflection.

"Right," says the professor. "May I introduce Soria Karadach. She teaches history at Ben Aknoun University and contributes to several learned journals here and abroad."

She offers me a firm handshake, which contrasts with the sweetness of her smile. "I'm delighted to meet you, Superintendent Llob. I've heard a lot about you."

The professor pushes a chair toward me.

"I've known Soria for a few weeks," he tells me. "I mentioned a journalist who was interested in SNP the first time you came to see me about the presidential pardon. This is her. She turned up as soon as I began to draw the threat posed by my patient to the attention of the authorities and the press. Then she disappeared, and I thought she'd got cold feet. Well, I was wrong. Mrs. Karadach is tenacious. She went on investigating. I think she has some revelations to pass on to us."

"Not revelations," the woman corrects him, "but a number of details that are, in my opinion, quite relevant. The truth is that I've been interested in the charismatic personalities in our revolution for several years. I dedicated most of my studies to them, and at the moment I'm preparing a feature on their feats of arms which I intend to publish. I came upon SNP's case by chance. I was doing some research into the post sixty-two period when the story of a serial killer threw me for a loop. The press decked him out with a fancy name at the time, 'The Dermatologist,' and convicted him out of hand before the trial even started. The court case was rushed. That's how the file was closed before it had even been properly opened. When Professor Allouche wrote to our editor protesting at the release of a potentially dangerous prisoner, I got in touch with him right away. SNP was already in my notes. I thought this was an opportunity to add to the few facts I had been able to gather here and there; but no. Apart from the man's psychological side, nothing tangible. Then there was this business of the attempt on Mr. Thobane's life and SNP's appearance on the scene. And then everything changed."

"What changed, *madame?*" I ask her, lighting a cigarette.

"I believe there's a connection. Tenuous perhaps, but real."

"Do you know that my main partner is involved, *madame?*"

"Of course."

"How can you know that? Nobody in the press has been allowed to mention it."

The woman is taken aback by the abruptness of my question. She looks over at the professor for a couple of seconds and then gathers herself. Her flashing eyes seem to be sending out a warning. "I am a historian and an investigative journalist, Mr. Brahim Llob. I have friends at various levels in Greater Algiers. My sources are more reliable than press reports that have been given a superficial gloss by censorship and cant and then issued in accordance with the propaganda message of the day. I'm here to make a deal with you, not to denounce anyone or waste my time. I could have continued my research alone, but unfortunately, a woman in our society is often excluded before she even starts. Before we continue this conversation, I'd like to make something clear: I'm an active participant in this affair. Either you accept me as part of your team or I go home as if all this had never happened."

"I insist on seeing what you have first."

She waves her file. "I have here a list of names that could crown my work as a historian, and yours as a policeman, with success. In my files, SNP has a surname, a first name and a birthplace. It turns out that Mr. Thobane was born in the same godforsaken place. I have witnesses who can't wait to cooperate. If you agree, let's settle our course of action and our respective roles right now and investigate together, hand in hand, no tricks. Otherwise..."

The professor is frozen.

I imagine my emotions aren't too well hidden either.

"You've been able to identify SNP?" the professor blurts out.

"Maybe. Now, it's time to say yes or no. I know I'll get there, but it will take me months, maybe years, on my own, which would make the significance obsolete and uninteresting. With Mr. Brahim Llob and his experience, we can strike while the iron is hot. He has an officer to save, I have a story to put together."

I examine the huge ember at the end of my cigarette.

"Just because two people are born in the same place, it doesn't necessarily mean they share the same destiny," I tell her.

"That's not all there is, Superintendent."

The professor stares at me intently, shocked by my prevarication.

"Nothing ventured, nothing gained," he says.

I pretend to think. In truth, I don't know what to decide. The woman seems sure of herself. The way she grips her folder bespeaks implacable conviction. Perhaps that's what unsettles me; I feel so diminished in the face of her assurance, one war too late and too tired out to catch up. I also feel as though my efforts have been wasted on too many fronts, following trails that weren't trails. My defeats have plunged me into a kind of loser's despair, which takes away all desire to start anything from scratch.

The woman is waiting for my response. She can see clearly that it will be long in coming, but she doesn't give up. She must see that I have no alternative and that my pathological curiosity will win out over all other considerations.

Long after my cigarette has given up the ghost in a final wisp of smoke, I crush it under my shoe and say, "So far I've only heard what you want me to hear."

"I have two witnesses who are prepared to talk to us. A former prisoner who shared a cell with SNP during the nineteen seventies, and an ex-sergeant who remembers a boy who turned himself in after a series of murders he said he'd committed and which have never been confirmed."

I don't like Soria Karadach's witness number one from the start. He's shriveled, with hairy ears, arms that are too long, and a con man's face—he has a way of looking at you sideways and telling you nothing worthwhile; he's the type who would trample over his mother's body to get to a pot of jam.

His name is Ramdane Cheikh and he owns a grocery store in one of the most unsavory areas of Blida. You must bear a heck of a grudge against yourself to choose to live in a hole like that.

The man is dozing at a surreal counter with shelves crammed randomly with boxes of preserves, packets of lentils, floor cloths, cans of oil, detergents, cookies, slippers, powdery sweets, rat-traps, loaves of bread and other bits and pieces of rubbish with no sell-by date or instructions for use—all no doubt bought off the back of a truck at two cents apiece and, for want of a better method, thrown together in this dangerous manner, though without causing any apprehension among his customers, let alone the city authorities charged with food hygiene and public health.

"Well, well, *madame* is back," he chuckles, sitting up lazily.

Soria introduces me: "This is the friend I mentioned."

The shopkeeper looks me up and down. His thick lips pull back to reveal a sewer-like mouth fit to suffocate a deep-sea diver.

"Your friend has the look of a pig, *madame*."

"Bullseye," I confess. "Is that a problem?"

The shopkeeper shrugs. "I don't see any. As far as I'm concerned, cop or pizza delivery boy, it's all one to me. What can I do you for you, lady and gent?"

I look him in the eye.

"Madame says you know SNP?"

"That's right. I spent seven years in jail, of which three were with that asshole."

"Would you mind telling me why you were locked up?"

A frown gathers over an outraged expression. "And then what? Do you want me to tell you how I married my wife, while we're about it? I sinned and I paid the price; the rest is none of your business. Are you here for me or for someone else?"

"For SNP."

He holds out a paw to Soria.

"Same price, *madame*."

"I've already paid."

"One ticket doesn't give you the right to see the film more than once."

"There are continuous showings," I warn him.

He twitches, because he wasn't expecting the quickness of my response.

"Not mine, pal," he replies.

"It's not wise to try to rip off a cop."

He opens his camel's eyes wide and, throwing his head back, bursts out in exaggerated laughter. "Listen to me, pig. Cops, stool-pigeons and the laws of the republic: fuck them upside down and sideways. When I'm starving to death, that bastard mayor won't pay any attention. And when I'm late with the rent, nobody's going to throw me a lifeline. Everyone takes care of his own business any way he wants, or manages as best he can. Coming on like the bogey-man is a waste of time. Either you hand over some cash and we talk; or we just have a bit of a chit-chat, and I'm not in the mood. Frankly, if the lady had told me you were a cop I wouldn't have agreed to see you. Not because I'm scared or anything like that; just out of principle: I can't stand cops. Whenever I see one I feel seasick for a few days."

He turns to Soria. "The cash, *madame*."

She takes two notes out of her bag.

"For the pig too. The management makes no exceptions."

I want to tear his throat out, but I'm afraid of hurting my fist, it looks so armor-plated.

Soria pays up.

The man holds the notes up to the sunlight to check they're authentic, folds them in four and slips them into his pocket. His smile broadens and his eyes shine with unhealthy satisfaction. "What do you want to know?"

"Everything you know about SNP. I warn you, if we don't get our money's worth, we'll demand reimbursement."

He shows me his putrefying teeth in a grimace and starts: "As I told the lady, I knew SNP in prison. He'd just been given a life sentence. He was twenty, twenty-two years old, give or take. We knew why he was there. The warders told us what was written in the rags. Since he had a reputation for being vicious, they put him in solitary. Long enough to get an idea of how dangerous he really was. Apparently, he wasn't convincing. Afterwards, they put him in my cell. The governor had it in for me. In the best tradition of the prison service, he was probably trying to get rid of me. For the first few nights, I was on my guard—after all, he came with a heck of a reputation. The moment he got up for a piss I was standing up, with my back to the wall. After a while, since nothing happened, my stomach cramps started to let up. Two months later, I realized that my roommate was far from a disaster. Of course, it wasn't in my interest to shout it from the rooftops. While the others were shitting their pants, I had an easy time in my bed. I even added to his legend, by letting the others know that the guy was ultra-unpredictable and that the day someone stood in his way would be a total nightmare. All this time, SNP shut himself away in silence. He never said a word. Neither shit nor thank you. He was a nutcase pure and simple, no doubt about it. He pondered his plans and guarded them jealously. Once, in the showers, I passed him my soap. Against all expectations, he didn't reject it. He didn't say thank you, but for me it was as if someone had lifted a rock off my chest. Then one night, just like that, for no particular reason, he told me his name and where he came from and talked vaguely about a massacre he'd witnessed. I couldn't get over it. The next day, while we were having a meal in the canteen, he came up behind me and stuck a ten-centimeter piece of glass in my side. I still don't understand why. I was taken to the infirmary in a coma. When I got back, SNP wasn't there any more. He was put in solitary for a while and then sent to a lunatic asylum."

Soria opens her notebook and reads, "His name was Belkacem Talbi, wasn't it?"

"Yeah, that's right. And he was born at Sidi Ba and lost his whole family in a massacre."

"How come you remember his name after so many years?" I ask abruptly.

"The only time I've come close to death was thanks to the blow he gave me. If there's a name I won't forget in a hurry, it's his."

"Was it him who told you to keep quiet about his secret?"

"I don't take orders from anyone. If that bastard had been hanging around in my quarters when I got back, I'd have had his hide in a minute. I've never forgiven him for what he did to me…if

I haven't said anything until now it's because I didn't see the point. It wasn't until *madame* came to stir up memories that I discovered they might be interesting."

"So what did he tell you about the massacre?"

"It happened at night. Armed maniacs showed up at his house. They said they wanted to take him and his family to a safe place. They took them out into the forest and slit their throats, one by one. SNP took advantage of the confusion to escape. Two men ran after him but didn't catch him."

"Did he give any reasons for the massacre?"

"No, it was like he was delirious. It didn't feel like he was talking particularly to me. He just talked, that's all."

"He didn't mention any names, refer to anything, some event that might put the massacre in a particular place?"

The shopkeeper thinks.

"Who were these armed men?" Soria asks.

"I didn't ask him. You want my opinion, it happened during the war of liberation. Only during that period were people armed to the teeth."

"Did he ever have visitors?"

"Him? Not once. He was an alien."

Soria looks at me to see if I have any more questions. I don't, but the man has revived my enthusiasm; I promise him I'll come back.

"The price will the same, pig," he says. "If you want to subscribe, I could give you a good price, with a bit of luck."

The second witness is called Habib Gad. He lives in Mouzaïa, a tiny colonial town west of Blida, where he runs a property contracting business.

He is not overjoyed to see us invading his little enterprise.

He's a fairly well preserved old man, tall and thin as a flagpole, with a face like a knife blade and the eyes of a sparrowhawk. More to hide from prying eyes than from Muslim charity, he invites us to follow him into a kind of large plywood box he calls his office.

With a gesture of his head, he sends a secretary out to take a walk and she scurries out faster than a mouse; then, taking a deep breath to gather himself together, he closes the door and leans back on it.

"Something wrong, *madame*? I do you one favor and you come back the next day to give me a hard time?"

Soria, taken by surprise, is thrown off balance by the man's attitude. She doesn't understand, and tries to work out what she has done wrong.

The old man wipes his wrist nervously, sniffs, and shakes his head.

"If this goes on, *madame*, I'll soon have an army of penpushers on my back and then, maybe, the radio and the TV people too," he protests. "I thought you were working on a book."

"That's the truth," says Soria.

He waves his arm in an angry circle and points it at me. "So what's this guy doing here? I know him, he's an Algiers cop."

"You're a sergeant, right?" I ask.

"Ex...ex-sergeant, please. I retired ten years ago. Now I have my own business and I don't want any trouble."

"What's going on?" Soria asks him. "Last time, you were friendly and cooperated fully."

"Last time, I thought I was helping a historian. So you lied to me." He sits down on a metal cabinet, grabs a newspaper and slams it down on the table. "You weren't after a book, *madame*, you were after a scoop." His finger points out a headline on the cover: *ATTEMPT ON HAJ THOBANE'S LIFE.* "I bet it was you who wrote this article."

"I can assure you it wasn't."

"I don't care. I never suspected that SNP was behind that attack. Otherwise, I wouldn't have let you through the door of my company. I've got hassles enough with taxes, the city, customers, creditors and my own kids."

He's beside himself.

Only my presence prevents him from grabbing Soria by the hair and dragging her along the floor. His expression is murderous and his mouth is itching to bite.

Soria tries to calm him down; he stops her with an imperious gesture. "Get the hell out of here! For good! I never want to see you again, do you understand?"

"Have you been threatened?"

My question provokes him fiercely, unleashing a multitude of twitches at the tip of his chin. "Threats? What are you getting at? I'm telling you I have no intention of getting mixed up in this business. Even small children know who Haj Thobane is. It's not good for business."

"No one's asking you to stand up against him."

"God forbid. I don't give a damn about this attack. If he's done away with by some former prisoner or a hit-and-run driver, is that my problem? I refuse to have my name mentioned in any way whatsoever where Haj Thobane tops the bill. It's bad luck. The guy is a bad omen. Whether it's for a charity reception or a circumcision, receiving honors or in the shop window, I don't want my name linked with his. It's not complicated. I've worked like an ox to get my business up and running, and I don't intend to blow it all sky high when I'm a hair's breadth away from finally making it. Clear out of here, right away. As for you, *madame*, I've never seen you in my whole goddamn life."

"We promise—"

He throws the door open angrily and growls, "I beg you, leave."

We don't insist, but go back to the courtyard, where a truck is unloading some illegally imported cement. Soria jumps into her car, opens my door from the inside and starts the engine. The way she revs the engine gives an insight into the fury rumbling inside her. She gets her sunglasses out of the glove compartment and shoves them onto her face.

I glance back over my shoulder and catch the ex-sergeant watching us from his box with his arms folded and a poisonous expression on his face.

"I can assure you I'm aghast at his change of heart, Superintendent," Soria confesses as she moves off. "He was a model of correctness and consideration the first time I saw him."

"When was that?"

"A bit over a week ago."

"He didn't know."

"Apparently not. He said he was willing to help me and left me two phone numbers so that I could get hold of him at any time. He was very flattered because I promised to name him in my book. Do you think he's been threatened?"

"It was just something to say…so, how did you actually track him down?"

She waits until she has overtaken a van and then says, "Elementary. SNP was tried and convicted, right? The archives still exist. I looked up the date and place of his arrest; the rest followed automatically. Sergeant Gad was posted to El Afroun between nineteen sixty-nine and nineteen seventy-three. He was the first person to hear what SNP had to say. He was on duty that night. At first, he thought he was crazy. But SNP refused to leave the station and demanded that they lock him up in a cell. The sergeant had to call in his boss."

"What did he tell you that was interesting?"

"That he didn't believe this serial killer story at all. It's true that there had been some murders that had plunged the area into mourning. According to Gad, they were a settling of scores between rival families. Things had become a little crazy, and the local authorities, who were more irritated than worried, were ordered by Algiers to put a stop to the blood-letting, which was standing in the way of the forward march of the revolution. The press pounced on the story, concocting a special series of melodramatic articles in an effort to entertain their readers, who were dazed with lies and demagoguery. It wasn't long before 'The Dermatologist' was baptized as the bogey-man of the Tipaza–El Afroun–Cherchell triangle. Gad's boss had become the official hunter of the Beast and, by extension, the darling of the newspapers. When SNP showed up at the station to turn himself in, it was as if he had been sent from heaven. The superintendent had the chance of a lifetime in his grasp; he pushed the boat out to speed things up. According to Gad, he was the one who forced SNP to confess to murders that have never been confirmed, or even recorded, in the area. Gad was sure SNP would have confessed to anything to get himself locked up. He was scared to death of being released. He hid whenever anyone came into the station, as if he was being hunted. The superintendent didn't see anything wrong with this; on the contrary, he led the enquiry in the direction that suited him best. Algiers was all too happy to shut down a rumor that was gaining supernatural proportions, and stood by the policeman's story. The case was closed with a simple telephone call."

"It's a rather simplistic version, don't you think?"

"I don't agree, Superintendent. We live in a country where everything is decided by a nod or a telephone call, both big plans and purges. I have personally looked into files that are so improbable they become hilarious, and yet they're as official as my identity card. Something tells me SNP wasn't on Haj Thobane's road by chance. Ramdane Cheikh wasn't making things up either. I went to the town hall at Sidi Ba two days after speaking to him, and looked up Belkacem Talbi on the electoral roll. I found him. Born twenty-seventh October nineteen fifty, abducted and missing since August nineteen sixty-two, along with his whole family: father, mother, four brothers and a sister."

"And where does Haj Thobane fit in?"

She slows down, drives the car onto the hard shoulder and stops under a tree. She stares at a shrine on a hilltop for a long time. Having weighed up the pros and cons, she switches off the engine and turns to face me.

"If I wasn't sure I was onto something serious, Superintendent, I would have let it go. I'm not the type to paddle about in a glass of water. I'm well aware of the implications of this affair; you don't get off lightly when you attack a *zaïm*. So I can't afford to get it wrong. But I trust you. I'd be lying if I told you I hadn't had a look at your file. You're the right man for this situation. But it's out of the question for me to put you on the right track and then find myself left by the wayside. This story excites me no end. If you want in, I want to hitch you up to my train. I'll give you all the information I have. For your part, you won't hold back any detail that might help me in my work as a historian and journalist.... Will you give me your word now, or do you need a few days to think?"

"Lino wouldn't forgive me if I hesitated."

She offers me her soft hand. "I'm relieved, Superintendent, and above all happy."

"Yes, but you still haven't answered my question."

She looks deep into my eyes, as if seeking to lift a veil over what I have in my head. I don't bat an eye; she nods, and says, "Haj Thobane was the military head of the Sidi Ba region during the war of liberation. People say that what he did to the civilian population and the *harkis** was beyond imagining. SNP didn't make the attempt on his life by chance, I'd stake my life on it. The way he was prevented from doing any further harm takes my breath away. There's something fishy going on, Superintendent, and my hunch isn't based only on journalistic flair. I'm sure a little trip to Sidi Ba would put a little wind in our sails. Some people suggested a few addresses; it's up to us to see where they lead."

"May I ask who's hiding behind these 'some people'?"

She flashes me her most brilliant smile, starts the engine up again and, engaging first gear, purrs, "Credible and honorable people who prefer to remain anonymous so that the truth will have the greatest possible chance of coming to the surface. I trust them as much as I trust you, and you'll have to believe in me too."

---

*   *Harki*s: Muslim Algerians who served as auxiliaries with the French Army during the Algerian War (1954–1962). Since independence, *harki* has been used as a derogatory expression tantamount to "collaborator."

Chapter sixteen

The sign at the entrance to the village has been altered. Someone has crossed out the word *Welcome* and replaced it with "*Wilkoum** to Sidi Ba," a settlement which, in the space of a few years, has become a huge and shapeless town trapped among saw-toothed mountains between Algiers and Médéa.

To get here, you have to negotiate a thousand perilous hairpin bends, climb hundreds of hills, each more twisted than the last, and curse the potholes that mine the road every five seconds, ruining your shock absorbers and the cartilage in your vertebrae. The worst thing is that in the end you realize, to your cost, that the hike wasn't worth the trip. Because Sidi Ba is the kind of dump that kills any desire you might have to see the country. It's ugly, it's ignorant, and when you finally get there you are haunted by a single obsession: get away!

I've seen a lot of bullshit in my time, but the kind made manifest by Sidi Ba is worth a special award; the town is proof that men have reached the peak of their genius and, having run out of ideas, are embarking on the human adventure in reverse, which is to say

---

*   "Misfortune be yours."

backwards to the Stone Age, with an enthusiasm equal to the first cave-dwellers. Except that, at Sidi Ba, the laying of the first stone marking the beginning of the decline has been extended into an urban anarchy that exceeds comprehension. The rushed construction of buildings to house a rapidly expanding population has mobilized every crook in the region to throw himself body and soul into scams the devil himself couldn't think up, encouraged by a deeply felonious administration. Phony enterprises are set up overnight, led by elected predators and seconded by architects with dubious qualifications—welcome to the move-over-or-I'll-push-you-myself building site.

When I open the window of my hotel room, a torrent of dissonant sounds hits me in the face, followed by the traumatic spectacle of a vast slum of leprous streets, scabrous sidewalks and sinister alleyways that twist and turn vertiginously: a ghastly maelstrom. Not a speck of green space, not a decently constructed building; nothing but rudimentary dwellings, warped fences, hovels thrown together in contempt of the basic rules of masonry. A buzz of activity fills every space in this concrete chaos, aggravating the madding to and fro of pull-carts and motor cars.

"I wouldn't choose to write my next book here," I say.

"Are you a writer, Mr. Llob?"

"You're not going to tell me you didn't know!"

"I didn't know. What do you write?"

"Detective stories."

"Not really my thing, but I'll make an exception in your case."

"That's very kind of you, *madame.*"

Soria comes up to the window and contemplates the hubbub in the square.

"I'm sorry, it's the only hotel in town."

"Just as well there is one."

I close the window.

The room is cramped, the wallpaper is faded and there is neither bedcover nor curtains. The bed, scarcely wide enough for a hunger striker, is equipped with a mildewed mattress over which someone has folded some sheets of dubious hue. Opposite stands a metal wardrobe flanked by a broken table and a remarkably ugly bathroom.

"I hope there's running water?"

Soria makes a slightly embarrassed face. She arrived yesterday to book rooms and prepare the ground, and she feels guilty that she couldn't find anything better for me.

"Don't worry," I say reassuringly. "I brought some pebbles* to wash with."

"There's a Moorish bath nearby."

"Glad to hear it. What's your royal suite like?"

"Same layout, but the window looks out over a very busy carpenter's workshop."

"What floor?"

"We're on the same floor. It's the room next door."

I light a cigarette and say, "I must say you're rather unwise. I'm a sleepwalker, you know."

"And I'm an insomniac."

It's hard to know how to take this reply. Soria's direct gaze doesn't help me; I drop the subject.

"May I have a little nap?"

"Of course, Mr. Llob. I'll leave you to rest. It was a hard journey; what awaits us won't be a walk in the park."

She waves and disappears.

The first address we have entails a visit to the old quarter of Sidi Ba. It is inaccessible to cars, so we go on foot. It is obvious that the populace is not accustomed to the swing-hipped walk of women with their buttocks shockingly clad in tight trousers. Street urchins interrupt their games, amazed. Some of them take us for Western tourists, shrug their shoulders and go back to their racket; others, less emancipated, stay out of our way for fear of the evil spirits they can "see" floating around our horned silhouettes. Scandalized faces appear in windows and doorways, over people's shoulders; the excitement wanes as we approach a workshop and fades away entirely as all eyes converge on some old men sitting at a table on the terrace. The men, solemn beneath their turbans, turn toward us as we pass and take turns to spit on the roadway.

---

* Pebbles are an alternative to water, sanctioned by the Prophet.

Soria is aware of the disturbance she's creating; she's walking less gracefully, but it's too late to turn back. She takes shelter behind her glasses.

A mechanic is stripping a rusty old wreck. Bent double under the hood, he is cursing a corroded radiator hose that won't come loose. His large behind is moving about in all directions, shocked by the tenacity of the recalcitrant part. I cough into my fist. He stands up quickly; his head hits the edge of the hood. His pain is swiftly dissipated by his surprise at finding himself face to face with a woman from the city.

"Don't they sell *hijabs* where you come from?" he asks me reproachfully, ostentatiously turning his back on Soria.

"Is this the Omari household?"

"What do you want with them? You're here about the taxes, right?"

"We've come from Algiers. We would like to speak to Hamou, Hamou Omari."

He frowns and wipes his grease-stained hands on a cloth hanging from the back pocket of his overall. "Are you a medium?" he asks me.

"Not necessarily."

His threatening look shuts me up.

He wipes his nose with his hand and mutters, "My father died three years ago."

Upon which he dives back into the car's maw to take it out on the hose.

"That's why it's difficult for a woman to carry out her research," Soria sighs when we get back to the hotel. "Here, people only talk to men and among men. Yesterday, I wasn't allowed into a single restaurant. They don't want women in public places, even if they're escorted. The receptionist had to get me something to eat herself."

I am exhausted, and I keep my comments to myself. My feet are burning in my shoes. We have walked all afternoon, in vain. Hamou Omari is dead, and so is Haj Ghaouti. The third witness has moved out and the fourth, one Rabah Ali, has traveled to Médéa and won't be back before the weekend.

"Your sources should update their information," I say, with a note of resentment.

"They haven't set foot in Sidi Ba for a long time."

"Very wise."

I lie back on my bed and take off my shoes.

Soria is standing in the doorway, thinking. "Do you think we shouldn't have come?"

"We should have discussed it first."

She folds her arms across her breasts, which are generous, and throws her hair back suddenly. She is very attractive, this Soria. She has beautiful eyes. "What are we going to do?" she says, girlishly.

"We're here, and we'll stay here. I won't go back to Algiers empty-handed."

She nods and stands lightly on tiptoe. "Good," she says. "I'm in my room. If you need me, at least you know where to find me."

I go back to the old quarter, alone, the following day. Yesterday's experience sticks in my craw. Soria wasn't just grumbling. Her presence beside me reduces our chances of progressing, and she knows it. In Sidi Ba, people's mentalities will have to suffer quite a few more cataclysms before they evolve; here, when one mentions a woman, one does so with respect.

The old *maquisard*'s codename had been En-Nems, and he receives me eagerly in his studio. As soon as he realizes that his war stories have some chance of interesting me, he releases his two workers, closes the door and draws the curtains so as to have me all to himself. He is a worn-out weaver, almost old, with enlarged eyes behind thick glasses. His emaciated face is lined with deep furrows, but his astonishingly white teeth are in good shape. Like many who find themselves in the spotlight after being long ignored, he starts by adopting an exaggerated solemnity.

With his chin up and his lips firm, he tries to be dignified.

"If it's for a film, I agree. If it's for a book, I don't," he warns me from the get-go.

"Most cinema is inspired by books," I say enticingly.

"Not in this country. Besides, cinema hardly excites me. There isn't one in Sidi Ba. The nearest one is eighty kilometers away. And they only show moronic films. What interests me is the TV. Everyone has a TV…."

He sticks two fingers in his mouth to adjust his false teeth.

"I'll never forget the film *The Survivor of Jenien Bourezg*," he says, challengingly. "Now that's a documentary. The brave *mujahid* is arrested by the French army, beaten up, taken off to a dump and shot in the back of the head. He is pronounced dead by the administration and the brothers inscribe him in the register of martyrs. Fifteen years later, it's the survivor himself who tells his story to millions of amazed viewers. He became a saint overnight…. If it's a TV documentary with that many viewers, count me in, right away; if it's for a book, it's a no."

"That depends on what you have to give me as a witness."

He puffs out his chest like a rooster; he waves his arm in a wide circle: "You won't find a better one for hundreds of kilometers around. I was Commander Lefty's closest collaborator. The Lefty's not just anyone; he's a living legend, an epic figure. All France used to tremble at the very mention of his name. Shit! When he showed up somewhere with his Mauser and his bandolier, it was a sign that all hell was going to break loose. He would charge into enemy troops like a hurricane. Before he even unsheathed his sword, the paras would take to their heels and swim across the Mediterranean to hide behind their mother's skirts…. As for me, I joined the ALN* in fifty-five. At almost the same time as the Lefty. He recruited me. It wasn't a hard decision. I knew that with men like him we were bound to win. There were no more than fifteen fighters in the *maquis* at Sidi Ba at that time. And we weren't all armed. When we went down into the villages for supplies, we would lug small tree trunks wrapped in canvas and pretend they were bazookas. The bluff worked like a charm, because volunteers joined us. Me, I had a pistol stuck in my belt, and no bullets in the cylinder. That didn't stop me picking fights with the settlers. I wasn't afraid of anyone, didn't run away from anything. It wasn't until the ambush of February fifty-six, when we

---

* ALN: *Armée de libération nationale* (National Liberation Army), military wing of the FLN.

killed around twenty French soldiers, that we managed to get hold of some proper equipment...."

He launches himself on an epic tale I imagine to be dysenteric. You have only to keep your ears open to hear unbelievable stories like this, elaborate because they're unverifiable, all the time. The official stamp of approval and today's propaganda campaigns encourage them to proliferate because they exhort every has-been who ever took the oath, to invent them in industrial quantities, thus ensuring the longevity of historical legitimacy.

I decide it would be wise not to let the conversation degenerate into sterile fantasies and get right to the point: "It's the period after the fifth of July nineteen sixty-two that interests me, Mr. En-Nems."

He starts, incredulous, shocked by my lack of interest in the founding period not only of the Algerian nation but also, and above all, of the idea of freedom among the oppressed peoples of Africa and elsewhere.

"What? There's nothing after the fifth of July, my friend. The revolution ended on that date. The proof is that we've been regressing at full speed ever since."

"Did you know a certain Talbi?"

This time he freezes; a death mask replaces his features.

"What Talbi?" he cries, his voice cracking.

"He lived in Sidi Ba until August sixty-two. Then he was abducted and went missing along with his whole family."

En-Nems gulps. He goes pale. In the silence of the studio, his breathing reminds me of the wheezing of a boiler.

He points his finger at the door and yells, "Get out!"

*   *   *

My question about the Talbis brings the same reaction from two other witnesses. Keen, at first, to give a fresh shine to their feats of arms, they change their minds completely when I mention Talbi's name; as if I had kicked their sandcastle into the air. One of them asked me never to set foot in his house again; the other swore that he would split my skull with his pickax if I ever mentioned the name of "that traitorous dog of a bastard" again.

When I get back to the hotel, I find Soria engrossed in her notes and files. She had been due to meet a *mujahida*; the woman canceled as soon as Talbi's name was mentioned.

"Three days, and we haven't progressed one inch," I say.

"At least we've flushed out our prey," she replies.

"I admire your optimism, but I don't see any hares running."

"I do. At least we know that the Talbis worry quite a few people."

That evening, I'm told there's a visitor for me at reception. I ask Soria to keep an ear open in her room and hurry down the stairs.

The visitor waiting for me in the lobby looks to be just turned fifty. He seems harassed. Salt and pepper hair brushed forward, he is a fine figure of a man, well dressed, with a tie, and shoes polished to a military shine. A thin moustache underlines a gaze that is gentle and open despite a pair of peaked eyebrows.

He stands up promptly when the receptionist points me out. "I'm Rabah Ali," he says, introducing himself in an anguished tone. "My sons told me you were looking for me. I hope it's nothing serious."

The way he hangs on my words betrays the terrible anxiety he has been suffering ever since his children told him about my visit. I bet he headed for the hotel as soon as he got home, in order to get to the bottom of whatever it was. He must be a tormented soul, perpetually on the alert, like a hunted animal, a manic depressive like so many of us in this country.

His fingers twitch in my hand, clammy and trembling.

"It's not an emergency," I reassure him quickly. "We're not from the justice department or the revenue. My colleague and I are gathering eyewitness accounts from former *mujahedin* for a piece of historical work."

He relaxes. His Adam's apple returns to its place instantly, and his complexion returns to its normal color.

"I thought you wouldn't be back until the weekend, Mr. Ali."

"My business trip was cut short."

He becomes confused again; his cheekbone twitches repeatedly. He breathes hard to compose himself, discomfited by my intent look.

"Forgive me," he mumbles. "It's absurd to lose control for no reason, but I'm going through some difficult times at the moment and I don't have the strength to keep my cool."

"You're not the only one to get stressed over a simple yes or no, Mr. Ali. Nothing is really calm in this country, neither in our heads nor in our streets."

He nods, chewing his lip, and looks at me for three seconds as if waiting to see what's coming next.

"You shouldn't believe everything you hear, Mr…?"

"Llob. Brahim Llob."

"What can I do for you, Mr. Llob?"

"Whatever you can."

He grabs a handkerchief, his hand still trembling, and wipes his forehead.

I invite him to sit down in the hotel's clapped-out sofa. He accepts willingly, but not without glancing at his watch.

"This won't take long, Mr. Ali."

"I'm listening."

"It's about what happened here between July and August sixty-two."

He thinks for a moment, chewing a fingernail. My interest in that period doesn't bother him unduly. He's just uncomfortable. He looks back at me.

"I'm afraid I can't be of much use to you, Mr…?"

"Llob," I repeat. "Brahim Llob."

"I won't pretend the subject isn't embarrassing for me. Personally, I don't have much on my conscience. I took part in the war from beginning to end, without excesses and without cheating. I saw some terrible things, too. But I have no desire to turn the knife in the wound, Mr. Llob. They left some indelible marks on the people around here. Even today, echoes of those dramatic events can arouse rancor, and sometimes fresh blood is spilled. I have the reputation of being a man with no stories to tell. In fact, I don't feel I have the strength to take them on. Maybe it's cowardice; as far as I'm concerned, it's abstinence. Sometimes attitudes like mine shock other people, but they keep those who adopt them sane."

He stands up. "I'm sorry to disappoint you, Mr. Llob."

"I respect your decision. But we're very frustrated. We have no intention of digging up dead bodies or reopening wounds. Our work is of great importance, please believe me."

"I don't doubt it."

He holds out his hand to say goodbye. I seize it and hold it in mine. Rabah Ali tries to pull his hand away, but I won't let go.

"Can you at least suggest some people who might be able to help us with our enquiries?"

He tries to extricate himself from my grip; I don't give up.

He says, "There are lots of survivors who want nothing more than to throw themselves at microphones and show off. But how many of them are sincere? If you want statements about heroic struggles and honor, all you have to do is spread the word and you'll have them in ecstasy. I'm sure that our unhappiness stems from the pride we take in it. That's what pushed me to close that book forever."

Our eyes meet; he gives in first: "If you promise not to mention my name, I know someone who's still paying the price. He lives in the forest."

"The forest is thick, Mr. Ali," I say, tightening my grip.

"First right after the Roman bridge at the north exit from Sidi Ba. Follow the road to the end. Seven or eight kilometers. It's a farm, or rather a big barn where they keep chickens."

"And who is at this farm?"

"His name is Jelloul Labras. You can't miss him. An honest man, even a good man."

"Do you think he has something of substance to tell?"

His Adam's apple scours his throat. "I think so, Mr. Llob."

I relax my fingers; he recovers his own, turns to leave, changes his mind, comes back to me and repeats, "Don't tell him I sent you."

"Cross my heart and hope to die," I promise.

Soria's Lada lurches along the track, plunges into a young forest, slaloms from one obstacle to the next for several kilometers and finally emerges, more or less unscathed, onto a deeply rutted road. We continue down a valley of fairy-tale loveliness. In the distance, a reservoir of water sparkles in the glare of daylight. Flocks of sheep graze on green pastures, and a man on horseback gallops flat out in pursuit of bliss.

Soria winds the window down and lets the wind ruffle her hair. Her sunglasses sit gracefully on her profile, and her smile lights up at the wonders of the landscape.

We climb several hills before we finally end up at a farm deep in the forest. A tall and robust-looking man in overalls and rubber boots is working in the yard; he is feeding an army of chickens.

He stops his work when he hears us arrive; since our car is unfamiliar to him, he goes back to tossing out big handfuls of grain.

Soria parks under a tree and waits in the car.

I walk up to the yard with my hands in my pockets.

"*Salaam!*" I call out.

"Good morning," says the farmer.

He is fairly tall, with a well-tended beard, and looks as though he gets everything he can out of his sixty-odd years. The few white hairs flecking his temples and chin don't make any difference to him; he moves with ease and his face radiates health.

"They look healthy, your chickens."

"Thank you...the vet didn't think much of them."

"He was probably just a quack."

"I'm not sure I'd go as far as that."

He lunges at a too-greedy rooster and pours a load of millet into the midst of a clump of pathetically aggressive chicks.

"Is it about a delivery?" he asks.

"Not exactly. My colleague and I are just passing through the area. We're doing some research for the university."

"Archeologists?"

"Historians."

He tips an imaginary hat: "Hats off to you! Intellectuals are few and far between around here. I'm pleased to see that not everyone has been blinded by fool's gold."

"There are more serious things in life."

He agrees, and cuts open another sack of millet.

"Do you live here?" I ask him.

"I was born here. May I ask what wind brought you this way?"

"My colleague and I are looking into some events that took place in these mountains just after independence."

His arm stops still over a poultry assault.

"Did you come here by chance or did someone send you?"

"Both. We're going virtually door to door. Some witnesses interest us, others less. Someone suggested we speak to you."

"Does he have a name?"

"We don't remember. Would you mind giving us a bit of your time?"

He glances at Soria, who has just got out of the car, examines me for a moment and then, since we don't look like anything in particular, smiles. "If you can wait until I've finished feeding my chickens, it would be a pleasure. Under that eucalyptus there's a low table with some dates and a dish of curds on it. Help yourselves while you're waiting."

"That's very kind of you, *monsieur.*"

Soria comes to the foot of the eucalyptus with me. We contemplate the plain, and the forested slopes undulating around it. The sky is a perfect blue. It reminds me of my youth at Ighider, when I used to give my mother the slip and climb as high as I could up the hill, with a *tarboush** about my head and my *gandoura*** undone. I used to love loafing about on the Grand Rocher, picking my nose and swinging my legs in the air, and would stay there until nightfall, contemplating the magical jigsaw puzzle of the fields and watching the shepherds coming home with their flocks in front of them like sated armies. When the frail Arezki Naït Wali***—later a well-known painter—joined me on "my" tower, I was surprised to find myself waxing enthusiastic about the slightest rustling in the depths of the bushes, the slightest chirrup carried along on the breeze. Sometimes I would crouch on my unrepentant climber's calves, form a megaphone with my hands, and send long calls out over the valley to hear them

*   *Tarboush*: felt hat/turban.
**   *Gandoura*: robe.
*** See *Autumn of the Phantoms* by Yasmina Khadra.

ricochet about in the distance, mimicking each other in a surreal fugue. Arezki didn't pay any attention to echoes. He would follow the light and shadow of the copses with his eyes, making canvases in his head and dreaming of paintings that would be more intense than the hunger gnawing at his guts. We were young and poor, but we had eyes to see and to imagine radiant kingdoms only we knew about; a pair of awestruck kids, one a budding poet, the other an artist in the making, and even if we didn't watch the cattle together every day, because we weren't always needed, we had in common our love for the hills that stretched all the way to the horizon, the orchards that spread out as far as the eye could see, the ancient almond trees, the taciturn olive trees, the clinking of the goats' bells, the river like a mythical serpent among the serrated ridges, and the hieratic mountain watching over the tribe....

It's fine to believe that your country is the most beautiful in the world—deserving it is another matter.

The farmer joins us, wiping his hands on his thighs.

"Isn't it spectacular!" he cries. "Nature has genius; it's men that disfigure her in order to remake things in their own image. Just look at that village over there. It looks like a big stain on a magic carpet. I would never go and live in a dump like that. Here, there's healthy work, clean air and peace. I don't have any neighbors, so no nuisance, no arguments. And sometimes, when I lie down in my bed at night, I can hear the planet turning."

"You're a poet, Mr. Labras," Soria tells him.

"Just a primitive man, *madame*. I like communing with nature. I feel in my element, and I don't feel I'm waiting for anything or that I lack anything. I was lucky enough not to go to school, and at an advanced age I came to know some enlightened people who taught me to read and write. I've taken advantage of this to limit myself to the essentials."

"Was there no school in your village?"

"Let's say my father needed a shepherd; I didn't wait for him to give me lessons. I love animals. Nevertheless, I still have a tremendous passion for books. Now that I'm a hermit, they've become my prophets."

"Do you live alone?"

"I was married, thirty years ago. My wife died very young. It was terrible for me. I didn't dare try the experience again. What is it you want to know?"

Soria comes round me to get closer to him.

"We're working on a piece of historical research," she tells him. "In particular, the excesses that led to bloodshed after the fifth of July sixty-two."

Labras purses his lips. His expression becomes dark with painful memories. He digs his chin into his chest and, with the tip of his boot, digs out a stone hidden in the grass.

"It's a very controversial subject, don't you find? It's hard to find anyone who goes into it without attracting reprisals. I hope you know what you're getting into."

"It's high time we come to terms with that war," says Soria. "The only way to do it is to look it in the eye. Evil was done. To exorcize it, we must first admit to that. My colleague and I are certain of it. We have a duty to remember; nothing will throw us off the course we have chosen, neither curses nor the executioner's sword."

The farmer looks up. Soria's argument makes his eyes shine.

"You seem sincere, *madame*," he admits sadly. "That's rare nowadays."

"Perhaps that's because of what we don't say."

"Maybe…. Some silences are unbearable. With time, you try to get used to them. That's not enough. If you lie to yourself you stop being yourself and become a stranger."

He crouches down, picks up the stone he dug out and throws it far away.

"Haven't you ever thought about leaving?" I ask, to relieve the uncomfortable tension his suffering has caused between the three of us.

"I've thought about it, but the thought doesn't last longer than a cigarette. I find it difficult to imagine myself far from these mountains. At the same time, I can't tell you what keeps me here. Before, it was terrible; now, it's unhappy."

"That's what I think too," I confide.

That stirs him. He digs out another pebble, rolls it in his palm and stands up. "And yet you could live well here, once," he acknowledges. "Sure, we were poor, but we weren't wretched, as we are today. Then there was the war. It didn't spare anyone on either side. When the ceasefire was announced, everyone was relieved. Alas! The party was pretty short. As soon as the French soldiers started evacuating the area, the atrocities started up again with twice the ferocity. Families were hunted day and night by the people who were supposed to set them free. The *fellaghas* went crazy; they set fire to the losers' homes and fields; summary executions turned into mass purges on an unprecedented scale. Every morning, 'traitors' whose noses and lips had been cut off were forced to file down the streets before their heads were cut off in the village square. I'll never forget the hundreds of mutilated bodies rotting in the orchards, those poor bastards handed over to the vengeance of the people, stoned and spat on by street urchins, those women and terrified kids fleeing into the mountains, from which they would never return...."

"Are you talking about massacres of *harkis*?"

My question shocks him.

He looks me up and down, horrified, as if he has never seen me before. "What's a *harki*?" he asks indignantly. "What is it really? Go on, explain to me. What is a *harki*?"

Since he doesn't see any answer coming from my side, he shivers and goes on: "It's someone who was down on his luck and made the wrong choice when nothing would go right for him. That's what a *harki* is. History's whipping-boy, then her scapegoat.... He who pulls the devil by the tail has no chance of occupying center stage, Mr. Historian. He ends up selling his soul or getting crushed underfoot. Defeat on all sides, rout, ignorance in its raw state. Apart from a few educated people and a handful of enlightened citizens, nationalism was a mystical affair. Who were we, in those days? Muslim Frenchmen with our spines bent so low under the colonial yoke that we found ourselves grazing on the same grass as our donkeys. Natives, that's what we were; poor wretches, ragged and scarred, with our hands shredded by hard labor and our trousers so patched that we wore them like shackles; haggard ghosts whose wives would light candles at the corner shrine every Friday to appease the spirits, while their children begged breathlessly in the shadow of damnation. We said we would kill not to starve to death, and death would often take us at our word. Some of us became stable boys, serfs, shepherds, fly-swatters; others descended on the barracks to become *goumiers, spahis* or *zouaves,** not because they wanted to make war but to help the family stewpot bubble every now and then. It was a hell of a time. People would collapse on roads leading nowhere; children would give up the ghost the way others hang up their tools. Who were we, really? Poor relations or natives, victims of expropriation, or abortions with no right to legitimacy? The legends our mothers told us to distract us from the grumbling in our stomachs didn't enlighten us. What we knew of our tribes was limited to our graveyards. Our great-grandfathers had themselves cut to pieces in eighteen seventy for the sake of France; our grandfathers had themselves gassed in the trenches between nineteen fourteen and eighteen for the salvation of France; our fathers had themselves blown to bits on all fronts during the Second World War for the honor of France; as for the survivors, their reward was to be slaughtered like diseased cattle on the eighth of May nineteen forty-five,** while the whole world, finally rid of Nazism, was crying 'Never again!' from the rooftops and in the public squares. For the average garbage collector or shoeshine boy, for the hardened peasant or the shopkeeper in a negro village, France was the *mother country*. The inequalities were staggering, of course, and something wasn't quite right among all those slogans and promises,

*   *Zouaves*: corps of French infantry first raised in Algeria in 1831 and recruited solely from the Zouaves, a tribe of Berbers from the mountains of the Jurjura range. *Goumiers, spahis*: other corps of indigenous north African soldiers in the French army at various times.
**   On this day, mass demonstrations linking the defeat of fascism with the end of colonialism took place all over Algeria. At Sétif, a demonstration was broken up by police, leading to general insurrection throughout the region. Large numbers of settlers were murdered and wounded. Martial law was declared, but the violence dragged on for weeks, with Foreign Legion and Senegalese troops, aided and abetted by settler vigilante groups, killing and pillaging indiscriminately in retaliation. The final death toll was between 1,020 and 1,300, according to French statistics, or as high as 45,000, according to Algerian nationalists. (Summarized from *Algeria: Anger of the Dispossessed*, by John Phillips and Martin Evans.)

but we were too poor and too stunned by our wretchedness to think about anything else, really. The only fixed point we had was that photograph clumsily pinned up on the cob wall, slowly turning yellow and visibly curling at the edges, that showed us the epic story of this or that relative strapped tightly into his French uniform, with a moustache the size of his pride and his breast covered with medals. When the All Saints' revolution broke out, few took it seriously. Rise up against one's *mother*—and one of the great powers of the world, at that? You must be joking. And the worse things got in the *maquis*, the less you knew which way to turn. On the one hand, the *fellaghas* were ratcheting up their reprisals against the undecided; on the other, pacification was taking its toll on the most deprived. It was madness, and that didn't help anyone to see the appalling mess for what it was, a rebellion without end. It was an atrocious war, vile, absurd, and no one could believe for one second that he was on the wrong side."

"And which side were you on?" I ask him.

My question cuts him off in full flow, stopping him like a hammer blow. It's as if a storm has suddenly blown itself out. A leaden pall blots out the ridge. Soria is frozen. She is staring at the farmer open-mouthed. Worn out by his speech, he is panting as if he has been running headlong. His face is pale, his mouth is dry and his gaze is empty.

"Why did you come here and spoil my day?" he sighs.

There is so much suffering in his exhalation that Soria chooses to give in. She lowers her head and hurries toward the car.

I realize my blunder, and the disaster it has just caused.

I try to recover: "Dirtiness is part of war, Mr. Labras."

He doesn't hear me. He stares at a bare hillside at the foot of the mountain for a long time, nods, and then, ignoring me, goes back to his chickens, who start moving about again when they see him coming.

Chapter seventeen

I don't expect you to be a diplomat, Mr. Llob," Soria tells me in the car, "but I do expect you to show a minimum of courtesy."

"It just slipped out," I confess.

Her eyes flash with anger. We have drawn a blank on every expedition. The one time we come across someone interesting and cooperative, I'm the one that cancels out our good luck.

Soria forces her car through the gravel. The potholes stoke her resentment. She shouts at me, "History has had a spectacular vomiting fit up here, Mr. Llob, and we are splashing about in the leftovers. No one will come out smelling of roses. Okay, so you're a former *maquisard* and it's hard for you to face yesterday's enemies, but today we have to rake over these unimaginable atrocities and listen both to those who carried them out and those who suffered them. It's not about forgiving or condemning; it's about reconstructing the events so that we can learn the lessons we have so far failed to learn. For my part, before I jumped into the water I left my prejudices in the changing room, so that I could approach these events with that measure of objectivity without which no serious work is possible."

"I told you it just slipped out," I protest, enraged.

"I'm not deaf!" she yells, yanking at the steering-wheel.

The car swerves violently off the road and runs into some shrubbery, throwing us against each other. My leg straddles the gear shift and my foot lands spitefully on both Soria's foot and the brake pedal, stopping the car dead.

"I forbid you to raise your voice to me!" I shout at her.

She pushes me back, outraged by my loutish behavior. "I am not your subordinate, Superintendent. I don't have to accept any prohibitions from you."

We glare at each other in a silence crackling with electricity. Insect sounds buzz in our overheated ears.

As the last few skeins of dust fall back to earth, Soria gathers herself together again. She pushes back a lock of hair that has fallen over her right eye and relaxes.

"All right," she concedes. "We're both exhausted. Let's try to behave like grown-ups."

I mumble my agreement and drop it.

A group of sinister-looking gentlemen are waiting for us in the lobby. They get up en bloc and intercept us. The stockiest, whose jutting jaw marks him out as the leader, positions himself in front of me with his lips pulled back against two rows of gold teeth.

"Mr. Llob?"

"Yes?"

"Can we have a word, just us men?"

The implication doesn't escape Soria, who leaves contemptuously. We wait until she disappears into the elevator cage, then the stocky one asks me to follow him to the back of the lobby, with his praetorian guard bringing up the rear.

"To whom do I have the honor...?"

"The dignitaries of the town, Mr. Llob. A town which is beginning to ask questions about the precise purpose of your presence among its population. My name is Khaled Frid, president of the Association of Former *Mujahedin* and Disabled Veterans of the War of Liberation. I am also a political commissar, a member of the Assembly and mayor of Sidi Ba."

"In short, you're a one-man National Assembly. And who are these gentlemen?"

"Former officers in the ALN and members of the Party. They insisted on coming with me to see exactly what this was about. Our sources tell us that you and your assistant are stirring up murky waters, trying to bring as much mud to the surface as possible. That upsets us, because it's what we're doing our utmost to prevent. Our region suffered greatly from the colonial war, and we're not keen on having outsiders come in and lift our gravestones and interfere with our dead. I don't know who you are. I telephoned Algiers yesterday and this morning, and no one could be bothered to tell us what you're up to or what's behind your little scheme. At first blush, your plans reek of spite, and we have no desire to hold our noses until you clear off. To sum up, you're not welcome, and your sordid intentions are greatly irritating to our sensibilities."

The others mark a period at the end of their leader's words with grave nods, which lends a note of grotesquerie to their theatrical solemnity.

"I don't see why a work of remembrance should disturb you," I say.

"You can call it what you like; as far as we're concerned, it's subversion. I'm sure you haven't even considered the significance of your venture and the consequences if you continue to pursue it. Therefore, in the name of the citizens of Sidi Ba and of the members of the association of which I am president, I request that you pack your bags and go back where you came from."

"Am I to understand that you're threatening me?"

"You said it, not me."

He looks at his watch, takes inspiration from the solemn silence of his companions, and decrees, speaking clearly enough for there to be no misunderstanding, "It is not traditional among us to show strangers the door; when their behavior is as shameless as yours, however, we give them an hour, at most, to leave. It is now twelve fifty-two. Someone will come here at one fifty-three to make sure that you have gone for good. No need to pay the hotel bill. I've taken care of it personally."

I don't have time to say a word in reply. The man turns on his heel and leaves with his four marionettes in his wake.

I stand pensively in the middle of the deserted lobby.

The receptionist watches me on the sly from behind his counter. Not once does he openly look at me.

At about two o'clock, someone knocks at my door—a repulsive and brutal-looking ape with flaring nostrils and knuckles down by his ankles. He blocks the corridor all by himself. He starts off by putting his hairy mitts on his hips and throwing out his chest, then looks me up and down and growls out of the corner of his mouth, "Do you know what time it is, pal?"

"Why?"

"What do you mean, why? Are you sure you're all right in the head? You're not going to tell me you've got amnesia?"

"And you, are you sure you've got the right address?"

"You're Llob, right?"

"That's right."

"Then I've got the right address, pal. Besides, I'm never wrong. It's two o'clock and you, you're still on your bed, wrapped up in your blankets."

"So what?"

"So what? There's obviously something wrong with your head, pal. I'm here to throw you out."

Soria appears in my doorway. The gorilla looks at her with consternation. Turning back to me, he continues with his mulish script: "Are your bags packed, pal?"

I gesture with my head to Soria, advising her to go back to her room; then, having first pushed my finger into the brute's invasive belly, I say confidingly, "You've come to the wrong circus."

And close the door.

Before I turn my back, the landing is shaken by a disturbance. The big monkey has just kicked his way into my territory. Without breaking his stride, he lifts me up and slams me up against the wall. My legs wave about wildly in the air.

"Nobody hangs up on me, pal."

He flings me across the room.

"Your bags, on the double!"

He grabs my washbag off the sink and throws it in my face, opens the wardrobe, seizes my suitcase and starts rifling through my things. That's when he feels something metallic pressed against his neck; when he pivots round, he comes face to face with my Beretta.

I've seen chameleons change color, but I didn't know gorillas could do it too. Kong's nostrils flare so wide that I can see the maggots in his brain. It's probably the first time he's encountered civilization since he came down from his tree.

"The mayor didn't say anything about a pistol."

"The mayor probably doesn't know what a pistol is, any more than you do."

Arms above his head, he retreats into the corridor.

"It's all right, pal. Those things can go off by themselves, I warn you. Point the gun away a little, will you?"

"That depends on you. If you promise to go back to your jungle and never come back, I'll holster my gun and the incident is closed. On the other hand, if you come back and upset my timetable again, the mayor won't be able to keep you in bananas any more."

He nods and runs down the stairs like a circus strongman being pursued by a wasp.

Soria, leaning against her doorframe with her hair down to the curve of her thighs, applauds me. She is so proud of me that she has forgotten to do up her blouse. Her rounded breast, lovely as a pear, troubles me. A prickly shiver starts at the level of my navel, without warning, and spreads like a shockwave through my whole body. Since I can't tear my eyes away from the sinful splendor lurking beneath her embroidered neckline, I hurriedly thrust my gun back into my belt to prevent an explosion of any kind.

Kong almost faints when he sees me in the crowd milling about in the foyer of the town hall. He thinks I'm there to sort him out and flees through an emergency exit. Another ape tries to stop me going upstairs. I bring out my badge; fortunately, cops are still held in high regard in rural areas, because he starts bowing and scraping forthwith and rushes to clear my path to a padded door. A heavily made-up secretary stops filing her nails and looks at me like a sultry seductress. She guesses I'm in a hurry; her chin points down a corridor, at the end of which I emerge into a large, splendidly philistine room where three men are yelling at each other around a table covered with telephones.

The two clowns with their backs to me turn round and stiffen, amazed at my intrusion. The biggest one immediately shuts the top of an attaché case stuffed with banknotes; the other just hides behind his opaque sunglasses. I don't need to consult a tarot-reader to guess what's going on in the mayor's office. The two wise guys reek of funny business from miles off. The identical black pinstripe suits, the awful, clownish, yellow ties and the patent-leather shoes identify them as *nouveau riche* products of scientific socialism, Algerian-style, which is to say, members of the brotherhood of visionary lowlifes who have managed to convince the apparatchiks that it is necessary to abuse their power and construct financial empires in order to enter the new world order better armed and forewarned.

"You could have waited your turn, Mr. Llob," grumbles the mayor. "Can't you see I'm busy?"

"I can see it all too well, Mr. Mayor."

The two clowns sense danger. They gather up their things and leave. The mayor is very upset by my tactlessness; he takes his chin in his hand and looks at me with hostility. "I can't stand inconsiderate people," he announces.

"Well, I can't stand being pushed around. You shouldn't have sent your circus animal to my hotel. Thanks to him, I didn't get my afternoon nap and I don't quite feel myself."

"I didn't know you were here on a mission," he says, hopefully. "People on a mission normally come to me first. They've never regretted it. I put my human and material resources at their disposal and spare no effort to make their visit as pleasant as possible."

He stands up, comes round the table and takes me by the wrist. In Algeria, this is a conciliatory step. When your adversary takes you by the wrist and makes you follow in his footsteps, it means he is ready to bury the hatchet, and you along with it.

"If I'd known you were with the *Mouhafada*...."*

"I'm with the police."

He frowns. "The police? Has there been a murder in my town without my knowledge, Inspector?"

"Superintendent."

He pushes a chair toward me and starts pouring me a cup of tea. "I don't understand, Superintendent."

His hand is shaking.

The pit bull terrier that was going to devour me whole a short while ago, in the lobby of the hotel, is pulling in its claws. He has chosen to talk things over.

"I'm looking into the events of July/August sixty-two."

"I don't see the connection with the police."

"You don't need to, Mr. Khaled.... Did you serve in this area during the war?"

"Of course. I joined the FLN the moment the armed insurrection broke out. I was a liaison officer to begin with. My job was to give aid and assistance to our commandos when they passed through the province. Sometimes I put them up, and I also arranged their movements. In fifty-six, an informer denounced me. I was arrested, tortured, and condemned to five years in jail. I managed to escape with a group of other prisoners. In fifty-eight, I was in the *maquis* in Chréa, then I asked to be moved closer to home and the regional command transferred me to the mountains of Sidi Ba. I worked as company chief of staff, under the Lefty. In fifty-nine, our battalion commander was killed in a skirmish with some French paras. The Lefty replaced him, but I stayed with the company until the end of the war."

"Did you know—?"

"The Talbis?"

My astonishment amuses him.

He explains: "The whole town knows, Superintendent."

"Did you?"

"Did I know them? In those days, Sidi Ba was just a name

---

* *Mouhafada*: regional cell of the FLN.

on a map. Everyone knew everyone. We're almost in the same tribe. The Talbis lived in a small house near the Roman bridge. They were peaceful people. The father, Kaddour, was a livestock merchant. The son, Ameur, who was about my age, was a student at a school in the town. We weren't friends, but we'd have a cup of coffee together every now and then, when we bumped into each other. When the father died—he was swept away in a flash flood—the son found he was in debt up to his neck. His father's creditors ruined him. Xavier Lapaire, the settler who ran the biggest farm in the area, took him on as a bookkeeper. As far as I know, Ameur hadn't taken sides; he was neither for the revolution nor for pacification. The purges of July sixty-two didn't affect him. I don't remember ever hearing a *muhajid* having anything to say against him."

"So he wasn't a *harki?*"

"Not to my knowledge, no."

"So why was he slaughtered, along with his whole family?"

"I tell you he wasn't worried. The massacres of *harkis* didn't drag on around here. The whole thing was settled in three days and three nights. When the French soldiers decamped to the heights above Sidi Ba, the *harkis* tried to follow them. But the Lefty and Lieutenant Barrot had agreed on a course of action. The French officer was not to take any Arabs with him. His unit's vehicles were checked by our guys, and they managed to winkle out a traitor. The Lefty wasn't happy, and burned him alive on the spot. That same day, he gave the order to hunt down all traitors. By the end of the third night, the count was one hundred and fifty-nine dead in the municipality of Sidi Ba alone. The Talbis were not among the victims."

"They were killed at the beginning of August."

"Who told you that nonsense, Superintendent? Until proven otherwise, the Talbis were abducted and are missing. No trace of them was ever found; no bodies, no forwarding address."

"Our witnesses say some armed men came to get them during the night and drove them somewhere, from which they never came back."

"It's possible, but not to kill them. The massacres didn't start up again. Some excesses had been noted, and the order came down to stop all punitive expeditions against the families of traitors. Besides, the *harkis* who were arrested later weren't executed; they were handed over to the republic's jailers. But some undesirable families may have been forced to leave the area. That's probably what happened to the Talbis. I think they settled somewhere else, like thousands of other families who felt threatened where they lived."

"What did people have against Ameur Talbi? You say he didn't collaborate with the French army."

"Maybe that he was friendly with Xavier Lapaire, the settler. The Lefty hated the French, and Arabs who sought out their company doubly so."

"There's a story that one of Talbi's sons, Belkacem, who was about twelve at the time, managed to give his abductors the slip that night."

"I've heard the story, but I'm not sure it's true, because no one ever saw the boy again."

"It is true. I've picked up the boy's trail."

The mayor shrugs. "What does that change?"

"Many people's stories."

"So bring him in and we won't talk about it any more."

He doesn't believe me, or else he's trying to make me believe that the demolition of his story leaves him indifferent, because he's got nothing on his conscience.

"In your opinion, Mr. Khaled, what could have made that boy run away if all he had to do was simply move somewhere else?"

"I confess I have no answer to that. It's true, if the family was just asked to leave Sidi Ba, the kid had no reason not to go with his parents. Especially given the dreadful things that were going on in the area. But the boy was never found, and there's nothing to prove these stories aren't just invented by enemies of the revolution who want to cast doubt in people's minds, any way they can, to tarnish the pages of our history."

"I've found him."

"Others have shouted the same thing from the rooftops, but in vain. We've seen so many ghosts around here that no one believes in them any more. At Sidi Ba, we're quite sure that the story of the young Belkacem Talbi was invented, from start to finish, by certain malcontents trying to damage Haj Thobane's reputation."

"What's the connection with Haj Thobane?"

"Haj Thobane is the Lefty."

I get out my little notebook and scribble "Haj Thobane = Lefty." A whimsical gesture, perhaps, even an unusual one for a cop who works by instinct, but it allows me to hide my amazement.

"Who would want to undermine a national hero?"

"Revolution doesn't only give birth to valiant souls, Superintendent. The internecine quarrels that ravaged our ranks during the war are still going on today. Within the same party, people loathe and plot against each other. Nobody likes the ones who have been successful. The Lefty has been successful. He attracts the envious, the critical. People try to destroy his legend, to sully his past, to dispute his charisma. We're aware of this in Sidi Ba, and we suffer. To some extent it's a symbol of us that is being disfigured, you see. Haj Thobane is a gentleman. His generosity is enormous. Everyone at Sidi Ba owes the best part of his wellbeing to him. Thanks to him, this hamlet has emerged from economic stagnation. Our *douar* is on its way to becoming a town, maybe even the capital of a *wilaya*. Malicious tongues speak of regional favoritism, nepotism. They think our hero is too rich, too greedy, too suffocating. It's not true. Haj Thobane is a good man, caring and charitable. Personally, I hold him in veneration."

I bring my glass of tea to my lips, sniff at it, then put it down without tasting it. The mayor twitches but doesn't express his hurt. He must be finding me more and more disagreeable, because his moustache, which previously drooped downward, is now bristling.

I light a cigarette and watch a wisp of smoke making its way toward the ceiling.

"How could the story of a boy tarnish the image of Haj Thobane, Mr. Khaled?" I ask him suddenly. "Is there a link between the Talbis and our hero?"

My questions don't put him off his stride. He pours himself a cup of coffee, to give himself time to think. He says, "Since Haj Thobane, the Lefty, was the military commander of the region during the war, people try to pin every blunder and every messy story that took place here on him, that's the link. A tissue of vulgar lies. The war is over, Mr. Llob. What's done is done. Regrettable or not, it can't be undone. We want to turn the page and rebuild the country. Everything else, the fabrications and the idiotic insinuations, shouldn't put us off. I assure you there's nothing to it. If you insist on finding out for yourself, go ahead. But be careful, people's sensibilities are only just below the surface around here."

As he pats his temples dry, the mayor notices that his hand won't stop shaking, despite his efforts to keep calm and to moderate his language. He puts his handkerchief in his pocket and stands up. "Why don't you come and have dinner with me tonight, Superintendent? We can talk about all this again, calmly. I have a pile of administrative files to deal with right now; this office is going to swallow me whole."

"What a pity, I have problems with cholesterol."

In the corridor, the two crooks from before are waiting for me to leave so that they can go back to the mayor. The bigger of the two, whose gaping shirt can only just contain his belly, throws a smile at me that's as fake as his Lacoste belt.

I lean over to him and murmur in his ear, "You should put some underpants over your face."

There is a man waiting by the car in the municipal car park. He is unkempt and unshaven and seems to be in an advanced state of inebriation. As soon as he catches sight of me, he snaps to attention and brings his hand to his temple in a formal salute.

"Is it you who's making trouble with the citizens of Sidi Ba?"

"That depends," I say, opening the door.

The man jerks his thumb over his shoulder. "That mayor is a son of a bitch of the first order. He thinks he's God and believes the whole town belongs to him. I knew him when he was twenty. He was a hick, a spineless wonder, a loser. He tells everyone he spent time in prison for his revolutionary activities. It's not true. He never fought with the FLN. He didn't know what it was, before independence. He was a rustler, a common sheep thief, no more. He was arrested by a farmer trying to sneak into a sheep-pen."

I start the engine.

The man pushes me out of my seat and turns the key. "I'm not talking to the wall and I'm not a halfwit. Let's do like this, okay? I talk, you listen. I've been waiting for a man, a real man, who doesn't have cold eyes and who goes where there are mines without protection for his balls or a bullet-proof vest; you won't disappoint me, will you?"

I start the engine again; he jumps at the dashboard and switches it off again.

"I'm not a lunatic. Have I asked for money?"

"What do you want?"

"I've heard, in town, that you're looking for the truth. I'm in possession of part of it. Don't take me for a tramp either. I know I look like a rag-and-bone man, but I wasn't like this my whole life. I've worked right at the top, me, and I've gone around in luxury cars. You know how life is in an abortion of a republic like ours. One day you're praised to the skies, the next you're up in smoke. If I've slipped down the ladder, it's thanks to my integrity. Honest people don't last long among predators and opportunists. That's the cause of my ruin, my friend. Because I was upright, they broke me. I'm not the only one, and you won't contradict me there. So, this bastard 'truth,' are you still interested in it?"

As I hesitate, unsure how to take this, he thrusts his arm under his worn cardigan and brings out a bundle of papers held together with a rubber band. "This here is my former *maquisard* card. I was a cadet in the ranks of the ALN. My face my have changed, but I've kept my name and family. This here is my party membership card. I was office manager at the regional level. And these here are my orders when I was appointed as a Sub-Prefect by the president himself in nineteen sixty-three...."

A small crowd is forming around us; a few kids at first, then some passers-by turn up, intrigued by my interlocutor's gestures; judging by the sniggering and open laughter flaring up here and there, he can't have a very good reputation in the neighborhood. Kong shows up too, truncheon in hand, to disperse the curious. He doesn't manage to worry everyone.

"Get in," I tell the stranger.

The man buries his bundle under his coat again and salutes his audience before slumping down in the passenger seat.

"Bastards! They'll be hearing from me."

"Where are we going?"

"Wherever you like. Fuck them, anyway."

"My hotel?"

"Why not?"

The crowd won't part to let me through. Some kids, probably egged on by the adults, throw missiles at us. I engage reverse gear, go the wrong way up a one-way street, find an exit and escape at top speed, far from the shouting that has started up behind us.

"You mustn't think people don't like strangers," my passenger says. "They're people who are incapable of judging things for themselves. If someone says some bad things about you, they'll vomit all over you, right there and then; if someone says you've been sent from heaven, they'll throw themselves at your feet, you see? They're just weathervanes, reacting to the gusts of the wind. When the air is calm, it's hard to believe that they're flesh and blood and still breathing."

"Do you think someone set them against me?"

"Here, manipulation reigns supreme. Everyone in the town knows why you're here, you and the little woman. They say you're here to bring the town into disrepute, that you're communists, atheists and enemies of the Revolution. That what you write is insane, and that you're trying to drag our martyrs through the mud. It's always the same story when strangers take a close interest in our intrigues. So they stir up the mob against the undesirables, and let anger take care of the rest. If misfortune follows, you can't punish a whole mob."

"And has it followed?"

"Misfortune? This is its home."

Soria isn't wearing a blouse any more. She has replaced it with a tightly buttoned burgundy shirt with a Mao collar. Her hair is gathered up in a chignon, leaving her willful brow uncovered, and her eyes, highlighted by mascara, shine like jewels. She is even more beautiful in her velvet trousers, which define the shape of her thighs with great skill. This woman stops me concentrating; I realize I haven't thought of Mina for several nights in a row. Next time, I swear, I won't take a woman on my team.

"Do you mind if she stays with us?" I ask my guest. "She is my colleague and our conversation will interest her as much as me."

"Why should I mind? I'm not macho."

I thank him and have him sit on my bed. Soria occupies the only chair in the room; I sit on the corner of the table.

"Don't let that asshole of a mayor intimidate you," the unkempt fellow advises us. "He's got a big mouth, and he's got no more education than a donkey trainer. Sure, when it comes to counting pennies he could give an electronic calculator a run for its money. But apart from that he can't put together a simple memo."

"Looks to me like he gets by just fine."

"He's crafty. The phrases he comes out with, he memorizes them for official speeches and recites them cleverly so that he passes for an educated man. He's never set foot in a school, I tell you. He's illiterate in three languages, our mayor; he signs documents automatically, without bothering to decipher them. I know him. We grew up in the same dead end. He was a smelly little brat who wore the same rags in winter that he wore in summer and emptied every sheep pen within a fifty-kilometer radius. That's all he knew: stealing livestock and selling it on somewhere else at a tenth of the price. At the end of nineteen sixty-one, he came out of prison. On the nineteenth of March nineteen sixty-two, with independence visible on the horizon, he joined the ranks of the ALN as a common foot-soldier. The bastard had seen which way the wind was blowing and made his move. Result: it worked."

"Had he taken part in massacres of *harkis*?"

"For sure. It was a scramble, my friend. Everyone was in on it."

"Even you?"

"I wasn't active in this area. And I didn't wait until the nineteenth of March to take up arms. I was one of the few educated men to join the *maquis*. I went to high school, and I set fire to my institution before I went to war. In nineteen fifty-seven, if you please. I was wounded twice." He undoes his jacket and lifts up his undershirt to show a chest decorated with two blackened holes. "I was an officer cadet in nineteen sixty, and I was appointed as deputy commander of the company at Melaab, in the mountains of Ouarsenis. I came back to Sidi Ba a week after the mass killings. But I was there for the Talbis."

Soria is trembling from head to foot.

"My name is Zoubir, *madame*, Tarek Zoubir. You're a historian, aren't you? At least, that's what they say in the town."

"It's true."

"I want to help you. We absolutely have to smash these bastards. They're equivocators, base creatures, dogs, starving wolves. What with all the money they've amassed, they continue to flourish. This region was the breadbasket of the country when the French were here. It provided forty percent of the red meat on the north African market. It's because I tried to save it that I was made destitute and handed over to the mob. I raised the alarm in nineteen seventy. This region was made for agriculture, as I say. Messing it up with factories was out of the question. I had prepared a report, which was endorsed by a formidable group of experts. No good: Haj Thobane was bent on industrializing the land of his birth. As far as he was concerned, that was emancipation. He wanted to abolish the profession of shepherd, which reminded him of his former status. I opposed his plans. With a snap of his fingers, he had me relieved of my duties and instructed his clique to make my life difficult. I'm at rock bottom today because of him."

"Why don't you tell us a little about the Talbis?"

"I'm getting to them. This business isn't only about the Talbis. There was also Allal Kaïd and his family; they were abducted and went missing too. And the Bahasses, who made the best olive oil on the High Plateau; abducted and missing. And the Ghanems, who had several thousand head of cattle; abducted and missing. In one night, without trace and with no sign of life since. As if they had vanished into thin air. The people around here have worked out what happened to them, but they're afraid to talk about it. Afraid to think about it. Afraid to remember it. There were similar disappearances in the early years of independence. Not rich people, just curious people who tried to understand what happened on the night of the twelfth to the thirteenth of August nineteen sixty-two. They were never seen again. Me, I'm not afraid. What have I got to lose? I don't have any kids and my wife left me for a big shot more than two decades ago. I don't have any real existence and I don't really want to extend it. I should have died in the *maquis*. It's no life, nowadays. So if I'm going to die, let me die, as long as it's for the right cause. I'd be the happiest of victims if I could bring Haj Thobane down. He's a criminal and a bastard of the highest order. His financial empire is a direct result of that night-time purge in August nineteen sixty-two, I'd bet my life on it."

"That's a serious allegation you're making."

"It's nothing compared to what he's done."

"Did you know him personally?"

"I certainly did!"

"You think he's directly linked to this business?"

"As closely as he is to the devil."

I grimace dismissively. "Surely you don't make whole families disappear just so you can appropriate their property? There must be something else, otherwise tongues would have loosened since then."

"They were comfortably off families, and they were wiped out for that reason."

"Because people were envious?"

"Because people resented their good fortune. Freedom had been won; now we had to get ourselves out of the shit. To get started on the right foot, you had to put on other people's boots, Mr. Historian. The Thobanes were the barefoot type. They were starving to death before the war broke out. The father slaved as a stable boy for the Lapaires. They say he was killed by a mad horse. The son, Haj, worked as a shepherd for the Ghanems. Two of his brothers were killed in Indochina, in the French army. Haj inherited unbelievable poverty. I remember him very well. He would often go roaming about the barracks to glean ration packs. That's how the war started for him. He had got to know the Muslim soldiers and had managed to radicalize a few. With them, he mounted an ambush against a military supply truck. Complete success. First glorious feat of arms, with the bonus of seven soldiers killed and supplies diverted to the *maquis*. The Lefty had just entered into legend, through the front door. He went on to reign as absolute leader of the whole region. After the war, he turned it into his personal fiefdom. He appropriated Allal Kaïd's lands, the Bahasses' presses and the Ghanems' livestock pens, and no one felt he had gone too far. After all, wasn't he the savior of Sidi Ba?"

"And what did the Talbis' fortune consist of?" Soria asks him.

"That's the gap in the story, *madame*. As far as I know, the Talbis were ruined. They were living on the threshold of poverty. The father was working as the Lapaires' bookkeeper, it's true, but he didn't earn enough. Why they came for them on that night is a complete mystery and a stumbling block. None of the old people around here can come up with the feeblest of theories. Because Talbi was neither on one side nor the other. He had a handicapped wife and sick children, so he was left in peace. But I think there's someone who could enlighten us. A cut-throat for the revolution turned full-time drunk, a certain Rachid Debbah. He lives like a hermit in the woods. He's flat broke and an alcoholic, so if you slip him a few coins he might make the effort to regain his lucidity."

"Can you take us to him?"

"Of course. I'd have to speak to him first. He's suspicious and pig-headed when he decides not to cooperate."

"He can name his price," says Soria.

He stands up to take his leave. "If you promise to follow your investigation all the way to the end, I'll go and see him right now. And tomorrow, you'll find him fresh and willing at my house. I live ten kilometers from Sidi Ba, on the road to Médéa. You can't go wrong, my place is visible from the road. About a kilometer past the petrol station, you'll see a shrine on your left. Further on, a ruin by the side of the road. My place overlooks it. There are no other houses around. I'll wait for you there, with Rachid."

"Nine o'clock?" I suggest.

"Not so early. Rachid doesn't get up before noon. Let's say two o'clock."

Gratefully, I offer my hand. "Tomorrow then, two o'clock sharp."

He holds his hand back. "We can shake hands when we've finished with these bastards, Mr. Historian. Not before. I want these villains to pay, I want the country rid of their carcasses for ever. Don't think I'm getting revenge. There's a bit of that, of course, but I don't feel like I'm settling scores. I love this country. You don't have to believe me, and I don't give a damn whether you do or not. The only important question for me is how to get you to pursue your investigation all the way to the end. Because if you pull out like limp chickens it will be the end of everything, for me and for anyone who believes there is justice on this earth."

"It's true that I sometimes feel I'm being kept in the dark, but I'm no chicken."

"I realized that as soon as I saw you coming out of the mayor's office."

"See you tomorrow."

"That's right. See you tomorrow, historian. Without fail."

I show him out.

When I get back, I find Soria standing by the window looking worried. She's looking at the swirling square with frowning eyes and a single line across her forehead. Without turning round, she says, "Can I have a cigarette, Mr. Llob?"

Chapter eighteen

It's true: you can see Tarek Zoubir's place from the road. To get there, all you have to do is follow the track leading up to the shrine, whose green and white dome dominates the hill. We turn onto a winding road and follow an avenue of shrubs. It's ten to two. The sun beats down on the countryside like an animal. Soria is driving; she looks exhausted. She spent the night pacing up and down in her room and scribbling endless notes in her files. When morning came she was still bent over her papers, so absorbed that she didn't hear me knock or come in. It's hard to say what's going through her mind. She hasn't said much since last night and has lost a huge amount of her enthusiasm, as if this business is suddenly beginning to get on top of her. She tries to hide it, of course, but the shadow over her expression fools no one.

Tarek Zoubir's patio is silent. Soria honks the horn. Nobody comes out. We wait for two minutes, and then I step out and go and knock on the worm-eaten door. Nothing. I listen, but don't hear a sound on the other side. I call the man; my voice ricochets around the cob walls and dies away without arousing any interest. I try the lock; it opens. Through the half-open door I can see one end of the courtyard and a dog stretched out on the ground. It doesn't move. Of course not: its head has been blown off. Soria starts when she sees me get out my weapon; I tell her not to leave the car and enter the house on tiptoe. A small table has been overturned on the floor; a shoe has been left in the hallway. With my back to the wall, I move in, listening out for suspicious creaks. The window is wide open; it gives onto a wretched living room. The few pieces of furniture are out of place: signs of a struggle. I move in further, step over a bench with my Beretta in front of me, and come into a bedroom that has been turned upside down. I raise my head and find him. Tarek Zoubir is hanging from a beam, his naked body covered with bruises and his arms dangling. Streams of blood branch out from his chin and his chest. His neck is twisted by the knot in the rope, and he is staring at a corner of the room with part of his tongue sticking out through his lips. His executioner cut off his nose before hanging him.

I rush through the remaining rooms, come back into the courtyard and search the surroundings; not a soul.

Soria arrives, curious.

"I don't advise you to go any further," I say.

She pushes my arm aside and heads for the living room. I hold her back by the wrist.

"Get your hands off me!" she screams, beside herself.

"It's not a pretty sight."

"I've seen worse."

She goes into the bedroom.

I expect to see her back out with her tail between her legs, or else bend double and throw up, but Soria doesn't panic. Her legs hold firm and she faces the mutilated corpse with a calm that gives me goosebumps.

"This is no coincidence," she mutters.

"Doesn't look like it."

She holds her head between her hands without taking her eyes off the hanged man. Rage makes her eyelids puffy. In the silence of the house, her breathing seems cacophonous. I sense that she's a couple of heartbeats away from imploding. After meditating on our bad luck, she turns to me, her face crumpled.

"They cut off his nose," she says.

"I saw."

"Do you know what that means?"

In Algeria, the nose is the organ of pride. During the war of independence, the *maquisards* used to cut off traitors' noses before forcing them to march down the street so that people would get the message. The signature and the message were clear in those days. It's seeing it again, twenty-six years later, that shakes me.

"Do you think this is a joke, Superintendent?"

"Whatever it is, it's in bad taste."

"They're trying to scare us."

"Are you scared, *madame*?"

"No. Are you?"

"A little, but not enough to discourage me."

The superintendent at Sidi Ba is furious. He's trying to intimidate me, but he isn't up to it. He's a dried-up little runt with a face carved out of granite, who talks with his hands and feet and explodes like a spring every time I try to get a word in edgewise. He must be very harsh, because his shouting wreaks havoc in the police station, an ill-conceived edifice, like the profession carried on therein. The two inspectors helping him are standing at attention. The taller of the two, a beanpole with a mean expression, has it in for me because I'm getting his boss all worked up. The other, a sweating great tub of lard, can't stop scratching his backside. He looks mean too, proud of his military moustache and his gluttonous pig's belly. It's high alert in the office, whose french window looks out onto a graveled courtyard. We are constantly interrupted by telephone calls. It's the fat tub of lard who answers. If it isn't the mayor, it's his secretary. The inspector's discomfort betrays the dissatisfaction reigning among the powers that be. The superintendent refuses to take the calls. "Can't you see I'm busy," he shouts, every time the inspector holds out the receiver. As for me, I just stand there aghast. I did right to leave Soria at the hotel. With clowns like these in the police, she would finally have lost the small amount of respect she still has for me.

"So there you have it," the superintendent of Sidi Ba explodes.

"You show up and hello corpses. Things were calm on the whole, and then you arrive on your high horse and sow your fantasy in a field of nettles. You're not in Algiers, comrade. This is *my* town. If you have a problem, you come to me. You have no right to step on my toes. There are regulations, and administrative divisions."

"Would you mind turning down the volume?" I say to him. "You can be heard at the other end of the town."

He stops dead.

The superintendent can't bear the idea that one might not show him the proper respect in front of his subordinates; he is writhing with apoplexy.

"I don't quite understand," he squeals, hoping to get me to beg his pardon.

"That doesn't surprise me."

Cut to the quick, he froths toward my belly. With a trembling finger, he threatens me, "Save your arrogance for the little people, pal. I wasn't born yesterday. I crush jokers like you every day. I'm so used to it it bores the pants off me. So calm down."

"Fuck you."

He moves to throw himself at me, but holds back at the last moment. He's reached boiling point; his teeth are chewing at his lips and his hands are shaking.

He tries a different tack: "Do you think, because you're from Algiers, that you scare me?"

"That's about the size of it."

His Adam's apple clicks in his constricted throat. He realizes he's hit upon a tough nut and that it's not in his interest to push his luck. As a precaution, he orders his inspectors to clear off. Once we're alone, he undoes the top button of his shirt and goes back behind his desk.

He is deflating, the loser.

"I shall inform the minister, Mr. Llob."

"You can drop a word in the president's ear, if it would give you pleasure. I'm here to work. Furthermore, Superintendent, I categorically forbid you to treat me as you just did a moment ago. I know you run your ship your way around here, far away from indiscreet ears and therefore with total impunity, but that doesn't give you the authority to hit anyone you want with your oars. Stick to polishing up your little scams. You're lucky you're not already rotting behind bars. My short stay in your magnificent whorehouse has given me an insight into your activities. You don't do things by halves, and that's to your credit. But rest assured, I'm not here to stop your little games. So if you want to avoid my investigation straying off the beaten track, I suggest you don't get under my feet."

The man has stopped breathing. He has turned to stone in his chair, with his hand suspended over the telephone. From his distorted point of view, he must be wondering whether I'm bluffing. We look at each other for a long time, both looking for the chink in the other's armor. There's no doubt that the bastard in front of me is cunning, but not bold enough to throw my audacity back at me and see what it's based on.

"I suppose you're well protected, Mr. Llob."

"You amaze me."

"May I see your orders?"

"In your shoes, I'd give that a miss."

He pushes the telephone back.

"I get it," he groans.

"If it's not too much to ask…will that be all?"

He spreads his arms in surrender.

Before leaving I glance back over my shoulder. You can't imagine.

The next day, we go into the woods, Soria and I, looking for Rachid Debbah, the famous cut-throat Tarek Zoubir was going to introduce us to at his home. We manage to unearth him late in the afternoon, thanks to some young shepherds. He lives in a hovel on the other side of the hillside, surrounded by undergrowth and a heap of garbage. The goat track that leads to him is too narrow for the Lada. We abandon the car beside an orchard and clamber up the slope on foot. Soria climbs faster than me, as if afraid of arriving too late.

The place must have sheltered a few families before it was completely burned out. The disaster must date back an eternity, judging by the ruined shacks, which are overrun with wild grasses and rats. A thin stream of foul-smelling water leaks out of a dilapidated tank and disappears behind a wall of cactuses. Here too, the carcass of a dog is becoming rank. Further back, the hovel. Its door is lying in the ditch. The buzzing of flies tells us nothing we want to know. Soria is dismayed; she utters a curse and sinks onto a rock.

"It can't be," she moans, "it can't be."

And bursts out sobbing.

I go into the hovel.

Rachid Debbah is lying curled up on a mattress, at the end of a bare room bathed in a dazzling glare. The only furniture is an upturned crate put to use as a nightstand. There is a candle on it, drowned in wax, beside an empty wine bottle. The sleeping man stinks; he hasn't had a bath since Noah's flood. His bare feet, which the tiny fringed blanket doesn't manage to cover, are covered in a thick layer of filth. I crouch down to pull back the blanket and uncover the poor devil's head: someone has smashed in his skull so hard that fragments of his brain have spattered the wall.

The blood has drained out of Soria's face. She says nothing, holding back the rage welling up inside her. *Don't touch me,* she says through gritted teeth when I offer to help her down the steep path. Not another word after that. Nothing but the spasmodic working of her teeth, ferociously grinding up the screams that leap to her throat. She refuses to take the wheel. I drive, looking straight ahead while she stares into the distance, stubborn, turned in on herself, with her arms folded over her chest, like a sulky little girl.

Our trip back to Sidi Ba takes place in a silence weighted with storms; the slightest spark could set off the powderkeg. Something tells me she holds me responsible for the bad luck that dogs us, that she thinks I'm a bad omen.

I drop her off at the hotel and go to park the car in the carpenter's yard. Night has fallen. The feeble lamp accentuates the darkness at the base of the buildings. I switch off the motor and light a cigarette. Just as I open the door, a shadow pounces on me uttering a deafening *Son of a bitch.* A blow to the back of the head, another to the jaw, then blackness…

When I come to again, I recognize the ceiling of my room. I'm stretched out on my bed with a barbecue grill at my temples. The walls are undulating gently around me. I touch my face with my hand and find patches of fire and lumps under my ear and on my cheeks. Trying to get up I manage only to set my migraine off again and give up immediately; that's when I remember I was attacked.

Soria arrives with a saucepan full of ice cubes. She sits down beside me, dips some compresses in the cold water and applies them gently to my wounds.

"What happened?"

"The receptionist heard you cry out. If he hadn't come running out, the bad guys would have lynched you. They were kicking you in the kidneys while you were lying on the ground."

"Would he be able to identify them?"

"It was dark. They ran off as soon as they saw him."

My jaw hurts like hell. Suddenly, I look for my gun in my belt and can't find it. Soria reassures me: "I've put it away…. You didn't have time to see them?"

"I didn't see anything coming."

"You're getting old, Superintendent."

"I think so too."

She is wearing a diaphanous gown, pale and transparent, within which stirs a splendid body. Her bewitching breasts, beautifully contained in their lacy brassiere, look like a pair of suns emerging from behind a cloud. When she leans over me to apply the compresses, they quiver like jelly and almost pour out over me. She really is a magnificent woman. Now that she seems to have digested her anger, her face is restful and her eyes, sparkling jewels that they are, fascinate me. Her scent makes my whole being lose its equilibrium; I have the vague sensation of being carried along on a stream toward some enchanted shore. She leans over again, and the nearer breast overflows a little, with her nipple like a cherry on a cake. Suddenly, she catches me looking at her, and her expression leaves me flustered. I try to beat a retreat, like a child caught in the act; her smile comforts me, disarms me, strips me naked; I can't find the strength to fight the strange wave breaking over me from all sides. Soria sees that I'm in disarray and exploits it without encountering any resistance. Her fingers drop the compresses and spread out over my face, stroke the bridge of my nose, slide over my lips, arousing a multitude of tremors in my flesh and as many flying sparks in my spirit. Her breast is now completely free; it's hovering over my chest, like a forbidden fruit. My throat is dry and my heart is fluttering about in its cage like a frightened sparrow. She leans over some more, then more still, letting her hair drop over my face; her breath mingles with mine in a muted ballet; her hand slides slowly down my belly, logical and in control, goes lower, fearlessly and without reproach, as if moved by some invincible force. I am writhing and trembling, completely out of my depth. Soria's lips come and brush against mine, stilling their quivering, drinking in their fear. I'm being carried along toward a state of dizziness, caught up in delicious torment. Just as I begin to flounder, her hands roughly grab my belt, instantly breaking the spell. I pounce on her wrist: "Mina would be angry with me."

"She'll never know," she murmurs, her mouth against mine.

"I'd know. I'd never be able to look at her the way I used to. In the end, she'd suspect something and be very hurt, and as for me, I'd never forgive myself."

She doesn't insist. "Mina is very lucky," she says, standing up.

Chapter nineteen

Kong leaves the town hall at five thirty. He reaches the center of town on foot, recognizable by his sloping shoulders and oafish gait. Looking at him, you understand right away what a brute is. People cross the street when they see him; kids pick up their balls and make themselves scarce when he approaches; shopkeepers address him with elaborate *salamaleks*. In short, he is intimidation personified. When he gets to the *souk*, he orders some grilled kebabs from a street vendor, eats them on the spot, standing at the counter, and leaves without paying. That's what they call having an easy time of it at the republic's expense. Then he goes into a seedy-looking café, sends a dominoes-player packing and takes his place. At the end of the third game, he has a go at his partner, who didn't manage the return match well. Toward evening, he stocks up in a grocery store and, with his arms full of purchases he hasn't paid for, climbs a repellent alleyway and enters a vile-looking building. The moment he opens the door to his slum, I bundle him inside and hit him over the head with my gun. He collapses like an electrocuted bear. His shopping bags burst open on the floor, littering the floor with tangerines and cracked eggs.

"Hello, Kong. I was expecting to find you up a tree, but you choose to vegetate in a cage. You're way ahead of your species, I must say."

He shakes his head to order his thoughts.

My .45 flashes and lays him out again, nose to the tiles.

"Lie down!"

I switch on the light in the room, close the door and crouch down beside him, my Beretta on the alert.

"What do you want from me?"

I show him the lumps on my face. "How am I going to pull any girls, now that you've messed up my looks? Is that any way to behave?"

"I don't know what you're talking about."

"You're breaking my heart, Kong."

"I swear I don't understand."

I grab him by the hair and pull his head back sharply. His neck cracks and his eyes bulge with pain.

"You and your friend have made a serious mistake."

"You're wrong, Superintendent. I'm not crazy. The first time, I didn't know who I was up against. But as soon as I found out you were with the police I kept my distance. I know my limits."

I stand up and survey the hovel; it's a shabby room where housework is rarely done. A metal bed, a bench, a low table overloaded with dirty plates and glasses, a dust-covered television and a fridge comprise the entirety of the furnishings. On the damp-stained walls, amid a bunch of pictures of naked women, an electoral poster showing a smiling mayor of Sidi Ba.

Kong takes advantage of my inattention to pounce. He tries to disable me with his arms. I dodge him and follow up with a series of lefts that don't have any effect on him. He charges again, falling on me and yelling. His fist slams into my ear, exactly where it hurts most. The pain stokes up my anger. I strike out blindly, short-armed, with the butt of my gun. Kong collapses. I go on hitting him. Each blow I land fills me with the idea that I am contributing to the salvation of humankind and, by the same token, carrying out a sacred duty to the good Lord.

"Okay, okay, I surrender," he gasps.

I order him to back up against the wall; he obeys, cramming

himself into a corner and wiping his forearm. I have messed up one of his eye sockets and smashed his nose. Blood is smeared all over his face.

"The two guys who attacked you are not known to our battalion. They came here from Algiers three days ago, and claim to be members of Military Security. The mayor received them in private."

"What do they look like?"

"Well, like everyone else."

My .45 digs into his gut.

"I only saw them once, I swear."

"Describe them to me."

"Strong-looking, shaved temples, broken noses. Classic bouncer profile. One of them has a scar on his upper lip; the other one has short legs and limps a bit. They give you a chill up and down your spine when you first see them."

"How did they get here?"

"What do you mean?"

"Their car?"

"Gray Peugeot 405, Algiers plates."

"Are they the ones who did Tarek and Debbah in?"

Kong moves; I push him back with the toe of my shoe.

"That's not a question for me, Superintendent. I'm the mayor's bodyguard. It's true, I do some bad things, but never anything really serious. I don't know who's behind the murder of those two poor bastards. And even if I did know something I'd keep it to myself. I don't play with fire, me."

"Let's make a deal."

"No, no, I don't want to be mixed up in this business. Don't rely on me."

"I want their names."

"You know very well that guys like that don't have names. They just have codenames, and no address or family. You can beat me up all night, but you'd be wasting your time. I won't say anything. Already I don't remember who you are, and you've never set foot in my home."

Turning his back on me, he grabs a rag, thrusts it onto his face and crawls miserably back into the depths of his hole.

Soria has been listening to the account of my interview with Kong without interrupting. A line on her forehead shows that she is worried about how I will act on it. She's holding her breath, with her hands clasped on the stack of papers.

"I won't force you to take any serious risks, Mr. Llob. You're free to take whatever decision you feel is right. As for me, it's out of the question to stop when I've come this far. An army of secret policemen couldn't make me back off. I'll go right to the furthermost point of my limits."

"I'm not a gutless worm myself."

"That's not the point. Anyone can pull out if he thinks the stakes are too high. There's no shame in that."

"Can you tell me what your motivation is, right now?"

"What motivates you when you carry out your duties, Superintendent: the truth. I've never been so driven by a story. I've made it a personal matter."

"Why?"

"I can't stand injustice. People have been killed...."

"Abducted and missing."

"Come on, Superintendent. What does that really mean, abducted and missing?"

It's ten o'clock, and the town is hunkered down in impenetrable silence; the streets are deserted and the shops are shut. Once in a while a car goes by and vanishes immediately. Soria has dark rings under her eyes. With her little pocket tape-recorder next to her files, she goes back to checking her notes, confirming certain points and adding huge question marks over others.

"I'll leave you alone," I say to her.

"You're right. A good night's sleep will bring us the answers."

I leave her, promising to snore less loudly.

Once in my room, I release the safety catch on my Beretta and place it on my nightstand. I have no intention of sleeping soundly tonight. The presence of the two guys from Algiers in Sidi Ba worries me. If they're behind the murders of Tarek and Debbah, nothing will prevent them from visiting me in my hotel. I switch on the lamp and stretch out on the bed with one hand behind my head.

In the morning, I decide on a solo visit to the town. The only way to bring some order back to my thoughts is to locate the famous gray Peugeot 405 with Algiers plates. By noon, I have gone down and lurked around the town hall, then taken up a position by the police station. No sign of my two attackers. Halfway through my investigation, I realize I'm being followed. The fat tub of lard from the Sidi Ba police station is glued to my heels. He's trying to be discreet, but he isn't helped by the frenzied scattering of merchants in search of safety triggered by his passing.

At the corner of an alleyway, I catch him off guard, grab him by the throat and thrust him against a wall.

"It's for your own good," he gurgles without struggling.

I let him go. He straightens the collar of his shirt and says, "If it was up to me, I'd be getting laid instead of trotting along after you like a puppy so you don't get royally lynched by the mob. Except the superintendent insists he doesn't want to have to pick you up in little tiny pieces. He doesn't want any trouble on his watch, you get me? I can assure you it's not out of team spirit nor because he likes your looks."

"Frankly, with two corpses on your hands and two dangerous lunatics in the town, don't you think there are more important things to do than go round sniffing at my ass?"

"As far as the dead are concerned, they've been buried and the investigation continues. As for the two bastards who attacked you, they've flown the coop."

"No kidding."

"It may not look like it, but we had nothing to do with those crooks. We're cops and we carry out our duties with the few resources we have at our disposal."

"How touching."

He looks at me with disgust in his eyes. "I seldom lack respect for my colleagues, but right now I'm dying to punch you in the mouth."

"So die and let's get it over with."

He snickers, with his mouth curled into a sneer of distaste. "You poor fool!"

I get my left ready. He is saved by a group of women emerging from a patio. We stare at each other. He backs down first, shakes his head and retreats with his finger erect. "Watch your step, Superintendent. You're strutting about in a minefield."

"You're in a worse position. I feel sorry for your mirror."

He recovers his finger, uses it to tug at the bottom of his underpants and waddles off.

That afternoon, Soria insists that we go back to the home of Labras, the chicken farmer. I subject her to a complicated route, in the hope that the gray Peugeot 405 will appear in the rear-view mirror. After we've been on the road for several kilometers, we agree that we're not being followed. We retrace our steps as far as the Roman bridge and go back through the forest until we reach Jelloul Labras's farm. We find the latter sitting on a rock by the side of the road, as if expecting our visit. His welcome is less than generous. Soria asks me to leave it to her and gets out of the car. I watch from the car as they carry on a conversation. The farmer isn't very warm. His weary gestures and the way he rolls his eyes at me are not encouraging. Soria doesn't let herself get beaten. She plays her strongest cards: her charm and her arguments. The man moves limply, paying less and less attention to what she is saying. Finally, by some miracle, he stands up and heads for the eucalyptus. Soria gestures to me to follow her; it's in the bag.

The farmer puts out three folding chairs around the table at the foot of the tree. He doesn't address a word to me. He avoids looking at me. I sit down beside Soria; he positions himself slightly to one side. Suddenly, he says, "I was at Tarek Zoubir's burial. His death affected me profoundly. He was a good man."

"Did you know him?"

"Yes…. He had fallen a long way, it's true, but once upon a time he was respected. He was a local authority in the nineteen sixties. An idealist, clean. He believed in the renewal of Algeria. His promises didn't survive long in the face of those greedy vultures. When he tried to oppose the Lefty, who had grabbed the region for himself and his gangsters, he found himself in the gutter. He's lucky he wasn't done away with sooner. I owe this farm to him. I was starving. Nobody would give me a job. Nobody, in the town or anywhere else, could stand the sight of me. I was like a plague victim; I still am, even if people don't throw stones at me any more. I had no work, no relatives and no support, my house had been confiscated by the *fellaghas*...."

Fellaghas! The word explodes in me like a bomb, blowing apart my equanimity. My expression darkens in a fraction of a second, and my temples burn. I stand up and indignation gushes forth: "What did you say those freedom fighters were called?"

"*Fellaghas*...."

This time, it's my guts that are on fire. I am overcome with incandescent rage. "Take it back, and do it now."

"It won't clear their name, you do know that," he says, somewhat intrigued by my reaction.

"I forbid you to call them that."

"Hey, makes no difference to me. I don't need your permission and I'll call anyone I want whatever I want. For you, they were heroes; for me, they were demons."

"Because the harkis were angels?"

"They were what they were, and at worst they weren't as barbaric as the *fellaghas*."

My fist flashes out. Labras takes it just below his left ear; he falls flat on his back. To stop him getting up again, I give him my .45 under the chin. Soria tries to intervene; I catapult her aside, against my better nature. Labras puts himself out of reach of my blows and points his finger at me. "Would you dare to raise your hand against me if you weren't a cop? I'd crush you like a ripe pumpkin. But the law's on your side, isn't it? It's made to measure for you, isn't that right, Superintendent? You strike first and then you hide behind the law. Don't you think that's rather a simple contest? Go on, put your badge and gun away and show me there's more than shit in your belly."

I take off my jacket and put my gun and badge down on the ground. He surprises me with a hook. A flash lights up my brain; a second hook follows. My legs wobble beneath his blows, but my pride forbids me to cave in. In an excess of rage, I attack again. We tangle with each other in a web of curses and inextricable contortions. He's very solid, this chicken farmer. The healthy country air helps him with the close work. Soon, my energy is being sapped by my ragged gasping; my grip on him falls apart, weakens, I'm grabbing for a hold any way I can. The pollution of Algiers hangs heavy on my legs. Labras realizes he is getting the upper hand, and slips his arm under my buttock to lift me up; I stick a finger in his eye and force him to put me down again. A sudden explosion brings us to order. It's Soria. She's holding my Beretta in both hands and pointing the gun at us.

"That's enough!"

We move apart, Labras and I, mesmerized by the barrel of the gun.

"Hey!" I say to the historian. "That's no toy for a woman, you know."

"Nor are you two. Your squabbling is getting on my nerves. And you're ridiculous. What's most frustrating is realizing that you don't see it in yourselves. Times have changed, gentlemen. The ideals you used to defend have no currency today, and what's happening to the country is the antithesis of your utopias. Have pity on yourselves and spare me your foolishness. I'm carrying out a serious investigation here. The last thing I need is pettiness, of which you two are sad examples."

"What became of yesterday's promises is not within my remit. But I won't allow anyone to call men and women who died for their country *fellaghas.*"

"And what have you done to honor their memory, you, the guardian of the Temple?" the farmer shouts at me. "The country they died for has been handed over to dogs and good-for-nothings and, apart from hunting down legless cripples and beating up men with no arms, what have you done about it, Mr. Freedom Fighter?"

"I was not a *fellagha.*"

"Were you just in the *maquis?*"

"What about this?" I roar, lifting my undershirt to show a bullet-hole two centimeters away from my heart. "Do you think that's a cigarette burn?"

"What about this?" he retorts, pulling his trousers down to his groin. "Do you think that's my eunuch's badge?"

My breath is cut short.

Soria doesn't turn away. Though shocked by the man's naked-
ness, she seems turned to stone at the sight of his groin, which is
densely covered with pubic hair, as if to hide his affliction: the farmer's
penis and testicles have been cut off.

The silence of the tomb falls on the ridge.

Labras pulls his trousers back up and sits down again. Panting but calm. He turns his back on me, as if to expel me from the
universe, and addresses Soria and Soria only: "You should have left
him in his zoo, *madame*. Wild cats get very agitated when you take
them into the forest."

"I'm truly sorry, Mr. Labras."

He winks at her sadly. "It's not too bad. In a way, it's even a
good thing: at least I'll stay faithful to my dead wife to the last. For
Tarek Zoubir," his tone changes suddenly, "I'll make an exception.
He didn't deserve to end his days like that. I owe him a lot. He was
the only person in authority who was willing to see me. He listened
to me, and it was him who suggested I move in here, far from men
and their rancor. If it hadn't been for his personal intervention, the
bank wouldn't have lent me enough to buy some rope to hang myself.
The bastards who killed him won't get away with it. I'm ready to
risk everything to make them pay. Tell me what you want to know,
madame, I'm ready."

Soria hands me my gun. I slip it under my belt and go and
get some air a little apart from them, but at a distance from which I
won't miss any of the conversation.

"Tarek Zoubir was going to introduce us to a key witness on the
day he was murdered, Mr. Labras. A witness to the disappearance of
the Talbi family, who disappeared on the night of the twelfth to the
thirteenth of August nineteen sixty-two. He really wanted to cooperate fully. Unfortunately, they got there ahead of us. And Debbah—"

"Don't talk to me about that dog. He died the way he had
always lived. He was a butcher, scum of the worst kind. Many innocent people went under his knife. Just thinking about him makes me
want to go and shit on his tomb."

Soria raises her arms. "Sorry. I didn't know you hated him."

"Hated him? That would do him too much honor."

"Very well, Mr. Labras. I take back what I said."

"There's no point wasting time on that, *madame*. What must be remembered once and for all is that the people who were abducted that night and are still missing were executed, with the exception of a child who managed to escape, a child whom the Lefty's men hunted for months, maybe years, and whom they never found. I was there, *madame*. I will never forget what happened that night. Never. I can remember the tiniest details, every curse uttered by the Lefty's *fell*...henchmen, the tears on the cheeks of the women and children, every prayer of the men who were about to be liquidated.... I had been arrested two days before. They found me in the woods, where I had been hiding since the first mass killings, the ones where my wife, my father and two of my brothers were finished off. I was hoping to get to a port and sail to France, but FLN troops were scouring the region, putting up checkpoints on all the main roads and checking all travelers without exception. The hunt for *harkis* was at its peak. I was one, and there was a price on my head. I don't know how many days and nights I hid in the forest, eating plants and wild berries. One morning I came down to a spring to quench my thirst, and the Lefty's henchmen pounced on me. Some of them wanted to slit my throat on the spot, the others insisted I should be brought before their leader. They took me to a disused look-out post and tied me up in a cave. That same day, three more *harkis* came to keep me company. One of them had been badly beaten; he died from his injuries before sunset. The next day, after a mock execution, they took us back to the cave. That evening, a tractor arrived with a hefty escort. I recognized Allal Kaïd and his family, as well as the Ghanems. They had their belongings in suitcases and didn't understand what they were supposed to have done wrong. A few hours later the Bahass family arrived, on foot. I remember that the oldest child was carrying his grandmother on his back. Straight afterwards, a truck unloaded Talbi and his family. None of them understood why they were there. It seemed to me that not even the kidnappers knew. They were waiting for the Lefty's orders. It wasn't until they saw Debbah the Butcher show up, with his bag full of long swords, that they began to get the picture. As it was getting late, a rumor started to go round that the Lefty couldn't come and had ordered us to be put to death. We and the two *harkis* decided to sell our lives dearly. The killers began with the Kaïds. The scene played itself out in a clearing, under the light of a moon that was bright as day. When they started tying up the children, Allal Kaïd shouted out, 'They're going to slit our throats.' There was panic. The three families spread out in the general chaos. The Lefty's men started shooting left and right. My two companions and I took advantage of the confusion to make our getaway, overcoming the two men standing guard in front of the cave along the way. There were already a few bodies laid out in the clearing. All the kids, and the women who had been caught by their pursuers, were screaming. Bullets were whistling about my ears. I ran as far as I could. My bound hands weren't much help. I ran into a tree and slid into a ditch. Three armed men caught me. 'This one's mine,' Debbah said. The other two pinned me to the ground while Debbah pulled down my trousers. He emasculated me there and then. There was more screaming nearby, so he ordered the youngest to let me suffer a while before blowing my brains out. I hadn't passed out. The pain was so atrocious it kept me conscious. And there was the screaming of the victims. The guy who had been told to finish me off was trembling like a leaf. I begged him to put me out of my misery. Sobbing, he shook his head. His rifle was shaking in his arms. He aimed the barrel at my head, then turned it away, shot to one side and fled.

"Why the Talbis?" Soria persisted.

"I don't know. I've often asked myself that question. There have been some speculative theories, most of them fantasies. Some are very serious, often improbable. I have my principles: this country has got us so used to manipulation and disinformation that, in order to keep my head on my shoulders, I'll only believe what I can touch with my hands and see with my eyes. The Talbis? I don't get it. The others? They were rich, and people had it in for them because they hadn't supported the armed struggle financially. Their refusal to participate in the war effort was seen as high treason."

"Tarek suggested it was so that the Lefty could appropriate their wealth."

"That's what he went on and did. The official version remains the first one."

"The Talbis weren't wealthy."

"Exactly. That's the flaw in the theory. Later, there was a rumor about them, but it fizzled out."

"Why's that?"

"It might just have been tittle-tattle."

"Tell us anyway."

"I don't have the right. I know someone in a better position than me to answer you."

"Does he live around here?"

"Yes, but I don't know whether he's willing to talk to you. He was very friendly with Tarek in those days. And he's a man of integrity. In my opinion, he knows a large part of the truth."

"Can you take us to him?"

"I must ask him first."

Jelloul Labras comes to fetch us at the hotel at about midnight. He advises us to leave the Lada where it is and to make our way through the maze of narrow streets that disappear into the old town. On several occasions he goes on ahead and scrutinizes the area; sometimes he pushes us into a doorway and heads back to see if we're being followed. He's not frightened; he's just on his guard and doesn't seem to be exaggerating. These excessive measures aren't being taken to protect our movements; Labras must have promised our witness that he wouldn't be exposed to any risk. Although I'm impatient to reach our destination, I leave him to feel out the territory as he sees fit.

There is a car waiting for us. Labras asks us to climb into the back seat, jumps behind the wheel and drives the vehicle onto the tarmac with its headlights extinguished. He doesn't turn the headlights on until after we have skirted round the city walls. We leave the town behind and turn toward Médéa. The night is dark, the sky threatening. We don't encounter a single car on the road. The countryside is buried in shadows, the silence pierced here and there by the howling of wild dogs. We reach a junction, make a detour because a bridge has been damaged by floods, and head down a track. Labras switches off the headlights and gets out to listen. He comes back after three minutes, sure that no one is following us.

Headlights still switched off, he starts up again smoothly and heads for a copse of trees. A bolt of lightning streaks across the distant sky, followed by a gust of wind that is swallowed up by the trees. The first few fat drops of rain spatter the windscreen. The headlights, now switched on, illuminate a deeply rutted road hemmed in by thickets. The creaking of the shock-absorbers covers the sounds of the forest. Soria looks straight ahead, holding her breath. Her hands slide anxiously up and down her thighs.

"Is it far?" I ask.

Labras doesn't answer. He is maneuvering the car skillfully among the ruts, one eye on the state of the road and the other on the rear-view mirror. We drive on for about twenty minutes, until we start to make out some far-off specks of light indicating a few hearths that are as distant from each other as my way of thinking is from the chicken farmer's. At last, just as we emerge through a hedge of spindly pine trees, barking breaks out. The dog's eyes gleam in the darkness. Behind it, there is a building where someone has just switched on a light. A silhouette comes out onto the terrace and tells the animal to be quiet. I recognize Rabah Ali, the man who came to see me at the hotel and suggested I get in contact with the chicken farmer. He has changed since the other day; he seems to have cheered up. Nothing like the fearful man who couldn't wait to get away. This time he cultivates an aggressive manner, with frowning eyes and a heavy mouth. I wonder whether his confident look isn't down to his hunting garb—mesh trousers and a brightly colored nylon jacket over a wool sweater, finished off with an impressive studded American belt.

He leads us into a living room strewn with Chaoui rugs illuminated by bronze lamps in sconces. We sit down on padded benches. Jelloul Labras chooses to remain standing by the window.

"As far as my children are concerned, I've gone partridge hunting," Rabah Ali explains in a stuttering voice that contrasts with his carefully calculated appearance. "Which is not untrue. In a few hours, some friends will join me. At four o'clock we will set off for the woods. All of this so as not to attract attention. I've already told you, Mr. Llob. I want to stay out of this business. Even if I think it's high time to lance the boil. Jelloul didn't have to work hard to persuade me. I've had it up to here myself, and I'll be glad when it's over with. But before we go any further, I have to ask a few questions."

"That's fine," I say, "only I've got one important one. After that, I'll let you take over and have the floor."

Rabah Ali frowns. He looks at Jelloul, who nods.

"Go ahead, Mr. Llob."

"The first time around, it was you who steered us toward Labras. Tonight, he's bringing us to you. Would you mind telling me what the connection is between you?"

Jelloul raises his hand, asking our host's permission to answer in his stead. The latter accepts. The chicken farmer addresses Soria: "The armed man Debbah ordered to blow my brains out on the night of the twelfth to the thirteenth of August was this man, Rabah Ali...."

Soria is dismayed by my behavior. These details don't interest her. She's desperate to get to the heart of the matter. She turns to Rabah Ali. "May I take notes, Mr. Ali?"

"I don't see why not."

"Thank you."

She gets a notepad and a pen out of her bag, switching on the tape recorder she has hidden there as she does so. Totally in control of her movements and feelings, she opens the conversation: "I'm waiting for your questions, Mr. Ali."

"Do you know who you're up against?"

"Haj Thobane, otherwise known as the Lefty, a person of national influence and a member of the Political Bureau."

"Very good, *madame*. How far are you willing to go?"

"Me, all the way," says Soria.

"Meaning?"

"What it means."

"Are you sure you're a match for Haj Thobane? If so, how?"

"Would you mind telling me what this is all about?" I growl.

"Please, Superintendent," Soria breaks in. "I know exactly where he's going with this and he's right. Two men have already been killed because of our investigation. I swear that their deaths will not go unpunished. You're wondering, Mr. Ali, how I intend to cross swords with a god like Thobane, who flourishes by doing whatever he likes with no respect for laws or the people who want to apply them? I'm not alone, believe me. I have solid backing, important people in authority who are up to date with my research and wouldn't hesitate to back me up if I discovered anything serious enough to put Thobane up against a wall. I would never have started on this business if I hadn't been sure I could mobilize people who could carry it through to the word 'end.'"

"I won't keep anything from you: that's what I thought. It gives me complete reassurance, now that you confirm it. Because I've got some revelations for you, and they're major."

His voice suddenly goes husky. The moment he has been fearing has arrived. He has just remembered the dangers that await him and a glimmer of doubt flashes across his face. Soria looks at him intently, as if to breathe some of her determination into him. Rabah Ali's proud demeanor is somewhat diminished; he hesitates slightly, tries to pull himself together. There are beads of perspiration on his forehead; his lips are dry.

"You have to go ahead, Sy Ali," says the chicken farmer encouragingly. "I trust this lady."

Rabah Ali thinks about the farmer's exhortation and somehow manages to overcome his misgivings. He goes into a neighboring room and comes back with a small spiral-bound notebook, which he slaps down onto the low table in front of Soria. "I've kept this for twenty-five years. Now I want nothing more to do with it."

"What is it?" asks Soria, turning pale.

"It belonged to Ameur Talbi. I was the one who was ordered to escort them that night," he tells us. "And I mean 'escort.' I didn't know there was going to be any rough stuff. I was barely twenty years old, and my hands were still clean. I was ordered to find the Talbis and tell them to pack their bags. A truck was put at my disposal for the mission. In those days, I didn't argue with orders or ask myself questions. At nine thirty, I knocked on the Talbis' door. My rifle wasn't loaded. That shows how little I knew what was going to happen. Ameur Talbi wasn't expecting our visit. He said there was a misunderstanding, that the Lefty would never send anyone to his house. I said I had strict instructions and that I had to drive him and his family to post number thirty-two. Ameur Talbi told me he couldn't come anyway, because his wife was semi-paralyzed and his younger son had a forty-degree fever. I had no radio or telephone to talk to my superiors. Seeing my uncertainty, Ameur Talbi gave me this notebook to prove that I had the wrong person. I opened the notebook to read it. At that moment a jeep drove up. It was an NCO. Without getting out of the vehicle, he shouted at me to hurry up. I tried to explain that we might have the wrong person. He yelled at me that if I wasn't at post number thirty-two by ten o'clock he would tear off my skin with pliers. Ameur Talbi had heard. The orders were clear. I told him that everything would be sorted out once we got to post number thirty-two and that there didn't seem to be any reason to panic. He nodded and fetched his children. Two of my men helped him carry his wife. We went up to post number thirty-two and I missed the rest. Jelloul must have told you what happened afterwards."

Soria wants to know what the Lefty had against Ameur Talbi. Frightened by the seriousness of what he has revealed, and knowing he has gone too far to turn back now, Rabah Ali slaps the notebook down on the table again. "What, you still don't understand? Ameur Talbi was the Lefty's closest collaborator, his most trusted confidant: he was his treasurer."

A thunderbolt exploding in our midst. The shock is such that the pen Soria has been holding in her hand snaps in two. Her face is a waxen mask.

I am numb, and the rest of Ali's words fail to reach me. It's enough for me to watch his mouth working his gall. Cosmic hissing fills my ears, blotting out the screams of the wind in the trees and the drumming of the rain on the roof.

Chapter twenty

I can hardly recognize Soria. A strange blend of rage and intense joy has altered her features. She didn't utter a solitary word while Labras drove us back to the hotel. I could only feel the constant trembling of her body, transmitted to me through the leather of the back seat. She didn't even thank the chicken farmer when she let him go. Once in her room, she threw herself at her suitcases in a sort of frenzy and started rifling frantically through her things.

"What's got into you?" I ask her.

"I'm packing up and getting out of here."

"Do you have any idea what time it is? It'll be dawn soon."

Her mouth twists as she straightens up. Her staring eyes look me up and down. "Don't you get it yet, Mr. Llob? For the first time in his life, that monster Haj Thobane is in a hole, and I'm dead set on turning it into his grave. To do it, I have to strike while the iron is hot. One tea-break, one delay, one distraction and he could turn the situation in his favor. I won't give him the chance. I'd rather die. I want him to fall, and the sooner the better."

"We need some sleep. It's a difficult drive, and the weather outside is foul."

"No rest until the war's over. May I remind you that you have to rescue a lieutenant who's languishing in the shit? In his situation, time is worth more than gold; it's survival. In any case, I'm so excited I couldn't possibly sleep anywhere. If you're tired, I'll take the wheel. I promise to get you home in one piece."

"What about my car?"

"Give me the keys and papers. I'll send someone to get it tomorrow."

There's no point arguing. She's already elsewhere. I put a brave face on it and go back to my room to pack.

I don't last long. About a hundred kilometers in, I slump down in my seat. Soria wakes me as we enter Algiers. She needs me to direct her to my home. I direct her in a daze. She drops me off in front of my building and vanishes, forgetting that my bags are in the trunk of the Lada.

My watch says it's five o'clock in the morning. Somehow, I climb the stairs. On the third-floor landing, I struggle in vain to overcome my dizziness. This makes two nights in a row that I haven't shut my eyes. Mina opens the door, her pretty face puffy with interrupted dreams. I collapse into her arms and let her take care of me. I have a vague recollection of her taking my shoes off. My head buries itself in a pillow and immediately drags me down into a wonderful abyss.

I sleep like a log. The sun is on its way down when I come back to my senses. Mina is sitting on the side of the bed and smiling at me. She has touched up her make-up and emphasized her eyelashes with kohl.

"I've run you a bath," she chirps.

"I certainly need one."

While she's soaping up my back, I ask whether there have been any phone calls.

"Apart from Monique, no one."

"What did she want?"

"There's a wedding this weekend. I said I'd think about it."

By the evening I'm fit to be tied. Soria hasn't shown any sign of life. What drives me mad is that I didn't once have the presence of mind to get her address. I don't know where she lives, or how to get in touch with her. The more the telephone continues to brood in silence, the worse my mood gets. I'm so disappointed I don't touch my dinner. Toward midnight my temples start throbbing again. Mina begs me to come to bed. I dig my heels in. In the end, I collapse on the padded bench in the living room.

Same again the next day. I stare at the telephone all morning, like the dog in His Master's Voice. Apart from routine calls, nothing. Soria persists in her neglect. I speak briefly to Baya, to see if a woman has tried to reach me at the office; the answer increases my disquiet.

Mina avoids confrontation; she has learned not to rub me up the wrong way when my jowls look like a constipated mastiff's.

Late in the afternoon, Fouroulou, the neighbor's son, tells me there's a woman waiting for me in her car in front of the building. If anyone had timed me getting dressed, I think I would have earned a place in the Guinness Book of Records. Mina has hardly had time to turn round before I'm out in the street.

Soria is done up from head to foot. Certain that she's holding the winning cards. Squeezed into a breathtaking suit, with her daring breasts and her dazzling manner, she plants a greedy kiss on my cheek.

"Careful," I say, to calm her down. "Do you want my wife to drag me to court?"

She throws her head back in a laugh that embodies true happiness, all by itself. She slaps my thigh, hard.

"I've hit the jackpot," she cries. "I spent yesterday knocking on doors and my prayers have been answered. As of now, we have three solid supporters. Two politicians and the most powerful lawyer in the country. They won't back down. They're known for that. And I haven't even told them everything. They know I have the bull firmly by the horns and they're happy to hear it. I guarantee they'll march beside us to the bitter end. But that's not the best of the good news. Guess who called me less than two hours ago."

"I'm too exhausted."

"Che!"

"Chérif Wadah?"

"Himself."

That wakes me up.

"If that man is with us, the match is as good as won," I tell her.

"He is. He's expecting us at his home."

"When?"

"Now."

And she takes off like a shot.

I can't remember seeing anyone so euphoric, except perhaps for Inspector Bliss on the success of some particularly brilliant piece of chicanery.

"We're going to blow him sky-high, that cardboard monster, Superintendent," she cries in jubilation. "I promise you they'll be gathering him up with tweezers."

"Better not leave the car in the road," Joe advises us, having first looked right and left to be sure the way is clear. "I'll open up the garage."

A big wrought-iron gate judders as it opens onto a tiled court-yard. Soria backs up a little and slides her car under a canopy of bougainvillea. Joe shows us where to park and hurries back to close the gate.

Chérif Wadah, looking serious, is standing at the top of a short staircase, with his hands in the pockets of his bottle-green dressing gown. He has put on some weight. Freshly shaved and with his hair brushed back, he has recovered some of his former charisma. When he sees me heading toward him, he spreads out his arms. "The great Superintendent Llob."

We greet each other in the dignified terms that befit the war-riors we used to be. He is very happy to see me again. Soria waits her turn on the top step, a satchel at her chest. Our host invites her to embrace him. She doesn't make him ask twice.

"You're magnificent, my beauty," he whispers. "If I were twenty years younger, I'd marry you four times over."

"Give me a break!" the historian replies, laughing.

"I didn't know you knew each other," I say, feeling jealous.

"Soria is my muse," the old *zaïm* tells me. "I love her like my own daughter. We first met five or six years ago—"

"Eight," Soria corrects him.

"She studied me a lot, even wrote a book about me."

"Two," the historian explains. "A biography and a volume of conversations."

"That's right." He leads us into an enormous living room strewn with handmade rugs. The walls are covered with huge, very old black and white photographs in which our host may be seen, sometimes in his *maquisard* getup, with a machine gun slung around his neck, sometimes tieless, in baggy worker's clothes, posing beside the great figures of our revolution. In some of them, the late President Houari Boumediène is recognizable, in others President Tito of Yugoslavia, the Vietnamese general Giap, Fidel Castro, King Faisal Ibn Saud, King Hussein of Jordan, the Libyan leader Muammar al-Gaddafi, and President Nasser of Egypt. Chérif Wadah has been shot from all angles in the company of these great men, sometimes laughing out loud with some of them. Impressive.

"So, my lovely princess, what can you tell me that's good? I got the call this afternoon. It seems you're in possession of an atomic bomb."

Soria spreads the contents of her satchel out on a small table. "You won't believe your ears, my dear Che."

First she hands over her notes. Che studies them attentively while the historian lays out her argument. After half an hour the old man is no longer nodding his head. Shaken by her revelations, he is holding his head in his hands and listening to Soria's report without interrupting. His forehead is deeply furrowed. I intervene with a word here and there. I tell him about the various stages and the difficulties we encountered in our investigation. Tarek Zoubir's story makes his face crumple. He sighs with vexation and looks up. His eyes glow; beneath them, his cheeks twitch with indignation.

"Unbelievable, unbelievable," he mutters.

He stands up. With his hands behind his back, he paces up and down the room, furious and stunned at the same time.

Feverishly, he says, "God gave men the best of Himself. He made the world like a water-color painting for them, so that their eyes would be awakened to beauty, put stars in the sky to guide them, built enchanting horizons around them to arouse their interest. But

He forgot to put a brake on their need for cruelty, and all His generosity went for nothing.... God shouldn't have rested His hopes on the very creatures that excel in disfiguring His image. He should never have believed for one second that we were incapable of ingratitude. All the unhappiness in the world stems from that misplaced trust."

Soria now gets her tape recorder out of her pocket.

"And now the climax of the show," she announces, pressing the button.

Che sits down again. Rabah Ali's voice pours into the room like a river of lava. The universe retreats around it, fragments, dissipates. There is nothing left but the tiny reel turning in its cassette, setting free, bit by bit, the unbearable narrative of our key witness at Sidi Ba. It is several minutes before Che notices that the reel isn't turning any more. His face cloaked in inscrutability, he rings for Joe and orders him to fetch his pills. The former boxer complies. Having swallowed his medicine, the old man asks leave to retire to his office to think. We tidy up our papers and wait an eternity for him to return. Through the window, the evening has dismissed the last glimmers of daylight. A moonless night is preparing to magic the city away.

Che catches us fretting. He is himself again, and his features are relaxed.

"Algeria and God wouldn't forgive us if we filed this matter away," he decrees. "Such atrocities will not remain unpunished."

Soria is relieved. The old man suggests that she shouldn't get too carried away, saying, "It won't be a cakewalk."

"We've got enough to ruin him," cries the historian.

"Haj Thobane is no ordinary citizen; you don't just turn up at his house with a warrant and some handcuffs. He is a permanent member of the Political Bureau."

"You're a member of the Political Bureau too," I remind him. "Your charisma is as huge as his influence."

"Things don't happen the way you think they do in the higher realms. It's more complicated than that. Personal interests are closely linked, as are complicities and networks. If one pillar comes down, there's a chain reaction, a domino effect. Many of the regime's dinosaurs would feel themselves directly threatened if one of them, whether an ally or a dissident, was targeted. The System has survived so long only because the mini-universe it has made for itself is watertight. Within the centers of power, you can disagree, or even shoot each other down from time to time—all's fair in war—but when the threat is external, all those enemies close ranks and form a single bloc, compact and solid. Besides, a heavyweight like Thobane doesn't only have interests; he controls an army of disciples and pawns who wouldn't want to see the manna that flows from his heaven compromised. It won't be easy to unseat him."

"Easy, no, but possible," says Soria. "He's just a crook with blood on his hands. He's strong because no one knows how he got where he is. What we have will expose him, naked as a worm, to public opinion. His closest friends will drop him. When the stockade has been breached, everyone tries to keep his head down. I'm sure of it. What you say is true, Sy Chérif. But only if the conspiracy is exposed or aborted. When the worst happens, you go back into your shell and keep out of sight. Up there, in the higher realms, U-turns are terrible. Let's not allow ourselves to be intimidated. We're within spitting distance of our objective. Let's go on. I've already written the article for my newspaper. With your support, the editor will accept it for publication. You know very well that no one can stand that vile and ugly reptile Thobane, not even his own family. He's scum, and he isn't held in high regard, but feared like the plague. The country will be grateful to us for ridding it of him. It would be awful if we didn't carry it through after so much effort."

"Who said anything about throwing in the towel?" asks Che calmly. "If anyone here never gives up, it's me. I know what this individual represents for the future of the nation: the worst of all disasters. The problem lies elsewhere. What is the best course to follow? That's the real question. One false step, and it could all be turned against us. He would come out of it stronger than ever, and no one would dare stand up to him. It's double or quits time."

"Will you agree to help me publish my article?"

"In all the main newspapers," he says emphatically. "In Arabic, French and Chinese, if that's what you want. But it won't be enough."

"I'll need a television crew too. I'm going back to Sidi Ba

tomorrow, to cover the excavation of the mass grave. Labras is driving me. We'll film the exhumation of the bodies and the whole world will see it on the television news."

"Whatever you do, don't rush it," says Che.

"I don't care; we've got to act fast, very fast. Our success depends on timing. If that bastard suspects anything serious, he'll get in ahead of us and block our exits."

"Do you think he isn't already aware?"

"He doesn't know the most important thing. He thinks we've drawn a blank, that our arm-waving is just much ado about nothing. Otherwise, he would have set his dogs on us already."

Che asks us to calm down. Our discussion goes on for several hours: Soria will have her television crew; her article will appear in the major national newspapers. But we need some additional evidence, without which our enterprise will fail. *"And that's where it's up to you to pull out all the stops, Superintendent,"* Che says to me in an aside. Upon which we shut ourselves up in his office to iron out every tiny detail of our plot.

Algiers is radiant. The purity of the sky inspires her. She relaxes and gives in to pleasure, spangled with light, her bay like an immense smile. The sunlight of broad day shows off its muscles on the square. As for me, I'm full of myself. I feel good in my mind and good in my body; I'm off to topple a god from his Olympus and, by the same token, enter into mythology. Anxious not to blow it, I check regularly to see that my Beretta is still there and that the mike is still securely taped beneath my undershirt.

I have made an appointment with Haj Thobane at three o'clock sharp. At three o'clock sharp, I park my Zastava in front of number 7 Chemin des Lilas. The grille rattles the moment I press the buzzer, confirming to me that I am very much expected. A stocky individual, size extra large, blocks the doorway and then stands aside to let me through. As soon as he has closed the door, he proceeds to search me.

"We're not at Roissy airport," I comment.

He pays no attention to my remark, feels the folder I have in my hand, runs his expert hands around my ankles and between my thighs and discovers the surprise beneath my armpit.

"No firearms here!" he barks, holding out his hand.

"I'm on duty."

"Give me your gun, please."

"Out of the question! A cop has to keep his weapon about him even when he's getting laid."

Another extra-large specimen, on guard duty on the terrace, signs to him to let it go. The gorilla grumbles. He moves on ahead, limping slightly. Like a newsflash, Kong's story of the two heavies spotted in the gray Peugeot 405 at Sidi Ba sparks in my mind: *the other one has short legs and limps a bit...* We cross Haj Thobane's property, which produces wonder after wonder. A whole country: marble avenues through a tropical forest, low stone walls dancing around miniature palm trees, sculptured lampholders every five paces, rectangles of magnificent garden bounded by tiny babbling brooks, a small zoo with peacocks strutting about in a group of quadrupeds: a pair of gazelles, a doe, two caged fennecs, a young zebra and other cute little animals brought in from distant lands.

Haj Thobane is sitting in an imposing wicker throne, facing his fellow animals. He is wearing a desert robe, with his belly in his lap and a fat cigar in his mouth. At his feet is one end of the most beautiful swimming pool I've ever seen in my entire lousy life.

He dismisses my escort with a wave of his finger. "You wanted to talk to me, Superintendent?" he bellows, getting straight to the point.

I don't panic; quite the contrary, I thrust my hands in my pockets and spend some time admiring the landscape.

"All you need is a flag, and farewell to the republic," I suggest.

His eyebrow twitches. He turns his head slowly and stares at me. "Have you been to see a doctor, Mr. Llob?"

"Yes. He said I was certifiable."

"I think so too."

"I don't, Mr. Thobane."

"Are you sure you think anything?"

"Why wouldn't I?"

He crushes his cigar in an ivory ashtray shaped like a shell. And sinks into a disturbing silence, the way a storm does.

"I went to Sidi Ba," I tell him. "Shame an agricultural area should go in for uncontrolled industrialization. It has ruined its poetry and corrupted its minds. But I wasn't bored."

"I know. Others have been there to mess about with my legend before you. They ruined their voices as well as their teeth."

I move closer to him. His face convulses with indignation. Either he's a hypochondriac or he can't stand the proximity of nobodies.

"Still, it's an area that suffered greatly from the war," I continue with detachment. "All you'd have to do is scratch the ground at random and you'd find human bones."

"Do you think freedom is delivered like a pizza, Mr. Llob? Algeria's cost at least a million and a half martyrs."

"There weren't only martyrs."

"I don't count enemy losses. That's not our problem."

"There weren't only enemy losses."

He turns his whole body toward me, hoping to put me in my place. I wink at him to show how determined I am. He looks through me like an x-ray. I can tell by the way his left eyelid is twitching that he's beginning to smell trouble. Nobody would dare hold a conversation with him in such a casual way. Except a madman. That's what he thought of me to begin with. But the clarity of my delivery explodes that theory. Haj Thobane knows I've come to do battle; what unsettles him is that he doesn't know what weapons I hold, how they will perform in practice. Who's behind me? A wretched poacher or the whole forest? An unweaned bear or a fox on the point of bolting? My overt, even zealous, self-confidence is a massive gesture in itself. Why, he asks himself. Is this a fishing expedition or a stupid blunder? He is used to shouting for silence among those around him, and, throughout decades of abuses and cruelty exercised with the most impregnable impunity, has hardly ever encountered any resistance or argument, so he can clearly see the drift of my combativeness; it's just that he doesn't know what strategy to follow. So he waits for me to stumble, and let him gain the upper hand. Even I am surprised by his stoicism. Is it his age or is he too accustomed to excess? In any case, he seems improbably disconcerted, as though a destructive foreboding was secretly sapping his morale.

"Would you mind getting to the point, Mr. Llob?"

"Many innocent people were sacrificed too."

"Come on, that was inevitable. Where there's disorder, people will get hurt."

His philosophy doesn't convince me. I don't try to hide it. He works out that it's going to be difficult to change my mind; he can see where I'm headed and has read my coded insinuations loud and clear. He looks me in the eye for a long time, trying in vain to make me look away. With a sigh, he agrees to defend the indefensible:

"It was war. There were no guilty or innocent people, no executioners or victims, just people who were in the wrong place at the wrong time and people who took other people's lives in order to save their own. Sure, some people shouted louder than others, and some cried victory at every opportunity. But in fact the whole nightmare was having a laugh at their expense. In the end, there were neither winners nor losers, just those who lost everything and those who played their cards right, but even they didn't escape completely unscathed."

I carry on, stubbornly, "Some of the innocent people didn't just happen to be passing by, Mr. Thobane, and they weren't really just unlucky."

"It happened. It's unfortunate, but that's the way it is."

"The most unfortunate thing is that the executioners have never had any reason to worry since."

"What good would it do? You can't bring the dead back to life. What's done is done. Today, with the benefit of hindsight, you realize you could have avoided quite a few excesses, with a minimal amount of good sense. Hate and anger were in the ascendant, and nobody could do much about it. We were in a hurry to get it over with, and we botched everything that came our way. We weren't even supposed to ask questions. There was only one dazzling horizon: the independence of our country. The rest—our lives, our deeds, our gestures, our mistakes and our abuses, were carried away on the tide of our commitment. We didn't stop along the way, we put our heads down and charged toward freedom, and if we knocked a few things over on the way, or walked over the corpse of a friend, we didn't say sorry. We wouldn't have expected apologies if it had been us being trodden on. That was the agreement. When you take up arms, you take things as they come; good or bad, you have to accept them. That's the only way you have any chance of forcing destiny's hand.... Besides, I'm not telling you anything new. You were a *maquisard* and you know what it was like."

"It's true, I was a *maquisard*, but my motives weren't even close to yours, no matter which way you look at it. I was fighting for independence, not for what I intended to make out of it afterwards. For me, surviving the war was the finest gift God could give me. I was overcome by the idea of being reunited with my family, my house, my little foibles. Other people looked further ahead. They were already dreaming of sharing in orphaned fortunes, influential jobs and the privileges they guaranteed. It's not the same thing, you must admit. Putting up a flag outside the new town halls wasn't enough. Some people wanted to substitute themselves for what it represented: they wanted to become masters of the country. Because they were shepherds before, they didn't know how to become governors, and went on treating people like livestock. But that's not what we're here to talk about, Mr. Thobane.... I've come to stir up some shit for you."

I expect him to fly off the handle, or at least to order his men to beat me up and then show me the door; instead I am granted a sad and tired look, the look of an old god who is beginning to realize that he is mortal. Not even the vulgarity of my language has shocked him. It's as if he has understood that I am not drawing on my investigator's logic for my strength, but on the stealthy gathering of forces that has gone on behind me, of whose determination my person represents a sample. Haj Thobane is a first-rate crook. He has overcome more tests than a titan, avoided traps in industrial quantities; if he has survived this long, in a country where machinations are of surgical precision and treachery is soberly calculated, it's not just because he was born under a lucky star.

"Carry on, Superintendent. I can assure you you have no idea of even a hundredth of the shit you're about to land yourself in."

"You have thrown a lieutenant of police into a dungeon, Mr. Thobane. You have accused him of making an attempt on your life out of jealousy. It turns out this poor cop is there for no reason at all. That you have been the victim of your past, which has finally caught up with you. I don't know how he obtained my colleague's weapon, but your attacker had every reason to have it in for you. He was trying to avenge himself, and his family, who were executed by your orders on the night of the twelfth to the thirteenth of August nineteen sixty-two, near Sidi Ba, where you went by the name of the Lefty. That night, three other families were wiped out; none of them managed to escape. The Kaïds, rich landowners; the Ghanems and the Bahasses, owners of the biggest fortunes in the region. No survivors, no heirs. Their property became the spoils of war, which were, in their turn, diverted to personal ends—yours. The other family, the Talbis, left a survivor: Belkacem, who has been in confinement since nineteen seventy-one, under the name of SNP, and who was granted a presidential pardon last November. This boy, who was only about twelve years old at the time of the mass killings, survived only in order to find you and settle the score. He may have missed, but I won't."

"The families you mention had collaborated with the enemy. They were tried and convicted by an FLN court-martial. Their fortunes didn't interest us. The Talbis were as poor as Job. Everyone in Sidi Ba knows it. So why were they executed, if the object of the exercise was just to get hold of the guilty parties' property?"

I brandish my file folder in the air before I slap it down in his lap.

Coolly, he takes out a bundle of photocopies.

"What is this?"

"Read it. It will refresh your memory."

He turns toward the interior of the villa and orders someone to bring him his glasses. The limping gorilla hurries up immediately. Haj Thobane puts on his glasses—the lenses enlarge his eyes out of all proportion—leafs through the documents and doesn't seem to be bothered by them.

"I don't see what this means, Superintendent."

"You're looking at a copy of the accounts kept by Ameur Talbi during the war. Every single cash deposit handled by him on behalf of your battalion is entered, as well as every disbursement signed by your hand. We can easily calculate the income and expenditure, the totals of various donations, subscriptions and other financial contributions from citizens, Muslim and Christian—extortion, too—collected in the Sidi Ba region between March nineteen fifty-six and June nineteen sixty-two. To wit: forty-five million old francs in cash, one thousand and thirty-seven gold louis, twelve kilos of loose gold, fifty-two precious stones with a total value of three million...in short, all the loot you never declared to the FLN and which you pocketed once the war was over."

"Get out—"

"Ameur Talbi was your secret treasurer. You executed him, along with his family, so as not to leave any traces—"

This is the last straw. Haj Thobane is on his feet, shaken, distorted from head to foot, with a gun in his hand.

"I have a microphone on me, and several people are listening to our conversation with interest as we speak. Sorry, but I had to take certain precautions. Two men have already been killed this week, in Sidi Ba, for less than this. Their murderer forgets—like other murderers—that you can kill witnesses in their thousands, but you'll never completely kill the truth."

The fist with the gun in it goes pale at the knuckles and trembles.

"You're not going to shoot me, you see."

"I'm not likely to dirty my hands with the blood of a dog," he growls. "Other people are paid to carry out that chore."

"I'll try to be vigilant."

"Too late."

"Do you think I made a serious mistake in coming to you, Mr. Thobane?"

"Get out of here. Go get your lump of sugar, before your masters change their minds."

The two gorillas grab me by the shoulders and manhandle me toward the exit.

I twist round to gloat at the vulgar god: "You can keep the documents as a souvenir. The originals are in a safe place. See you very soon."

"Get lost!" drools the gorilla at the back of my head.

Haj Thobane's tenebrous eyes watch his men drag me through the tropical forest. He must be asking himself two questions: what sauce to serve with me, and, most important, when to come to the table.

Soria calls to tell me she is back from Sidi Ba and everything went well. Her three-page article will appear tomorrow in the main national newspapers. She advises me to remain glued to my armchair and not to let the small screen of my television out of my sight; her report will be on the television news at eight o'clock. At five to eight, I declare a curfew in my house. Mina and the kids, just as tense as I am, join me in the living room. I haven't told them anything, but my over-excited state has got them wondering. Only my youngest stays in his room, cursing as he crosses swords with his homework. The television news opens with a single headline: *Mass grave uncovered at Sidi Ba; 27 bodies found, 15 of them children.* The pictures are of a bulldozer turning over the soil, men digging up human skulls, various piles of bones, witnesses telling their versions of events, the same ones, learned by heart; panoramic view of the mountains of Sidi Ba, close-up of the town, damning commentary. Archive pictures take us back to the war years: groups of *mujahedin* marching through the snow, French airforce planes dumping napalm on Muslim villages, burnt faces, peasants fleeing their devastated villages, women and children huddled among their belongings on rough carts; then it's back to the mass grave, where a quavering old man tells the dramatic tale, pointing out a path and the surrounding area. The reporter expands on the statements of the witnesses who were interviewed earlier, then disappears, to be replaced by a recent picture of Haj Thobane, immediately followed by older ones, taken within the *maquis*, of the famous Lefty showing off a field radio-communications post captured from the enemy in an ambush, taking aim at a target with his machine-gun, the whole thing narrated in the cavernous tones of a funeral oration…. All around me, frozen silence. My two grown sons and my daughter are turned to stone. Mina is holding her cheeks in her hands, and her eyes are swollen with tears. The noise in the apartment next door has stopped; normally, at this hour, it's hard to tell which is louder: the shouting or the crashing about of children. The whole building is holding its breath. I think it must be the same in the rest of the country.

"Dad!" my youngest yells from his bedroom. "How am I supposed to go over my notes with this racket going on? The phone's been ringing for hours."

I feel as though I'm emerging from a cave, and it takes me a while to absorb what my son is shouting. Finally, the sound of the telephone gets through to me. I run to it and answer; it's Haj Thobane.

"You idiot," he says in a remarkably serene tone of voice.

After a short pause, he goes on, "Tell your sponsors that they shouldn't count their chickens before they're hatched."

He hangs up.

Mina finds me in our bedroom, holding the phone queasily in my hand and staring into space.

At five forty-five in the morning, the telephone makes me sit up in bed.

It's Nedjma, Haj Thobane's little friend. "Come quickly," she sobs. "Something terrible has happened."

Part three

"Dying is the worst thing you can do for
a cause. For there will always be a race
of vultures hanging over the ruins and
the sacrifices, cunning enough to pass for
phoenixes. They won't hesitate for one
second to use the ashes of martyrs to make
fertilizer for their Edens, or the tombs of the
missing to make monuments of their own,
or the tears of widows to make water for
their mills."

Brahim Llob, *Autumn of the Phantoms*

Chapter twenty-one

Daylight spreads itself carefully over Chemin des Lilas. The night must have been worrisome around here. People probably took tranquilizer shots in order to get some sleep. It's natural: when your neighbor is lynched, it means the anger of the masses isn't far away. I imagine the shock the nabobs of Algiers must have felt in front of their televisions last night. It wasn't the Haj Thobane scandal itself that churned their guts from top to bottom, but the realization that nothing is truly hidden. If someone has dared to strip a living legend naked, it's proof that any petty tyrant can be easily stripped. Which explains why staying in bed is the preferred option in this little slice of paradise. You won't leave the house before making phone calls right and left to ascertain the magnitude of the shock wave that's about to break over the city. In the meantime, you stay in the warmth, breathing in the smell of your blankets or sniffing at your own perspiration, since the streets aren't safe anymore.

Outside, the sky is livid. Not a cloud to hide its face. Soon, the sun will focus its beam on the scale of the destruction. It's not every day that a dinosaur is dragged through the mud; the gigantic streaks will be perceived a long way away. One is curious to know what sort of chaos one is in for.

I park my Zastava in front of number 7. Here, in particular, the silence augurs something irreversible. A bit like the one that surrounds you when you realize you're right in the middle of a minefield. I don't let it get to me. Having crushed my cigarette stub out in the ashtray, I step out of the car and shut the door firmly to give myself some impetus. I am lucid. In possession of all my faculties. It's going to be a beautiful day. A few birds, buried in the foliage, are tuning their vocal chords. There's no hurry.

Nedjma opens the door before I've finished fondling the doorbell. She is showered, made up, coiffed: she doesn't look as if she's about to go into mourning. In her state of undress, surrounded by the most delicate of scents, she resembles a fairy emerging out of a cloud of smoke. Her eyes, sparkling like jewels, are those of a poetic muse, and her lips look like temptation itself. Now that I permit myself to look at her close up, I can't remember ever seeing such complete beauty. Her twenty-five years crown her freshness like a diadem. Everything in her is nigh on perfect: the regularity of her features, the tilt of her cheekbones, the clarity of her gaze and the excellent design of her figure. Quite a specimen.

"How are you?" I ask.

"I haven't asked myself the question yet, Superintendent."

She asks me to follow her. Lino would have followed her all the way to hell. When she walks in front of you, this woman blots out the rest of the world, starting with its snares and pitfalls. If she walked on water, you would find yourself skimming over it yourself. Her grace is a joy to behold, her appearance an epiphany.

I try to keep my head screwed on; it's impossible to tear my eyes from the mesmerizing dance of her hips.

I look for the gorillas, or at least a flunkey on the prowl for an order or a signal; not a soul in the gardens.

"Are you alone?"

"Yes."

"What happened to the bodyguards?"

"Haj sent them all away yesterday."

We go into the palace. I don't think even the king of Jordan would last long if he started strutting about here. The magnificence on display would make the gods on their comets envious. It's incredible what men will gather around their minute persons during their ephemeral lives. Even more incredible when you think that, after such ostentation and such blasphemous riches, they consent to rot at the bottom of a dark hole for the rest of eternity.

Nedjma leads me straight to her lover's private den. Haj Thobane is there, surrounded by his mahogany treasures, his crystal knick-knacks and his hard-currency paintings. He is sitting in a padded chair, wearing a dressing gown, the upper part of his body slumped over the desk, his head resting on his left arm on top of a newspaper, his right arm dangling over the armrest with a huge revolver in his fist. The bullet smashed his temple and took away half his skull, fragments of which have sprayed the wall with a skim of brains and blood.

I move closer.

The newspaper is open to a double page completely given over to the mass grave at Sidi Ba.

"I think reading this paper finished him off," sighs Nedjma.

"That's what it looks like at first glance," I agree. "Can you tell me what happened?"

"I was asleep when I heard a shot. I ran down and found everything as you see it now. I didn't touch anything."

"What about the servants?"

"I told you. Haj sent them all away yesterday. He wanted to be alone. He asked me to go away. I refused to leave him in the state he was in."

"How was he?"

"Strange."

"Meaning?"

"When they started shooting him down in flames on the TV, he didn't move. Or say anything. He just asked for a glass of water. He stayed in his armchair, calm, as if he was watching something completely banal. Of course, he didn't miss a single word of what was thrown at him during the news. But it was like someone else was being torn apart, someone he didn't know. Afterwards, he turned out the lights and told his servants and bodyguards to go home. He was calm. He just wanted to be alone to think about what was coming down on him. He came over to me, kissed my forehead and asked me to pack my bags and leave. I refused. He didn't insist. It was like he was suddenly tired of life. Once the staff had left, he called you, hung up and locked himself in his office. I decided I hadn't stayed in order to take refuge in my apartments and leave him alone with his grief, so I went to his office to comfort him. He was standing by the french window, with his hands behind his back, staring at the moon. I think he was expecting phone calls from his friends. Several times, he turned round toward the telephone and stood there, lost in contemplation. Since nobody was calling, he picked up the receiver, checked for a dial tone and put it back down, smiling at me. It was the saddest smile I have ever seen in my life. It tore me apart and I ran to him. He took me in his arms. He was more bitter about his friends than angry about those who had conspired against him.... You know how it goes, in our country. Every god is worshiped until his vulnerability is exposed. Immediately, those who used to lick his boots start hungrily snapping at his heels. That hurt him a lot."

"Did he spend the night in his office?"

"I managed to get him into the living room. We talked about the times we had shared together. He asked if I held anything against him, if he had been improper toward me, if he had hurt me somehow or other. I said that on the contrary, I had been unable to be worthy of his kindness and generosity, that he had indulged me so far that he had almost spoiled our happiness. I wasn't lying, Superintendent. He was a good man, charitable and emotional. He couldn't bear other people's suffering, and anyone could ask him for anything. The people who pushed him to suicide are dogs; their fleas will devour them faster than their remorse."

We go into the living room. Set up as if for a ceremony. No sign of violence, not a single false note.

"Why call me?"

She spreads her arms wide:

"I was Haj's mistress, not his secretary. I don't have access to his diary. His friends were not my friends and I was forbidden to answer the telephone when it rang. He was discreet, not jealous. When I found him swimming in blood, I panicked. Who to call? I don't know any of his relatives. Then I remembered the last phone call he made. It was you. I pressed 'redial' and you were on the line."

"Am I to understand that no one knows about this drama?"

"No one."

"We're going to have to stir everyone up."

"Do what you have to do, Superintendent."

"How long did you stay in the living room?"

"I don't know. Until midnight, maybe."

"And then?"

"We went up to our bedroom. I could see that something terrible was running through his head."

"How, for example?"

"His calm was intriguing. It wasn't a habit of his. He would roar for a yes or a no. He was even impulsive. His anger kept him stable. After a good bout of shouting he would recover his aplomb. That night, his silence frightened me. I feared the worst."

"Did you have the impression he was going to kill himself?"

"That he would react with extreme violence. Kill himself or kill both of us. I know him very well. I've never seen him the way he was yesterday. It was distressing, very distressing. He lay down on the bed. I put some sleeping pills in his fizzy water and kept watch until he fell asleep. You know what happened after that. A shot woke me up. Haj had just committed suicide."

"So you fell asleep yourself?"

"After an evening like that, of course I did!"

"Nobody came here in between?"

"No one."

"Maybe you didn't hear them."

"Impossible. If someone had shown up here, the bell would have alerted me. The intercom is on my nightstand."

"So who brought him the newspaper, at a time when the kiosks are still shut?"

Nedjma becomes confused. It's about time. Her unruffled demeanor seemed excessive for a mistress who has just lost her patron saint. Her delightful eyebrows frown as she racks her brains for ideas and can't manage to find a way out. As she lifts her eyes to me, I notice that her lips are distorted, twisted by a discomfited grimace.

"You're right," she admits. "Maybe he went out while I was asleep."

"The kiosks aren't open for another thirty minutes."

"Sometimes, when there's important news, he calls the printers. He knew the prints would follow the television news—"

"That explanation doesn't hold water. If he had called the printers, you would have reached them when you pressed 'redial.'"

"In that case, someone brought it to him this morning," she concedes.

Nedjma is embarrassed.

I ask her to show me the room where they spent the night. She obeys, with her mind elsewhere. The business with the newspaper is awkward for her. She hasn't given it the attention it deserves. I follow her along a corridor lined with revolutionary frescoes glorifying the bravery of our resistance fighters; paintings with no real talent, but jingoistic enough to force one's respect. Nedjma walks ahead of me. Her progress has lost its nobility; it's as though she is fleeing, or trying to pull herself together.

The bedroom is huge, with no fewer than four french windows enveloped in velvet curtains held back by imposing gilded ropes. A large four-poster bed covered with silk drapes occupies the center of the room, flanked by two nightstands and a roman-style couch. Opposite the bed, a monumental mirror reflects the daylight back across the room. The walls are painted off-white. As for the two chandeliers cascading down from the high ceiling, they are absolute marvels and must have cost the skin off the backs of a thousand honest civil servants.

Nedjma asks my permission to leave the room for a couple of seconds; I grant it willingly. Relieved, I inspect the place at leisure. I spot Haj Thobane's reading glasses on a chest of drawers, a glass on the nightstand—this I slip into my coat pocket—a spiral-bound notebook by the foot of a lamp; I rummage about in the drawers, shift a few stacks of files, find a few insignificant things, nothing really interesting. The sound of the toilet flushing brings me to my senses. Nedjma finds me admiring an oil painting showing the deceased at his peak.

"It was done by Alessandro Cutti, a famous Italian painter," she informs me with a hint of aggression.

"I would have been surprised if it were by Denis Martinez."

"Who's that?"

"A famous Algerian painter."

The doorbell interrupts our discussion. Nedjma frowns and goes over to answer the intercom.

"That must be the forensic team from Headquarters," I tell her. "I asked them to meet me here."

"Why a forensic team, Superintendent? It's suicide."

"Just a formality, *madame*," I assure her.

Haj Thobane is handed over to the gravedigger in less than forty-eight hours. I don't know whether this is to follow Muslim tradition or swiftly to turn the page on this odious episode in the legend of our revolution; in any case it is done remarkably quickly. A burial permit issued by a slovenly municipal official, a few spadefuls of earth, a pair of grotesque flagstones instead of a tombstone, all preceded by a funeral march. No fanfare, no guard of honor, not so much as a glimpse of a crown. The notables of Sidi Ba are absent, most conspicuously the mayor. There's not much of a crowd; fifty-odd dust-covered peasants, rushed in from their villages as an emergency measure, a group of former fighters, senile-looking and trembling with decrepitude, and an obscure *imam* who keeps getting his verses wrong and strutting about, very much on his dignity. Some visitors go back and forth in front of the gathering, picking their noses. The ambulancemen wait impatiently so that they can get their stretcher back and leave. An old man in the background is the only one to sob, held up by a young boy. This must be the deceased's brother. The occasional comrade tries to console him, without conviction; some resent the spectacle he is making of himself.

The ceremony is abbreviated, reduced to the absolute minimum. People are there to be sure that the monster is well and truly dead, not to tell stories about his little peccadilloes. No party officials have seen fit to bestir themselves either. The dead man doesn't have the right to the respect due to his rank; the scandal has automatically stripped him of that. I notice two or three journalists, one of them a short-sighted photographer. The evening papers will give him a paragraph next to the obituaries. Just enough to confirm the rumor and give the survivors something to think about.

As the remains are being placed in the grave, I turn on my heel and head for the parking lot, where Serdj is keeping watch over my wreck. He didn't want to go to the funeral; graves make him ill, he says.

"What are we doing?" he asks.

"You choose."

He suggests a cup of coffee by the sea front. I shrug. On the way, he realizes I am depressed fit to grind down a tank and decides it is wiser to drop me off at home.

Didou is waiting for me at the entrance to my building, looking crestfallen.

"What is it now?"

Didou is a taxi-driver by trade. Not a week goes by that he doesn't get a ticket. "I swear I didn't do anything this time," he begins. "I was carrying a passenger, and when I came to a junction I got stuck in a traffic jam. The guy behind me started honking his horn and flashing his headlights at me like a machine gun. He seemed to be in a hurry, but I couldn't move forward or move over to one side. So he called me every name under the sun. I didn't react, I swear. I followed your advice."

"Not entirely, I see. What do I mean by that? You still insist on beating about the bush."

Didou takes off his mangy hat and rubs it. My impatience makes him uncomfortable, and he doesn't like taking short cuts.

"It was a police sergeant, Brahim. He confiscated my papers and impounded the one tool of my trade. The kids don't have anything to eat any more. I swear I didn't do anything. There was a traffic jam...."

Then he gives me this persecuted-victim look I've never been able to resist. I find myself promising to take care of it first thing tomorrow. Didou is so relieved he takes my head in his hands, almost sobbing, and kisses the top of my skull.

That's Algeria for you: one tyrant lost, a thousand recruits hot on his heels. Abuse isn't an aberration for us, it's a culture, a vocation, an ambition.

Mina has prepared a feast for me: a wild-mushroom omelet. I eat my portion, hers and some of the children's, then I go to my room to ruminate. Just as I am reaching the deepest part of my slumbers, my daughter shakes me.

"Dad, it's Headquarters."

I stagger into the hallway and grab the receiver.

"Yeah?"

"The guys in the lab want to you to get in touch with them," Serdj tells me.

"What time is it now?"

"Twenty past three."

"Would you mind coming to pick me up? My car's at the mechanic's."

"I'll be in front of your building in a quarter of an hour."

The police forensics laboratory is in the basement of an administrative building adjoining Headquarters. It used to be a store-room, where all sorts of things were shoved away, a sort of chute down which you could push compromising files, worn-out typewriters, stale ideas and even new thumbscrews. Then there was a flood, and it was necessary to clear the basement out from top to bottom. Since the police had just acquired some new investigative equipment that was sophisticated and coveted by other branches, the bosses decided to set up a laboratory. Ever since, the men who slave away there contract all kinds of illnesses, and nobody knows whether it's because of the equipment they use or the damp.

Bachir, the director, welcomes us in his cubicle; the glass I removed from Haj Thobane's home the previous night is in prime position on the desk. From the way he's blinking, I sense that he has hit the jackpot.

"Well?" I ask.

"You were right, Brahim. There was a big enough dose of tran-
quillizers in the contents of this glass to put a mule to sleep for two
nights in a row."

"Are you sure?"

"The analysis is definitive. It's Stilnox. A powerful drug. One
tablet and you can go through a catastrophe and not notice anything."

"In any case, he didn't survive it. And on the gun?"

"Only the dead man's fingerprints."

I take Serdj by the elbow and go out into the fresh air. What
I had feared is catching up with me. I would have preferred things
to calm down so that I could go back to a normal life. Not a chance:
the Thobane affair is bound to break cover again, and I'm not sure
I'm flexible enough to catch it in mid-flight.

"Something wrong, Superintendent?" says Serdj, worried.

"How about you take me down to the sea front? I feel like a
really good cup of coffee to get my ideas in order."

"Are you sure one cup is enough?"

"As long as I'm not paying."

A maid, no longer young, but fresh out of her wrapper, opens the
door. I give her my particulars. She doesn't understand my gibberish
and asks me to repeat it. I suggest she goes and gets her mistress and
tells her Superintendent Llob would like to see her. She comes back
a few minutes later and takes me to the swimming pool. Nedjma is
stretched out on a lounger, with her sunglasses up in her hair. She
is reading a fashion magazine, with her dressing gown open over her
perfect legs.

"Good morning, Superintendent."

"Morning, *madame*."

"Isn't it a glorious day?"

"If you have the means."

She puts her magazine down and faces me, her elbow on a
cushion. I can't say it often enough: this girl is temptation in its most
acute form. Her wide eyes cast a spell over me. I can feel my calf
muscles twitching below my carcass.

She offers me a chair beside her. Why not? I say to myself.

There's no law against dreaming. I undo my vest to give my belly some freedom and lie down near these sulfurous influences. Suddenly, my lounger turns into a flying carpet.

The maid appears with a tray loaded with fruit juice and imported cookies. She puts it down on a small table and leaves.

"Is she Algerian?"

"I think she's from Yemen. She worked as a cook in the Algerian embassy in Aden. A diplomat friend recommended her. She can do anything. She's amazing."

I watch the maid walking away.

Nedjma sits up to serve us. The top of her gown falls open, revealing firm round breasts like apples plucked from the Garden of Eden. I try to take an interest in a pair of gazelles, but I can't tear my eyes from the splendor within reach of my fingers. Nedjma notices the confusion developing in my soul and conscience; her falsely modest hand rearranges her gown.

She holds out a glass of orange juice.

I swallow a mouthful and smack my lips admiringly. "Excellent."

"Isn't she amazing?"

"Everything here is amazing."

She rewards me with a smile that would arouse a legless cripple. "You really think so, Superintendent?"

"I certainly do!"

She leans back again, puts her sunglasses over her eyes and, without carrying the nectar to her dazzling mouth, says, "Did you just happen to be passing?"

"To tell the truth, *madame*, I never *just happen* to pass through the wealthier areas. It has to be a real necessity for me to venture there. I hate rich people. Their good fortune makes me sick."

"Pity."

"Why a pity, *madame*?"

"You don't deserve to suffer because of other people's happiness."

"It's often a trap, you know."

"As long as there's enough to eat and drink, we don't generally give a damn."

She decides against her drink and puts it down on the

table. Suddenly, she despises me. "Would you mind telling me what gives you the right to come and depress people around here, Superintendent?"

"I'm here to clear up three or four fuzzy details, as part of my investigation."

"Investigation into what?"

"The death of Haj Thobane, of course."

She frowns. I watch her hands; they stand up to my examination very skillfully. This woman, I think, has character; she knows what she wants and how to get it.

"Are you serious, Superintendent?"

"Have I said something foolish?"

"You must have. Since it was suicide. The press reported it—"

"The press writes what it's told to write, *madame*. We're in Algeria, in the socialist era, don't forget."

"Where do you see any socialism? In this heavenly residence?"

"In the practices of the day, *madame*."

She tosses her hair down her back. Her profile, that of a goddess, extends her elegance all the way to her high, full breasts before flattening her majestic belly, which is graced with a navel that is so delicate one would unquestioningly accept it as the sign of the Lord himself.

"What is it that bothers you about this suicide?"

"A bunch of dead ends."

"For example?"

"The gun in his right hand."

"What of it?"

"Haj Thobane was left-handed. That's why he was called the Lefty in the *maquis*."

"I've seen him use both hands without difficulty."

"Perhaps. But have you seen him read a newspaper without his glasses?"

She starts.

"His glasses weren't on his desk, beside the newspaper, *madame*. They were in your bedroom, on the nightstand."

"Perhaps he left them there when he went to fetch the gun."

She will always surprise me, this Nedjma. The liveliness of her intelligence is a feast.

"Perhaps, again. The problem is, how did he manage to wake up, given the dose of sleeping pills you gave him? According to our analyses, a nag from the Aurès mountains wouldn't have survived it. Haj Thobane can't have woken up or dragged himself to his office, never mind being clear-headed enough to think about what was happening to him. He was practically incapable of lifting his little finger to scratch himself."

"What are you getting at, Superintendent?"

"This: your story doesn't stand up. Haj Thobane was murdered, *madame*. With or without your assistance."

Nedjma sits up, her fingers clasping her knees. Her sunglasses hide the expression on her face, but they can't hide the twitching of her cheekbones. Her fury comes boiling up to the surface; she doesn't attempt to contain it.

"Do you realize what you're saying?"

"Absolutely."

"I doubt it, Superintendent."

She stands up and, unwilling to waste one more second with an overdressed killjoy like me, picks up her towel and struts back to her apartments in a gust of wind.

I can see the maid coming back, so I raise my hands and come down from my flying carpet. "No need to worry about me," I call out to her. "I know the way out."

I haven't had the strength to check my mail. There are three files lying about on my desk, between the telephone and the blotter. They've been there for days, sealed like oaths. Baya comes in from time to time to check that I'm still alive. The expression on my face bothers her. Twice she has tried to remind me of something and then held back. The portrait of the president opposite me seems to be poking fun at me. Whenever one of us catches the other's eye, my heart hiccups oddly. I don't know what to do with myself. Yesterday, after leaving Nedjma, I went for a walk along the sea front. I walked for kilometers without noticing. There's no doubt that Algiers offers fate that is blind; as you walk, she slips away before your cares, like a disturbing mirage, even as the depths of your discomfiture open up behind you in proportion to your disillusionment.

The boss isn't back yet. His courtiers say that his convalescence still has a good way to go. Despite the fall of Haj Thobane, his anxiety refuses to go down even a notch. I thought about going to visit him at his home, but I was afraid of aggravating his condition. I'm so awkward when it comes to being polite.

In the boss's absence, Bliss has taken the place over. He rules the roost with an iron fist, the pitch of his scream higher than the flag on the façade of the building. He's only a lowly inspector, a nobody on the hierarchical scale, and yet the staff neither grumbles nor argues. Among us, the interregnum is often filled by men who can be trusted—boot-lickers and yes-men—seldom by ranking officers.

I miss my Lino.

Funnily enough, just as my eyes happen to fall on the lieutenant's office, Ghali Saad calls me. He starts, in his cheerful way, by congratulating me on the job I've done, talks to me about how my success has begun to sweep away the grayness of the years of lead, about the relief of the laboring masses, now rid of a tyrant, about his certainty that he will see the country rediscover the magic of former times… when I don't respond, he asks whether I'm still on the line. I assure him that I am still there, at the end of my rope, like a hanged man. He finds my metaphor too much, and turns it aside with a sugary laugh. The receiver is heavy in my hand. I feel like hanging up and going somewhere far away, where no one can reach me. Ghali Saad gets down to business. He begins by informing me that he wore out his fist banging on the desks of the biggest of the bigshots to get a hearing, and that after staggering feats of special pleading, backed up by well-constructed reports and emotional statements, he has managed to win the day: Lino is free!

* * *

My lieutenant has left his septic tank for a clinic on the heights above Algiers.

I cross the city in a whirlwind, provoking curses at every turn.

I even run two or three red lights. The doorman at the clinic raises the barrier as soon as he hears my tires screaming. A kind doctor explains that the officer arrived early in the morning in an indescribable state and that he is in the best room in the institution and in excellent hands. I ask to see for myself. He rings for an assistant and hands me over to a huge nurse who looks as though she is trying to touch the ceiling by standing on tiptoe.

We walk down a number of glistening corridors. A few sick people hobble about here and there, under the watchful eye of a medic who looks like a prison guard. Lino isn't in his room. A nurse has taken him out in a wheelchair for a breath of air, we are told. We retrace our steps and go into a garden. Lino is there, under a tree, with a blanket over his legs, looking like a torture victim in an electric chair. With his arms crossed limply over his knees and his back bent under the weight of the nightmare he has experienced in the jails that don't exist, he is staring at a corner of the lawn and not moving. On his ascetic face, marked forever by man's infamy, is an expression of suffering. The handsome lad of Bab El Oued is a feeble vestige of his former self. I wouldn't have recognized him if I had come alone.

"We'll get him back on his feet very soon," the nurse promises.

I turn on my heel to get out as quickly as possible.

"You don't want to see him any more, Superintendent?"

I look at her. "Not in his present state," I say, swallowing hard. "He would resent me for it."

She nods. "Yes, I understand," she sighs.

I have already left.

In an effort not to isolate myself with my anger, I take Mina with me to visit Monique. I have no interest in shutting myself away in my room and continually seeing in my mind's eye the picture Lino presented. A private conversation with myself, in a situation like that, would finish me off.

Monique greets us with her usual friendliness. She is very pleased to see me and won't stop fooling around, in the hope of driving away the veil of bile covering my face. I try to take the bait, but I can't find it in the troubled waters of my bitterness. Mohand watches me from his corner. He sees that I'm primed to go off like a bomb and chooses not to rub up against me too much. After a while, the flow of Monique's stories slows down, and finally dries up completely in the face of my black mood. Dinner is eaten in a disconcerting silence. At about ten, Mina asks permission to take me home. She is disappointed by my performance. We found our hosts in a jovial mood and we spoiled their serenity.

As they are seeing us out, just as I am preparing to go down the stairs, Mohand suddenly says to me, "You still haven't told me the story about the gravedigger who wanted to become a caver."

I give him a look for a moment and then grumble, "Don't you know it?"

"No," he says.

"He changed his mind."

Upon which note I go down the staircase, feeling as though I'm dissolving away in my troubles.

The next day, I hear that Nedjma has flown off to Frankfurt: now I have nothing at all.

Nevertheless, I go back to number 7 Chemin des Lilas. I must know what really happened. The maid hesitates a long time before letting me in. With her mistress gone, she behaves a little as though the house is her own. Her apron is in the wardrobe, her hair is loose, and she is living the dream in broad daylight. Judging by her tanned skin and bloodshot eyes, she must be spending her time in the swimming pool and lounging in the sun, sipping endless pitchers of fruit juice. My unannounced visit seems to spoil her pleasure; worse still, she endures it like a crisis of conscience: she feels guilty about abusing *Madame*'s privileges while the latter is elsewhere.

I exploit her inner weakness to wrong-foot her:

"When did she leave, exactly?"

"No more than an hour after you left."

"She didn't behave like someone who was about to fly off somewhere. Did you know she was planning to leave?"

"No, *monsieur*."

"Do you think it was because of me?"

"I don't know, *monsieur*. When you left, she went into her bedroom. Probably to make a phone call, because she called me right away to pack her bags."

"How was she?"

"What do you mean?"

"Was she nervous, excited, calm…?"

"Normal, as usual. She was neither rushed nor angry. She took a shower while I was getting her bags ready. I helped her do her hair and make-up. She was calm. When they came to get her, she was ready."

"Was it a taxi?"

"No, it was a big black car with tinted windows. A tall gentleman took her suitcases and put them in the trunk. Then he opened the door for *madame* and they left straight away."

"Did she say where she was going?"

"No."

"Or when she would be back?"

"*Madame* never tells me anything."

"Did she take a lot of baggage?"

"Enough for a long stay."

I hold my chin with my thumb and index finger, to show the maid that the situation is a massive problem for me. Seeing my discomfiture, she gulps and starts fidgeting with her fingers. I choose this moment to get down to business. "May I see her bedroom?"

She starts visibly, as if taken by surprise, and looks around. "I don't know whether that's proper, *monsieur*."

"I'm a cop, I have every right."

She can't deny it. She's just going through the motions. I am touched by her voice when she says, timidly, "Can I come with you?"

"Of course. I just want to make a phone call."

"There's a phone in the hall."

"I'm allergic to draughts."

She raises her arms in surrender.

I go into the bedroom, where everything has been carefully tidied away, pick up the telephone and press redial. Immediately after the first ring, a siren voice chirps, "Good morning, general secretariat of the Bureau of Investigation."

I put the receiver down quickly, as if I had opened a trapdoor and come face to face with the ghost of an ancestor. The maid is taken aback by the violence of my movement. I reassure her with a wave of my hand:

"It's nothing. I'll call from my office. It's safer."

Chapter twenty-two

To understand what goes on in Algeria, you have to imagine the following picture: in an Olympus whose higher circles have fallen into disuse, in the absence of the loving God, four demons are trying to gain control of the interregnum—Beelzebub, Lucifer, Mephistopheles and Satan. Below, the people are reduced to base influence-peddling; they are on the point of giving up their souls, which each of the aforesaid demonic creations wants to damn.

Superintendent Dine isn't following me. As far as he's concerned, literature and philosophy are on the senile side of human folly. By his own admission, he's never touched a book apart from scientific texts and manuals. He abhors them, and almost pities me when I'm polishing up a manuscript. Right now, strangely, his Adam's apple is trembling. He has immediately guessed that this is just an opening gambit. The expression on my face would make an alley-cat's whiskers stand on end, it's true, but it's the dancing flames in my eyes that worry him. If he only knew, poor man, he would have stayed at home eating lettuce leaves until he turned into a rabbit. But he chose to invite me to a lavish meal, and now discovers that the tax, which he hadn't foreseen, exceeds the bill. He must be chewing his fingernails to the bone. With me, you always get your money's worth. So I spill out what's on my mind. In a single vomit. Taken aback, he doesn't have time to put his smile away. First he frowns, then sucks in his nostrils. The more I spill the beans, the more his hair stands on end, even the hair in his ears.

"Do you hate me that much, Brahim?"

"I don't hate you."

"So why do you come here and add to my troubles with your idiotic story? I just wanted to see you and have a laugh or two over a friendly meal."

"I thought you might like to know the truth."

"The what? You're the one turning your back on the truth, that whore. If you want my opinion, you spend too much time with your books, and that distances you from reality. The real truth is that you're just a big fat disgusting flea, puffed up with air, that loves rubbing up against thorns. You just have to play the mischief-maker. Even if there's no water in the river, you have to go looking for eels under rocks. What's the point of this nonsense? Even the devil would hang up his hat. I warn you right now: I didn't come here to listen to rubbish. I get enough of that from my wife."

"Nevertheless, he was killed."

Dine panics.

"Not so loud," he begs.

"As far as I'm concerned, Haj Thobane was well and truly murdered," I emphasize, unmoved.

"I heard you…for heaven's sake speak quietly."

I touch my chin to the table and whisper, "He was ex-e-cu-ted."

"That's enough. Cut it out now."

He looks round at the few customers at nearby tables. They seem fine, absorbed in their desserts. The girl in the corner gives us a wary smile; she can't hear us, unless her hearing aid is very sophisticated. The waiter ignores us; he's facing the kitchen, waiting for a dish that has been ordered.

Dine takes a deep breath. "You're imagining things, Brahim."

"Maybe—"

"Haj Thobane committed suicide."

"Oh no he didn't!"

"He killed himself for good and all, you'll see."

"It's not true. He was eliminated."

Dine wipes his neck with a napkin to get rid of the sweat that has just appeared there. My stubbornness terrifies him. In the little restaurant at Belcourt, where he invited me to celebrate Lino's release—a place where, he wants me to understand, he is well known—my every word sets off a series of stinging sensations.

"You're not well, Brahim. You've blown a fuse. Haj Thobane put a bullet in his own head. Dinosaurs don't survive when their universe burns down around them. He hadn't expected this disaster, it's as simple as that. He'd never thought it possible and he hadn't prepared for it. He held himself above the fray, far from unpredictable annoyances. And bang! He's thrown. He didn't get up again. What else could he do? Defend himself? He didn't know what it meant. Deny it? A waste of time. Pick up his routine where he left off, as if nothing had happened? People like that don't know how to say sorry. Either they grab everything or they give up everything. Thobane couldn't be satisfied with a life disrupted—especially not after he'd been flattered for decades. He couldn't bear having people look him in the eye and question his historical legitimacy. He understood that the die was cast, that there was no conceivable retreat. All or nothing. That's the law of the hydras that rule us. It's a law that doesn't go into the particulars. And nor do those who have chosen it. Thobane died the moment he and his aura parted company. His extreme act was just the natural extension of a process of withdrawal. He chose to die the way he chose to live: with no appeal."

"That's the summary. The script for the scene is more developed."

"Only in your warped mind."

"Why won't you just think for a couple of seconds, Dine?"

"I hate that kind of brain exercise. It always degenerates. Personally, I don't give a damn what really happened at number seven Chemin des Lilas. What's in it for me, besides a lot of shit?"

Dine is beside himself. He thought he was offering me a moment of relaxation; I'm turning it into torment. I don't like disappointing him, but I can't help it. It's important to me to know whether

I can rely on my friends. On my own, I won't get any further than the end of my nose. Right now, I'm dying to do battle. I've been an ordinary little puppet in this business, and it bothers me day and night. Why me? Why Lino? I can't reconcile myself with the notion that the lieutenant's idyll was a simple crush, of the kind people get all the time in these years of serious sexual frustration. Lino was thrown into Haj Thobane's path deliberately. His gun was found on SNP's body as part of a plan to reel in a sucker.

Who is the king of suckers?

Probably a resentful old cop who was fed up with twiddling his thumbs and felt ready to pounce on any new case to get back in the saddle. He wanted trouble, so he got buried in it. Unceremoniously. Almost with a laugh, even. Otherwise, what was the significance of the string of blunders that followed? Those summary executions, carried out "as if they were formalities" don't necessarily indicate amateurism. Maybe it comes down to over-confidence, as if the killers and their sponsors had nothing to fear from a turning of the tables.

"Brahim," breathes Dine, exhausted. "It's over."

"What do you mean?"

"Shelve the case and go back to your kids."

"I've been used."

His belly shakes with a short dry laugh. "Somebody's always being used, Brahim. That's how things happen. There's no need to feel cheated. When you put on a uniform, you take off your pride. Besides, they're two irreconcilable attitudes. There's no point beating yourself up about it. You're a cop, and like all cops you go where you're sent. When you investigate, you're following a profession, not necessarily a vocation. Whatever you do, don't try to see what's behind it. You'll be overcome with vertigo."

"I'm not a tool."

"That's where you're wrong, Brahim. We're all just pawns on a chessboard. Supposing you're right and Haj Thobane was murdered—God, the idea gives me the willies," he grumbles, wiping his temples, "what do you care? It's the bigshots' business. Small fry aren't invited. A few higher-ups are having a kind of clear-out in the harem. Hell, they can do what they want, it's their home! You were brought in to play a small part in the purge. The toilet has now been flushed. Now you wipe yourself, go home and try to lock your door properly, that's all. It's not complicated, for crying out loud."

"Is it you giving me this speech, Dine?"

"And what am I if not a mouthpiece, Brahim? What were you expecting? That I would congratulate you on your cleverness? If you came here to hear me glorifying you and encouraging you to go into the lion's den, you got it wrong. I've got kids and a fine wife at home. My work ends where the territory of the gods begins. As long as my bosses order me to carry on, I move forward. If suddenly there's radio silence, a red light goes on in my head. I know my limits. I've gone down some strange paths myself. Sometimes, you find yourself in forbidden clearings. That's when you sound the retreat, and I can promise you I'm the first to turn back, as quick as I can. I'm neither a prophet nor a dispenser of justice. I'm a superintendent and I obey orders, period, the end."

He grabs me by the wrists.

"Strictly between you and me, Brahim, would you be big enough to stand up to them? They've just eliminated the man everyone thought couldn't be toppled. Just like that, with a snap of the fingers. He was a guru, that man. He had friends at every level and armies of followers. Better protected than a holy fortress. And look how they messed him up. From one day to the next, it's as if he never existed…. We don't belong in their game. It's too big for midgets like us. The odds are huge, and we're microscopic. Trust me, Brahim, and drop it. You're just a fly buzzing around a cow's ass; a simple fart would blow you to pieces. If you want another piece of advice, don't tell anyone else what you just told me. In our country, trust is the first step on the way to perdition."

The waiter brings our steak frites and disappears. Dine continues to wipe himself with the napkin, his lips almost white. He pushes his plate away with his other hand.

"You've taken away my appetite."

"Sorry," I say, digging my fork into a piece of potato.

"Honestly, Brahim, what is it that attracts you to the shit?"

"Let's say my idea of honesty is different from yours."

"I'm honest."

"Really?"

"About myself, to start with. Knowing your limits is already a way of not abusing yourself."

He stands up.

"Are you leaving?"

"I'm getting out while I can, Brahim. I'm going to ask for two weeks' leave to go somewhere a long way away from your heedlessness. I don't want to waste my meal every day."

He leaves his napkin behind the way you might throw in the towel, goes off to pay the bill, and leaves the restaurant without looking at me.

I feel a bit left to my own devices, like a spore at nature's whim. Soria Karadach hasn't shown any signs of life; Chérif Wadah has gone abroad, so I'm told; the boss has granted himself a sinecure at Hammam Righa; Headquarters is like a sheep-pen, open to the four winds, and Algiers is behaving like a straitjacket. I go back to the clinic to see Lino. He hasn't got his color back, but he's coming back to life bit by bit. The conversation wasn't long. I sat down on the edge of his bed and we looked at each other and couldn't find the words. The doctor joined us. After a few kind words, he noticed that we weren't in the mood. He left with a funny look over his shoulder, no doubt wondering whether we came into the world just to spoil the few joys that still exist here.

I went back to work the way the proverbial Halima returned to her comfortable old habits. Neither too early in the morning nor too late in the evening. My irritability is still present, but I don't see the need to make a meal of it. What today keeps to itself, the future will tell us. This doesn't mean I'm disheartened. In this life, it's not enough to know what you want; the important thing is to get it. For the moment, I don't know how. So I wait.

Serdj has taken over the files that have been stagnating in my drawers. He's a good man, Serdj. If I lost my false teeth, he would offer to serve as my jaws. I've seen inspectors expend themselves unstintingly, but none of them come up to his ankles.

Baya has put on a bit of weight. Her breasts have expanded and the generosity of her hindquarters is more and more distracting to the staff. Every morning, she arrives with a handbag full of Swiss chocolates. From this I gather that her new stallion has learned his lesson better than his predecessors. Those damn redheads! Their intentions are so explicit they make their hair burn.

Bliss, for his part, is taking himself very seriously indeed. He watches over the place with rare devotion. The interregnum has whetted his appetite. Ever since the boss came close to swallowing his shirt, Bliss has been behaving like an absolute monarch. He has bought himself a shiny new three-piece suit and a pair of certified authentic Ray-Bans, and his severe tie lifts his chin considerably. We met once in the corridor, and he got upset because I walked past without saluting him. It's extraordinary how the heights can go to their heads, especially when their reign is subject to chance. A few minutes later, he called me to assign a minor task to me. I realized I had to remind him of the proper order of things, because at this rate he would soon be holding out his hand to be kissed.... Fortunately, matters are going to go back to normal. The latest news is that the boss is doing wonderfully: he was caught with his tongue up a nurse's pussy; which goes to show that he's regaining his sanity and his taste for sinful pleasures.

One morning, at about a quarter to ten, someone calls me on the telephone. His voice is very faint. At first I can't make anything out through his panting; he speaks so quickly I can't keep up. The man explains that he can't stay on the line very long and begs me to meet him at Café Nedroma, not far from Headquarters. I ask him who he is. He hangs up, insisting I keep our appointment. I weigh up the pros and cons. It's very hot in my office and the air conditioning is out of order. Ten minutes of hurrying later, I reach the café in question, which is opposite the bus station. A sparse few customers decorate the interior: crippled old men, a few travelers waiting for their bus to arrive, and one or two disillusioned boys. Apart from the fat cashier watching me from behind his counter, none of them seem to pay any attention to me.

I look at my watch: I'm on time.

A man walks in, a basket on each arm, looks around all the tables for a familiar face and leaves, cursing.

Not my man.

Three minutes later, the telephone screams. The cashier picks up, listens distractedly and growls, "Your mistake, *kho*. Wrong number."

Hardly has he put the receiver down before it rings again. This time, the cashier wakes up. His face becomes more and more flushed as the crackling in the receiver goes on.

"Hey!" says the cashier irritably. "I didn't hang up on you, okay? I just said it was a wrong number. This is a café and not the police-station switchboard. Your cop doesn't work for me, okay? So stop yelling because I hate it."

I yank the receiver from his grasp.

"Hey! You…"

I show him the gun under my vest, which is considered the most intelligent short-cut for showing your professional credentials. The barman retreats against the mirror, holding up his paws.

"It's not a hold-up," I say. "I don't even have a bag to put your pathetic money in."

He nods in agreement but doesn't dare put his hands down.

At the other end of the line, the stranger is still complaining about the cashier's lack of cooperation. He is hopping mad and shouting so loud I'm afraid my otitis will flare up again.

"It's all right, it's Llob. Why aren't you at the café?"

The stranger calms down. After a couple of sniffles, he squeaks, "I can't come to the café."

"What? You make an appointment with me and then you stay home?"

"That's not it, Superintendent. I wanted to talk to you. I don't trust the phones in the office. They're all bugged. I never intended to go to the café. I just preferred to have our conversation on more reliable equipment."

"What about?"

"I'm in the shit, Superintendent. They're after my blood. I've been on the run for three weeks. I'm going crazy. I can't go home and I can't go to a hotel. If you could only see the state I'm in."

"I don't even know who you are!"

I can hear him panting, with loud traffic and people talking; he must be calling from a call box. "My name wouldn't mean anything to you," he says, clearing his throat. "I'm not in any of your files."

"What's the problem?"

"I killed a guy."

" . . . ."

"I want to turn myself in."

"Do you need the address of the nearest police station?"

"Don't make fun of me, Superintendent," he says, angrily. "It's very serious. I'm being hunted by the *High*, and I need someone to protect me. I want to surrender right now, but not just any old how."

"First of all, what's this *High*?"

"*High Society*, of course!"

"I don't get it."

"The upper echelons, for crying out loud!"

"I still don't follow you, pal."

He's sniveling into the handset. His trembling is drowned in the roar of a truck.

"I can't stay here long, Superintendent. They'll find me and do me in. You're my only hope. I turn myself in to you and you promise me a fair trial."

Judging by his feverish tones, the flames are licking at his heels.

"All right. I'll wait for you in my office."

"Stop making fun of me, Superintendent. If I show my face there I'm finished."

"What do you suggest?"

"That you come and get me. Alone. I don't want anybody with you. And you come immediately. I mean immediately. Or else I leave. Don't try to make a plan, Superintendent. You don't need one, because I'm turning myself in. To you, nobody else."

"What do you find in me that you don't find in the others?"

"You're not a crook. You don't know me, but I know you. I trust you."

"Where are you?"

"Over by the Castors."

"Not a place for picnics."

"That's right."

"You think I should trust you?"

"I promise you it's not a trap."

"It's big, the Castors."

"On the north side there's an old building site: two unfinished buildings. It's easy to find. If you're coming from Bab Ezzouar it's on your left. After the waste ground, you can't miss it."

"I know where it is."

"Very good, Superintendent. I'm already here, waiting for you. But remember: no escort. No friends. No colleagues. I have a view over the whole area. Anything suspicious, and I clear off." And his gasping voice cracks, becomes almost tearful: "Are you going to come and get me, Superintendent? On your mother's life, can I trust you?"

"I'm like a rock."

The building site covers half of a piece of waste ground at one end of a suburban area that seems to have emerged from a nuclear cloud. The track leading to it crosses a public garbage tip before breaking its teeth on a shantytown with its roofs gone and its windows filleted. The hideousness of the place recalls the worst heartbreak despair can bring. Heaps of rubble rise in the midst of the devastation like monstrous carbuncles, so awful that even the stray cats stay away. I check the area; as a no-go zone, you couldn't ask for better. My hand instinctively checks that my gun is in its holster; the coldness of its butt calms me down. I park my car behind a stripped-down site office and wait, ears pricked. On my left, an abandoned cement-mixer sits rusting among a mass of scrap metal and rotting girders. A mutilated fence does its best to mark out the zone, here standing up on swaying posts, there lying on the ground. On my right, a clump of shrubbery covers the ground for a hundred-odd meters and then merges with an immature copse of hirsute trees. In front of me, the two unfinished buildings look like misfortune herself, gray, skeletal, distressing.

A shadow appears from a bed of wild grasses.

I was expecting to meet a man, but it's a ghost I see before me. With his rumpled and dirty clothes and his worn-out shoes, this terrified man would make a conspirator run away quicker than a police raid. His long greasy hair is plastered against his temples, framing an indistinct face, pale as a dying man's. His swollen eyes won't stay still.

He drags himself warily to a position in front of the hood of my car.

I open the door; he leaps back, on his guard.

"Don't you want to get in?"

"Not immediately," he mumbles, wiping his nose with his sleeve. "Your colleagues might turn up."

"I came alone."

"I don't have to believe you."

"Don't you trust me anymore?"

He retreats, a pathetic sneer on his lips. "In my job, that's a deadly sin."

"And what is it you do?"

He stands up on tiptoe to check the surroundings, focusing on the copse. His fear distresses me.

He stares at me and murmurs, without emotion, "Occasional hit-man."

"Is that all?"

He clears his throat and spits a considerable distance.

His gaze, which seemed lost, hardens.

He says, icily, "Everyone does what he can to get by."

"What is an occasional hit-man exactly?"

He plunges his hands into his pockets and frowns heavily. He must be wondering whether it's a good idea to carry on with this conversation. Now that he has me in front of him, he's no longer sure of anything. A thread drips elastically out of his nose; he pays no attention.

He steps back five meters, shooting hunted-looking glances around the place.

"Superintendent," he goes on, insistently. "You must understand that I want to turn myself in. I've shot people and now I want to pay. Without remission."

"That's your right."

"The people who hired me are after me to eliminate me. That wasn't in the contract and I have no intention of allowing myself to be beaten to death."

"Spare a thought for the small amount of brain I have left. Tell me first of all who you are and why they're out for your blood."

"I was recruited by some higher-ups. I had killed a rival, the leader of a gang of thieves, who ran part of Tilimli. I was arrested and thought I was in line for the firing squad. That's when someone suggested I work for the higher-ups to atone for my sins. The offer was tempting. Not only could I start with a clean slate, but also I'd go up in the world. At twenty, you don't spit on everything. I dived in without hesitating. Well paid, well dressed, well housed. And easy jobs: awkward mistresses, intrusive gigolos, indiscreet servants. I found them and killed them. Nothing really complicated. I went back home and picked up the envelope in my mailbox. The rest of the time, I spent my cash like a lord. For ten years, life was sweet. Correct, I was. Not particular about my methods. And now, all of a sudden, my employers are trying to get rid of me. I don't think I've broken any of the rules. I can't explain what's happening. Three weeks ago, they kidnapped my girlfriend. I thought she'd dumped me. Wrong! My employers told me that if I wanted to see her alive again I had to surface. Was I hiding? Since I hadn't done anything wrong, I calculated there must have been a misunderstanding and surfaced. They took me to a house in the country and told me to keep out of trouble. They said things were turning sour, that I had to leave the country and that they were getting me a passport. I said okay. Later on, a gorilla turns up. I ask him if he has the passport. He says 'yes,' getting out his gun, and adds, 'it's even got a visa,' as he screws a silencer onto the barrel. I didn't need to fill in the blanks. I hit him. I ran into the woods with Warda, my girlfriend. The gorilla and another ape came chasing after us. They shot at us and told us to stop. Warda got a bullet in the thigh. I couldn't do anything for her. I don't know what happened to her. Me, I carried on running. This has gone on for twenty days. I can't go home. I don't know where to go, and I'm living like a dog."

"And who did you kill last? Maybe that's where your problems started."

"Some nabob's driver. The revolutionary who killed himself recently."

"Thobane?"

"Something like that. My contract said I should wait outside his villa and whack his driver. That's exactly what I did. I don't know why they want to get rid of me."

"Look, it wasn't you," I say to regain some lost ground, time to get my thoughts in order, because what I've just heard has knocked me sideways. "The killer was called SNP and had just come out of prison. He was liquidated."

"Rubbish. I'm the one who whacked the driver. And there's no way I missed him."

I search my pockets feverishly for my pack of cigarettes. My frantic movements frighten him; he thinks I'm going for my gun and gets ready to clear off.

"Just a cigarette," I yell, showing him the pack. "Do you want one?"

"It might be doped."

"Suit yourself."

"No, I won't take the risk."

I light my cigarette and suck on it greedily; the first few puffs warm up my ideas and ease the trembling of my hands.

"Why did you shoot at the passenger seat then, instead of the man who was at the wheel, if you were after the driver?"

"I was given a counter-order by radio. A tire had blown out on the way. The driver had sprained his wrist changing the tire. They told me right out that it wasn't him at the wheel. The rest wasn't rocket science."

He has just passed the test with flying colors. A confusing multiplicity of thoughts crowd jostling into my skull. None of them stand out in particular. Like a drunk when he wins the jackpot, I lose my bearings and find myself wanting several things at the same time. This man is the missing piece in my puzzle. And yet I can't work out how to bring him on board, nor where to start. I feel certain I have a terrifying bomb in my hands, and I realize I'm not a bomb-disposal expert. Suddenly, I understand how loaded with good sense Dine's words in the restaurant at Belcourt were. A burning hot iron takes up residence in my stomach. Sweat trickles down behind my ears, soaks my collar and starts eating away at my neck.

"I'm completely stunned," I say, to control the fear that's taking hold of me. "You shot him with your own weapon?"

"I've never carried a weapon. My employers give me one when it's time to do a job."

"Do you know that the weapon you used belonged to a cop?"

"That's none of my business. In my profession, the less you ask questions, the more chance you have of waking up after a good night's sleep."

"How did they get hold of it?"

"I don't have an answer to that, Superintendent. The guy gave me the gun in a little plastic bag. He was very insistent that I keep it like that. There were prints on it. I was supposed to wear gloves when I used it, put it back in its wrapper immediately afterwards and then leave it in a particular trash can...."

Noticing that I've stopped breathing, he thinks I'm playing a dirty trick on him.

"What is it, Superintendent? Doesn't my story interest you?"

"It's not that."

"So what is it?"

"I'm thinking."

"What about?"

"About what you've just told me."

"If you promise to protect me, I'll confess it all in court."

I gesture to him to keep quiet for a minute. I need to aerate my brain.

"So now what?" he says impatiently. "I'm not planning to hang about here."

The end of my cigarette burns my fingers. I've smoked it in fewer than ten puffs. My throat is burning and my palate is bitter with the taste of nicotine.

"Would you be able to identify your employers?"

"Not a hundred percent. They're two clever guys who come out only at night and stay in the shadows when they give me my orders. In all the years I've been working for them, I've never met them in the street, on the beach, in the airport or in a restaurant. And yet I'm a man who's always out and about. And I've not once found myself face to face with them. It's always them that know where to find me when they need me."

"If you can't even recognize men who have been using you for years, your story doesn't have a chance of standing up. This is a very serious business. It's out of the question for us to reach an agreement on the basis of fairy tales that no one can verify."

He lifts his head suddenly, and takes his hands out of his pockets. "What the hell's going on here?"

I turn to see where he's looking.

A cloud of dust has just risen up behind a bank of dirt, to the accompaniment of a rumbling sound.

"Son of a bitch," the ghost says angrily, "you promised."

A car appears at the end of the track. It's heading for us at full speed.

"I don't know who this is," I tell him.

"Like hell! You're all the same...."

The car, a big, black, hellish body, is eating up the road at a ferocious clip. The man is going completely green: "It's them. They've tracked me down."

Before I have time to get out of my vehicle, he has taken to his heels and fled toward the woods. I start pursuing him, but give up right away: the occasional hit-man has a nuclear reactor up his ass. He clambers up a heap of gravel in a single bound, runs along the fence and then starts sprinting at unbelievable speed, straight ahead, with his vest streaming out in his slipstream. I turn toward the mad car, with my Beretta in view. The driver sees me right in the middle of the track and applies the brakes but fails to slow down; the locked wheels gouge at the ground, slipping and sliding in a tremendous skid. Taken aback by the clumsiness of this maneuver, I remain standing in the dust. The huge body threatens to run me over, spins, passes within a meter of me, and smashes its front end into the cement mixer with a crash of metal on metal.

Stunned, I wait for the dust to settle before thinking about the disaster I have just escaped.

The driver opens the door, groggy but unhurt. He's just a kid. "I didn't see you, *monsieur.*"

"What the hell are you doing in that crate? Did you steal it?"

"Oh no, *monsieur*! It's my father's. He lets me take it sometimes so I can learn to drive, around here, where there aren't any people. I swear I didn't see you, *monsieur.*"

I run toward the woods, hoping to find my exhibit A hiding there. Despite my reassuring calls, my friend doesn't reappear. He must already be in hiding on the other side of town by now.

I went back to my office and waited. The next day I clock in at daybreak and ask to be left alone with my telephone. The stranger doesn't call. Not on the following days either. At the end of this wasted time, I face the facts; luck doesn't ring twice at the same fool's home. I put a cross against the call in question and decide not to worry about it too much. In the evening, I go out with Mina to change my outlook; during the day, I try to make sense of the things of this world. Yesterday, the doctor informed me that Lino is making a fight of it. He's still mistrustful of the nurses; on the other hand, he's getting on wonderfully with the other patients. And that's something.

On Thursday, early in the morning, Serdj announces that a body has been found in a scrapyard. We travel to the site together. The place is on the way out of town, on the road to Tizi Ouzou. We get there after an hour of slaloming about cursing. It's on the other side of a hill, on a pothole-filled piece of land where a few lonely trees despair of their birds. There are hundreds of cars crammed into less than a hectare, some of them nearly new, others in an inconceivable state. A barred gate, topped with a strip of barbed wire, opens onto a small yard with a bleached-out watchman's hut falling apart at its center. I honk my horn to announce my presence. The watchman comes out and peers at us and then goes back to fetch his keys. He is a big man, compact and sullen; his chest bulges beneath a leather waistcoat stained yellow with sweat in places. He is flanked by a scrawny dog that is too pathetic to act fierce without bringing down ridicule on itself.

He heads for the gate, undoes a big Chinese padlock and pulls the chain through the bars.

"I was about to hit the sack," he says reproachfully, unhappy at being disturbed.

"It's only just nine in the morning," I tell him.

"But I work nights."

He throws the gate open wrathfully and lets us through. I drive my car up to the hut and switch off the engine. Serdj gets out first, with me hard on his heels. The watchman chases his dog away and joins us. He has the sinister look of a man who knows nobody likes him and doesn't give a damn. He walks in front of us without looking at us, the scent of a rabid animal like an aura around him. He must pack a good hundred kilos into his one meter sixty, as well as concrete shoulders and thighs strong enough to tow a trailer. His shaved skull rests on a bulging neck, like a medieval cannonball on a worn-out shock absorber.

"Was it you that found it?" I ask him.

"Do you think there's an army of us here? I don't even have a stand-in."

He leads us through corridors cut through car bodies. The ground shakes beneath his feet. He's in a hurry to get it over with and go back to his nap.

"Why isn't the ambulance here yet?" he grumbles.

"It's on the way."

"I hope the ambulance men don't stop and get something to eat along the way. I want this crap taken away from here pronto."

"Are you so rude because your arms are too muscular?" I say in exasperation.

"I didn't ask you to marry me," he replies without slowing down.

"Cool your jets, big fella. I don't like the way you talk to us."

"Normally I don't talk, I punch."

"Your dog?"

He stops dead, walks back and looks me up and down. "So tell me, pig. Are you looking for trouble?"

"That's enough," Serdj interjects.

"Me, I don't go looking for trouble," he warns me. "I'm happy in my hole, okay? Do I make trouble for people? So stay well clear of my fist, pig. Whether you're a *houkouma** or you clear out monkeys' asses for a living, it's all the same to me. Nobody messes me about, you get me? I'm a watchman, not a tradesman's entrance."

Serdj slips between us, to reason with the ox and handle the pig. The watchman swallows his belligerence and walks off ahead. He arrives at the remains of a van and sets his hands on his hips.

"There he is. Up to you to take him away. Me, I'm going back to bed and having a snooze."

"Not so fast," I advise him. "We need to ask you a few questions."

"I'm not the one who did him in. I don't need a knife for that, pal."

"You found him, right?"

"My dog did. Ask him. I didn't see anything or hear anything. Max howled. I came. The dead guy was there, exactly like he is now. I haven't touched anything. I called the management. The management got in touch with you. That's all there is to it.... Shut the gate on your way out."

He leaves, short-necked and stoop-shouldered. His dog comes to meet him, wagging its tail. He kicks it in the ribs and shouts, "You always have to stick your nose in everything, don't you!"

I pay no attention to him and crouch down by the body.

It's my "occasional killer."

His hands and feet are tied up with wire, his torso is naked and his throat has been slit from ear to ear.

---

* *Houkouma*: functionary, regimental flunkey.

Chapter twenty-three

The fingerprints taken from the body at the scrapyard don't produce anything. A photograph, taken with care and distributed to all the police stations in Algiers and the suburbs, is a dead end. I have sent Serdj and other inspectors out to sniff around in the night clubs and swanky bars where young hoods go to blow their cash, without success. The array of dragnets organized around the matter come up empty. My "occasional killer" is completely unknown. I remembered Tilimli, how he told me he behaved like a chieftain when he was a young delinquent, and went there myself four times in the space of a week; the downturned mouths on the people I approached almost trickled down their chins. After trying everything else, I bring in the press. There too, the publication of a picture of the unknown man in the main national dailies, with the headline "Help identify him," finds no takers. Just once, a hoaxer called the switchboard and sent us down a blind alley.

My activities end up arousing the inescapable Bliss's curiosity. Now that the boss is getting ready to take up his post again, his dedicated spy would like to spice up the report he intends to submit. Needless to say, he has noted all the unexplained absences of his colleagues, the petty disputes and the transgressions, but that's not enough. He must have noticed the frenzy that has gripped my department and absolutely insists on knowing what's going on. That way he will have an answer to everything, proving his remarkable prowess as a guard dog for his master.

He comes in on tiptoe, rubbing his Ray-Bans on the back of his grenadine tie. After beating about the bush for a while, he gets to the point: "I asked for car number fourteen yesterday, and the head of the carpool told me you had requisitioned it."

"What of it?"

He puts his glasses back on his ratlike face. "Car number fourteen is untouchable, Llob. It doesn't leave the garage except on the minister's personal order. I thought maybe there was a delegation of VIPs to be driven somewhere. But no, there wasn't. I said, what's got into the superintendent, that he's driving around in a bulletproof car, classified as untouchable, without the authorization of the chief of police himself?"

"And you're here to find out the answer?"

"That's right.

I look him up and down for a moment. He looks as though he's come straight from the beautician. He's dressed up to the nines, freshly shaved—which further emphasizes his pixie-like cheeks—and smells stronger than a gathering of ten whores. The shoes showing beneath his sharply creased trousers are of a foreign brand; I've never seen their like in the shops I frequent.

"Was it the boss who gave you the combination of his safe?"

"Don't change the subject, Llob. A car from the restricted category left the Headquarters car pool without my knowledge. It's a serious breach of regulations."

"My car broke down, and my department's vehicles are hardly in better shape. I had an investigation to carry out and I took number fourteen for the morning. If you think that's worth including in your report to the director, go right ahead."

"An investigation, did you say?" he says, taking off his sunglasses. His yellow eyes glitter like a snake's when it finds a plump little mouse trapped in a hole. His reptilian tongue passes over his lips, his nostrils flare and his ears prick up.

"You heard me," I say.

"An investigation into what?"

I push my chair back to give my gut a rest from being pressed up against the desk, and sneer at him. "I thought I made myself clear the other day, Bliss. The boss left you his throne, but that doesn't mean you're the king. Even you wouldn't be stupid enough to think so. There's a hierarchy in this whorehouse. A ladder that gets ridiculed as much as our scale of values, with the difference that it's still in force. We all appear on an organizational chart, all the way from the big chief down to the security guards, and we're paid according to a clear and precise order of battle, without which we'd be chewing each other's heads off at every turn. Me, I'm a superintendent. You, you play your little games several grades beneath me. If it pleases you to forget it, that's your problem, not mine. Here, you're in *my* department. And you're not welcome. If I were you I'd go back to being a poodle on the third floor and wait for someone to whistle for you."

"There's a standing order that in the absence of the director, Inspector Nahs Bliss will act in his stead."

"You're right. There was one on my wall. It gave me the runs so badly I used it to wipe my ass. And another thing, Inspector. I know the regulations, and when an idiot of a director tramples them underfoot I'm under no obligation to applaud. Putting you at the helm of Headquarters is illegal. As long as it just gives you a hard-on, I don't mind. If, on the other hand, you're unwise enough to come into my office and remind me of the anarchy reigning in our various administrations, you don't have a chance of getting out unscathed. My advice is simple: go fuck yourself and don't tell anyone about it."

Bliss retreats, waddling. He waves a casual finger at me, threateningly, and giggles.

Once in the doorway, he turns round. "I almost forgot. I've got excellent news for you. You're going to Bulgaria for some training. The telex arrived this morning. Signed by Ghali Saad himself. With recommendations at that level, you'll be well placed in the harem. To think you hated big shots so much."

"I didn't ask them for anything."

"No kidding?"

"And I want nothing to do with this training. I'll cede my place to you."

"Unfortunately, I'm not a superintendent yet."

"That's the first intelligent thing I've heard from your mouth since the oil industry was nationalized."

He winks and disappears from sight.

Baya arrives on her stiletto heels. She has made herself up like a rubicund goddess and put an inflammatory red on her lips. Her tight blouse makes her breasts leap about like two fat rabbits caught in a net. First she listens to Bliss's steps as he leaves, then says enthusiastically, "Is it true, what I just heard?"

"That depends how long you've been there with your ear glued to the door."

"You're very unfair, Superintendent. I don't get involved in arguments between my superiors."

She puts a big envelope down on the blotter. "This came in the mail," she explains.

"I don't see a sender."

"Well, it wasn't me."

She picks up a completed file and presses it to her chest like a schoolboy with his comic book.

"Is it far, Bulgaria?"

"It's not next door."

"It must be a nice country."

"Why do you say that?"

"Well, of course it is. You'll change your ideas, see new faces, new towns, new ways of thinking. Me, I'm game for any new horizon. I really need to get out of here."

"That low-cut dress suits you."

She blushes with pleasure. "You noticed, Superintendent?"

"Of course! Now take cover, honey. The envelope might be booby-trapped."

She nods and goes back to her cubicle.

I tear the envelope open and take out a creased old photograph in which five *maquisards* with rifles slung over their shoulders are saluting toward the lens. They are in a clearing. In the background there is a kind of blockhouse or cave camouflaged with branches. The men are rather young, and pleased to be so. The tallest sports a thin moustache. He's giving the thumbs-up as a gesture of satisfaction. The others seem proud to be posing beside him. The enlargement, which must have been made from an original print rather than from the negative, exaggerates the defects of the original. I try to identify the characters, but none of them ring any bells. My magnifying glass doesn't reveal anything in particular. There's no caption, no accompanying note, not even the usual greetings establishing the context. I ask Serdj to come over. He looks at the photo from all angles and then gives it back.

"Maybe it's a former comrade in arms who thought he recognized you in it," he suggests.

"He could have written something on it."

"That's true, pretty stupid."

"Look carefully. None of the faces remind you of anyone?"

He takes the picture again and studies the five fighters. "I don't see anything."

"Do you think it's a coded message?"

"Meaning?"

"That it might have something to do with recent events?"

For the third time, Serdj leans over the photo. "It could be anything, Superintendent. A simple mistake, a moment of forgetfulness. The person who sent it probably forgot to put in the letter that goes with it. There's nothing to worry about, I don't think."

"Do I look like I'm losing it, Inspector?" I yell.

"That's not what I meant."

"So drop it. I asked your opinion about the photo, not my state of mind."

Serdj gets the measure of his blunder and escapes as quickly as he can.

I glance at the photo one last time, throw it into a drawer and ring for Baya to get me a cup of strong coffee.

Two days later, a telephone call catches me at home. It is remarkable to what extent death, life, the progress of one's career, sackings, declarations of war, crises of love, in fact everything in our country can hang on a telephone call. A voice with a strong eastern accent tells me not to hang up in its face.

"I'd have to see it first," I tell the voice, still swallowing my piece of chicken.

The voice becomes bolder: "Thank you for hearing me out."

"I can't guarantee you that. I've just sat down to eat."

"Sorry I interrupted your meal. Would you like me to call you back?"

"Not necessary. Be brief, and we'll manage."

The voice clears its throat and gets to the point: "Did you get the photograph?"

"Which one, Mr...?"

"My name wouldn't mean anything to you. I sent you a letter in the mail a week ago. With a photo inside."

"You forgot the text that goes with it."

"There wasn't one."

"So what's the story?"

"It's too long to tell, Superintendent. Can we meet? I have some interesting revelations for you."

"About what?"

"Not on the telephone, Sy Brahim. It's very very important."

"I'm in the office every morning."

"I'm busy in the morning. I suggest we meet tomorrow at eight o'clock, at the Pyramids restaurant."

"I don't know which suit to wear to such an august establishment."

"There's no need. Should I reserve us a table, Mr. Llob?"

"If it gives you pleasure to be eaten under the table by a pig..."

"It's an honor, for me, to invite you to dinner."

"That's great. Tomorrow at eight, at the Pyramids."

"I thank you with all my heart, Sy Brahim. Goodbye."

Mina, who has stopped all movement to watch me, searches my face for worrying signs. I flash her a reassuring smile. "Just a charitable soul inviting me to a fancy restaurant tomorrow. I'm going to stuff myself with those gourmet dishes until I throw up."

"Do you think I don't feed you enough?"

"Let's say this will be a welcome change."

Mina raises a disapproving eyebrow. "You won't eat like a king on the pennies you dole out bit by bit, after endless negotiations."

"Are you saying I'm stingy?"

"Worse: you're poor."

"That's not true," says my youngest. "My dad's not poor, he's honest."

"It comes to the same thing," his older brother tells him.

Mina lifts her chin and brings the kids back under control. I sit down in my seat again and go back to chewing on my drumstick, thinking about the ins and outs of the strange phone call.

The next day, in the evening, I put on my least worn-out shirt, my only suit—which I only get out when I have to—and my tie which bears the crest of a British club, which I bought from a second-hand-clothes dealer in Bab El Oued, and present myself at eight o'clock sharp at one of the most exclusive restaurants in Algiers. The receptionist can't see how well my threadbare moccasins and my flannel trousers go together, tries twice to find me in the reservations book and forgets to demand my documents. When he realizes it really is me, he hands me over wholesale to the arrogant penguin in charge of seating the customers. The latter accepts the responsibility the way a man who has used up all his trump cards accepts a compromise. He invites me to follow him with an obsequious wave of his hand. My table is at the end of the room, in an alcove protected by satin curtains, with a big painting behind it and an outstanding view of all the comings and goings in the room. The flunkey asks me, in educated French, whether I might perhaps trouble myself to take off my jacket; then, after a flustered glance at my neighbors—as if to apologize for being forced to seat such a clod so close to their idyll—he leaves without sliding back my chair. My closest neighbors, two taciturn nabobs sitting beside a fat sow draped in silk and precious stones, stare at me, baffled by the vulgar incongruities occasioned by my outfit. I bare my teeth in a bestial grin and sit down, ignoring them in a dignified manner.

A heavily made up waitress, her bust measurement equal to her hip measurement, hands me a menu on which bewildering delicacies are listed in a string of exquisitely phrased subtleties designed to stimulate one's desires and titillate one's fantasies: lamb steak in pastry, thyme *jus*; slice of smoked duck's liver; and other refined garbage that reminds me how far behind I am when it comes to emancipation. Since I can't decipher the menu, I suggest we wait for my host.

"And as an apéritif?" she pesters.

"What do you mean?"

"A small glass of champagne?"

"Oh no! I'm a believer."

"Some water?"

"With pleasure."

"Still or sparkling?"

Why is she persecuting me like this?

"Er, sparkling," I say at random.

"Mouzaïa or Perrier?"

"Miss," I beg her, increasingly horrified by my neighbors' ostentatious curiosity, "my palate has been so ruined by the bad food in the canteen that it wouldn't know the difference between marzipan and modeling clay. Not worth bringing me any at all, okay?"

Her smile disappears so fast that she's left speechless. She confiscates my menu and leaves me to my fate.

Some fifteen minutes go by amid the clattering of forks and the billowing of curtains. The ambience of muted hubbub, punctuated by the laughter of young sirens in search of a Ulysses to lead astray, is soothing. The beautiful people leave me alone with my frustrations, and my mysterious host is taking his time to appear, so the time starts to hang heavy on me. I have nibbled at the little savory biscuits and the slices of bread spread with something that dissolves on the tongue before giving up its secret; nothing in sight. Suddenly the penguin rushes to welcome a dream couple, obviously regulars. My Adam's apple comes up against the knot of my tie, and I almost swallow a crumb the wrong way. The man is exceedingly dashing, and a few reverent heads turn his way. He is tall and charismatic and seems to command great respect. As for his companion, who is squeezed tightly into a magnificent outfit, she shines with a thousand flames. Of course, it isn't her great beauty that leaves me bewildered, but the way she sticks to her man as if she wanted to merge with him. And what intrigues me to the highest degree is how a remarkable woman like Soria Karadach, a well-known scholar who, to my mind, is the embodiment of moral and intellectual integrity, can cling so closely, in full view of the world, to an individual with as little to recommend him as Ghali Saad.

The penguin leads them to the other end of the room, behind a mahogany screen, to protect their intimacy from prying eyes. Before he disappears from view, Ghali Saad puts his arm around the historian's waist and she, flattered by this evidence of his affection, gently rests her head on the shoulder of this man who can make it rain or shine at the Bureau of Investigation and, by extension, throughout the republic's nervous system.

I start when the waitress, whom I had not seen arrive, hands me a telephone.

"It's for you, *monsieur.*"

Still flabbergasted, I struggle to recognize the voice at the other end of the line.

"Sy Brahim?"

"Yes."

"Are you astonished?"

"I certainly am!" I say, coming to my senses. "Is this my host?"

"Sorry I'm late, Superintendent. In fact, I don't think I'll make it in time. So don't wait for me. This evening, you'll dine alone. Don't worry: the meal is on me. You won't have to pay anything."

"What is this, a joke?"

"It's up to you to work it out, Superintendent. It's right up your street. Admit it: you weren't expecting it at all. Soria Karadach, the famous historian, on the arm of a crook like Ghali Saad. Inconceivable, no? I'm not trying to manipulate you, Sy Brahim. You've been manipulated enough since the start of this hoax, and I have no intention of abusing your naivety myself. I'm even sorry for you. It's true that I used to bear a deadly grudge against you, but in a situation where there's no escape, the wise man gives precedence to the way of reason over the emotions of the heart. We know you're not in

bed with the dogs who drove to suicide so brave a son of the revolution as Haj Thobane. You joined in the plot despite yourself. You
had to save your lieutenant. Besides, your partner didn't find himself there by chance. He was entrapped in order to entrap you. The
people pulling the strings knew that the only way to drag you into
this business was by baiting you with a goat, in the shape of one of
your men. Since the fate of your lieutenant depended on your commitment, you were free to get to the bottom of things. The proof
is that he was freed without investigation or trial, as if nothing had
happened. Do you find that reasonable? ...Hello? Are you still there?"

"Go on, I'm interested."

"Many of us suspected the plot and condemned it. It was a
very cruel act. Of course, there are often disagreements among the
higher echelons, that's to be expected, but to bring about the death
of an enemy, that's against the rules of the game."

"So it's a game, as far as you're concerned."

"It's just a manner of speaking."

"You called it a plot?"

"Come on, it's obvious. A historian who shows the suicidal
temerity to profane the secrets of the gods: it's unheard of. She couldn't
be working alone. She didn't stand a chance of setting a trap without
being swallowed up in the abyss. She was super-protected, and I don't
mean by you.... Have you read her books?"

"Not a one."

"I suggest you have a look. She can't stop singing the praises of
every single one of the people who govern us, painting fantasy por-
traits of them, putting up monuments to them, tracing revolutionary journeys worthy of Mao or Gandhi. And yet, one *zaïm* has never
found grace in her eyes. She doesn't mention him in her scholarly
papers or newspaper articles."

"Haj Thobane?"

"Got it in one, Superintendent. So why did she have it in for
him so badly? Why did she hate him so much that she would deny
him the right to be included among our heroes, someone who is inex-
tricably associated with the epiphany of November fifty-four? And by
what squalid chance did she find herself the architect of his death?"

"You think she was the one who started—"

"I don't think anything; I ask questions."

"It comes to the same thing."

"I won't pretend I don't feel hatred for that woman, Mr. Llob. She has contributed to a misfortune that's about to turn our lives upside down."

"Is that a question or a statement?"

"I have nothing on my conscience, Mr. Llob. I have never wished for or agreed with anyone's death. You're the one who should be feeling some remorse. On your own initiative, you opened Pandora's box. Darkness will soon cast its shadow over our future and transform our city squares into fields of combat."

"Pity I can't see you face to face. I like your style."

"My name wouldn't mean anything to you. I don't represent a clan or a faction. I'm just an Algerian who's worried about the future of his country. I know that war has been declared among our leaders, and that its consequences will be dire for all of us."

"Is there a connection between your fears and the photo you sent me?"

"That photo has no value of any kind. It was just to arouse your curiosity and lead you to this restaurant. I wanted you to see, with your own eyes, the historian woman and that bastard in each other's arms. They've been lovers for several months and come to the Pyramids for dinner every Monday. Now, these are two viscerally materialistic people. Feelings have no place in their calculations. Their kind knows nothing of love; only complicity brings them together, only self-interest binds them to each other. What role does each play? In Soria Karadach's case, it's unclear. As for Ghali Saad, his professional ambition is limitless. Look at the way he rushes at everything. His presence is not a coincidence. We're sure he's no stranger to the situation—"

"*We?* I thought you said you weren't acting on anyone's behalf."

"It's just a manner of speaking."

"What are your suspicions based on?

"All you have to do to find out is start again at the beginning, Mr. Brahim Llob."

He hangs up.

I whistle for the penguin and ask whether my supper is paid for. He goes to check and comes back to confirm that it is. I ask him, therefore, to list for me my benefactor's origins and contact details. He informs me that it is not within his remit to give me that kind of information. When I threaten to cause a scandal, he goes and gets the manager. The latter, a bald and effeminate individual perched on legs that resemble those of a wading bird, explains that the person who invited me did not wish to be identified, and that one of the fundamental principles of the Pyramids is that it scrupulously respects its customers' requirements. His smile is affable, but his piercing gaze, which ends where his fragile facelift begins, tips me off that I have a better chance of surviving a bite from a cobra than a kiss from him.

"Fine, I understand," I say in surrender.

"You would show an even finer understanding if you went and dined elsewhere, *monsieur*."

"I am a superintendent of police," I warn him.

"There are two government ministers and three very high dignitaries of the regime in this restaurant, *monsieur*. They would like to have a delightful evening, and that's what we're here for, *monsieur*."

"You think I'm no longer entitled to the dinner that's been offered to me?"

"I'm afraid not, *monsieur*."

The two nabobs and their companion are watching with interest, delighted to hear the manager shut me up. The glittering courtesan is on the point of getting up and giving him a medal.

"Okay," I say, making as if to push back the table.

Satisfied, the manager lifts up his nose and stands there, solemn and strict, waiting for me to get out. Amateur error! My hand dives under the tablecloth, slips rapidly between his thighs and grabs him by the testicles. The poor fool jumps; his body lurches backwards as the pain exploding below his waist turns him to stone, while his already rubicund face turns completely scarlet. Since he cannot cry out or struggle, he freezes into a grotesque position half-way between a genuflection and a fakir's somersault. The courtesan at the next table clucks with indignation; her companions don't hear her, they're so shocked by the obscenity of my deed.

I tighten my grip to make the manager lean forward even more. When his ear reaches the level of my lips, I whisper, "Your ministers, I don't give a damn about them. Your balls, like your fate, are now in my hands. What will you choose? To apologize to me and serve me with the greatest diligence or to go home with a runny omelet in the bottom of your underwear?"

"*Monsieur,*" he moans hoarsely, "a little decorum, I beg you—"

"That's not the song I requested."

He gulps, trembling with pain, tries to hold out, but finally puts one knee to the ground. "I beg your pardon, *monsieur,*" he says quietly.

"Superintendent, sir," I breathe.

"Superintendent, sir."

"Superintendent, sir what?"

"I beg your pardon, Superintendent, sir."

"There you go, you've got it."

I let him go, stand up and leave the room in a lordly manner.

As I cross the exterior courtyard, I walk in front of a bay window behind which our two turtle doves are drinking a toast. As she brings her glass to her lips, Soria sees me in front of her. Her face darkens. I wink at her and disappear before Ghali Saad turns round.

I rifled through Soria Karadach's file from top to bottom. For three days. Nothing compromising. On the contrary, the scholar's career is littered with honors. Outstanding schooling in an orphanage—she was the daughter of a *chahid.*[*] Top of her class at Ben Aknoun. Graduate of the top European universities. Heads a militant organization called "The Relief." Godmother to minor currents within the young revolutionary movement. Exemplary reputation, both personally and professionally. Her chief editor worships her. The rector bows down before her qualities. In short, the cream of the crop!

Could a saint sleep with an incubus without losing her soul?

I search for reasons that might lead an *éminence grise* to fall for an obscure eminence of the Ghali Saad type, but in vain. Ghali Saad is not known for his erudition. He left school with no more

---

*   *Chahid:* martyr of the war of liberation.

than a diploma and signed up as a lowly administrative officer at Staoueli, a branch of the Security Services' Communications Center. His training over, he's an underling in an auxiliary service. His boss has a crush on him—malicious rumor has it that it was love at first sight; he covers him, literally and figuratively, and sends him abroad on a management training course. When he comes back, Ghali is appointed secretary somewhere in the Ministry of the Interior. He marries the daughter of a high official and rises meteorically up the hierarchic ladder. He is charming and cunning; his detractors criticize his lack of education and challenge his authority. They can do this because he has shown them all the door. Behind his courteous façade, he is said to be machiavellian. His closest collaborators only last as long as their first bit of intrigue; he fires them on the slightest suspicion. Women can't resist him; he features in the filthiest jokes told in Greater Algiers. His reputation as a skirt-chaser is such that a woman as refined as Soria Karadach must have protected herself against him. Of course, feelings are not based on rational considerations, and yet, having spent time with the historian and knowing her fervent dislike of crooks, I find I can't work out the precise nature of the couple they make.

On the fourth day, taking my stubbornness in both hands, I decide to shake the tree to make the rotten fruit drop. After working hours, I go and ring at Soria Karadach's door. Her maid tells me she won't be back until eight o'clock. I ask her to tell her that I came by and that I would return later.

Soria was expecting me.

At about nine o'clock, she receives me in her living room, which—let it be said in passing—would not be unworthy of a nabob. Knowing the poverty of our country's university professors and the penury of our journalists, who have to wear protective clothing against the wolf snapping at their heels, I am stunned at the sight of the luxury in which our friend lives the good life. But the ways of the Lord are mysterious, and the loving God giveth to mortals and taketh away as He wishes, without having to justify Himself.

Soria has put on a sober housecoat. She has removed her makeup and let her hair fall down her back as if planning to go to bed. She welcomes me without ceremony. Everything leads me to believe she wants to get rid of me as soon as possible. I have the feeling she's been waiting for me to turn up ever since our eyes met at the Pyramids.

She seems relaxed, in control of her faculties, and my visit doesn't worry her overmuch. She is no longer the daring historian who took her chances with me and shared in my mood-swings at Sidi Ba. Her expression is cold, her attitude neutral.

"You wish to see me, Superintendent?"

Her voice sends ice down my spine.

"Am I disturbing you?"

"It's always disturbing when people don't come to my home in friendship."

"Where do you see a hatchet?" I ask her, spreading my arms to show that I'm not carrying a weapon.

"In your eyes, Superintendent."

She offers me a place on the sofa. We stand facing each other, she on one side of the big table, I in the middle of a Persian carpet.

"I was very happy to work with you. But now it's over. We both move on."

"You used me," I retort abruptly.

Missed! She doesn't move a muscle.

She gives me a distant smile. "We made a deal, Superintendent."

"You had a hidden agenda."

"Perhaps, but the goal didn't change. We succeeded in our mission. Now it's up to each of us to make use of it as we see fit."

Her self-assurance is irritating, it chips away at my composure. It's as if she's thumbing her nose at me, telling me to go to hell.

"Willing accomplice or manipulated victim?"

"I beg your pardon?" She looks at me piercingly, her eyebrows compressed almost to the eyes themselves. I absorb the look without flinching. My vigilance prevents her from trying to change the subject; she knows I haven't come here to exchange idle chit-chat; that I have something important to get off my chest.

Her blood-red lips tighten slightly; suddenly she is undecided, even unsure. Now she is trying to become the historian of Sidi Ba again, energetic and beguiling. A wasted effort. My eyes are driving her into a corner, crushing her, binding her. A strange expression crosses her face. She feels she's about to lose ground and is trying to regain the upper hand. I don't help her, contenting myself with folding my arms across my chest.

"Anyone would think you had it in for me," she says weakly. "Have I done something wrong?"

I refuse to cut her any slack: "How much did they pay you?"

"Ah! Finally!" she says, shaking her head.

"It took me a while, but I got there."

My coarseness doesn't bother her overmuch. Curiously, it seems to stimulate her. She goes from hot to cold with amazing ease. She must have prepared herself for this. This woman is pure intelligence, without a shred of bone or an ounce of fat. What class, what talent, what a force of nature!

She takes a step toward me and decides to lance the boil. "What do you want to know?"

"How much they forked out to reel you in."

"They didn't have to. I would have sold my soul to be a part of it. They think they manipulated me, and so much the better. In fact, I played the game because the setup fit me like a glove."

"Throw me a line here. I think I'm beginning to go under."

"The water isn't deep enough, Brahim. All you have to do is put your feet down and you'll see."

"Unfortunately, I'm flat on my back."

"I don't believe you. You're the one making your life complicated. We created thunder, and we've every reason to be proud of it."

"Pride is a way of consoling oneself, but it doesn't settle anything much; its only value is that it flatters our disaffection by making a travesty of our aspirations, since it can't invest in them."

"Probably. As far as I'm concerned, my goals have been achieved, and I congratulate myself. I've played a part in putting the lowest scum that used to flourish in our country out of commission, so he can no longer do any harm."

"Scum like him are legion. One discarded, a hundred recruited. I'm afraid that eliminating him may well favor the proliferation of the species."

She smiles.

What a gem that smile is. Why does it cause me pain? Why do her immense eyes, her generous features, her voluptuous figure create in me suffering that is unbearable and inexplicable at the same time? What makes poison from the fruit of so much grace, death from the opacity of what she is concealing?

I notice that my fist is clenched, my jaws are tense, that I feel like being unpleasant. I'm afraid of what is scampering about in my head, I'm suspicious of the sensation that's insidiously taking me over, contaminating my inner self and cutting off my breathing. I feel like a cuckold who begins to sense his unhappiness inexorably intruding, to the point that every beat of his heart rips out a piece of his soul.

Soria is an experienced woman. She knows her subject better than anyone, and doesn't need a map to work out what is disturbing my voice and clouding my eyes. Coolly, she fishes a cigarette out of a mahogany case, lights it and stares at the cloud of smoke corkscrewing gently up to the ceiling. After a few emphatic puffs, she lies back on the sofa, revealing the curve of her long, well-toned thighs.

She pays no attention to this display of nudity, but goes on smoking, her eyes riveted on mine.

"Why?" I ask her bluntly.

"I'm a historian. Certain historical facts weren't in the right places. I put them where they belonged."

"What is your place in *our* history?"

"Whatever I've chosen to allocate to it."

Suddenly, her voice fails her, while distress spreads bit by bit over her lips, her eyes, her cheeks, her whole being.

She starts her story: "All my life I've been waiting for this moment. In fact, I've only survived because of it. I chose the least rewarding subject at university. They wanted me to do medicine or economics. I said history. I wanted to know where I came from, who I was and where I was going. I had a score to settle with my country's past, which was ruining my present and compromising my future. As a historian, I had a chance of obtaining the missing pieces of my puzzle, which felt like open wounds to me. That's how I knocked at forbidden doors and took my place in the court of the gods. Those

321

who rule our country have their little weakness: glory. I went to see them and magnified their feats of arms, and they loved me for it. I dedicated wonderful articles to them, seminars as sensational as rhetorical jousting matches, and told their stories in kingly tomes. Suddenly, I had become their eternity; their happiness hung on the finest lock of my hair. That's how I conquered Che, the president, the *zaïms* and all their eunuchs. And yet there was one god who never found favor in my eyes. I didn't hide it, so that the whole world would know. Because I knew that one day my brooding would lead him to his downfall."

"Haj Thobane?"

"The late Haj Thobane, may he rot in hell...."

"Was it you that killed him?"

"I caused his death, and that's gratifying. I expected him to disappear, but he went one better: he killed himself. Like the coward he always was."

"So you believe in the suicide theory?"

"You're not going to tell me he killed himself by accident? That would spoil my day."

Her sincerity leaves no room for doubt: Soria believes in the suicide theory.

"Did you know his days were numbered?"

"I hoped so. With all my strength. And his day came. His enemies needed helping hands to unseat him. I was one, made to measure. You were the other, Superintendent. History and the Law. Two marvelous marionettes. You, to save your lieutenant. Me, to rehabilitate the revolution.... A charismatic man had chosen to raise his pedestal on a mass grave. Was that the best foundation? What was in that mass grave, what secret, what glory? People had been executed, without trial. Like diseased animals. I wanted to know whether they were comfortable in that place or if they felt cramped. Did they deserve to die in a communal ditch, with no gravestone or epitaph? Or to be transferred to a proper cemetery, with decent burials; a cemetery where one could go and meditate over their graves without having to knock down walls? These questions tormented me day and night. I wasn't certain of anything. I had to settle it once and for all. I hoped to get justice for them. I would have been unhappy if I had done anything else. Rabah Ali's revelations the other night, at Sidi Ba, exceeded my hopes. I don't regret having cheated. A little, with you. Not enough for it to bother me. As far as the others are concerned, we're even. They lured me in. I took the bait with pleasure. They followed my research like a sighting line. The addresses they gave me led straight to their victory. Except they didn't know it was mine too. Right now, they think they used me. I'd like them to go on thinking so for ever."

"You think they knew all about this killing business?"

"Some of them even took part."

"Why dig up the dead now, after decades of silent complicity?"

"Because Haj Thobane was becoming a nuisance and was jeopardizing their plans."

"What plans?"

"The devil only knows."

"If Thobane was such a problem, why not just kill him? They had an embarrassment of choices: an accident, poison, any number of dirty tricks would have done the needful. Why all the rigmarole, the historical shit-stirring, the intolerable scandal?"

"Revolutionaries have their own ways of settling scores. An accidental death, or a murder blamed on some nutcase, would have brought the man down, but not his legend or his followers. He had to die both in the flesh and in the respect of others. Who, today, could describe himself as a member of the Haj Thobane faction, who would dare boast that he was his friend or confidant? The scandal has destroyed everything around him, like a radioactive cloud. Even those who used to sponge off him will have to go elsewhere to sharpen their fangs. Haj Thobane will arouse disapproval wherever his name is mentioned. History has rejected him, the nation's memory doesn't want to hear any more of him. He's not just a great traitor any more, he's already forgotten. His empire will leave no ruins, it never existed. That way our glorious revolution can recommence its martial progress, its conscience renewed, proud as a young bride."

"What I don't understand is your ferocity. Why so much hatred for a man who's no more reprehensible than most of the people whose bravery you parade in your books?"

She stubs out her cigarette in a glass ashtray and stands up. Her breath envelops me, her nose is up against mine; her lips look as though they're getting ready to devour me.

She says: "On the night of the twelfth to the thirteenth of August nineteen sixty-two, a member of the Talbi family managed to escape the killing. The murderers hunted him for months, maybe even years. Sometimes, they passed right beside him without recognizing him. They were looking for a little boy. But the survivor wasn't a boy, it was a girl."

Thor's hammer wouldn't have hit me so hard.

My voice is unrecognizable when I cry, "You?"

Chapter twenty-four

I twist in my bed like a worm in its fruit. In my head, the pen that broke in Soria's hands in that hidden-away cabin in the depths of the forest, somewhere near Sidi Ba; and her voice, which, just a handful of hours ago, seemed to emanate from beyond the grave. *My brothers' screams still ring in my ears. I ran into the woods, ran and ran. Branches scratched my face, slashed at my legs, tore out my hair but didn't slow down my headlong flight. The moon was as big as a funeral urn that night. It shone its beams down on me, directing my pursuers. However much I ran, it was always there, above my head, like a bad omen. If I had had wings I couldn't have run any faster, looking back at the clearing where they were just finishing off the massacre of everything that was dear to me in the world. I've never been able to look straight ahead since that night. Wherever I go, whatever I do, I can't look away. At the orphanage, at university, in Algiers, in Barcelona, studying, teaching, my head remained stubbornly turned toward that clearing, my neck cricked with a pain that cut into me like a yoke.... I had to go back in time, back to that box that was the source of my unhappiness, dig up the mass grave, tear my family from its grip, free them from their suffering, let them rest at last and, at the same time, soothe my soul....*

"Why aren't you sleeping?" groans Mina.

"Maybe because that's all I've done all my life."

I throw back the covers, put on my slippers and go into the kitchen to get a glass of milk. I find the fridge and plenty of glasses on the draining board, but not a drop of milk. One of my offspring has even gone so far as to eat the orange I had put aside. I go back into my room. Mina is twisted up in the sheets, her face tormented. I decide not to spoil her sleep and retreat to the living room. I smoke cigarette after cigarette, stretched out on the padded bench. It's two o'clock in the morning. Outside, some oaf honks his horn at something, with no consideration for children asleep with their fists bunched up or for people recovering from illness. I go to the window. The oaf carries on making his racket for two minutes and then launches his car at breakneck speed across the neighborhood. It's probably a drunk who can't find his way home. The silence, dazed, returns from a distance. On the sidewalk, a beggar woman tries to wrap a few rags around her children to keep them warm. A dog walks past her, pretending to look elsewhere in the face of this incomprehensible human destitution.... My God! It's so sad it makes you want to die.

And you, Algiers? Why are you so sad to be alive?

I go back to the bench and stub out my cigarette in a saucer. I hold my head in my hands and try to get my thoughts in order.

If Soria was Belkacem Talbi, the survivor, and the real Belkacem Talbi was dead and gone, who was SNP? A celebrity without a name, of course! A virgin past, a blank page on which any story could be written. So he was lent the story of the massacre victims. And everything fell into place. Just as *they* wanted it to. All that remained was to believe it. And I believed it, to the hilt. What an idiot! I who prided myself on having got the hang of all the countless wheels that nearly ground me down, who thought he had seen everything and could never end up blind, here I was, back on my ass.

"Would you like me to make you a cup of coffee?"

My poor Mina! Always making her own life difficult because of my torments.

"Did I wake you up again?"

"Don't worry about it. I wasn't sleepy anyway."

"Come and sit beside me."

She obeys. I wrap an arm around her neck. I press her to my chest. Hesitantly, modestly, she puts her arms around my waist. I bury my face in her neck and let myself melt into her breathing. Outside, the oaf starts honking in the street again. He can go on stirring up the city; I'm already lost to the world.

Mina slumps in my arms. With all possible care, I lay her down on the padded bench, cover her with a blanket and go into our room to change. Cost what it may, I have to lance the boil too.

*   *   *

I drive through the sleeping city without stopping at traffic lights. The deserted streets lend me wings. With my foot to the floor, I plunge right ahead.

At about four o'clock in the morning, I arrive at the asylum. I park my car in the lot and jump out. An epileptic wind comes down from the mountains, heavy with dust and dead leaves, and pounces on the trees like an addict on his hallucinations. In the sky, where a mass of swollen clouds is just beginning to disperse, the moon imagines it is bigger than its fear. It's as if the night doesn't inspire it with anything worthwhile. A long way away, on the horizon, a storm is attempting to create a diversion; its hullabaloo doesn't even cover the sound of the orchards.

Leaning over against the gusting wind, I stagger among the dark huts. I feel as if I'm crossing the no-man's-land of my folly.

I arrive in front of Professor Allouche's office-bedroom. No light shines behind the shutters. I bang on the door fit to scrape the skin off my knuckles.

"All right!" a voice splutters finally. "I'm not deaf."

A key turns in the lock.

The professor is taken aback when he sees me on his threshold.

"Brahim? What are you doing here?"

"I was just passing through. Am I disturbing you?"

He looks over my shoulder.

"Are you alone?"

"Like a grown-up, Professor."

"Do you know what time it is?"

"I thought friends didn't need an appointment."

"Yes, but there's no need to push it. I assume you have a good reason to drag me out of bed so early?"

"I couldn't close my eyes at home."

He looks at me curiously, then stands aside to let me by.

"What's happened, Brahim?" he says, switching on the ceiling light.

He is in his pyjamas, with the trousers revealing a considerable amount of his buttocks. His sheepskin jacket, worn to a couple of straps, hangs over the prominent ribs of his pale torso, which reveal the toll taken by his advancing years. My friend the professor is already an old story; I'm almost ashamed to have to bring it up again.

He looks at me with his hangdog expression. "You seem disoriented, Superintendent. What's wrong?"

I offer him a chair. "Sit down, Professor. You won't be able to take this standing up."

"Is it that serious?"

"Please, sit down."

He hesitates, then obeys. "Yes?"

I hold my finger up, asking him to be patient. He raises his hands to indicate his consent. My breathing is ragged. I pause briefly to bring it under control. Once focused on my subject, I open the hostilities: "Stop me whenever you want, Prof. Are you ready?"

"...."

"We take a prisoner with no memory, whom we'll call SNP. We graft onto him a past that suits our friends, and together we arrange for him to be granted a presidential pardon. In parallel, we stir up the city to think that this release is a grave step, because the person concerned is a potential danger to society. Result: everyone is on the alert. Starting with a certain superintendent of police. Then, the machine swings into action. Once on the outside, our SNP suddenly gets his memory back. He remembers the man who caused his disappearance, along with his family's, and tries to kill him. Unfortunately, he misses his target and kills his victim's driver. But it's not just any victim. Haj Thobane is in a real state, and the state doesn't know which way is up.

328

The finest sleuths, whole teams of them, are charged with finding the killer. They go one better: they eliminate him. Except that, amid all the chaos, it's a lieutenant of police who gets it in the neck. Since no one knows how his gun came to be found on the killer's body, the complicity theory finds favor. Good old Superintendent Llob is forced to extract his deputy from the hornet's nest he's landed up in. He'll try to establish a link between the target and the killer, in order to exonerate his colleague. And that's where the past that was grafted onto the prisoner with no memory, whom we called SNP, comes in. If you need to create a made-to-measure history for someone, there's nothing better than an amnesiac, is there? And if, what's more, he has no relatives and no friends, you can get rid of him without leaving a trace. Piece of cake! The perfect crime. Especially when the Superintendent has other worries: his pal is languishing in the jails of no return. The more time goes by, the more the poor bastard rots. Urgent measures are required. We must pull out all the stops, cut straight to the heart of the matter. The ground was prepared ages ago, and all the old cop has to do is follow directions, to the killing ground at Sidi Ba. What a horror, that killing ground; and what a scandal! The macabre discovery is described in technicolor on the TV news, and the newspapers take on the task of spicing it up, as usual. Haj Thobane, who had massacred SNP's family and couldn't handle his past as a monster, commits suicide. Of course. What else could he do? He's had it, no way out; the nation spits him out. So Good gets its revenge on Evil. Just like in the educational leaflets. The crook is buried like a dog. Justice is served. The lieutenant of police is rehabilitated. The curtain falls, the show is over, everyone goes home....

"What do you think of my synopsis?"

"I don't see what you're getting at, Brahim."

"Really?"

"When I saw you turning up at an impossible hour in the morning, I said you must be going soft in the head. I wasn't wrong."

He's taking it well, the prof is.

As if someone has briefed him.

He runs his fingers through his sparse hair, grimacing. He is embarrassed, all the same.

"How long have we known each other, Allouche?"

"We go back a long way," he sighs.

"You've had your ups and downs, haven't you?"

"It hasn't been a walk in the park."

"Has my attitude toward you ever changed one iota?"

"You're a good man, Brahim. You've always shown me the same kindness, through the best and the worst times."

"Do you think it's down to congenital stupidity?"

"Why do you say such a terrible thing?"

"Because it's exactly what I'm asking myself, Professor. I'm asking myself whether my uprightness isn't just proof of my idiocy. Because you have to be a hell of a fool to go on loving and trusting in a country where everyone else does his utmost to abuse everyone else to survive."

"Oh dear, oh dear! You're getting depressed—"

"Put your white coat away and stay on the sofa, Professor. I didn't come here for a session of hypnosis."

"So what did you come here for?" a voice explodes behind me.

I turn round.

Chérif Wadah is standing in the doorway of the room next door, wearing a dressing gown he hasn't quite done up. His face, still puffy with sleep, twitches spasmodically.

"Mr. Wadah?" I say. "I thought you were abroad."

"My enemies think so too, and so much the better."

"So this is your hideout?"

"Mind your own business, Superintendent. What story are you telling the professor? What is this rambling? Do you have any idea how incoherent you sound?"

He's trying to intimidate me. I don't walk into his trap.

"The incoherence is in the facts as they have recently emerged, Mr. Wadah. So very awkward!"

Chérif Wadah does up the knot of his dressing gown and walks toward me. He is furious, but tries to keep his cool. He picks up an alarm clock and turns it over.

"Shit! It's four o'clock in the morning. You have to be ill to come here at this hour and talk nonsense to people who just want to get some sleep."

He tries to stare me down, his features engorged.

"You're losing the thread of the story, Mr. Llob. I know you've gone through a particularly distressing period of turbulence, but that's over now. If I were in your shoes, I'd think about something else. A new life is beginning in our country. You should rejoice. You've done a masterful job. You've been fantastic. Why be suspicious of what you've undertaken with self-denial and intelligence?"

"Careful, you're flattering me. I might have an attack of the vapors."

"You deserve all the world's respect, Superintendent. And you'll get it from one and all. No one will miss the call. I'll take care of it personally. Thanks to you, a new era will be ushered in. Don't look for the answer where the question isn't even being asked. That will distance you from the essence, and from people's esteem. Forget this story and go to Bulgaria—"

"Well, well, so you know!"

"I'm the one who interceded with Mr. Ghali Saad on your behalf."

"You could have asked my opinion."

"I wanted it to be a surprise."

"What surprises me is that I can't shake Ghali Saad off. He's everywhere I go. After a while, it becomes wearing."

"You're barking up the wrong tree, Superintendent, I promise you. There's no conspiracy. Haj Thobane's past caught up with him. We decided not to help him, that's all. He was just a dirty beast. He has caused our homeland enormous trouble, stopped it progressing, stood in the way of reform, of every measure that might improve working and living conditions for our citizens, and held the people hostage. He saw every political or economic proposal as an attack on his financial empire, and focused his efforts on keeping society in a state of stagnation and mental decay. I assure you, your work is blessed by the gods. Come on, you knew him! You can't tell me you feel sorry he's gone. That man had to go, one way or another. It was

him or Algeria. History made its decision. The coward put a bullet
in his head, and life goes on."

"So he did put a bullet in his head?"

"Why, do you doubt it?"

"Maybe someone helped him."

Chérif Wadah explodes. His cheeks start quivering. Suddenly,
he grabs the alarm clock on the table and smashes it against the wall.

"Now you're really talking nonsense, Superintendent. What you
say is very, very serious, so watch your step! The pathologist's report
was definitive: Haj Thobane committed suicide. That's official and
final. And it's the truth. It's dangerous to put forward fantasy theories
whose implications you don't grasp."

His eyes are bloodshot. Froth ferments in the corners of his
mouth.

Something gives way inside me. An invisible lock closes over
my guts, and my calves go soft. I can't recall ever feeling so over-
whelming a fear as comes over me now.

Professor Allouche is embarrassed for me. I'm disappointing
him. He stands up, goes all the way round the table and sinks back
into his chair, doubtless worn out by my 'ramblings.'

"I beg you, Brahim," he says shakily, putting his finger to his
temple. "Sy Chérif is telling the truth. You should be happy. What
you've done is extraordinary."

"And you a professor, an educated man," I say to him. "How
did a man with your learning let himself embark on this business?"

He smiles sadly and gives me a harassed look.

"An educated man, Brahim, a professor? Do you know what that
means, in a country dominated by megalomaniacs and rich bulimics?
Learning is the worst misfortune that can befall a man in a country
ruled by charlatans. You've seen them at work, Superintendent, you've
seen them demolish me and demolish anyone who isn't like them.
My ups and downs, Brahim? The occasional applause; a lot of abuse.
If anyone should be the first to dive into 'this business,' it's me. It's
more than a duty, it's an obligation, a question of survival. Have you
ever been dragged out of bed at some absurd hour of the night by a
bunch of pumped-up goons who just barge into your house and get

your wife and children first upset and then frightened? Every night, for years on end? Do you have the slightest idea what kind of hell that is? They shove you down the stairs, barefoot, in your pyjamas, while your children sob and hide their faces behind their fists. And you, you try to reassure them but you can't because some poor idiot is hitting you and calling you a dog. How many times was this circus show put on, in the middle of the night, bringing the neighbors out onto their balconies to watch the secret police bundle me into the trunk of their car and drive off at top speed, through my delirium? I was tortured, shackled, humiliated, showered with urine and dragged through my own excrement. I was forced to sit down on bottles. I was so disfigured, so wretched that my wife couldn't take it anymore. She couldn't bear to see me reduced to a piece of shit, Brahim, she'd had enough of sharing my anxieties. One morning, she took my kids and disappeared. She never came back, never showed any sign of life. For more than ten years I haven't known where she is or what she's done with the children. And you ask me what the hell an educated man is doing in the middle of this business? This business wouldn't make sense without him...I don't want the best of us to be persecuted by the worst we have any more. I don't want my work to be used as a substitute for toilet paper in latrines any more. Because it's happened, Brahim. I've been forced to wipe myself with my own books. To apologize to my torturer, to call lowly jailers 'sir.' All this because I was an educated, honest, conscientious man who offered his services to gurus who didn't know what to make of them. Well, it's over, the reign of the philistines. I don't want such abuses to go on, I don't want good men to shit themselves whenever some crook looks at them too closely."

Since I don't say anything, he looks down and leans forward over the table. He can't quite rouse himself again, so he gives up and contents himself with sharing his conclusion: "You're wrong to let yourself get discouraged, Brahim. I promise you, you have every reason to rejoice. Sy Wadah isn't just flattering you. What you have done is priceless. Thanks to you, a healthy metabolism is establishing itself in our country. Good is finally getting the upper hand over Evil."

"Good?"

"Yes, Good."

"So tell me why I feel like throwing up every time I think about the people who propose to dispense it to us. Tell me why their goodness horrifies me, why I'm afraid to see them try to save us?"

In the distance, a storm breaks out, renewing the wind's assaults on the huts of the asylum.

Chérif Wadah nods. "So, you don't notice the transformation the nation was waiting for—"

"Nobody believes your pitch, Mr. Wadah," I break in. "Having been royally fucked by your demagoguery, hope no longer has the strength to join in your games. And don't talk to me about the nation, whatever you do; you don't know what it is. The country's only remaining chance is for you to leave, the sooner the better. You're driving us mad with your lousy speeches. The world is changing, that's true, but only where you're nowhere to be found. The obstacle is in your mind. If you think that Thobane's death is the best thing that could have happened, follow his example and let the younger generation take control of its own destiny. You can't make a feast out of yesterday's leftovers, Mr. Wadah."

"It's our Algeria," he thunders, rushing at me.

"Which one?" I roar to drive him back. "The one that used to inspire poets, or the one that sends a chill down one's spine? The one where foreign delegations used to be received by painters and writers, or the one where minstrels are locked up in jails? The one where giants used to come and bow down before its monuments or the one whose colossuses have feet of clay? The one that revered Tito, Giap, Miriam Makeba and Che Guevara, the real one, or the one that harbored Carlos and terrorist organizations?"

He's taken aback. His hand goes briefly to his heart; he recovers himself and challenges me to the end.

"I feel sorry for you, Sy Brahim. I don't think we have anything more to say to each other. Leave now."

"That's what I was intending to do, *monsieur*. I just came to remind you that no crime is perfect. You can cover up your tracks and shuffle the cards, mix up the clues and the evidence, blind people's minds and eyes, but sooner or later, inevitably, like Haj Thobane, the truth will catch up with you."

"What truth are you talking about, Sy Brahim? There never was one."

That slipped out. His flared nostrils twitch. His forehead glistens with sweat and his jaws grind silently, like millstones. He can't decide whether to keep arguing or leave it alone.

To the professor's great displeasure, he opts for the least profitable of initiatives: speechifying. He comes over and shoves his carnivorous leer in my face. His breath besieges me as he tries to melt me in the furnace of his eyes.

"We're just a tissue of lies, Mr. Llob. We believe we know where we're going, but no one can guess what awaits us around the corner. We proceed hesitantly in broad daylight, dazzled by our shimmering vanities—that's when we're not being seduced by the mirage of our perdition, trusting only in our hallucinatory instincts, like gnus galloping flat out toward unfeasible pastures riddled with traps, violent death and madness. We're as much to be pitied as those gnus, Superintendent. The traps of the past have taught us nothing. Our memory retains nothing about the things that have destroyed us. We've never stopped lying to ourselves. Maybe that's where the secret of our survival lies, in our refusal to correct ourselves."

He raises his hand level with my face and moves his fingers in a way that suggests a spider on its back, then forms his hand back into a vengeful fist. "What has changed since the first murder, who has settled down since Noah's flood? We continue to race to our deaths, caring not a damn about what might become of us…one war after another, suffering on all sides, more dramas and accidents than you can handle. Why? Why so much unhappiness, so much terrible and pointless misery? That's the question. Unfortunately, the man who knows the answer wouldn't be able to implement the solution."

His fist relaxes, turning on itself so that the fingers come free. "So where the hell is it, Superintendent, this sainted Truth of yours? In the lessons men have never managed to learn? In the trivialization of tragedies, to the point where the surviving generations feel left out and demand their share of damnation? In the piety that expects to get from the stars that which the earth offers, in vain, every day? If Truth came to see us one morning, we'd die of boredom before nightfall. It's falsehood that helps us keep going. It's the only thing that understands us, that takes pity on us…falsehood is our salvation. What are hope, tolerance, dreams; what are fraternity, equality, loyalty; what are forgiveness, justice, repentance, if not exquisite falsehoods that allow us to experience the same setback several times without registering that something is out of kilter?"

His peroration has left him out of breath. He draws back to catch his breath. I don't let him off the hook. Looking him right in the eye, I tell him point blank, "You spend too much time in this asylum, Mr. Wadah."

At that moment, as if pushed over the edge by my insolence, Joe appears from somewhere with a hunting rifle aimed at my temple.

"Shall I blow his brains out?"

He is mad with rage. His face is crawling with nervous tics, and his finger has trouble keeping still on the trigger.

"Put your gun down, son," his protector advises.

"He showed you disrespect. I won't allow anyone to show you disrespect. Not even my mother. He's just a bastard cop. He has no right to raise his voice to you."

"Put your gun down, I say!"

Joe trembles at his godfather's order. His eyes act like a scourge on my entrails. I feel as though I'm vanishing in a puff of smoke. A cold sweat trickles down my back. After a long tremor, the finger falls still, moves off the trigger bit by bit and folds back on itself. Nevertheless, it's not until the barrel is well away from my temple that I feel myself again.

Joe steps back, reluctantly, and disappears behind a door, furtive as a ghost.

"I see everyone's up for a fight, Mr. Wadah."

"I told you he wasn't all there."

"He's not the only one, alas!"

"Let things take their course, Superintendent," says the professor. "A train is getting ready to set off into a new landscape; if you stand in its way, it means you accept that it will chew you up and spit you out. There are some things the ordinary taxpayer doesn't know about. He often doesn't realize it's for his own good, for the good of generations to come. The death of one man shouldn't kill a whole nation's chances. Alive, Haj Thobane was blocking them all. From now on, it's essential to make good use of our room to maneuver. That's what we're going to do right away."

"In your shoes," Chérif Wadah adds, to show I belong to him, "I'd go home and pack my bags. Bulgaria's a beautiful country."

"I don't need this training course."

"We can find other destinations for you. France, Italy, Russia, the United States—"

"I'll have nothing to do with that kind of thing, *monsieur.*"

"Pity."

As I reach the door, the sound of Wadah's voice holds me back.

He addresses me with the familiar *tu*: "You have no reason to doubt our project, Brahim. It's inspired by our mistakes and promises to recapture lost time. The country is going to be reborn, beautiful and healthy. Experts will have somewhere to work again, and merit will be sacred. A new politics promises to elevate us in the symphony of nations. Genius, forced into exile because of the self-centeredness and banality of certain leaders, will come back to us. Our schools and universities will rediscover the nobility of their vocations. Our artists will have a wonderful time, and all talents will have ways of expressing themselves fully. Everyone will have his chance. The best will rise to the heavens. We're finished with despotism and cant, nepotism and preferential treatment, favoritism and exclusion. Parties will spring up everywhere—this is not a utopian dream; some are already forming in secret, I promise you—and those in power will have an effective opposition, which will demand accountability and keep a close eye on them. Democracy is the mature state of republics, it's the real solution. You're wrong to remain a skeptic, Superintendent. Salvation is here, within reach; all you have to do is grab it."

"You must admit that falsehood is the best seducer in this case too, Mr. Wadah."

His smile fades.

I open the door. Outside, a radiant moon whispers sweet nothings to the drought-parched orchards. The weather is marvelous for
sleepwalkers and insomniacs; as for the peasant, with his shredded
hands, it's already obvious that the harvest will be catastrophic.

Before I get back to my car, I find I still have the strength to
turn back to the guru of all our unhinged tomorrows and say to him,
"All that glitters is not gold, that's the law. I love my country and the
people that go with it. I'm unhappy when things go badly, and I often
find myself praying for us to get out of a tight corner without too
much damage. Like you, I dream of a beautiful and healthy country; I'm prepared to work like a mad dog for the sake of a smidgen
of improvement in the grayness of our days, but however fervent my
faith, I will not permit myself to be allied with prophetic movements
that legitimize murder."

I don't know what I did for the rest of the day. I remember only that
I walked around somewhere like a madman, my hands behind my
back and my eyes hooded. I had a headache, and a terrible stom-
achache. The sounds of the city rumbled around me. I didn't know
where to go, and yet I continued to wander, convinced that it was
the only way to get some distance between me and my uncertainties.
Perhaps I thought I could step back somewhat from my own "convictions," as a way of checking whether they could catch up with me.
Night caught me leaning over a slipway on the waterfront. It took
me forever to remember where I had left my car. I went back home
like a man who has journeyed far far away and isn't close to seeing
light at the end of the tunnel.

It is after eleven o'clock, and Algiers is suffocating. It's as if
hell is at the gates of the city. Slumped in my armchair, with my lap
supporting my sagging belly and a worn-out footstool supporting
my feet, I can't stop trying to get myself blind drunk with a Ham-
oud Boualem, a local soda which is our pride and joy but can't even
get us tipsy.

Through the window I can see the lights of the Casbah. Night,
in this ancient quarter, is like a renunciation. Stunned by the swelter-
ing heat, people find their minds heated white hot; their memories

are tossed about by their cares, their sighs are headlong flights. They have spent their day overloading their credit at the cafés, cursing both the dishwater they're served in the name of a cup of coffee and their future, which is looking the other way. The alleyways are empty, and crushingly sad; if they rush to go to ground where the foundations begin, it's only to hide their dreadful crawling from the stars. The shopkeepers have pulled down their shutters, the curtains are drawn on all gossip. Silence has taken over the place; that's what you hear rattling foolishly against the blinds.

Further down, Bab El Oued is guzzling down her bile. She lurks in the shadows and waits, with a spider's patience, to ambush arguments. If the lamps are not lit it's not out of modesty; black is the preferred color for conspiracies. Bab El Oued has an old score to settle. She doesn't give a damn what people think of the rules governing her sensitivity or the hygiene of her self-respect. She gathers her resentments and ignores the rest. She has the means at her disposal: a few rough and ready principles, rudimentary pride, stirring tenacity. Not enough to erect an obelisk, but enough to load a good number of gibbets.

In front of me, the Mediterranean stretches out as far as a rejected dream, dark as a fretful omen. A few ships play at station masters, waving their lights about to keep their spirits up, while a lighthouse casts its evil eye on the shadows, looking for spells to bring to life.

Normally, when I used to lean over the edge of my balcony, Algiers would move me. I would look at things with affection, and the noises of the neighborhood would hold me spellbound. I found it difficult to look at a street without seeing the sense it gave to my life. I felt as though I knew all the buildings, felt the heft of every paving stone. I didn't even need to leave home to travel. Algiers was a journey of which one never grew tired. The fragrance of *merguez* and the din of the restaurants would fill my thoughts with a wolflike hunger; I had only to look deep into the eyes of the street urchins to quench my thirst.

Algiers was beautiful, in the days when the seasons were blue. The slightest thing would pump us right up; the smallest scrap of song would make us proud. We were young, like our ideals, and we took the most hare-brained promises at face value. We had green fingers, we put our hearts into our work, and our naivety was pure; our ambitions were humble and our hopes confident; we just wanted to live and to love being there amidst the prayers of the mosques and the drunkards' shouts, to look for our image in the affection of others, to touch our childhood dreams with our fingertips, with one hand to pick a flower to offer someone and with the other to keep all our promises. We were so happy with the days that were born in front of us, amazed that we could recognize them despite the chaos of our nights; we were so moved when someone said thank you to us, for nothing healed our scars better than a simple smile. Why has everything changed today? What is this bitterness that ruins our lives? What warns Mina off stirring up the past; what turns the mares in the meadows into she-asses? How many murderous interrogations, come the evening of the day of reckoning, how many immense disappointments at the end of wasted labors....

There is no trench worse than a mouth that wants to bite, there's nothing more incautious than to lend it your ear. Tonight, and this is a promise, when Mina comes to bed I will hold her hand till morning.

*   *   *

A few months later, on the fifth of October of the same year (1988), after a strange speech by the president in which he incites the nation to rise up, huge protest movements develop across all the big cities of the country. The result of the confrontations is five hundred civilians killed. In response to mass anger and popular demands for jobs and a minimum level of decency, the government offers a multi-party system and a sulphurous democracy that will encourage the rise of Islamist fundamentalism, thus creating the ideal conditions for the unleashing of one of the most appalling civil wars the Mediterranean basin has ever known....

About the Author

Yasmina Khadra is the pseudonym of the Algerian author Mohammed Moulessehoul, who was born in 1956. A high ranking officer in the Algerian army, he went into exile in France in 2000, where he now lives in seclusion. In his several writings on the civil war in Algeria, Khadra exposes the current regime and the fundamentalist opposition as the joint guilty parties in the Algerian Tragedy. Before his admission of identity in 2001, a leading critic in France wrote: "A he or a she? It doesn't matter. What matters is that Yasmina Khadra is today one of Algeria's most important writers."

The fonts used in this book are from the Garamond family

Other works by Yasmina Khadra
available from *The* Toby Press

Autumn of the Phantoms

Double Blank

In the Name of God

Morituri

Wolf Dreams

The Toby Press publishes fine writing,
available at leading bookstores everywhere. For more
information, please visit www.tobypress.com